The Other Side of Silence

SILENCE AND SHADOWS BOOK 1

DODIE BISHOP

Copyright (C) 2022 Dodie Bishop

Layout design and Copyright (C) 2022 by Next Chapter

Published 2022 by Next Chapter

Edited by Fading Street Services

Cover art by CoverMint

This book is a work of fiction. Names, characters, places, and incidents are the product of the author's imagination or are used fictitiously. Any resemblance to actual events, locales, or persons, living or dead, is purely coincidental.

All rights reserved. No part of this book may be reproduced or transmitted in any form or by any means, electronic or mechanical, including photocopying, recording, or by any information storage and retrieval system, without the author's permission.

For my sons, Chris and Alex, who always believed I could.

If we had a keen vision and feeling of all ordinary human life, it would be like hearing the grass grow and the squirrel's heart beat, and we should die of that roar which lies on the other side of silence.

— GEORGE ELIOT, MIDDLEMARCH

Chapter One
SUSANNAH

Might it be possible? Sitting at the battered walnut desk in my Henrietta Street bedchamber surrounded by so much that is familiar and dear to me, I begin to hope. Can I not draw strength from it, somehow? The bed with its sage green velvet drapes. My first good watercolours lovingly framed upon the walls. Papa's small portrait of Mama. My gaze halts there, wishing she was with me still, so none of it would have happened.

From the window, the sky is a sharp winter blue above the only London home I have ever known. My fingers trace the constellation of nicks and scratches on the desktop, familiar with them as with keys to play a tune. Placed in the centre is a book bound in fine brown calfskin with intricate gilded tracery at each of its corners. On the frontispiece I have already written *Susannah Gresham*. A coal shifts on the fire, startling me from my musings. I open the book, but still I hesitate. Why? I dip my pen with a sigh, staring at the blank page, its very blankness seeming a reproof. How can it feel such a huge thing to make this first tiny stroke? Have I the courage? I make a mark. The ink blots, but I have begun.

Diary: November 25, 1675

I write this journal because I am about to move back into my life and wish to record it so perhaps my journey may be eased by seeing evidence of the steps I manage each day. All forward ones I pray. I refuse to countenance failure when there has already been too much. For I am trapped and must find a way to escape. And, yes, I do laugh at myself because of it occasionally, albeit in a mocking sort of way. For how can I not when my predicament is entirely of my own making?

I must admit here that I am quite cravenly afraid, for this day is not one I saw coming. Or not yet. Nowhere near yet, in truth. But is it not better this way when I would have hidden from it if I could? I gasp a breath and straighten my back. Today I shall steel myself to return to Whitehall Palace again for the first time in three years and present myself to my godfather, the King.

Papa has shown him some of my new miniatures – another step back to who I was – and they have pleased him, so he has commissions for me. A slight narrowing of his eyes told Papa – who is his friend of many years – he had seen through my ruse. Few do. For whom would not believe themselves a little younger or comelier or indeed more manly. Many have come to Henrietta Street to view their finished miniature and left with maybe a greater sense of self-worth if not heightened vanity. All this while I imprisoned myself here.

The church bells sound in St Paul's in Bedford Street and now, God help me, it is time to leave.

Returned at last to my bedchamber, I compose myself before taking up my pen to write by candlelight. I must note first that I am truly proud of myself for only I know what this day cost me.

It began with a musical performance in the Banqueting House. Ranks of fluted marble columns soared. Rubens' exquisite, panelled ceiling dazzled. Heavy glittering chandeliers plunged, luminous with candles. I tried at least to appreciate the beauty of it all again, but it was difficult. I walked in on my father's arm, assailed by a miasma of perfume and raucous voices, wishing myself invisible though perhaps James and Catherine's flamboyant dress meant I was to no little extent. Papa squeezed my arm with his to reassure me while I tried to maintain my usual detached expression, despite my loathing of any enforced time in the company of my stepmother and her son. Though it was not that, was it? I was not detached, of course, but rather sick with anxiety to be at the palace again. I must bring truth to this or what purpose will it serve?

I found the performance of Carissimi's *Jephte* heartbreakingly beautiful, though the constant chatter from the audience was unsettling. It was a reminder of what I most disliked about the court. The shallowness of it all. I saw the King seated at the front before the dais between his brother and his son, all three splendid in scarlet satin and gold lace. His head often tipped towards Monmouth, discussing the performance I hoped, for had he not commanded it? His brother's eyes were closed though, his chin threatening to fall to his chest until his duchess touched his arm, for he is known to lack Charles's eclectic tastes and would far rather be racing him on horseback at Newmarket.

In truth, I was much relieved when it was over, and I could attend the King at the privy apartments close beside the river. Though I approached the closet where I might swop my mantua for a painter's smock with some caution, knocking and opening the door but a crack to make sure it was unoccupied. Last time I had done so only to be confronted by the sight of a naked male posterior thrusting between a lady's thighs upon the sofa. I shuddered at the recollection, thankful that on this occasion it was empty, allowing me to change and collect my painter's box and easel needed for my work.

How thin and pale was my reflection in the mirror ... as Catherine never failed to point out to me. I blinked back tears, needing my mother just as much then as I had ever done. I could scarce believe it three years since her death and for each one, I have hidden away. Can I admit here how much it has been in anger? I must, of course. And how much I now despise myself for it.

The King's rooms were more lavish than when last I saw them as was one of his long-standing mistresses whom I am to paint. Though I had heard tell of his spectacular silver furniture, I was not quite prepared for its startling presence or indeed its abundance. I gazed at a console table embossed with tulips and scrolling acanthus leaves, his crowned cypher chased at its centre. On either side were matching candelabra stands, with a mirror above to reflect the light. Jesu. This lavish place felt ... outlandish. I took a deep breath in air heavy with a cloyingly sweet floral perfume, though its taste was bitter on my tongue.

Lady Castlemaine, Duchess of Cleveland, was to be painted sitting beside her son whom on reaching thirteen years, had been made Duke of Southampton by his father the King. How vexed my stepmother is that, though her first husband was a Villiers, he was but a distant kinsman to this one. Our lives might have been very different now should he have had closer connections. My poor papa would surely have escaped her clutches as a means of getting to court. My heart pounds with indignation for all the good it does.

After watching me begin my work and praising both his mistress and his son for their poise as sitters, the King turned to me. 'Why, Susannah, do you no longer speak? We remember you had plenty to say for yourself the last time you were here. What can have brought about such a reversal?'

I shook my head and looked to my brush, horrified by his sudden interest. This was why I had stayed away. These were questions I had no answers for. I chew my lip as I write. If any man has the look and stature of a King, it is he. Everything about his person exudes power and entitlement. He terrified me.

He sighed his vexation. 'What then if we should command it of you?'

Why in the name of Jesu had I gone there when I knew he

would challenge me? Not brave, merely reckless. I put down my brush, lifting the notebook I kept tied on a girdle at my waist, and with trembling fingers scrawled, 'Your Majesty. I cannot. It is not in my control.'

'But your father tells me you have had no injury or illness to bring about such an enduring deficiency.'

I clenched my jaw and scribbled, 'I cannot explain it, Sire.' How abjectly feeble, as I knew how very much he despised such weakness. When his eyes narrowed, I feared his temper was about to erupt. I had witnessed it once as a girl and never forgotten it. Papa, and others often at court, tell me it is now a more regular occurrence. The line between his fierce brows deepened, like an arrow pointing to his mighty nose. I held my breath, my stomach clenching at the prospect of his rage now directed at me.

Then, he smiled and shook his head, tweaking my cheek with his big fingers. 'A woman's mind is ever a mystery for want of male reason, if nothing else ... and we wouldn't have it different. We shall leave you to your task.' With a nod to Castlemaine and Southampton, he left the chamber trailed by his usual retinue. They seemed very little changed in the years I had been away. I pretended not to hear the sniggers from some fine examples of male reason as they passed by.

After breathing deeply for some moments to gather myself, I looked to my work again, standing resolutely at my easel until I had sufficient completed in watercolour to copy with enamel onto precious metal in Papa's studio. Castlemaine's cream satin and crimson mantua contrasted well with her son's indigo velvet and would be helpful to the portrait's colour balance. She was gracious when I told her we were done. Her boy had fallen asleep, his chin down upon his chest, and she woke him with impatient hands before coming to look at my work.

'You will make much of my fine white skin.' She touched her face more gently than she had her son.

I knew she thought of her younger rival, the Duchess of Richmond, whose face bore some ravages of smallpox, though without leaving her sufficiently disfigured to deter the King's affections. They all seemed so jaded for such activities. I shuddered at the thought of all that flesh released from its bejewelled encasements. Though such indulgent abandon befitted those rooms entirely.

Back in the Henrietta Street studio, soothed by aromas of hot metal and firing enamel, I became myself again, my racing heart slowing, and my breathing eased. Rows of worktables and shelves of metal oxides. Jars of powdered glass in vibrant colours beside flagons of amber oil. And key to it all, the kiln where we performed our alchemy. Everyone was busy and no one looked up at my arrival. *Good.*

Assessing my composition placed down on my table, I was surprised at its fluency despite my unease while painting it. Then, using my lens, I began applying my first colour paste – prepared by Papa's assistant, Edmund, without need to ask – to the gleaming gold disc. I sighed my relief. Yes, this studio had become my refuge. Too much so, I knew. It had become my hiding place. And, finally, my prison. Had I not withdrawn within myself, too, by not speaking?

The more I had thought of my predicament the more it alarmed me, for it would rob me of my life if I allowed it. So eventually, when one fear sufficiently outweighed the other, I went outside. I sighed again, knowing it was now time to address my silence, which meant confronting the why of it, and with some honesty at last.

When the longcase clock chimed four, echoed as always by the bells of St Paul's in Bedford Street, I put away my work and took off my smock before running downstairs to the receiving hall and tugging the bell pull to summon my maidservant. I hastily wrote on my pad, telling her I would go in her stead to Whitehall to fetch Penny home. She was visiting her friend whose parents had rooms off Wood Yard far from the King's where I had been earlier. I am truly determined to make myself go out whenever I can and here was another opportunity. I hope the more I do so the easier it will become, though it is far from that yet.

Bess had Papa's town coach sent round and I hurried to it in light already fading into evening, though the street was still lively with traffic. Coal smoke rose from every chimney to shroud the twilight and taint the air with its acrid odour. Inside, I pulled a rug over my knees for even through my fur-lined cloak, the air was chill.

Sam would soon be home from the French court, where he has been these last many months, and I longed for him in a way that almost overwhelmed me for I have known him my whole life. Loved him my whole life, and it felt a part of me was missing without him. 'Sam.' My breath misted the air in front of me. Yes, I can speak, though he is the only one to hear me now. And unbroken silence for so long has taken its toll upon me. So, this damnable thing must end, but I shall need his help to do it. Yet I laugh as I write. Why? Because he really should turn his back on me; I am so burdensome to him. He is too honourable to do it, of course.

It had begun when I lost my mother to the sweating sickness – well in the morning, dead by dark. Felled by shock and grief … and then impotent rage at her loss, my voice had truly deserted me for a time. I was twenty. Penny but four. I remember how powerless I felt, and silence gave me a sense of agency when it became something I could control. How glad I was for it, too, when Papa married Catherine Villiers just two months after her death. I used it to hurt then … and do still … so fittingly damaging myself most of all. Can Papa ever forgive me? For I know it must end now. And I must start by talking to him. Might it be that Sam's prolonged absence has taught me a salutary lesson by opening my eyes to just how much I too need the easy chatter not possible with pencil and paper?

Penny was ready for me at the Foyles' lodgings. I wrapped her in her own warm cloak and kissed her; she was so happy to see me when she had expected Bess. I smiled at her excitement wishing I could speak to her. What madness that I cannot.

As we crossed that icy court an odd young man came into view, appearing to dress himself as he walked. On hearing our approach, he looked up with such a strange expression on his swarthy face, I was quite unnerved. As I walked away towards King Street and my coach, Penny tugged at my hand.

'A pretty man.'

I have never felt so brittle, as though one sharp blow would shatter me. I exhale, allowing fatigue to sweep over me for it can never be this arduous again. Can it?

RAPHAEL

James Villiers led them through the crowd, turning heads with his dark and glossy handsomeness. He might have turned mine too, had my inclinations been such and I lacked knowledge of his reputation for violence and absence of scruples. No. Villiers seemed a man best avoided.

Yet many eyes both male and female followed him. Many lips were licked. While there is no doubt he is a very fine fellow, he had the look of a man too much reliant on his foppish clothing to get him noticed and in that he was not alone, of course. Though, as a Florentine not long to these shores, what did I know of English fashion and its artifice? My own clothes were tailored in Florence and sent by my father. Though I did appreciate the current English vogue for high-heeled shoes, which I adopted with deep gratitude. In truth, I know more of an English lady's clothing than of a gentleman's, I am somewhat ashamed to admit, with no little experience gained from its removal. I had moved away then, vexed by Villiers strutting; every stride, every arch sideways glance had the look of a performance refined before a looking glass. Although I turned back on hearing the name Susannah murmured through the crowd, intrigued to know who this might be and why her presence should cause such a stir.

Sir Richard Gresham followed behind James with his wife, Lady Catherine, upon one arm – just as polished and gem-encrusted as her son – and a slender girl on the other. So, this was Susannah Gresham. That I had never seen her until then was perhaps unsurprising considering the interest her attendance had provoked. It was her paleness that held my gaze. For I come from a land where such colouring is so rare and eye-catching, heads turn on the street to stare. Pale hair. Pale skin. Though with too little womanly flesh to be thought a beauty at court, she was without artifice in fine blue silk and a simple mantua. Should I not regret her lack of gems for I am here to sell them, after all? Yet she took my breath away.

I could not help but imagine peeling off those layers to expose more of that silky whiteness. But how was I back to such thoughts, as a man of seven and twenty, when I had once foresworn them? Though, Christ help me, I now took what was offered again. Which was plentiful enough. Though I do not know entirely why this should be.

Please do not think me unaware of my own shortcomings. Three elder sisters took care of that. I was only outstanding in my ordinariness and never at any stage in my life have I had sufficient stature. Hence, the heels. Still, I could not be entirely without charm. A warm body rolled in against me then, a small hand caressing my chest and moving slowly southwards.

'Raphael, my dearest, you must soon away. My husband expects me prompt to supper, so I should begin to dress for it.'

The hand, I am ashamed to say, found no work necessary and not through any effect of her presence beside me. Of course, I soon rolled over her and there my musings on Susannah Gresham should have been abandoned but, to my further shame, they were not. With eyes closed, a woman's body need not be her own, though I had to disregard some of milady's fleshly curves beneath my hands. I do occasionally doubt I am quite a gentleman.

Charlotte lay naked atop her bed while I hastily dressed, ready to vacate her rooms so she might summon her maid's assistance. She looked peevish and impatient as she twirled a strand of auburn hair around her finger. It was not a pretty look. Viewing her dispassionately – and all passion had by now entirely left me – she was a touch too plump, not forgetting she was ten years my senior. Nonetheless, she was generally willing and, indeed, more than a little able. When I smiled at her she returned it, looking quite herself again. I bent to kiss her, cupping her ample breast to let her know I would return another day and left her bedchamber, hastening through her ill-lit parlour with its paltry fire and whiff of mould, out into the freezing, gloomy court.

Away from the grand houses and lodgings, Whitehall Palace more resembled a ramshackle city quarter, and Sir Joshua's rooms were about as far away from the King's as was possible. Knighted for making him a generous loan – still outstanding, no doubt – Lady Canford had once caught Charles's eye. I felt certain he had, along with many others so lodged, now quite forgotten he housed them at all.

I stopped a moment in the dismal yard to button my Brandenburg when soft footsteps on the gravel claimed my attention. I looked behind me to see Susannah Gresham approaching, hand in hand with a small girl who appeared her very double. Both were swathed in winter mantles. Her sister, surely? I had not known she had one. I doffed my hat, which I knew from feel had been a little askew and bowed. '*Signorina.*' She brushed past me without acknowledgment. The little girl looked over her shoulder as they swept by and smiled. It was an enchanting smile and I had little doubt her sister's would look much the same. I wondered if I should ever see it. And, yes, encountering her in person, I was mortified by the thought of my all too recent base imaginings and more than a little grateful for the shadows in which to hide it.

. . .

Returned to my Cheapside house, the contrast these surroundings made with Charlotte's shabby and faded lodgings was certainly startling, not least for their Florentine décor with all its opulent white Carrara marble and gilded carvings. The fire was heaped high with blazing coals, the drawing room bright with candlelight. My father's house had been bought as a London investment, and as a place from which to ply our trade with King Charles's court. We sold him gems. We sold gems and jewellery to all of them and the only obstacle to this most pleasant and lucrative of relationships between a seller and a buyer, was their constant unwillingness to pay. This appeared to operate in direct relationship to their wealth. That is to say, the richest were most reluctant and the poorest most eager, so they may not appear lacking in funds.

Giuseppe, hearing the clatter of my footsteps on the marble stairs, soon arrived with wine and a letter from *Papà*. He held the silver tray balanced over his shoulder on one hand, the other placed behind his back. His black hair tied neatly at his neck. In the Rossi livery of green and gold, his face shone with his idea of the deference I deserved as my father's son. He had been my childhood companion and played the part of my obsequious servant … when he remembered it. Or, indeed, wished to. I took off the flowing wig I only wore at court and tossed it onto a chair, smoothing my own hair which now more resembled his. In truth, we had much in common in appearance. The same colouring and slender build, though he was my elder by three years.

'Wine first, *Signore*, eh? This letter has a bad feel to her, something *cattivo*.' He placed his salver down and crossed himself, blinking as though seeing something invisible to me.

I rolled my eyes and held my hand out for a glass, my thoughts still full of Susannah Gresham. '*Grazie, Nonna*.' I emptied it rapidly and held it out for him to refresh.

'Ah, you sense it, too, my dearest *Padrone*?'

'I sense nothing of the sort. It's a letter full of orders and complaints just as always. It can wait while I drink to an apparition of beauty.' I swallowed several large gulps.

'Ah, please God, a fine *vergine* this time. Not another old *puttana*, giving you the cock rot.'

I smiled. 'A very fine maid, indeed.' Though not in my imaginings.

He handed me the folded paper displaying my father's large seal, holding it gingerly by a corner. '*Signore*, if you please. I may be in your employ, but it is your father who remunerates.'

'Open it and hand it to me.'

'Pah,' he said, dropping it into my lap before sitting on a chair beside me, all pretence forgotten. 'Fuck me sideways, but I shall not. Open it yourself you little shit.'

I laughed at his excellent impression of a London accent and snapped the wax. 'Sell more.' I held up a finger. 'Make them pay sooner.' Another finger. 'Less household expense.' A finger. 'Find a rich wife.' Finger. 'A shipment is on its way.' Thumb. 'Gianna is dead … Gianna is dead of smallpox.' I stood, the letter dropping to the floor. 'Gianna. Not my Gianna.' I blinked back quick tears. 'It can't be true. *La mia bella sorella.*' Giuseppe rose to grasp me in his arms, his face already wet.

'I told you, this letter *è crudele*, eh?'

Grief-stricken, I took myself off to the Garter in Blackfriars to find some lively company. It seemed to me a very English way of responding to such a loss. On opening the door into the smoky tavern, I surveyed its dimly lit interior newly decorated in the classical style. Once again, I missed its old incarnation as a bawdy house, though I was never a customer, I had enjoyed the wine and the smiling, buxom girls happy to help me with my English when not occupied elsewhere. That night, I surveyed the men seated at marble-topped tables hoping to locate friends or at least acquaintances.

'Raphael.'

I turned on my heel.

A large arm waved, attracting my attention. 'Over here.'

'Tom.' I made my way through the throng of pot boys and serving wenches to his table under a night-dark window, but close enough to the fire to feel its heat. I was glad to find him alone, though he had not been so for long judging by the array of tankards in front of the three now empty chairs. Thomas Monkton was Lieutenant of the Yeoman Guardsmen at the palace and the first man to befriend me when I arrived at court past eighteen months since, now. He was dressed in his scarlet uniform, meaning he would be on duty later and, knowing his character, he would not drink more than to quench his thirst beforehand. 'I'm glad to find you here.'

'You look mighty dejected. What ails you, lad? Not milady Canford again? She seems a touch more trouble than is warranted, does she not?'

'It's my sister, Gianna.' I bit my lip, blinking back further tears, hoping he would not see it in the gloom. Englishmen seem little impressed with what they judge a weakness.

Thomas leaned closer across the table. 'Tell me.'

'Smallpox.' I shook my head to convey the outcome.

He gripped my wrist for a moment, giving it a reassuring shake. 'Sorry to hear it, my friend. She's the one you were closest to in age?'

'Five years older. Artemisia and Claudia, many years more. Artemisia is soon to become a grandmother.' I felt tears brim again when I thought of her two young girls left motherless and my mamma's grief. Poor Mamma. She was always so close to Gianna. They were very much alike, so quietly, sweetly loving. Though Gianna joined in my teasing with her sisters – who were old enough to know better I had long realised – her heart was never really in it. She would kiss away my tears when they had gone about their business. I would write to Mamma tonight. Though not to Papà. Would he even feel her absence?

'You have my pity. Shall you return to Florence for her funeral?'

'I doubt my father will permit it. There's another gem shipment on its way, and he'll expect me in the workshop to bring him a quick return. I fear my sister's laying to rest will be of little importance in the face of trade.'

'You'll have no difficulties finding buyers, Raphael. I'm told your designs are very fashionable. And they're Italian too, which is very much in vogue they say. All those noble lads and their so-called chaperones, debauching themselves around your fine cities. No, there'll be plenty of buyers, I'm sure.'

I frowned at the defiled cities and the prospect of buyers. For that would not be the problem. 'It's finding payers that proves difficult, alas.'

'Can't say it surprises me, Raph.' He waylaid a passing serving wench, seizing her around the waist, swinging her in close. His flashing smile and muscled bulk was enough for her to bite-back the vexed retort there ready on her lips, replacing it with a welcoming grin.

'What can I get for you two handsome sirs?'

'A jug of Rhenish for my friend here, and a tankard of small beer for me, my lovely.'

She cocked her head. 'Small beer, sweetheart? You sure?'

He gestured to his uniform, grinning. 'Indeed. For I must stay sober to keep the King's peace.'

She laughed, raucous and gap-toothed, throwing her head back with abandon. 'God love you, Sir. You be the only one at Whitehall who do, I'll be bound.'

SUSANNAH

Diary: December 1, 1675

I have found I cannot write every day for often there is nothing to say, or at least nothing I can bring myself to record. Not forward steps. Perhaps even some backwards ones? And I despise myself for it. But today has not been one of those. Today I have been truly happy for the first time in many months.

Sam has returned, thank Jesu, and straightaway came to visit me. I was standing beside the studio window checking my colours when I saw him leave his house to cross the street. My heart soared at the sight of him. He looked wonderful in a lapis blue coat cut in the longer French style, his glossy chestnut hair tied at his neck. He was a candleflame in my darkness. I left my miniature on the sill and clattered down the three flights of stairs to let him in. Then I was in his arms.

He held me away for a moment to plant a kiss upon my forehead. 'Sukie, forgive me. I've abandoned you for far too long.' He took my arm and led me upstairs and into the first-floor drawing room, where the fire burned fiercely in the marble-porticoed fireplace. All the décor was Catherine's; nothing of my mother remained. Gilded chairs and couches. Pale floral upholstery. Matching gold-framed wall panelling. Needless to say, I hate it.

When the door was firmly closed behind us, the relief of it left me quite faint. 'Jesu, Sam. I've missed you more than I can say.' Even though I must keep my voice low, it felt blissful. 'I think it sent me a little mad, speaking to no one.' Little? Understated, perhaps? I clutched his hand. 'But it drove me outside the house at last.'

He pulled me back into his arms. 'Well, I'm very pleased to hear it. And, how brave of you. I can imagine how difficult it must have been.'

I nodded, sighing. 'Having no life became too high a price, so I had to.'

'Sukie, I never expected to be away this long. It all turned out to be so much more complicated than we thought.'

'I know it wasn't by choice. Nor is it your fault I'm so disgracefully dependent on you.' I looked up at him and forced a smile. 'I hope it was all resolved in the end?'

He nodded. 'I think the King is content.'

I knew he could tell me little of it. These visits of his to the royal courts of Europe. Painting portrait miniatures proved an excellent cover for the secret discussions with courtiers and diplomats the King required of him. 'Now I must break my silence, or I fear it will break me.'

He stroked my back. 'I'm here now, so tell me how I can help?'

'I shall try to speak to Papa. And the first words I must say are, "forgive me."'

He grasped my shoulders. 'You were ill after your mama's death. Your voice deserted you. It wasn't your fault.'

'Sam, I spoke at my grandmother's and chose to stop again when I returned here. Because I was angry.' Grandmama and I had needed each other's comfort, even though it meant abandoning Papa and fleeing with Penny to Hampshire. Had this on top of his grief contributed to Catherine snaring him? It must be so, surely?

'Christ, you came home to the Villiers.' He shook his head. 'You wanted to punish your papa for it – I would have felt the same – so you refused to acknowledge them. I understand all of it.' He held my face. 'And I'll do everything I can to help you have a life again.'

'I know you will.' I took a deep breath. 'Now, come up and see my new work. I'd like your opinion of it.'

'With pleasure.'

In the studio, he was soon standing before my table holding his chin whilst he scrutinised my miniature for the King.

Finally, he spoke. 'You really are a sorceress, Susannah. The luminosity. How you do this is beyond me. I saw Castlemaine at court this morning when I brought letters to the King.' He shook his head. 'The rest of us try to give the sitter what they hope for ... hinting at greater beauty. Fewer years. Yet somehow, it's always clear it's been done. You do it and it's not. How in God's name do you know just the right amount to leave unchanged for them to not see what has been?'

I chewed my lip as I wrote, for we were no longer alone, of course, 'I despise that place. I hated being back there–'

He pulled me tight into his arms. 'Sukie, my sweet love.'

Penny ran in then, excited to see him as always and especially so after he had been away for so long. We broke apart and he swung her up into his arms, showering her with kisses. 'How big you've grown my poppet and how exceedingly pretty you are.' He turned to me. 'She gets more and more like you. No one could ever doubt you're sisters.'

I closed my eyes for a moment and smiled. 'Indeed, they could not.' I wrote. Yet I saw the blue eyes that were not mine and a sweet soul much kinder than my own.

I led him back down to the drawing room and when Penny ran off to fetch her new dolly to show him, I was able to whisper to him again before she returned. How I hate my silence with her. It shames me. 'The King saw through my trick.'

'Maybe, for once, your father boasted of your skill to him? Perhaps, to win his patronage for you again?'

'He wouldn't. He guards it closely. It's why my work is so in demand. Sitters must believe I make a true likeness.' We sat together on the couch beside the window looking down on a bustling Henrietta Street. Carriages jostled. Overladen farmers' carts headed for the arcades of Covent Garden. Crowds hurried about their business. Ragged boys wove between them at their peril to cross the gloomy street. Cartmen jeered at coachmen and both bellowed at pedestrians, picking their way through the horse dung.

Sam moved to the fire, adding more coals, and poking it vigorously. 'Will he see it when you do his portrait, or will he choose not to?'

When he was seated beside me again, I whispered, 'He'll see it but say I haven't worked my skills upon his person, knowing I won't be able to contradict him for he is the King.' I quickly moved away from his ear when the door burst open, frowning to see not Penny but James Villiers.

His frown quickly mirrored mine. 'Carter. I heard you'd returned.' He moved to the fire, holding his hands to it. 'I note it didn't take long for you to present yourself here.'

His speech seemed more affected than usual. For Sam's benefit, no doubt. I felt my lip curl at it.

Sam shrugged. 'I greatly missed my dear friends and hurried to see them.'

Now seated opposite, James watched us, sullenly. 'Did you find your miniatures more in favour at the French court?' He paused for a moment before answering the question himself. 'But you wouldn't be back in Henrietta Street had that been so. Perhaps you've come for lessons from Susannah?'

Sam laughed without any discernible edge of rancour. How he does so is a wonder to me when the man is such an odious dolt. 'No one is as good as Susannah, nor quite as expensive.'

I wrote and held up: 'True.' Neither Papa nor Sam have need to work for money, so have chosen not to. I, however, take payment from all bar the King. Does he ever pay anyone for anything?

Once again, the door flew open and this time Penny rushed in clutching her doll, the smile instantly leaving her face at the sight of James. Not, indeed, an unusual response to encountering him in this house.

She came to Sam to sit on his lap, holding out her doll to him. 'I've dressed her in her best gown for you to see.'

'Well, isn't she a truly wonderous creature?'

James grinned at the unease his presence caused her. 'Perhaps

Carter can make a living painting faces on little girls' dollies? Then he might spend less time at our table.'

What an insufferable wretch he is. I wrote quickly and held up, 'At Papa's table. Where he was welcome long before you. And he has no more need to earn a living than you do.' Sam's father is an admiral in the Royal Navy, his disappointment at his son's failure to follow him into the service was only exceeded by his dismay that a bequest from his mother meant no other profession necessary, either. Yet he has a secret one, intelligencing for the King.

James made a show of looking away in order not to see my words.

Sam ignored him. 'Susannah, perhaps you'll join me for dinner tonight? Pascal is pleased to have someone to cook for again at last. It'll give us a chance to catch up.'

I smiled, nodding.

James laughed. 'Well, won't this be a lively evening. I hope you enjoy the sound of your own voice, Carter, and the delightful scratch of a graphite stick on paper.'

Sam smiled at me, with no acknowledgement that James had even spoken. 'I've missed you very much. It will be wonderful to have your company again. To have you all to myself.'

'I feel the same.' I wrote.

At a light knock upon the door, James called out, 'Come.'

Bess entered carrying a heavy tray. Sam set Penny onto the floor and rose to help her, placing it down on the end table. She curtseyed to me but not to James, which visibly irked him.

'You make a good footman, Carter. Ever thought of taking it up?'

Sam laughed affably, which further irked him. 'Why have you brought our refreshments, Bess? Isn't it Robert's job?'

I was glad Sam laughed at James's taunt and also that he asked the question I was poised to write.

'Master James said to, Sir.' She began to pour the wine with a shaking hand.

James rose and moved to her, placing his hand on her shoulder, making her flinch and spill wine over the table. He scowled. 'Clumsy cun–' He glanced at Penny. 'Chit. I've a good mind to thrash you again.'

'No,' Penny shrieked.

Once more, the word I was about to write. Instead, I wrote, 'Again?'

'Run along now, Bess. I'll pour for us. You, too, Penny. Bess will find a cordial for you in the kitchens,' Sam said.

I walked to the door, closing it behind them before moving to Sam's side.

He turned to James. 'You've beaten her? What right have you to lay hands on her?'

'What right have you to question my actions? You, Sir, are not a member of this household.'

I pointed at my mouth and then at Sam to tell James he spoke for me. Jesu, I wanted to scream oaths at him. Yet I was powerless, trapped in my damnable silence.

'Bess is Susannah's maid. She doesn't serve the family. And in this house servants are not beaten.'

I nodded, vigorously. I am mute. Truly, I must find a way to end this.

'All servants are thrashed. It keeps 'em willing. This is Mama's household, and such decisions are hers. She'll decide if the chit needs a further dose.'

'My father's house.' I scribbled and thrust it in his face. He smirked at me and walked away.

Looking out from the window, he smiled. 'Ah, I see her coach approaching. I shall welcome her home. I'm sure she'll happily give you her decision on the matter.'

Then he strode across the room, and we soon heard his footfalls on the stairs going down.

'He won't hurt Bess again, will he?'

Sam moved to the door. 'I'll make sure he doesn't.'

I climbed the stairs back up to the studio as Sam made his way down.

When the doors to Sam's drawing room closed behind me this evening, I felt I had entered a different world where I was at once my true self again. I could speak with complete freedom, and it was joyous.

If our drawing room was a woman's – and a silly one's at that – here was a man's. A naval man's. Dark furniture upholstered in hard-wearing brocade. Brass ship's instruments and wood carvings – mementos of command – upon the mantle and side tables beside heavy brass candelabras. It felt an age since I had last been in there.

We sat close together on a couch before the fire, while I listened to his description of the French court at the Palais du Louvre and all the interesting people he had encountered there. The gossip. The rumours. The mistresses. The affairs.

'And you tell all this to the King?' And the rest he could not speak of to me, of course.

'I do. He believes it gives him a true flavour of the place. He was particularly interested to hear of Louis's building works out at the Palace of Versailles. I was lucky enough to be shown the plans. It will be truly magnificent.'

'Jesu. Pray God it doesn't give him any such notions.' I frowned. 'Though I believe he and Prince Rupert have plans for Windsor, even though Papa says the exchequer is in a rather parlous state again.'

'Too many wretched duchesses.'

We both laughed. 'Too much swiving before lavishing riches on them, getting children off them and then lavishing more. Riches he doesn't truly have.'

'Why, Susannah Gresham. I'm shocked to hear such vulgar speech from his own Goddaughter.' He nudged his shoulder against mine and we laughed again 'And with monies taken from the public purse at that. There are rumblings in Parliament again, I believe.'

'So, he'll prorogue it once more.'

He studied his fingers for a moment. 'I wonder if his wild extravagance – and Monmouth's too, thinking of it – comes from those years living with such limited resources in exile? There must have been times when their lives were greatly restricted by the constant need to rely on others' generosity.'

'James saw real hardship. His father never truly did.'

He sighed. 'And, in all honesty, it's little excuse for the venality now, never mind that William Chiffinch procures actresses or a pretty flower seller or two for him. There's something base about it all that undermines everything I admire about him.'

We were silent for a while, both lost in thought.

He turned sideways to study me. 'Stand up. I want to look at you.'

'No. You've already seen me. What's the matter with you?'

'Not dressed like this. He touched the damson velvet of my skirts. 'Not for rather a long time.'

'Very well.' I stood, feeling horribly embarrassed, a blush hot on my skin.

'May I say something to you, Sukie?'

I thought I knew what it would be. 'Of course.'

'You look very beautiful, as you always do.' He stood and held me close. 'But a little too slender, I'm afraid.'

And there it was. 'Would you care to add insipid to your assessment. Catherine barely allows a day to pass without reminding me of it.' I shook my head. "So thin and insipid, Susannah."'

'Catherine is a cunt.'

I patted his cheek. 'I cannot tell you how much I've missed hearing you say those words. I often try to imagine them emblazoned across her far too ample bosom when I'm forced to communicate with her.'

He laughed. 'In truth, I do believe I'd rather not imagine it.'

He pulled me down beside him again, his arm around my shoulders. 'James was insufferable this afternoon.'

'He told Bess she'd be dismissed if she reported the beating to me. She knows now not to believe such threats and that she must always come to me if he tries to harm her in any way.'

'Good. And I don't like to see the effect he has on Penny, either. It has become noticeably worse since last I saw them together.'

'He seems to truly enjoy how much he frightens her.'

He squeezed my hand. 'There is something wrong about him. The stories of him at court.' He pursed his lips. 'Well, some of them are hair-raising to say the least.'

'And Penny has to share her home with him. Though, thank God, he spends more and more time at Whitehall now Buckingham has taken an interest in him. You can imagine just how thrilled it has made his dear mama, bless her.' I slapped my forehead. 'No. I mean damn her.'

'Fuck her.'

We laughed like the children we once were together. I was a girl whose best friend was a boy. Jesu, but I know how to curse, too.

A tap on the door from Sam's valet, Connor, told us dinner was served and we followed him to the dining-room where the mahogany table was set for two, close beside the fire, the silverware sparkling in bright candlelight. Behind Sam was a portrait of his mother. How alike they are. I know he misses her still. Just one more thing we share. I was silent until the red-haired Irishman had served us and left, closing the door behind him. 'Pascal has cooked as though every chair is filled.' There were twelve.

'I rather feared he might, poor man. He doesn't enjoy enforced idleness.' He shook out his napkin. 'The servants shall eat well tomorrow and then Connor will know where to take the rest. There'll be many hungry mouths happy to receive it all, I'm sure.'

The large plate before me looked daunting. Though it was

but the first of them. Quail with garlic and prunes. 'He won't serve more to you tomorrow?'

'He has rather too high standards for that, which is unfortunate when Papa is used to food onboard ship, of course, and Winchester prepares one for anything, however rancid. What are school fees for, after all. This could feed me for a week.'

I moved the contents around my plate a little, but none had, as yet, found its way to my mouth.

He watched me. 'Susannah. What do you eat at home?'

I blinked. 'Well, I generally eat with Penny in the kitchen parlour. I have what she has.'

He blinked, too. 'But Penny is an eight-year-old child.'

I was suddenly madly enraged by him. 'God's blood I know how old she is, Sam. Damn you. You–' I clenched my jaw so I would say nothing further ... particularly something I might regret of which there was plenty to choose from. He meant it well. I knew he did. I took a long breath, my nostrils flaring. 'Forgive me.' I reached out to place my hand over his. 'I'm so grateful to you for this. I don't know what is wrong with me.' Just to be there with him. I had prayed for it for so long.

He took my hand and squeezed it, before bringing it up to his lips. 'You're unhappy, which is perfectly understandable under the circumstances. But, my Sukie, we're going to do something about it now. Together. So please eat. If only a few mouthfuls from each plate.' He raised his eyebrows. 'Will you at least try?'

I nodded. How many wretched plates could there be?

In the end it was a perfect evening. After I had eaten enough to satisfy him, we returned to the drawing room with more wine. Later, he walked me across the street to my door with Connor acting as our linkman, carrying a lantern now all the exterior household ones had been extinguished. He stood with me for a moment, holding me in his arms. 'I'm back now, Sukie, and we will overcome it all, you have my word.'

· · ·

How had I ever endured without him? And it was so wonderful to talk. I hope because I have after so long, it might ease me back to do so with Papa. I still wish he had never brought the Villiers into our home, but I rather suspect he might have some regrets of his own now.

RAPHAEL

I came to court on the first day of December hoping for another sight of Susannah Gresham. Sadly, she did not attend. That those I asked confirmed they had seen her but once in recent memory, did not fill me with much hope of making her acquaintance. Perhaps I could arrange for her to paint my miniature, but I doubted that would pass my father as an expense of trade. I smiled, picturing his outrage. James Villiers was there though, with his entourage of young men all in his own image. I stood with Tom Monkton just inside the entrance to the Banqueting House, watching.

'Who do you seek?'

'No one in particular,' I lied.

He laughed, knowing it. 'Well, you're not impressed with Villiers, that's plain to see. You should learn to guard your expression more, Raph. He has many friends here.'

My eyes had narrowed involuntarily at his mannered strutting. 'Then they've little taste, so explaining their choice of friend.' At that moment, I became aware of a small resplendent figure approaching in an indigo gown encrusted with some of my finest pearls. As yet unpaid for. Tom left through the doors behind us to take up his designated position outside.

I bowed low. 'Your Grace.'

'Raphael, my dearest.' She touched the ruby necklace at her throat. 'This is very fine. Your best yet, I think.'

Frances Stuart, Duchess of Richmond. Her beauty clear in

the ghost of her former face beneath cruel ravages of smallpox. Yet she did nothing to conceal the change. Her eyes still sparkled, and the King still favoured her it seemed. I had never heard her complain about her disfigurement, once telling me she was simply glad to live when so many did not. I thought then of Gianna. 'Thank you, Your Grace. I'm glad it pleases you.'

'I had hoped to see you here tonight. A little bird tells me a certain gentleman is alarmed by his wife's indiscreet dallying.' She tapped my arm with her fan. 'I think a short sojourn to the country might be prudent, my dear.'

I felt heat on my face, glad my dark skin would make it difficult to detect. 'I fear I'm unfamiliar with anywhere outside of the capital, Your Grace. Perhaps I might lie low in Cheapside for a while?'

She tilted her head. 'I fancy it will take a little more than that this time, Raphael.' She tilted her head the other way, now tapping her lips with her fan. 'I have some old jewellery at Kew Palace. You may accompany me there on the morrow. Perhaps you might inspect it with a view to resetting?'

I bowed again. 'Your Grace, it would be my pleasure. You have my gratitude.' Once again, her patronage came to my rescue. Had she not brought my pieces to court displayed upon her person, my business here would not have prospered quite so quickly or so well. She had been delighted, as had I ... and Papà, of course, when the Duchess of Portsmouth and the Countess of Castlemaine – themselves mistresses to the King – vied with her to secure my most valuable pieces, though they did not condescend to deal with me in person, much to my relief.

'The only benefit of the frigid winters we have had of late is the greater ease of travel with the absence of mud through the winter months. Nothing slows a carriage quite like mud.'

A cold journey together then, though one which might prove useful in prompting payment for all that now adorned her. I smiled and bowed, a final time. 'Your Grace.' I watched her walk away, lambent with my pearls.

. . .

Kew proved rather bewildering from my perspective as a Florentine with a somewhat different notion of what a *palazzo* should be. An old red-brick royal residence too small and decrepit for the King's use – he had a surfeit of the large and decrepit, I imagined – put at her disposal should she wish country air without traveling as far as her house in Kent. While not in the same league as his gift of Nonsuch Palace to Castlemaine five years earlier, it was generous enough to a former favourite he had once thought to marry when the Queen seemed near death years before, later even contemplating divorce for Frances Stuart. Could it be true she had not been his mistress then? She had no children off him, which was unusual considering how many he had acquired elsewhere bar from his wife, of course. Poor lady. The duchess, too, was childless and a widow, living on the King's generosity and as a Lady of the Bedchamber to the Queen. My father's research had been nothing if not thorough.

Though we arrived at dusk, the journey through the park was well lit for us with braziers along the gravel drive, and lanterns aplenty around the great iron-studded oak entrance doors. Inside was a Tudor Great Hall, with a mighty hearth and a blazing fire. Chairs were pulled up close and we soon shed our travel chill and were ready to dine. The duchess retired early, and I thought it best to follow her lead, signalling Giuseppe to wait upon me in my bed chamber.

After our barge with its gold fringed crimson canopy and its thirty liveried oarsmen, conveyed us from the Privy Stairs at Whitehall up to the Friarsgate Stairs, he had travelled in a second carriage to Kew with three of the duchess's ladies whom he told me later, always accompanied her on her journeys. Though they were all well passed the first bloom of youth, his expression as he climbed in to join them suggested he found this nothing to concern him. Knowing him as I did, I suspected he felt he could charm them with greater ease than younger and more discerning companions. Frances Stuart was close to my own age at twenty-eight or nine. Did these older ladies now make her feel her disfigurement less?

The next day, Giuseppe and I rode out on a pair of fine bay horses from Kew's stables into the old hunting park, soon relaxing back to our easy companionship once away from others' nosy eyes. I felt sure the English would disapprove of friendship between master and servant. Or at least would claim so. Yet I had noticed a distinct lack of reserve between the duchess and her eldest lady, Mary Warnock, which I raised with him.

'Frances is fond of her old Mary. She was her most beloved nursemaid at the old Queen's court in Paris, and she's stayed by her side ever since.'

'Then she must feel like a kind of *mamma* to her, no?' The thought pleased me. Her duke had died some years before, and I imagined she must be lonely for affection, especially when the King's favours were generously shared amongst so many.

We cantered on along a frost-hardened track through ancient trees. The December morning was bright but frigid and we wore fur-lined riding cloaks over our Brandenburg coats, with our mounts' breath blooming around us in billowing clouds. The track led to an open glade which, to my startled surprise, was already occupied by the duchess and her lady, Anne Hyde. I bowed, doffing my hat, hoping Giuseppe had done the same behind me. Florentine servants do not often do this without direct instruction. Or was that just mine?

I halted my horse alongside them. 'Your Grace.' I bowed again and turned. 'My Lady Anne.' Both were dressed in dark riding habits and wore periwigs, a peculiar English custom for ladies when out riding. The duchess's slight build and comely figure stood out against her companion's bulk. That lady's expression on registering Giuseppe's presence, showed it was by no means an unwelcome one.

'Raphael. It seems we have all felt the need of outside air this morning. The palace chimneys need sweeping, which accounts for the acrid quality of the air. Ride with me.'

'Your Grace.'

Her horse, an elegant dappled grey, moved away at a canter and I followed, admiring her horsemanship riding side-saddle with her cloak streaming behind her over the horse's rump. When we had left the others far enough behind, she reined-in and we walked our horses side-by-side along a wide frosted avenue between beech trees, their bare, white-rimmed branches arching over us like a soaring, glittering ecclesiastical ceiling. The horses' hoofbeats and the jangle of their bridles echoed in the still air.

'I wonder what you find quite so enticing about Charlotte Canford?' She gave me a hard stare. 'You could do so much better.' She must have read something in my expression for she threw back her head, laughing with some abandon. 'No, Raphael, I do not mean me.'

Heat flamed upon my face because that was just what I had thought ... and how much the prospect pleased me. 'Of course not, Your Grace ... not that ...' I delved desperately for something to say to draw her attention away from my embarrassment. 'There is a young lady at court who has caught my eye, Your Gra–' In my confusion, I spoke my own language rather than the French we had conversed in until then.

'Frances, when we are alone. And Duchess is sufficient when we are not, my dear.' She answered in perfect Italian, reaching across to touch my arm. 'So, don't keep me in suspense. Who is she?'

'Susannah Gresham.'

'Ah, yes. What a pairing you would make. You so dark and handsome, she so fair ... though perhaps she has a little height on you. She is a tall girl.'

Her mockery stung. I turned away. 'Your Grace.'

She drew a sharp breath and touched my arm again. 'Raphael, no. I speak honestly. You would look very well together. Truly.'

Again, I found myself terribly discomfited. It seemed I had misinterpreted her, so was in danger of appearing to seek compliments for my appearance, which left me full of confusion. And once more, I floundered for a way to divert her. I tried to laugh but there was no mirth in it. 'I don't think she favours me, anyway.' I closed my eyes, feeling my tongue escaping me. 'When I encountered her in a palace courtyard, she ignored my greeting.' Why, in the name of God, did I tell her that? 'Her young sister smiled at me, though.' *Cristo*. I was losing my mind. Her sister smiled at me? *Really*? Yet something hard and knowing flitted across her face and then was gone, leaving me doubting I had ever seen it.

'She does not speak, so you should make no assumptions about her meaning.'

'She cannot speak? Was she born so?'

'Not at all. I believe she became mute after her mother died. She is the King's Goddaughter, so I know something of her.' She pursed her lips in thought. 'He has some fondness for her. Richard Gresham was with him at Worcester and on the continent when other courts took his people in for a time. They are staunch friends, still.'

'Perhaps some malady took her voice?'

'She had not been ill – or only from grief at the time – so far as I am aware. The King believes she is now but wilful. Her grief began it and when Richard married Catherine Villiers so soon, she continued it ... to pain her father.'

I turned at the sound of horses approaching, followed by the trill of feminine laughter. Giuseppe and the Lady Anne.

Frances sighed. 'Come, Raphael, I shall show you my jewellery. The stones are good, I believe, but the settings are heavy and antiquated. I'm sure you can work your magic.'

The duchess had set off back to Whitehall Palace the next morning, telling me she would send word when it was safe for me to return. Yet with a courier expected at Cheapside, I could not remain away for long, and I was eager to start the work for her. The gems were spectacular, and she had given me carte blanch to re-cut them as well as create fashionable settings. Nonetheless, two days later, I still remained before the fire in my chamber – a draughty place with air smelling of mildew and smoke – its walls hung with faded arrases from a past era depicting saints and martyrs. Once again, the day was drear and chill and such visions of grisly death did little to lift my mood. Giuseppe snoring in the chair opposite, content after our morning ride followed by a luncheon of mutton and a jug of Rhenish, did little to lift my mood either.

With the duchess departed and finding myself again without occupation, and the novelty of it now quite gone, my thoughts returned again to Susannah Gresham. It was difficult to believe she would remain silent by choice. Who would? I did not have to imagine the frustrations of being unable to communicate as I had struggled with English on first arrival. How could I forget trying to make my way from St Katherine Dock by hackney through the teeming streets? When the coachman asked, 'Where are bats?' I had clutched my head in despair. I sighed. Could her father's anguish over it have made the King take such a harsh view of her misfortune? For he is known to have a kind-hearted nature, shown with many demonstrations of love for his children and even his pretty little spaniel dogs.

Giuseppe's snort woke him, and he sat up looking befuddled. 'Why you wake me, Raph? I dreamt of many women. Many, many all for me only. One, she about to suck my–'

'I didn't wake you, oaf. Your own snoring did. Get up and do your job. Serve me in some way.'

He grinned. 'You wanna me to suck you off, eh? Or there's a *bella Signorina* in kitchens, she is so nice an juicy–'

I laughed, holding up my hands. '*Tu stolto*. I can't decide which orifice is the more repellent.' I stood and walked to the window, looking down at dense woodland motionless as painted theatre scenery under a lid of pewter sky. 'We shall leave for London in the morning. I'll take my chances in Cheapside.'

Giuseppe began to pack for me. Perhaps he too was tired of inactivity? When a tap sounded upon the door, he was there to open it with surprising speed. He took the letter from the footman and brought it to me.

'The duchess's seal.' I broke it and unfolded the thick sheet of paper, quickly scanning it. 'The Canfords have gone to their house in Salisbury after having their lodgings withdrawn.' I shook my head, smiling. 'She had a word with the Clerk of the Green Cloth. What a wonder that woman is.'

'She *la lussuria* for you, no mistake, eh?'

'I know for a fact she does not, for she told me so herself.'

He laughed uproariously, bending to slap his thighs. 'You think a woman tell a man the truth of this?'

Sadly, in this case, I did.

Chapter Two
SUSANNAH

Diary: January 4, 1676

I shall enjoy writing this entry. I smile as I do so.

Today I made a new friend who came to Henrietta Street for Papa to make his miniature. His name is Thomas Monkton, and he is Lieutenant of the Yeoman Guardsmen at Whitehall Palace. I was busy at my table when Edmund brought him up. He is a bear of a man with a mane of his own dark hair tied at his nape. Papa's wig conceals his fuzz of grey hair, for which he is grateful. I wonder if it is true the fashion began because the King wished to cover his own thinning, grey hair?

Lieutenant Monkton was in his full uniform of scarlet and gold, with its crowned Tudor Rose, shamrock and thistle, and the royal cypher emblazoned upon his chest. Papa appeared slight beside him though he is taller than most.

He likes to work from life directly onto precious metal so his sitters must wait between each firing. And whilst he waited for Papa to finish his preparation – which he prefers to do himself – he came to my table.

'Do you mind if I watch you?'

I wrote, 'Please do.' I was unsure if he was aware of my silence, but he made no indication he was surprised by it. Unexpectedly, his presence did not discomfort me.

He looked at my watercolour. 'Lady Castlemaine is very beautiful. I didn't know she has green eyes.' He narrowed his. 'The boy favours the King, though.'

I nodded and began to build up translucent layers of red to achieve the depth of colour needed to suggest the drape of her mantua, upon the gold oval. This was the second of the two the King had requested. One for himself and one for Castlemaine.

'Would you tell me what you're doing? What sort of paint do you use and why only one colour?'

I took a moment to write, 'It is a paste made from powdered glass and metal oxides mixed with oil. Each colour must be applied separately.' I dotted another layer to deepen the colour in the fabric folds.

'Why?'

I wrote. 'When I've finished, it will be fired in the kiln. The colour needing the longest firing time must be done first with the rest added in the correct order.'

'I had imagined you'd work all the colours together, just like in other paintings.' He shook his head. 'You have such a steady hand with those tiny brushes. This sort of skill and delicacy leaves me a little unnerved.' He looked down at his own great paws.

'You have other skills, I'm sure.' I wrote.

He shrugged and began describing his typical day, weaving such a tale I found myself both enchanted and amused by his self-deprecation. Yet, oddly, his soft voice did not distract me as he told of his duties policing the court in the King's name, handling everything from drunken courtiers, assaults, and petty disputes, to running the King's spaniels in St James's Park at his whim. I smiled, not quite believing that.

When Papa returned to his table, he squeezed my shoulder as he passed though I did not look up.

'Come, Thomas. Let us begin. Oh, and could I ask you to persuade my daughter to attend tomorrow night's ball, if you can–'

I knocked on my table and wrote, 'I have already agreed it.'

'Have you now, my dearest girl? And whom is this worker of miracles who has prevailed upon you after we have so often tried and failed?'

'Frances Stuart.' I wrote.

Papa's eyebrows shot up. 'Richmond? Well, well. How unexpected. I wonder why she would ask you ... and why, indeed, you would agree?'

These are questions I have been asking myself ever since. When I visited court earlier with Penny, she had taken much trouble to engage me in conversation, pressing me to attend the Twelfth Night Ball. She was so effusive and warm, I had found myself agreeing to it. She had waylaid me waiting outside the King's presence chamber after he had asked for Penny, whom he had not seen for some time. Yet I could not understand why the duchess had done it when we had barely acknowledged each other before. Though I had been aware of her as a presence often beside the King when I had last visited court regularly and had painted her once, we spoke little then. In truth, it was almost as mystifying as my consent.

Diary: January 6, 1676

I attended the ball in the end last night, though I had often thought to change my mind. When Sam said he would accompany me, so I need not travel in our coach with my father and the Villiers, I relented. Catherine was not happy with my decision, insisting we should arrive as a family.

'We're not a family, though. Surely even someone with her

limited intellect can recognise it.' I said to Sam when we were alone in his carriage.

'You are still your father's daughter, Sukie, don't forget that. And Penny too.'

I felt myself redden, though not for the reason he would imagine should he see it in the gloom of the single candle lamp. 'Why then were we not sufficient for him? Why inflict the Villiers upon us?'

'Because he fell in love with her, perhaps? We can question his taste and we do, do we not?'

We smiled at each other.

'Yet was he not entitled to search for happiness? Though perhaps after a seemlier wait.'

I frowned. 'If he did fall in love, she manipulated it ... and certainly never reciprocated.'

His coach took us to the Holbein Gate, where we were waved in from the queue by an attendant checking for those warranting immediate entry. The Richmond coat of arms on the invitation prevailed.

Once inside, we made our way across The Court lit by blazing torches, to the Great Hall where the ball was already well underway, music and raucous laughter reaching us as we walked with many others towards the entrance with blazing light and the din of a multitude of voices flowing out to meet us. Sam looked well in his French finery. A coat and waistcoat of periwinkle blue edged with fine silver embroidery, white lace cravat at his throat. My pearl grey gown, violet mantua and skirts gathered to show violet taffeta petticoats, were not entirely unbecoming either. Still, we both looked a touch dowdy alongside many of our bewigged and bejewelled fellow guests.

Inside the Hall, the evergreen boughs and branches of holly hung with aromatic pomanders, added their scent to that of hot beeswax and perfumed revellers, but did not quite conceal the faint sour smell of too much overheated flesh. Though an orchestra played at the other end of the great chamber, and some were dancing, most paraded the floor both to show themselves and locate those with whom they wished to converse. Fans were fluttered beneath shining eyes. Lips licked and smiles flashed. Many glasses of arrack and claret were quaffed. While gentlemen guffawed and lit their pipes, ladies eyed each other with speculative disdain.

After some time meandering through the gaudy, rustling crowd, we found a quieter spot near an exit into a small, closed courtyard where we could watch. It was here Lieutenant Monkton found us, entering via that court with a companion. This man was of slight build, dark haired and tawny-skinned with a wide smile revealing straight white teeth as he laughed with the lieutenant. When he noticed us, he stood stock still, the smile falling from his face like a candle snuffed. I turned to Sam thinking there must be some animosity between them, but he appeared as puzzled as I. Thomas turned to see why his friend had stopped.

'Ah, Mistress Gresham. I am glad to have found you so easily.' He looked around at the milling crowds. 'We came in through a private entrance. I might be off-duty, but I still have my keys.' He tapped the pocket of his russet velvet coat.

I wondered why he was so eager to locate me and gestured towards Sam.

He bowed to Thomas. 'Samuel Carter.'

'My oldest and dearest friend.' I wrote for him to read aloud, which he did with a self-deprecating smile.

Thomas placed his hand on his companion's shoulder. 'And this is my friend Raphael Rossi.'

He bowed to Sam before lifting my hand to his lips, which were cool and soft. Raphael Rossi. I knew the name. The Italian Jeweller whom it is said beds ladies faded past the first bloom of youth in return for their purchasing his gems. He is much in demand I am told, and had it not been he I saw dishevelled in Wood Yard? I sighed. So many women believing themselves winning love when, in truth, they were mere playthings taken so easily with empty words. How had they become quite so complicit in it all? Yet most seemed content enough. Jesu, and what sort of paragon was I to grudge them such? Too scared of life to even live it.

I refocused my attention, finding Raphael Rossi only slightly taller than I, leaving our eyes almost on a level. His were large, dark lashed and an amber-flecked deep green. Truly, the green of winter moss. I had never seen their like before. Mine seemed involuntarily locked with his while he stared at me so intently. I began to feel some alarm until his gaze left me, suddenly. I turned to see the Duchess of Richmond approaching through the crowd, which parted for her tiny form as though choreographed to give her passage. She made quite a sight in her gown of crimson encrusted with pearls, gathered away from golden petticoats with a gossamer lace gorget around her shoulders. She greeted Raphael Rossi very warmly indeed.

'Raphael, my dearest. You look most fine this evening, does he not, Susannah?'

And he did, in a green satin coat and waistcoat edged by a wide band embroidered in gold thread, a combination that having now studied them, I saw closely matched his eyes. Was she his latest faded lady? Though, in truth, there was nothing faded about her. Her disfigured skin did nothing to dim her glowing beauty. If he were bedding her, I hoped they kept it from the King. He had refused to recognise Castlemaine's last daughter as his. He did not always share well. Yet the duchess had not the look of a woman easily conquered even though Raphael Rossi clearly would not often encounter resistance.

'Duchess,' he said, bowing before kissing her hand.'

Duchess not Your Grace. That told me much. They were definitely close. When she turned to me, I curtseyed, noticing Sam and the lieutenant had moved away before she acknowledged them, leaving me standing alone beside the jeweller.

'Susannah. I'm so glad you and Raphael have met at last. I hope you might get to know one another. You must have so much in common. You with your skill at portrait miniatures and Raphael's with gems.' She lifted a ruby necklace from her throat. The gold setting was as fine and intricate as a piece of lace.

I wrote, 'It's very beautiful. Like fronds of foliage hung with scarlet fruit.' His teeth flashed in a rather attractive hesitant smile, where one side of his mouth lifted moments before the other. There was something charmingly engaging about it.

'I used botanical forms as my inspiration, *Signorina*.' His deep voice was honeyed by an Italian accent, matching it to perfection.

I curtseyed again to the duchess and wrote, 'I should return to my friends, Your Grace.' I did not wait for her reply. My heart already pounding alarmingly without Sam beside me. I had seen them step out into the small court and followed. He stood alone in a patch of light thrown out from the hall. 'I still don't understand why she was so keen for me to come–'

When Thomas stepped out from the shadows, he became the second person at Whitehall to know I could speak, though I said nothing further once I knew he was there. I wondered if, indeed, I could. Yet I was not brave enough to find out then. He readily gave his word it would go no further. And I find I trust him.

RAPHAEL

I watched Susannah Gresham walk away, hearing the duchess's slight gasp when she did so rather impolitely. Though when I turned to look, her expression was quite serene once more. 'As I told you, Duchess, she's not interested in me.'

'Pah. Don't be so lily-livered.' She tapped my arm with her fan. 'At least now you have been introduced. You can proceed from here.'

'She could not wait to escape me.' I sounded tiresomely self-pitying, even to myself.

'If you covet her, Raphael, you must pursue her. For she will not pursue you.'

'How? When she is so rarely at court?'

She shrugged, impatiently. 'Make friends with her friends. Have her make your portrait. There are ways and you shall find them if you are eager enough to win her.' She tapped me with that fan again. Quite sharply, this time. 'Now, my dear, I must return to *my* friends. Good luck to you.'

I bowed. '*Duchessa.*' And then I was left quite alone. I took a glass of arrack from a passing footman, swallowed it in one long gulp, and made to follow Susannah and her companions through the door they had left by. I crossed myself before stepping out. '*Dio aiutami.*' Not behaviour recommended at a protestant court where papists were loathed with a peculiarly English kind of relish. I moved out into a shadowy yard, encountering a vague whiff of shit. I had heard courtiers thought nothing of availing themselves of any dark corner and made a careful note to avoid stepping anywhere near one. I could see only one person present, and it was neither Susannah nor Tom. 'I look for my friend, Thomas Monkton,' I lied, bowing to Samuel Carter again. I had not spoken with him earlier though we had been introduced.

'*Signor* Rossi,' he said, returning my bow.

The light from the open door now shone directly on him, allowing me to appreciate his quite startling beauty. Fine features. Large almond shaped blue eyes framed by long dark lashes. Of course, my attention had been focused elsewhere at our first encounter.

He pointed to a closed gate. 'Monkton has just left for the privy apartments. With the King about to leave the entertainment, his rooms must be searched before he enters them. I believe he requested him particularly, though he was off-duty tonight.'

'Tom must search the King's rooms? He hasn't told me of this duty.'

'It is more ceremonial than practical. Just something the Lieutenant of the Yeoman Guardsmen does, apparently. Susannah has gone with him to make her salutations there rather than have to waylay him while he tries to escape the melee.'

'Thomas tells me he is a keeper of the King's peace at court, which means despatching guardsmen to deal with most matters, leaving him to herd the aristocracy. I have never really understood what he means by this herding. I can only picture him harrying a crowd of grand people with several eager sheepdogs under his command.'

Samuel laughed. 'I just met him for the first time tonight, but that seems entirely feasible.'

I laughed too, until a shadow appeared across him when someone else stepped out into the court through the door behind me. I had caught his look of dismay before his face fell into shadow.

'James.' His voice was ice.

'Carter. Sorry to intrude on ...' He looked from one to the other of us. 'Whatever this is.'

James Villiers. Of all the people I had wished to avoid tonight, he was at the top of my list. *Merda*. 'I had hoped to find Thomas Monkton, but he has business with the King.' I said into a silence, which now felt dangerous.

Villiers' eyes stayed on Samuel. 'Thomas Monkton now is it, Carter? Safely married, too. How sensible of you at last. But what luck. An encounter with a pretty morsel who will suffice instead, no? Add a little spice, no?'

His speech was just as mannered as his bearing.

Samuel took a step towards him, smiling. 'We're not all as fetid as you. No maidens to coerce, James? No boys to corrupt. To swive?' His tone was light though his words held menace.

Villiers' hand went to his sword, his polished façade quite fallen away. 'Silence or you'll regret it. I shall make certain of it, you calumnious knave.'

Samuel laughed, appearing quite unconcerned.

Then, as he began to draw with real intent, Catherine Gresham rushed into the yard, cannoning into him. 'Stop, you fool. Don't you know to use a sword within the palace precinct can be high treason against the King? Do you wish the traitor's death?' She seized his arm as his sword dropped back into its scabbard. 'Come. We're leaving now the King has retired and Monmouth is left holding court as though he is a true prince and not just another damnable bastard.' She shook her head. 'Jesu, how have I got such a son.'

After his mother had swept him away, I turned to Samuel. 'I see you have as low a regard for James Villiers as I.' Which, in truth, seemed an understatement.

He laughed, again. 'Indeed. And I am sorry you had to witness our hostilities.'

'*Signore*.' I bowed and left him there alone to wait for Susannah. Lily-livered indeed.

The next morning, I sat at my workbench examining the diamond pendant I had just attached to complete the necklace. With the stones mounted in the more delicate setting the duchess favoured using a repeating bow motif set with diamonds and sapphires, I was more than pleased with the result and slipped it into a velvet bag. That the sun had finally broken through the slab of cloud, now marbled with streaks of blue, flooding the workshop with light through the skylight, confirmed it. I would deliver the necklace to her myself today. I had never done so before but, as I wished to talk with her about Susannah, it offered the perfect opportunity.

'Giuseppe.' He looked at me from his place further along the bench where he examined another batch of new gems with the aid of a magnifying lens. His skill at this more than matched my own, though I doubted my father would approve of such delegation. 'I'm going to Whitehall.'

He frowned. 'You tell me this, why?'

'Well, you are my man. By rights you should accompany me.'

Something that happened only rarely when I came to think of it. In truth, only if he wished to.

'You needing a nursemaid, now, *bambino*?'

I laughed. Any visage less like that of a nursemaid was hard to imagine, especially as he was in need of a shave and had been for some days. 'Have we been sent decent stock this time?'

He rocked his hand, noncommittally. 'Well, not *cack*, anyway.'

'Not shit.' I echoed. 'Not shit will have to do.' He had returned to his task and no longer gave me his attention. 'Giuseppe.'

He looked at me again. '*Che cosa*? You want me fucking do this shit or no?'

He knew quite well how little I enjoyed the job myself. 'Indeed, I do. But first I'd like you to have my coach sent round.

He stood hands on hips. 'You say all them–' He gestured at the gems. 'All them must go in *stanza forte* then out again coz you no shout "coach" yourself, you little gobshite?'

Gobshite? What? The word 'coach' was yelled at the top of his voice, drawing startled glances from the men and boys working at other benches, and was probably sufficient to have it readied for me without any further action needed. This proved correct when the sound of hooves on cobbles could be heard as the horses were brought out from the coach house stables in the mews behind the workshop.

Giuseppe grinned and made an elaborate bow. 'At your command, *carissimo padrone. Sempre.*'

There was some appreciative chuckling, which I pretended not to hear as I went out to the coach. Unfortunately, this was replaced by the bellowing of oxen slaughtered in the shambles, telling me the direction of the wind. My father knew nothing of London when he purchased the Cheapside house or its particular proximity to Smithfield Market.

The traffic was unusually heavy, so my journey to the palace took rather longer than anticipated. Rory sensibly chose not to risk Thames Street, a notorious bottle neck. I trusted him to find the quickest route to King Street as I stared out at a rare sight of old London that had somehow escaped the fire: ancient houses, stories added haphazardly, leaning in towards each other almost blocking out the sky. This soon gave way to new piazzas and the regal terraces of The Strand until, reaching the mansions of Bedford Street, we came to a halt, finding the road ahead blocked by an overturned wagon.

With the air now full of furious shouts rather than the ceaseless clatter of hooves and rumble of iron-rimmed wheels over cobbles, my mind wandered away and, of course, alighted upon Susannah Gresham. Where else? And for the umpteenth time, I relived the events at last night's ball. How could the duchess not see there was no hope for me with her? It was not just a question of finding a way into her life. There would be little point to that if she did not welcome me when I arrived there. Yet I could not help but hear the duchess call me 'lily-livered' once again. Maybe she was right. I straightened my back. I would not give up without a fight. Susannah barely knew me thus far, and I did not regard myself as difficult to like. In truth, I had much evidence I was not.

At last, the coach began to move again and in no little time we were approaching St James's Park. Feeling in need of fresh air and exercise now the sun was fully out, though the air was frigid, I told Rory to wait there for me. I walked down The Mall between the lines of winter elms and entered the park, making my way towards the palace. I did question, briefly, whether it was entirely wise when I carried a piece of valuable jewellery about my person, but it was well hidden in a body-belt designed for that purpose and I had my sword, though I had little skill with the wretched thing. It would be a different matter after dark, of course. St James's Park became a changed place then. A carnal place I had been informed but had no personal knowledge of this. Though I doubted such activity took place in the depth of this freezing winter.

I arrived at the Park Gate quite unmolested and was admitted after showing the duchess's warrant to the sentry there. Still recalling last night's encounter as I passed the privy gardens, I thought once more of Samuel Carter. Susannah had seemed very close to him. Her oldest and dearest friend she had said. Was there more than friendship there? I felt a sudden cramping in my gut at the thought she already loved another. Then stepping over a fresh dog turd, the stink made me think of James Villiers. I laughed out loud, pleased such a stench should bring him to mind. There was most certainly history between him and Carter. I was rather intrigued to discover what it might be. Perhaps the duchess might enlighten me?

In Richmond House, I waited in Frances's drawing room looking out from the large mullioned and transomed window down onto the deserted privy garden with its white marble statuary, and the bowling green rimed with frost still, where shadows lingered. No one played in winter, of course. I turned when the doors opened for the duchess with a footman following close behind, carrying a tray holding wine and sweetmeats piled high in a crystal dish. I moved to her, bowing to kiss her hand. 'Duchess.' Her gown was of dark blue taffeta, the skirts pinned back to show silver and white striped petticoats. Her golden hair was curled in tight ringlets falling over her forehead. Strangely, I did not notice her pitted skin only the lucent amethyst of her eyes, feeling a sudden stab of tenderness for her.

'I must say I am surprised to see you this morning, Raphael. I thought all you young ones would be yet abed, having caroused long into the night. Some of you certainly did, for I heard it myself.'

'We are of an age, Frances.' I said when the door closed behind the servant. 'And I left early.'

She led me to a green upholstered couch close to the fire, inviting me to sit and poured the wine herself, handing me a glass before sitting beside me with her own. 'So how goes it with Susannah? That you left early suggests not well.'

I took a long drink of claret. It was excellent, naturally. I told her then of my fears about Carter and recounted the incident in the courtyard. 'Villiers is a vicious brute.'

She tilted her head. 'You're not alone in that opinion, my dear.' She drank her wine, looking pensive. 'He's a new favourite of Buckingham's, but I doubt even he could save him had he been seen to draw his sword with intent within the palace precinct and the King decide on treason … and George Villiers' star is waning anyway, I think.'

Another Villiers? Were they all related? Christ. 'What a pity then that he did not.' Examining those words, I found I felt no guilt over them. What was it about the man that made me dislike him so? Hearsay and appearance only. Yet his encounter with Carter had served only to confirm my prejudice.

She sighed. 'As for Samuel.' She looked away for a moment. 'I know only they were childhood friends. He is a delightful young man. The King has always been very taken with him.'

I frowned in puzzlement. 'The King? How so?'

She smiled. 'His father is Admiral Rupert Carter, another close friend since the exile, made viscount after the restoration. Sam's a portrait miniaturist too. Richard Gresham tutored him alongside Susannah. Sometimes he visits other courts on Charles's privy business, though that must be kept between us.'

She had a wonderful smile. I wished I had seen it in her full glory. And did Susannah know of Carter's work for the King? 'As you wish, Frances.' I stood. 'Well, I should tell you I'm here with a purpose beyond intelligence gathering. I have something for you.' When I began to unbutton my waistcoat, I watched her eyes widen and a slight flush appear upon her cheeks. However, she did not avert her gaze and, Christ help me, I began to feel the first stirrings of arousal. 'A necklace, in fact,' I said to remove any ambiguity. I was soon glad my own blushes were harder to discern, especially when I had to root in an unseemly manner in order to extricate the velvet bag from the body belt beneath my shirt, a process entirely new to me. By this time, she was laughing with some abandon, especially watching me trying to tidy my disarray.

She rose and took the bag from my hand, shaking the necklace out and holding it up to the light. 'It is quite lovely, Raphael. Better than I could ever have imagined from that heavy old stomacher broach.'

'I'm glad you're content with it.'

She lifted her face for me to kiss before I left, which I did with a strong urge to move my lips onto hers. When she smiled, I felt certain she knew it. Had she felt the same? 'I shall send a note when I have more for you, so you may tell me if it is convenient to call upon you. Forgive me for not doing so today.'

When I walked again beside the bowling green on my way towards the Park Gate, I cursed myself for not bringing my coach to King Street as the sun had now entirely vanished behind massing clouds and the air was mightily chilled. I looked up, fearing snow but not, I prayed, before I reached it. I settled my Brandenburg more closely and increased my pace.

It was then I spotted a figure a little way ahead and a moment later realised it was Susannah. Sadly, my first instinct was to turn around and leave the palace by a different gate. Walking yet faster, I was soon upon her. As I was about to announce myself, she stopped and spun around, leaving me to all but cannon into her. I grasped her upper arms to steady her. 'Forgive me, *Signorina*. I didn't mean to startle you.'

She frowned, shaking her head, and pulling out of my grasp just as small flakes of snow began to fill the air.

'I have my coach nearby. Might I offer you a ride home, now the weather has turned?' She looked uncertain for a moment, but I watched pragmatism win the day upon her face. 'Henrietta Street, is it not?'

Looking a little alarmed, she nodded.

Why had I not asked her where she lived? Christ. For I had no reason to know it. Or none she was aware of. I wished I had been more circumspect. What would she think if she knew of my conversations with the duchess where she had been the central topic?

I smiled, offering my arm though before she took it, she raised her hood. Had I left Frances but minutes later, I would have been unaware of her ahead of me without that gleam of flaxen hair like a beacon in the gloom.

It felt odd walking with a silent companion. The King believed she had chosen it. Could this be true? Perhaps one day I might find out. I glanced across at her now, but her face was hidden by her hood. Looking down, I saw she wore buskins of fine leather and glancing over my shoulder, saw our sooty footprints side-by-side across the dusting of snow. How intimate they looked. I began to talk to fill the silence, telling her of my commission and all the work needed to create the necklace I had just delivered to the duchess. I was glad to see her nod from time-to-time, so I did not feel I talked entirely to myself.

When she slowed as we walked through the park, I followed her gaze to the canal where a crowd had gathered. 'What's happening, I wonder?'

She raised her eyebrows, a slight smile playing on her lips.

'Shall we investigate, Signorina?'

She nodded and we set out across the frost-crisp grass, now powdered with snow. As we drew closer, the sound of cheers and shouted wagers reached our ears. The crowd parted then, revealing a resplendent figure now mounted on the most extraordinary horse I had ever seen, prancing on the canal bank. The animal was pure white with black spots scattered across its head and body and a magnificent white mane and tail of astonishing thickness and length. The man himself was no less impressive, dressed in gleaming jade satin with extravagant quantities of silver lace, he had fine almost feminine features and waves of his own glossy light brown hair flowing down below his shoulders. He seemed a source of light with snow flurries billowing around him. 'Is that Monmouth? What can he be doing?' But as I spoke, he walked his horse down onto the frozen canal to the cheers of his companions.

Susannah scribbled on her pad, smiling. 'James is ever the daredevil.'

And her smile was indeed as lovely as her sister's. Monmouth rode the beast a goodly distance along the wide frozen expanse before turning it up onto the bank again, laughing and galloping back – his mount's white tail streaming out like a banner – to where his friends waited, and the sound of cheers and shouted congratulations rang out. The horse, white against white, had seemed an insubstantial thing, a streaking dark swarm of giant bees, its rider carried on empty air.

Susannah shook her head, still smiling, and pointed back towards the path. Once inside my coach, she lowered her hood. 'He'll do anything if challenged to. He's been so since first coming to court,' she wrote. 'Sam and I rather hero-worshipped him then,' she added.

Somehow knowing this gilded figure – the King's most beloved son – was her childhood companion, made me more aware than ever of the gulf between us, leaving me at a loss for what to say. I settled, eventually, for a banality. 'I hope you are not too chilled?'

She wrote, 'You have my gratitude, *Signor* Rossi. This is not an afternoon for walking far.'

'You would not take a hackney?'

She pointed at her notebook and then to her mouth.

I understood her difficulty in finding a coachman who could read. 'Glad to have been of service.' I tried to think of something more intelligent to say. 'What brought you to Whitehall today, *Signorina*?' I fear it fell a little wide of the mark.

She gave me a cool stare, before writing. 'A commission to

deliver. How long have you lived in England? This is not weather you are much accustomed to, I imagine?'

I raised my eyebrows. 'Approaching two years, now. It doesn't often snow in Florence. But I'm told the winters here are much harsher of late?'

'That is so.' The coach rounded the corner into Henrietta Street, the rattle of the horses' hooves quieter now over lying snow. 'Here will do,' she scrawled.

I rapped on the wall for Rory to stop, which he did expeditiously, and was soon there to let down the steps from beneath the carriage. I climbed out first, taking her hand to help her alight. She smiled again and nodded to me before raising her hood and hurrying away. As Rory already looked half-frozen, I felt it inconsiderate to linger long enough to see which of these fine houses was hers, so quickly climbed back inside allowing us to be on our way, once more.

∼

SUSANNAH

Diary: January 10, 1676

Though it is but days since I last wrote here, it feels much longer to me. I needed time to order my thoughts when so much has happened.

I fear I must write of another encounter between Sam and James. He had told me of their confrontation in the courtyard on twelfth night on our carriage ride home. I could not help but wish James had drawn his sword and brought down the King's wrath upon his head. How unfortunate the damnable Catherine had to be within earshot.

Where do I start with their next clash? I suppose I can only write it as I witnessed it. Yes, this time I was there. We had just left the drawing room after enjoying a glass of wine and private conversation. I had been interested to hear how taken he was with Raphael Rossi, and he found my speculation of a possible liaison with the duchess interesting but unlikely. We did, I'm ashamed to say, have a small wager on it. He agreed, of course, that if true it seemed a foolhardy enterprise for the duchess who, since becoming widowed some years before, had lived at court by the King's generosity. It was then we heard a chilling shriek echoing up from below. My first thought was Penny, until I recalled she was again with Kitty at Whitehall.

'Holy God.' Sam set off down the stairs.

I hurried to follow. Inside the kitchens I heard a shout and arrived in the scullery to find Bess on the table, her skirts up and her bodice down with James between her thighs, one hand engaged there and the other fixed around her throat.

Sam was already moving to shove him away. 'Off her you filthy scum.'

I went to Bess's aid immediately but not before I caught a repulsive glimpse of James's anatomy and rather more of Bess's before I was able to untangle her skirts and put her gown to rights. How shockingly incongruous it all seemed accompanied by the smell of the stockpot simmering on the fire-shelf.

'Whore,' James said, pointing at Bess, making no attempt to fasten his breeches. 'Not her first time by a very long count.' He seemed to flaunt himself when he thought my eyes were on him. How pitiful he is.

'Cover yourself, you piece of shit.'

'Want it yourself, Sammy? Shame to waste a good stand, no?'

Sam punched him in the face, causing him to stagger back against the dresser, clutching his nose to stem the blood whilst crockery cascaded around him, fragmenting tumultuously upon the flagstone floor.

Catherine arrived. 'What, in the name of all that's holy, goes on here?'

Sam and James both began to speak at once.

Catherine held up her hand. 'My son will give his account. This is his household after all and not yours, Samuel Carter.'

Well, to my surprise, it turned out to be a reasonably accurate one only leaving out Bess's most obvious objection to his attentions. 'Rape,' I wrote on my pad and held it up. Catherine's lip curled.

'You.' Catherine pointed at Bess. 'Fetch the master down from his studio.'

I nodded at her to give my permission, clearly vexing Catherine which was pleasing as it had been my intention.

'The chit is obviously a harlot. She must be dismissed. I won't have my son debauched by the likes of that.'

James smirked. 'She lured me in here asking for my help with a heavy pot, Mama.'

'My maid will not be dismissed,' I wrote. 'Rape.'

'Whores cannot be raped you silly girl. And your father will agree with me, I think you'll find.'

Sam stepped forward. 'Bess is no prostitute. She's been with Sukie since she was twelve years old. James forced–'

'Servants can't be raped either. They're always at fault,' James said, with a grin.

'I think you should leave, Mr Carter,' Catherine said. 'You're no longer welcome here.'

'My guest,' I wrote. I wanted to speak so much. I wanted to defend my friend. I have to find a way out of this oubliette I have made for myself. How loathsome that I only scrawled, 'He will not leave.'

'No, Sukie. I shall. I'll see you later.'

Having little choice, I nodded before following him to the door to see him out. 'I need to make sure Bess is safe first, then I'll come to you,' I whispered as he buttoned his Brandenburg. He kissed me on the cheek and ran down the steps, and watching him walk away, my heart was full of love for him.

I met Papa coming down the stairs with a tearful Bess

following behind. When she saw me, she ran past him and into my arms.

'I've been given a very garbled account of James misusing her and Catherine dismissing her. What in God's name is going on, Susannah?'

I held up my pad and pointed to 'Rape' and quickly scrawled, 'James.' This was where I should have been able to tell him exactly what had occurred before the other side were able to spout their poison. It is hard to put into words just how much I hated myself at that moment. And Sam had been sent away. Catherine knew exactly what she was doing. He could not speak for us. I wrote, 'Trust me to always tell you the truth.' Amusing, no? 'I saw. Catherine did not. James will lie.'

He nodded. 'Never fear, Sukie, I'll have the truth of it.'

Holding Bess's hand, I followed him into the kitchen parlour where Catherine and James were seated at the table whispering furiously. They stopped, of course, the moment we entered.

'The girl must go at once.' Catherine placed her hand on James's arm. 'She has debauched my son.'

'Forced herself on you did she, lad?'

I thought my father had a look of the King just then, with his lowering black brows and beak of a nose.

He pointed at Bess. 'That slip of a thing had her wicked way with you, yes?'

I grinned, which was not appreciated by the Villiers. *Good.*

Catherine gave me a withering look. 'Don't be absurd, Richard. She enticed him. I won't have a common harlot working in my house, leading my son astray.'

That ship has long sailed, went through my mind.

'Are you a whore, Bess? Did you set a price for my step-son to have you?'

'I did not, Master. On my life, I did not. He forced me.'

Tears rolled down her face and I put my arm around her again nodding my support, vigorously.

Catherine rose. 'Explain then her lack of maidenhead?'

Bess turned and buried her face in my bosom. I gentled her just as I would Penny, grateful she was not here to witness such a scene.

'Pack your box, strumpet, and leave this house at once.'

I saw Papa's eyes upon me and read sympathy for my Bess there. She had been my maid, and dear companion, for six years after being taken-in by Mama when her seamstress mother became too ill to work. I shook my head, pleading with my eyes. His slight nod filled me with profound relief. 'Thank you,' I said, forming the words silently with my lips.

He sighed. 'Bess is in Susannah's employ. Only she can dismiss her.'

'But–'

He held up his hand. 'Wife, I suggest you instruct your son to keep away from Bess and My daughter will do the same with her maid, though I doubt she'll need such instruction. The matter is closed. I shall now return to my work.'

It seemed safest to send Bess to her mother in Southwark, where she might stay for a few days. She visited her often now she was entirely bedridden with the same complaint that had lingered all these years, only worsening slowly. We concealed such visits from the rest of the servants, who would have been dismayed to learn of such bounty when they were allowed little respite themselves.

I saw neither Catherine nor James again before leaving to walk the short distance across the street to call on Sam. I was to dine with him again as Penny would remain with her friend for the night. The evening was bitterly cold, and I wore my thickest cloak even for so short a walk.

He let me in himself, relieving me of it, and ushering me upstairs to the fire in his drawing room. 'You did the right thing sending her to her mother. Yet it will be hard for her to return, I think. How will she live in the same house with him? Won't she be in a state of constant fear?'

'James will skulk at court for a while. I just wish he could remain there permanently.'

'Perhaps one of Buckingham's wits might give him rooms? He's part of that set now, I believe.' He placed his hands on my shoulders and pulled me against him for a few moments. Then we sat together on the couch before the fire. 'We'll think of something. Might your father speak to the King ... or I could try?'

I shook my head, desperate as always to find a way to end my silence. Then I could discuss it with Papa myself. 'I don't know what to do, Sam.' It was a conversation had too often. 'If I admit what I've done so many people will be hurt. How will Papa feel when he finds out? How can I claim to love him and have treated him in such a way? If only I'd recognised what a mindless trap I'd set for myself.'

'It wasn't your fault, Sukie. At first it was real. It was the Villiers invading your life that made you use it as you did.'

'You're far too kind to me. But I chose it. Nothing was forced on me.' We dissect it all again, whenever we spend time together. How tedious it must be for him. To say the same things to me over and over again. Trying to help, I know. Jesu. And it seems such madness to me now.

'What about Penny. How will she ever make sense of it?'

'I think she'll just be glad to find her sister has a voice.'

'Well, I think a lot of people including the King, perhaps – who is not fond of cowards ... or, indeed, liars – will think I have made fools of them.' Sam has no idea just how much of a liar I am, nor is he ever going to know. 'I truly deserve to feel so trapped and full of self-loathing because of it. I feigned this to hurt. I wanted to hurt Papa when I was so angry with him and now I'm stuck not being able to comfort him when I think him unhappy with Catherine.' How quickly my anger had retreated, seeing the bleakness in his gaze when he looked at her. I had spent so little time with them together. I wondered how long ago he had fallen out of love.

'I remember when you couldn't speak to me, Sukie. You tried

so hard. You were desperate. It was real to start with. Never try to convince yourself otherwise.'

I grasped his hand. 'Well, we keep talking of it and I keep promising action, but nothing changes. So, I shall speak to Papa tomorrow. No more delays. I can't live with myself if I do not. I even considered suggesting it a miracle, but only if I had the slightest hope he'd believe it.' I tried to laugh but could summon no mirth. 'All I can do is ask his forgiveness.'

'You shall have it and his understanding, too, I'm sure. He loves you very much.' He glanced at the clock on the mantle and stood. 'Now, let us dine. Pascal has prepared his seafood fricassee you're so fond of. And this time he's made sufficient for two only, or so he claims.'

I smiled. 'I shall be delighted.' Though the admiral rarely stayed in the house himself, his chef was always there to cook for Sam. I often think he lives something of a charmed life.

By the time I returned home across the deserted road, shimmering white with frost, everywhere was in darkness save for the full moon setting our path aglitter, with no need for Connor's linkman duties because of it. Sam took my arm and walked with me again. Our talk had lasted well past midnight. There was a night candle left for me in the hall and I found the fire still well alight in my chamber.

Before I finish this entry, there is one last thing I must note before I sleep. I have not told Sam of my ride home with Raphael Rossi. I think it is possible that I am beginning to change my opinion of him, not only because Sam thinks well of him but because I found I enjoyed his company. He talked so enthusiastically about his work for the duchess and the details of how he went about it fascinated me. I really feel I would like to watch him one day. Maybe the duchess is right when she said we have things in common?

Chapter Three
RAPHAEL

Frances awaited me in her Richmond House drawing room, after sending word my visit would be convenient, though she expressed some surprise I had decided upon it. The weather had been so especially cold over the weeks since I last called on her, with February no improvement, I had remained in the workshop glad of the heat from the bellows-furnace needed to work our precious metals. Though there was little snow, the bitter wind had proved too much for me. When at last it dropped a little, I had made it to the palace with the help of several fur rugs and well wrapped hot bricks, to deliver the many pieces I had by then completed for her.

'Raphael, my dear. How brave of you to venture out on my account. She patted the couch where she sat close to the fire, indicating I should join her there.

I lifted her hand to my lips. 'Frances, I've had more than enough of my own four walls, so much so even my work for you became tiresome. I needed to see a vista other than Cheapside, if only that of sky and winter-trees from my carriage window.'

I stood and moved behind the couch to remove the pieces from my belt. I had already decided I would do this out of her gaze, shamed by its effect the last time. She did not move but I felt certain she smiled. As I peeled back my layers to extract the pouch held against my skin, I saw her straw-coloured hair, pinned up with jewelled brights, had many threads of copper woven through it. *Dio aiutami*, I wanted to take out those pins and watch it cascade around her. I handed the pouch to her over her shoulder. 'I hope they're to your liking.'

She turned to look up at me. 'I have no concerns on that account.'

With the sun now shining on her face, I marvelled once again at her eyes, the true violet of amethysts. It was only later, I again realised I had not noticed her skin at all.

She shook the emeralds out onto the sofa beside her, holding the ring, two bracelets and broach up to the light in turn. 'Raphael, it really is a kind of alchemy you do here, turning the old and ugly into something so vibrant and fresh.'

I bowed. 'They are extraordinary stones. I think ... hope I've done them justice.'

She placed them back inside the velvet pouch. 'Now they can hold light inside them just as they should. 'Pull the bell-rope for me, would you. I think refreshments to set you up for your journey home.'

I did as she asked before returning to sit beside her.

'Susannah has begun her portrait of the King. There was some slight delay as Penelope has been unwell.' She looked away. 'She has been mother to her these last three years.'

We were interrupted then by the arrival of a footman to take her instructions. The sun was fully into the room on this visit, and I was able to appreciate its beauty. Gilded Sofas and chairs upholstered in green and gold. Black statuary around the black and gold marble fireplace. Black panels framed in gold with mirrors at their centre to reflect light from tall candelabra placed in front of them. 'I'm glad her sister is well enough for her to begin. I've never seen any of her work, though I hear it's very much sought after.'

She stood. 'I have one she did of me some years ago. Though

it is watercolour on ivory not the enamel as she does now. I'll show it to you.'

While she was gone, a footman arrived with a laden tray holding far more than just the coffee and brandy I had heard her request. Some prior instructions must have been given for there was buttered toast, eggs and bacon, and, incongruously, a large and elaborately iced cake. I admit I had helped myself to toast liberally covered with eggs and bacon rashers, all consumed by the time she returned.

I placed my plate down on the table and stood guiltily wiping my mouth on a linen napkin. 'Forgive me.' I managed to articulate from behind the cloth.

She laughed, gesturing for me to sit. 'It is there to be eaten not admired. I had a feeling you might be hungry on such a cold day.' She sat down beside me again and handed me the miniature portrait. 'I had some little difficulty locating it.'

I examined it whilst she made a plate for herself. The portrait was exquisitely done. I found it hard to believe Susannah could have been but fifteen or sixteen at the time. And Frances was radiantly beautiful, her violet gaze direct, sure of her power. I looked at her now, eating heartily from her loaded plate, and hoped that seeing her past self had not distressed her. If so, she did not show it and nor had it stolen her appetite. 'Exquisite. The work and the sitter.'

When she had finished, she set down her empty plate beside mine and took the little painting from my hands, smiling as she looked at it. 'Her new technique is even better. Somehow she is able to get still more luminosity.' She stroked the glass gently with her fingertips, her expression wistful.

'Frances, I–'

She held up her hand. 'I've already told you, it matters little to me. I lived when so many did not, and I thank God for it every day.' She smiled, wryly. 'Both the King and Castlemaine had it but are unmarked.' She sighed. 'Yet the King's brother and sister were ones who died.'

I touched her cheek. 'You haven't lost your beauty, it's just changed a little like a jewel in a new setting.'

She tilted her head, studying me. 'I think you're a rather sweet man, Raphael.'

'I'm an honest one.'

When she leaned towards me to kiss my cheek, it was impossible not to find her lips. How, then, could my hands not find her body? And how could I not lose myself in her fierce response to me? Though she would not permit me to have her fully, she allowed me to pleasure her, abandoning herself to me without inhibition until I had her whimpering – near silent – knowing servants were never far away.

After we were mutually gratified, for she attended to my own needs just as wholeheartedly as she had enjoyed mine whilst I looked down at her golden hair loose from its pins and buried my fingers there, its lengths cloaking my thighs. Then, with our clothing back to rights, we helped ourselves to slices of cake and large glasses of brandy. I touched my glass to hers, '*Saluti, cara mia.*'

She smiled, wryly. 'You're a man of many talents, Raphael.'

I nodded a bow. 'At your service, *Duchessa.*' She was rather skilled herself, but I did not feel it quite appropriate to tell her so.

She caressed my face lightly with her fingertips. 'This cannot happen again. Not here. If the King called and found me behind locked doors with another man, he might send me from court. Favourites are allowed to stray because he does so himself, frequently, but I'm no longer one of those. He doesn't call on me often, only when he needs some respite from the others who want too much from him. He comes to me for peace and I'm dependant on him even though I never ask anything more from him. I cannot risk displeasing him. And you should be pursuing Susannah, anyway, not dallying with me.'

I stood and began pinning up her hair again. 'But it is such delightful dallying. And Susannah is yet to show any interest in me.'

'Well then, I shall visit you at Cheapside. I'll let you know when.' She touched her hair. 'Many talents, indeed. How do you know this?'

'Sisters.'

∼

SUSANNAH

Diary: February 5, 1676

I have not written here for some time, mostly because I wished to be able to say all is well.

I did not after all speak with Papa as I had intended. He was busy with patrons and then gone each night to the gaming tables with the King or to Dorset Gardens for a new production at the Duke's Theatre. So, what with one thing and another – otherwise known as cowardice – it was some weeks before I found him alone in the drawing room, having returned early from Whitehall. He smiled and stood to hug me. This time I would not balk.

'How are you, my sweeting?'

With my mouth dry as August straw, I expected to say, 'I am well, dearest Papa.' My lips moved but no sound came from me. I tried once more to say, 'Papa.' Nothing. No sound. Not the merest croak. I began to tremble, quite unable to make sense of it.

He held me away to look at my face. 'Why, what's wrong? Why do you shake, child?'

With my mind spinning, I lifted my pad and wrote, 'It's nothing. Just a sudden chill.' I moved away from him and close to the fire, feeling his eyes upon me, still. I stared into the flames and tried again to speak. Nothing happened. I fought to compose myself and turned back to him, only to catch a look of such sorrow upon his face that I rushed to him and flung my arms around his neck, hoping my kisses would be sufficient to convey my love.

He held me close, stroking my hair. 'All shall be well, Sukie. You have my promise. Somehow, I shall make it so.'

We sat together for a while, talking. Well, of course, he talked, and I wrote. I learnt his luck at cards had deserted him and, more from what he did not say, that Catherine had spoken inappropriately to the King again. I knew she wrongly assumed his friendship for Papa extended to her. Charles was usually content to flirt when flirted with but had, for some reason, taken against her. I must note here how much this pleases me, which will come as no surprise. When a companionable silence descended, I had a sudden thought. Perhaps if Sam were here with me, I might speak just as I had in front of Thomas Monkton?

I quickly wrote, 'Please wait here for me. I need to fetch Sam.' I stood, adding 'If he's home. Was he at court?'

'I didn't see him, no. Come to think of it, I haven't seen him there for evening entertainments at all since he returned from France. But why such urgency?'

The longcase clock helpfully chose that moment to strike ten, quickly supported by the chimes of St Paul's in Bedford Street.

'And it's late.'

'I won't be but a moment,' I scribbled. 'Please wait here, Papa, I beg you.'

He smiled, shaking his head. 'Very well. How can I refuse such an earnest entreaty?'

I dashed from the room and out into the night without stopping to collect my cloak and was soon across the road, knocking on Sam's door.

Connor opened it, appearing quite taken aback. 'Be there somethin amiss, Ma'am? Master Samuel is in the drawing room.' He coloured. 'He's with company. I'll be tellin him you're here, then. Do be sitting yourself.' He pointed to a chair against the wall in the small receiving hall.

I sat, leaning forward to watch, wondering whom Sam's

company might be. Well, if he was in the drawing room they could not be of an amorous nature, surely? Looking up the stairs though, I saw him bypass the door to go up the second flight. So, Sam was, indeed, in his bedchamber.

After some time, hearing footsteps approaching, I sat back to conceal my knowledge of their deceit. I stood for Sam to take me in his arms and kiss me on both cheeks. Connor moved away, discreetly. Sam was impeccably dressed, as always, though I thought his colour a little higher than usual.

He tilted his head, scrutinising me with a hard-blue stare. 'What can I do for you, Susannah?'

I felt my face flame. How foolish my haste seemed to me now. I could barely bring myself to tell him. My heart swooped, suddenly fearing I really could no longer speak even to him. I watched his eyes soften, reading my distress. 'Forgive my intrusion. Had I known you had company, I would never have disturbed you.' Greatly relieved, I told him all.

'Very well. Let's go and try this experiment of yours.'

I took has hand and squeezed it. 'Thank you. And thank you for not scolding me for my impulsiveness.' He kissed my forehead and took a cloak from the hall press to place around me.

We hurried across the deserted street and soon entered another receiving hall very little different to the one we had just vacated. Sam followed me upstairs to the drawing room, staying close behind until I stopped, causing him to collide with me. I drew a sharp breath. Catherine and James were seated where my father and I had sat earlier and of him there was no sign. I moved away, closing the door. They obviously found our sudden appearance amusing as peals of laughter accompanied us walking away towards the stairs. 'Studio?' I whispered. 'Or perhaps we should leave it for now so you might return to your guest.'

'I'm here. It's worth a try.'

I climbed the two flights ahead of him again, feeling increasingly uncomfortable for dragging him away from … well, from whomever shared his bed. I opened the door and stopped once more. Papa lay on the couch kept there for his sitters waiting between firings, snoring softly. The room was always warm from the kiln.

Sam put a finger to his lips. 'Let's not wake him.'

'No.' I agreed, moving back onto the landing. 'Sweet Jesu, do you think he sleeps there every night?'

'I don't know whether to hope he does or hope he doesn't.'

'Whilst she sleeps in my mother's bed.'

He drew me into his arms. 'I'm so sorry, Sukie.'

'This is why I must be able to speak to him.' I pulled away and took a deep breath. 'Now you, my dear, must return to your friend who will be despairing of you.'

He smiled, a little smugly. 'I think not.' He touched my arm. 'I'll see myself out. You should take refuge in your chamber.'

Which, after watching him descend, is precisely what I have done. Though I cannot help wondering who Sam might be returning to. Is it someone known to me, perhaps? I give myself a few moments to test my feelings about it. I love Sam and he loves me. We are now like brother and sister, though we have not always been. I bite my lip. Am I jealous? Should I be? I sigh. It seems too complicated, so best left alone.

Diary: February 6, 1676

And so, to other matters. I have begun my portrait for the King and must note here my ease with this sitting compared to my earlier one. I smile as I write, pleased my diary is fulfilling its purpose. For, despite everything, knowing this fills my heart with hope.

. . .

On my visit to make the watercolour, he was in a fine mood. Louise de Kérouaille was with him in the privy presence chamber, bright with all those silver tables and cabinets gleaming in the morning sunshine. She paid him just the sort of compliments needed to give his countenance the good-humoured glow I needed from him, knowing exactly what she was doing ... and so, of course, did the King.

When I held up a note saying: 'Thank you, Your Majesty, I have all I need,' he came to stand beside me, lifting my painting carefully to examine it before handing it to his mistress.

'Oh, but you are such a pretty King today.' She chucked him lightly under the chin.

I did not think pretty a word that could ever be used to describe him, but it sounded well in her soft Breton tones and clearly pleased him.

He handed it back to me. 'You've done well, Susannah. We look forward to the end result.'

'A gift for me, non?'

I had though it a gift for Castlemaine. I smiled a little to myself, glad I need not witness that confrontation. Perhaps I should make two? I might suggest it, but what about Nell? I could find myself producing countless copies. I decided the King must resolve the matter himself.

Diary: February 7, 1676

Jesu, despite yesterday's optimism, I again feel close to despair as though trapped in one of those awful nightmares where limbs are impossible to move, however desperate the situation.

My next visit to Whitehall proved more noteworthy, though not because of the portrait. I was dissatisfied with the drape of the indigo silk fabric I had used as a background behind the King and needed him there to ensure his positioning was correct against the changes I made before I could begin the enamelling. He was affable, telling me of all the work he was having done on his yacht, even inviting Sam and me to sail with him and Monmouth when the better weather arrived. When I only smiled, noncommittally, he seemed not to notice.

I was soon away, satisfied finally, and heading back on foot to Henrietta Street. As I walked along beside the bowling green, I saw Raphael Rossi leaving Richmond House looking exceedingly pleased with himself and not a little dishevelled. So, I had won my wager. I briefly wondered whether to catch him up and see if he would offer me the use of his coach once again but decided, under the circumstances, not to. I pulled my cloak more tightly about me in the piercing wind.

'Susannah. Hold-up.'

I spun around to see Sam and Thomas Monkton walking together some way behind. I waved and waited for them. They arrived smiling; Sam kissing my cheeks, Thomas my hand.

Sam put his arm around my waist. 'This is well met, indeed. I am to take Thomas to Henrietta Street, having discovered he has business with your papa and now I can take you home as well. Let's get to my carriage and out of this damnable wind.'

Here, of course, I would have spoken had Sam been alone. Instead, I nodded, smiling my gratitude.

Inside his coach he looked from me to Thomas and back to me again. 'I wonder, would you object to me explaining your current predicament? The one we recently sought to explore?'

I felt heat on my face that the lieutenant should be made aware of my belief, until two nights ago with Papa, that I had chosen my silence as a means to hurt. Still, I needed to know if it could be broken, and Thomas had already heard me speak. I nodded, suddenly afraid. What if I could not?

After explaining the sorry thing, Sam pulled me into his arms. 'Close your eyes. Imagine we're alone.'

I turned my face hard against his chest, the scent of him as familiar to me as my own.

He rubbed my back, gently. 'How went it with the King today?'

I hardly dared to try, managing but a feeble clicking sound from my throat before bursting into tears. I cannot doubt I deserve this, for it seems an entirely fitting punishment for such cruel intentions, does it not?

'Perhaps you try too hard, Mistress,' Thomas said. 'Don't distress yourself.'

I had just about recovered my composure when the carriage turned into Henrietta Street. Thomas took his leave at my house, and I remained with Sam until Joseph dropped us at his door. We did not speak until we were alone in his drawing room where he poured and handed me a glass of claret before sitting on the couch beside me. I took a long drink, enjoying how quickly the alcohol arrived in my blood. 'Well, that went well.'

He smiled, ruefully. 'Didn't it, though.'

'I made something of a spectacle of myself.'

'No. Not at all.' He put his glass down and took my hand in his. 'You really are much too hard on yourself, you know.'

I closed my eyes, allowing my fragmented thoughts to settle. 'I feel as though, somehow, I have secretly ... and I mean secretly to myself if that's possible. That I've done this to free myself from the guilt of it. Somehow my mind is doing this, so it can seem I have done nothing wrong.'

He tilted his head, still holding my hand and stroking it with his thumb. 'Whatever the cause, Sukie, there is clearly nothing to be done at the moment. And torturing yourself over it seems particularly unhelpful to me.'

So here I am no further forward and without any idea of what to do next. I can speak, yes, yet it seems only to Sam. Sweet Jesu, how can this be?

RAPHAEL

After her letter came several days later, I awaited her arrival that same evening with all the anticipation of a virgin schoolboy expecting that state about to change. Yet such excitement did not prevent me apprehending how much my father would be enraged if he knew my conduct risked alienating the King. Perversely, a small part of me wished him aware Frances Stuart, Duchess of Richmond and royal mistress, desired me. For I could not forget how he had belittled me as a man, even trying to deny me agency in my own life.

To avoid the formality of the dining room, I had Giuseppe organise an intimate dinner in the drawing room, making sure I offered her the best Florentine fare and finest of wines. Fortunately, the cook had accompanied us at my father's insistence, enabling us to entertain patrons just as we would at home.

When she arrived dressed as a man, a small gasp escaped me on opening the door, glad I had done so myself. She wore a perfectly tailored set of the most fashionable male attire, her hair hidden beneath a fine wig. I smiled. '*Signore mio, benvenuta.*' I knew such disguises were in vogue at court where women seemed to find them thrilling. Perhaps for the response it provoked in men? Which I was beginning to discover for myself.

She smiled, too. 'I don't have quite the height for it.'

I led her inside before bending to kiss her on the lips. It was extremely disconcerting. I handed her cloak to Giuseppe, who managed to maintain his persona of an obsequious manservant, which was quite a feat under the circumstances. I showed her up to the drawing room, where our table was made ready for us. The other servants had been instructed to remain below stairs. '*Mi fa piacere vederti.*'

She seated herself on a couch beside the fire, stretching out her legs clad in russet breeches and pale grey silk stockings, her heeled shoes were of black leather with silver buckles ... and tiny.

She watched me looking at her, accepting a glass of Chianti. 'I'm happy to see you, too, Raphael.' She gestured towards herself. 'But unsurprisingly, you're somewhat startled by my appearance.'

I ran my hand up the inside of her thigh. 'I'm beginning to see some advantages, *cara mia*.' When she touched my cheek with icy fingers, I leaned in to kiss her properly. 'How soon must you return?'

'I can stay until tomorrow if you wish it.'

I smiled. 'I wish it very much. You'll not be missed at court?'

'Mary Warnock will say I have gone to one of Katherine Sheldon's natural philosophy salons. Her house is some distance from mine, so no one will question my absence as I often remain overnight.'

I tilted my head and she seemed to read my doubt.

'There is indeed a salon this evening and she will say I was there if called upon to do so.

Her events are mostly attended by women now the men prefer the atmosphere at the Royal Society. And women are not made welcome there.'

'You have an interest in natural philosophy?' This again did not fit with my father's appraisal of her. He had wanted me to inveigle my way into the Duchess of Portsmouth's circle – she was known to spend wildly on jewellery – though Frances chose me first. He described her as uneducated and rather silly. I had already established neither was the case. Once more, she appeared to read my mind.

'I came to Whitehall Palace when I was but sixteen. Before then I'd been at the French court. I was – or looked to be – a pretty, empty-headed child. I am, of course no longer that. Nor was I then, entirely, for I lived upon my wits. And all I had to trade were my face and my maidenhead.' She smiled. 'Both of which are no longer current assets.'

I kissed her then, taking my time. 'Well, it seems unlikely

you'd be here with me now, should that be so.'

She touched my cheek. 'I think perhaps you don't quite see yourself as others do.' She gave me a searching look. 'At one time in my life I was rather unpleasantly vain, I believe.' She moved her fingers to her own face. 'Perhaps God began to find me a little tiresome?'

After our second glass of wine, I summoned Giuseppe to serve us. 'Refined peasant food, in truth.' I shrugged. 'Not your usual fare, I'm sure.' Ribollita soup. Arista pork. Schiacciata flatbread and various vegetable and fruit dishes done in the Tuscan style. All were new to her. And, once again, I enjoyed seeing her appetite.

By the time I led her up the second staircase to my bedchamber we were both well fed and at ease with each other. I had instructed Giuseppe to leave a jug of wine and two glasses, and I poured for us, draining mine while she took but a few sips. The room gleamed with light reflecting off the gilded furniture – shipped from Florence like all the rest, yet it probably seemed restrained compared with such at court – so I snuffed a few candles to soften it a little. We undressed each other tenderly before the fire bathed in its soft glow, though removing male attire was extremely disconcerting, both familiar and almost transgressively unfamiliar. When she stood before me naked, I saw how very tiny she was. I cupped her breast, heavy for such a slight frame, feeling a touch afraid I might hurt her.

She placed her palm on my face. 'I won't break, Raphael.'

I smiled. How had she read my thoughts yet again? Then I carried her to my bed, where we were soon enjoying each other with no little relish. That she wished me to finish inside her proved an unexpected addition to my pleasure. I blocked a sudden memory of the last time, recoiling from it. Valentina. *Cristo.* I took a breath, forcing my mind away. 'You're well practiced in the act of love, I think.'

'As are you, my dear.'

When I felt her chuckle pressed close against me, I raised myself on an elbow to look down at her, smiling. 'What amuses you, *carissima*?'

'I think, perhaps, you have enjoyed an added satisfaction this evening?'

'It was that obvious? You know why I choose to–'

She put a finger on my lips. 'I do. I've never had a child and hold out little hope of it now, yet it saddens me more than I can say. I've had a husband and lovers, one a rather prolific father, no?' She shook her head. 'I fear I share the fate of his poor sweet wife. Though she occasionally gets them and cannot keep them whereas I, it seems, cannot get them at all.'

I stroked her hair back to kiss her forehead. 'I'm sorry it saddens you. It is ironic, because the King didn't get you with child many thought you were not his lover.'

'I never was before my marriage and then when I eloped with Richmond.' She raised her eyebrows. 'After Castlemaine had found us together in my bed – you can imagine her delight –and that I had chosen his distant cousin vexed him all the more, he banished us.'

How extraordinary she should have held him at bay for so long. My father had been disinclined to believe it. Questioning what other hold she could have had over him. Novelty, I now speculated. The novelty of being refused and the delicious anticipation of having her yield. 'So, you were reconciled only after your husband's death?'

She ran her hand down my chest. 'No, he came to me when I became ill. He was very much afraid I might die and when I did not, he brought us back to court ... and I have been there ever since. He posted Richmond to Scotland and then to Denmark. When he died there, I found myself facing destitution.' She smiled. 'He was rather too fond of the card tables ... and strong drink. But he was also extremely fond of me, so I could forgive him those things. The King came to my rescue once again, and most generously, with a good pension and allowed me to keep Richmond House.' She sighed. 'Though he settled the dukedom elsewhere last year for there had been no heir, of course. Louise's Charles. His youngest son.'

Her hand began to roam further until it came to rest tantalisingly upon my thigh, whilst I took in what she had told me.

'He came to my bed for the first time when he brought me back.'

Later, after events had once again taken their course, and her head rested on my chest, there was another question I could not resist asking her. 'Did he please you then? The King? Does he still?'

She laughed and moved to lie on her side, facing me. 'Yes, and yes. Who would expect otherwise? He is much practiced, after all. What people do not understand about him is that he likes women and enjoys their pleasure. As do you, Raphael. Believe me there are many who do not. Even some who think avoiding pleasuring a woman prevents a child. And also saves them the trouble of doing so, of course.'

I had heard of this from men I knew to have sired bastards. '*Sì*. Then when the child arrives, they blame the woman for pleasuring herself to make it.'

She snorted laughter. 'Then she will have fared better than under such a man's ministrations, I have no doubt.'

I moved down kissing her salty skin, parting her legs to kiss the moist inside of her thigh, making her moan and shift until my lips were where she desired them to be. 'But how will you fare under mine, *Duchessa*?'

The next morning after breakfast taken at the table in my chamber, followed by an enjoyable return to my bed, I took her down to my workshop via a short flight of stairs at the back of the house, while the apprentices were down in the kitchens for their midmorning small beer and bread. I nodded at Giuseppe to remove her finished pieces from the strong room. Once again, he maintained his servile demeanor, eyes lowered, as he laid them out on the black velvet runner. However, when Frances's attention was fully engaged perusing the new settings, he looked up at me grinning and made an obscene gesture with his forearm. I could not prevent my lips from twitching in response, even though it would serve only to encourage him.

'Raphael, I have no words. These are your best yet. I do so admire your botanical designs. Others are beginning to take it up, you know.' She shook her head, still gazing at the diamond necklace. 'There are tiny flames burning within them.'

'I've cut many additional facets, as you see.' I had set the stones in a pattern of small flowers. And how could I not be flattered that my designs were already being copied?

'You are truly a magician.' She lifted the necklace to the light once more, before removing her white lace cravat and opening the neck of her shirt. 'Fasten it for me, would you? I shall wear it home.'

I did as asked while she fitted the ring onto the middle finger of her right hand, admiring it as she did so. 'I'll see you safe back.' I retied her cravat.

'The rest hidden beneath your clothing, perhaps?' She quickly concealed the pendent earrings down the front of her shirt.

Giuseppe made a throaty noise that sounded just as obscene as his earlier gesture had looked. I jerked my head indicating he should make himself scarce. Though Frances covered her mouth, her eyes were full of laughter. 'Have the coach brought out,' I called after him.

'I shall not refuse you, my dear.' She looked out at the cold sky. 'I feel sure it will be warmer than a hackney.'

I shrugged. 'Well, I am *Florentino*.'

Once outside walking with her to my carriage, the frigid wind was again much in evidence, carrying grains of ice to sting my face like blowing sand, making me wish only to turn back. Perhaps it should have been a warning?

Chapter Four
NOAH

Noah Bartholomew, lying in bed on a chill grey afternoon, found time to reflect on recent events and foremost, of course, upon the beautiful lad now sleeping snugly beside him. The fire burned warm and frost-rimed branches framing the diamond-paned window served only to emphasise what a cosy shelter from the elements this room afforded ... as, too, did his bed.

They had met aboard the Mirabel, one of his brigs on its final leg home from Barbados, having stopped in Le Havre to unload sugar and pick up a cargo of Bordeaux. This interesting young man, taking a last-minute passage, had been invited to dine with him in his cabin in the aftcastle. They had found much to talk of, the lad having come directly from the French court and being in possession of all the latest gossip and intrigues afoot there.

Nothing had occurred between them onboard ship – other than a mutually recognised interest – for it would have been difficult. True privacy was hard to come by. And it was too soon, anyway. No need to rush it. He planned to remain in England for many months, or until Margaret became too hard to bear once more. Though he had made another quick trip across the channel to fill the Mirabel's hold with cheap but top-quality port wine, suddenly available after an importer went bankrupt. Margaret had been enraged he chose to be away for the Christmas festive season, so missing his sons' visits home.

He had finally met the lad again in London, where they had arranged to dine together, and had found each other physically soon afterwards in the comfort and safety of a bedchamber in a private house. After that they had met often, with much discretion and no little ingenuity. It had not taken long to find himself smitten. Unwise, he knew. Bit late now.

He looked down at the silky hair fanned-out on the fine white linen pillow and sighed, quietly. With his passion spent, the guilt arrived once more. The guilt about the risks he took. Fuck. For, in truth, he risked his family as much as himself. Yet the moment his wife had announced plans to take the waters at Bath, he had determined to arrange this tryst at their country house in Bethnal Green. He had, though, argued against her going for the weather was poor and the journey would be gruelling. But her gout was always worse in winter and Bath's hot spring waters all the more welcome because of it. He knew she would go, just as he knew this encounter would take place.

When the body beside him began to stir, the self-reproach started its retreat as desire flamed once more. 'Holy God,' he murmured, moving in again to slide his hand over a warm flank and beyond, smiling. 'Well, laddie, I am finding you more and more delightful.'

'I'm very glad to hear it, for I'm feeling much the same about you.'

Noah rumbled a laugh. 'So, let's see what we can do to delight each other further.'

'Do you know, I rather enjoy you calling me laddie.'

Noah grinned. 'I shall call you it because you're small as well as young.'

'Well, I'm most certainly not small. It is you who are a giant. The first moment I saw you I thought Viking God.'

'And I thought pretty laddie.'

They laughed easily together.

'Must we return to London today?'

'Aye, I'm afraid so.' Noah's short Yorkshire vowels were long gone. Though his father had hailed from Whitby, he liked to claim he had been honed by the sea. He ran his hands through his thick fair hair. He disliked having to conceal it beneath a dark wig, though his flaxen locks sometimes felt a little frivolous – not quite right for a serious and very successful merchant. The wig gave him more gravitas, somehow. 'I've a ship sailing on the morning tide. I should be there to see it out.'

A fine-boned hand with long slender fingers reached up to smooth the golden mane. 'You should always wear it uncovered. Its colour is a wonder. You have your own candleflame to light your way. The hand dropped away. 'May I ask you something?'

Noah nodded, almost certain he knew what was coming.

'Do you still–'

'Do I still swive my wife? No, I do not. Not now. And before you ask, did I enjoy it? The answer being, as best I could.' He had been asked these questions many times before. And Margaret was not an easy woman. Her gout brought her much discomfort he knew, which did nothing to help her temperament. If not for his sons, he could easily imagine leaving her. If not for his sons. Yet they were so nearly grown now, so might it not be different? After all, she would always be well provided for, and it harmed no one that he imagined living a happier life.

'Forgive me if I've offended you.'

'You haven't. I can understand your confusion that I could be with her and also with you. It is more common than you might think. In truth, extremely so.' There were many deceived wives, and he took some small comfort that Margaret had been better served than many.

'I don't doubt it for a moment ... it is just I know it can never be that way for me. I tried. Once–'

Noah laughed. 'Once? And how old were you on this momentous, life-changing occasion?'

'Fifteen. Neither of us liked it much. But it wasn't that which made me so certain. Something happened not long afterwards.' He took a sharp breath. 'A man forced himself on me.'

Noah matched the breath. 'Raped? At fifteen? Christ.'

'I suppose he knew what I was before I did myself. It was dark so I never ... I was at a friend's house during school holidays. But later I was strangely grateful to him–'

'Grateful for rape? That is wrong. So wrong. He didn't know what you were he just wanted his cock in you.' He smoothed chestnut hair back from a warm forehead. 'I'm sad for you. You should have discovered yourself in kinder hands.'

He caressed Noah's face. 'With you would have been nice.'

'Indeed, it would, lad. Indeed, it would.'

In the event, they had not set out for London until early the next morning, leaving at first light. When a messenger had arrived telling him the Cleopatra would be a day delayed waiting for a missing cargo, fate handed them the chance for another night together. He turned to look at the lad who slept with his head resting against his coaches' well-padded squabs. The horses made good time even if the passengers were rattled to within an inch of their lives, moving over the frozen rutted ground. Or he was. It had been as the rocking of a cradle for his companion.

Now the sun had risen higher, and the lad's face was in full light, Noah took advantage of his absence in sleep to look at him. Chestnut hair, loose about his shoulders, shiny as a conker. Dark lashes so long they cast a shadow on his cheeks. Lips, slightly parted, full and wide. He wanted very much to touch them with his own but knew what would follow and a rattling coach was not the place and broad daylight certainly not the time.

The lad woke as they clattered through Clerkenwell, moving ever westwards and down towards the river. He smoothed his hair, looking confused and then uncomfortable before frowning. 'Forgive me. I've been poor company.'

Noah tilted his head. 'You've had little sleep for which I must take the blame.'

They smiled at each other.

'I believe the blame is shared equally.' He held Noah's gaze. 'Are you certain I cannot tempt you to take luncheon at my house?'

Noah smiled, ruefully. 'You can tempt me, but I fear I must resist on this occasion.'

'Well, perhaps we might dine later in the week?'

Noah reached across to touch his knee. 'I shall try. I swear.'

'Send a note and I'll make sure I'm free.'

Finally, the coach entered Covent Garden and he asked for it to stop on the corner of Hart Street. Both men were, of course, very aware of the importance of discretion.

Noah later wished he had dropped him at his door and embraced him on his steps but the more circumspect part of him knew that he had not, had been very much for the best.

On his arrival in Rotherhithe, having taken the horse ferry to Lambeth so avoiding London Bridge, he was surprised to find his son, Henry, waiting in his office. He watched him for a moment through the window from the corridor. His eyes were closed and, just as earlier in his coach, he was able to study him unawares. He was a man. There was no other way to describe him. They shared the same build with Hal's hair not quite his own pale shade, but close enough. There was stubble on his face. When had that happened? Yet he had not seen him in almost a year and that, of course, was time enough. He would be eighteen now for the love of God. That meant Michael was sixteen. Christ.

He walked into his office. 'Hal. What are you doing here?'

He stood and hugged his father. 'Are you not pleased to see me, Papa?'

Noah held him tight and then moved away to look at him. Their eyes were level. 'Of course I am.' He kissed his cheek. 'Of course. My God, I've missed you. But aren't you up at Oxford now ... Corpus Christi?'

Hal frowned. 'Well, I should be ... but–'

'But?' Noah gave him a hard look. He could still read him like an open book. 'Come on. Out with it, Hal. No point in not.'

He ran his hand over his hair. 'After Mama's reaction, I admit I am a little reluctant.'

'You've seen your mother? Where?'

'At home. She has taken to her bed. She and Aunt Mary had another of their pointless scraps, so they turned the coach around and returned home. She's not at all happy you weren't there last night ... and she is especially not happy with me.'

Christ's fucking wounds. 'Well then, you better explain it all to me, no?

He looked down at his feet. 'I've been rusticated.'

'Rusticated?'

'Sent home for the rest of the term.'

Noah folded his arms and raised his eyebrows.

Hal would not meet his gaze. 'A whore in my rooms.'

Noah knew immediately it was not the truth. He touched his son's face. 'Look at me, Hal.' He did. 'You know what you risk, so–'

Hal looked away again. 'Please, Papa. I don't need a damn lecture from you. Where were you last night? Jensen said you hadn't slept here. So where?' He shook his head. 'Mama said, "The apple doesn't fall far from the tree," when I told her what I'd done.'

Noah went behind his battered oak desk and sat down with a sigh. He gestured for Hal to sit, too. 'I've been at Bethnal Green, if you must know.'

'Alone?'

He took a breath. How could he expect the truth from his son if he was not honest himself? 'No, Hal. But I wasn't with a prostitute. And I don't think you were either.'

Hal threw his head back to stare at the ceiling. 'It's all so damn ridiculous. It was nothing. It meant nothing.'

Noah waited.

'What's the point. You won't understand. You'll think it something momentous when it absolutely is not. Something shameful–'

Noah's heart lurched. 'A man?' Please God. He could not bear this for his son. He knew too well its grim cost in fear.

Hal's eyes widened. 'How did you know?'

He groaned, unable to help himself. It felt like a knife in his guts.

Hal smiled, hard and cynical. 'There it is. Just as I expected. And it was not a man it was a boy a year or so younger than me. I am not a sodomite, Papa, which is the conclusion you've jumped to and reacted to, just as I knew you would. I met him in the town. I liked him. We drank together and I took him to my rooms where we drank some more and talked about women, believe it or not. And then … well, the talking ended as it usually did at school. That is when the porter came in and saw us. Someone reported me bringing him in.' He shrugged. 'That's all it is. Means nothing, like I said.'

What they usually did in school? Holy God. He had gone to sea at thirteen. You were lucky to get a private toss without being belted. He took a deep breath. 'I understand, I think. So forgive my misapprehension.'

Hal still looked at him with contempt. 'Well, I can't expect you to know me when we have seen so little of each other over the years. Mama might not doubt I had the whore but at least she would never think me a sodomite.'

Noah understood then, he must explain himself. 'It wasn't about you. It was because of me.'

Hal frowned. 'I don't understand.'

Noah sat up straighter in his chair. 'You see, Hal, I was with a man. And I would tear my own beating heart from my chest to save you from it. My response came from fear. Fear for you.'

Hal began to smile but it froze on his face. 'I thought it was a joke.' He shook his head. 'It's not a fucking joke though, is it? You mean it. You're a–'

'I'm afraid I am.'

Hal stood, his face now a mask of disgust. 'Then, Sir, I shall say good day.'

Noah folded his arms on his desk and put his head down upon them. 'Christ.' It would have been far better to be a hypocrite than to have so shocked his son with this. What could he have been thinking? 'Christ's fucking wounds. I'm an imbecile.'

∼

RAPHAEL

Under a generous pile of furs with our feet snug upon heated bricks, we made it to King Street unfrozen and halted close to Richmond House.

Frances smiled and patted my hand. 'I shall try and visit you again, should you wish it, of course?'

I squeezed her fingers discreetly. 'What do you think, Carissima?

'Very well, I'll let you know when.'

I stood beside my coach watching her walk to her door swathed in her fur-lined mantle knowing, somehow, I must secure payment for my latest work from her. *Papà* insisted copies of all worksheets and bills of sale were sent to him each quarter. It would not be long before I received a letter telling me to pursue her for it.

I turned to Rory. 'Take me to Horse Guards and then wait. I have another errand.' I would go to Tom's office. Perhaps he might be persuaded to join me for a pie and ale in a nearby Ordinary? He would know which one was best. While the carriage creaked and the four sets of hooves rattled over the cobbles, I contemplated all Frances risked with our liaison and very much hoped Tom might be able to reassure me that with enough discretion it would be possible to keep her safe.

Once Rory lowered the steps again, I hurried across the yard to mount the stairs up to Tom's office beside the clock tower. With his door ajar, I saw immediately he wasn't there, though his clerk was able to tell me he had just left on his way to speak to a guardsman in Scotland Yard. I told Rory to take the coach home as it was too cold for him to wait. I could easily find a hackney on King Street, either after luncheon with Tom or sooner if he were not free to join me. I still wonder why I did not climb into the warmth of my coach and return home there and then. There was no urgency to seek reassurance from Tom and, as it turned out, I was unable even to ask for it for quite some time.

I was far from certain of the most direct route to take through the old palace's warren of roadways, alleys, and courts, weaving around the newly built stone and red-brick houses and terraces cheek-by-jowl with the old timber-framed York Place era buildings. I kept up a brisk pace because of the cold, especially with my erratic path taking me mostly through shadow where the frigid air felt painful to breathe and savage-looking icicles hung from eaves in windowless walls. I had just rounded the corner to enter another narrow passage which I hoped would take me from inner to outer Scotland Yard when I halted, confronted by man on the ground propped askew against the wall, his cloak splayed out around him. Disconcertingly, he was completely rimed with frost which sparkled in the dim light as though he were strewn with diamond dust. I knew then he must be dead, though I moved to him to make quite certain of it. His chin was resting on his chest which was crusted with a dark stain. Frozen blood? His rimed hair still tied neatly at his neck suggested there had been no fight, or not much of one. I held his icy head between my hands and lifting it, found myself looking into the very dead eyes of James Villiers.

'*Cristo Santo.*' I carefully set him back just as he had been, crossed myself commending him to God, and continued on my quest to locate Tom, though now for a very different reason.

It was not without some trepidation that I waited outside the much grander Horse Guards' office of the Captain of the Yeoman Guardsman, Sir Henry Willets, while Tom told him of my discovery and its circumstances. He had viewed the body himself beforehand but had left it in place, though under guard, as Sir Henry would wish to see it in situ. I understood he would also wish to interview me and, though Tom had not said it in so many words, I would be considered a suspect. I could quite see why a murderer might claim only to have discovered a body as a tactic to divert attention when, in truth, he was responsible for it and so then why said finder should be suspect. However, this did not prevent me from finding it a particularly uncomfortable situation.

It would not be in my favour either that I was both a foreigner and a Catholic though *Papà* had insisted I went through the motions of converting to Anglicanism once in England. Crossing the Thames I believe it is called, colloquially. Not to do so would have affected trade in terms of higher taxation and restrictions upon my travel. Though I doubted I was the only secret papist at court amongst those surrounding the King when the Queen and two of his mistresses were openly so, and his brother the Duke of York was likely a convert.

I made a mental note to run like the devil in the opposite direction should I stumble across another corpse. Yet, if witnessed, would this not look to be a sign of guilt? The obvious answer seemed never to find one again but then I had not intended to locate this one. Had I known my way in the palace, I would not have entered that benighted passageway. Did the fact that I had make me more likely to be guilty or less? It was hard to know.

The wind had risen again and blundered down the chimney

in the hall where I waited, sitting on a wooden bench. I adjusted my position, the sooty smoke blown out from the fire which seemed to offer little in the way of heat, making me cough. Though my eyes had been fixated on the door behind which my situation was being discussed, when it opened, I was startled enough to emit a rather high-pitched sound, much to my embarrassment.

An elderly clerk stood in the doorway, eyeing me. 'You are required within, Sir.'

My heart pounded uncomfortably, and my mouth felt dry as dust when I followed him into the office. '*Gentiluomini.*' I looked from one to the other. What had possessed me to speak in Italian? Tom looked amused while Sir Henry's jowls trembled with apparent outrage. Well, then, he was easily outraged. But not a good start.

The only difference I could discern in their uniforms was considerable additional gold lace on the latter's. In their persons, however, they were opposites. Almost comically so. Though not many could match Tom's physique, few were as slight as the captain. He brought to mind a shrivelled hobgoblin from a disagreeable fairy tale, his long thin neck and disproportionally large head adding something of the look of a dandelion clock.

Tom smiled reassuringly and pointed to a chair. 'Sit, Raphael.'

I sat. Sir Henry faced me across his desk while Tom sat on a stool to my right. From the heat remaining on my seat, I knew he had but lately removed himself from it. To my left was the clerk, pen in hand, ready to write down all I said. Sir Henry already held a paper which I imagined noted Tom's report. I trusted him to have carefully remembered all I had told him. Sir Henry's first question, though, took me by surprise.

'Please account for all your movements in the last twenty-four hours.'

I broke out in a cold sweat. The twenty-four hours in which I had bedded Frances Stuart. Something I was, of course, unable to speak of. 'There is very little to tell.' I thought then of my *papà's* business advice that when truth was not possible, stick as close to it as was feasible. 'I was at my workshop and residence in Cheapside all day yesterday and arrived at the palace this morning with some pieces of jewellery for the Duchess of Richmond. As I was here and it was nearing lunchtime, I decided to see whether my friend Lieutenant Monkton were free to join me. I was on my way to find him in Scotland Yard when I stumbled across *Signor Villiers*.'

Sir Henry steepled his fingers, frowning. 'How does this explain your presence in Bride's Cut?'

'Bride's Cut? I didn't know it had a name. I'm unfamiliar with the palace layout, Captain. I was attempting to find my way to the outer part of Scotland Yard.'

'But Bride's Cut would not take you there.'

I shrugged and smiled, ruefully. 'So I discovered.'

'And just where did the passage lead you, Master Rossi?'

'To a closed court. If it has a name, it is unknown to me.' I glanced at Tom, who appeared relaxed, and took heart from it.

Sir Henry leaned forward. 'Can anyone confirm your whereabout yesterday, particularly during the hours of darkness? Where did you dine? Did you have company? That sort of thing.'

'I dined at home alone. My manservant can vouch for it.' Giuseppe would confirm my story, but no other servants were in a position to do so. Would this arouse suspicion if discovered? I must pray it would not. 'I can tell you nothing further, Captain. I trust I'm now free to go?'

Sir Henry smiled, revealing a snaggle of unpleasantly discoloured teeth. 'Most certainly not, Master Rossi. You will be confined here in the guardhouse while I make further enquiries into the matter. The coroner must examine the body and you may need to account for additional time periods after we establish how long ago the victim met his death. When he was last seen. That sort of thing. Then, of course, I shall need to confer with the King.'

Tom stood. 'Sir, I believe I might be–'

'Take this man to the guardhouse, if you please, Lieutenant Monkton.'

As there seemed nothing to be done, I stood and allowed Tom to usher me from the room. Once the door closed behind us, I stopped and turned to face him. 'I need to speak to you privately,' I whispered.

He nodded, leading me outside and across the wind-blasted yard to another entrance and down a passage to an empty office serving as a storeroom. With no fire, it was bone-achingly cold.

'Please don't tell me you did it, Raphael?'

'Holy Christ, no.'

Tom slumped a little, smiling his relief. 'Well, that's the most important thing. Now, what do you need to say to me?'

I told him everything, my breath misting in front of me, but could not bring myself to look him in the eye while I did. 'I can't see her involved. You understand that?' I finally looked up.

He gave me a hard stare. Very hard.

'You disapprove of me, my friend?'

He shook his head. 'It's not for me to approve or disapprove. Yet I cannot help wishing you hadn't risked her the way you have. But I will do my utmost to keep her out of it.'

In truth, at that moment, I felt no little shame and vowed when I was freed, for her sake, I would end our nascent affair.

SUSANNAH

Diary: March 9, 1676

With my hand shaking as I try to write, I have to move the pen away before a blot splashes down onto the page, whilst I struggle to order my thoughts sufficiently to turn them into written words. But to set it all down, firstly I must discipline myself to begin at the beginning.

. . .

Just a little over two weeks ago, I worked as usual in the studio when the screaming started. We all froze and looked at each other in some alarm. There was a woman shrieking and sobbing, too, somewhere below. Papa swore under his breath and left his table – where he worked on replica portraits for patrons to distribute as gifts – to hurry from the room. The sound, we quickly discovered, was coming from the drawing room.

'Catherine?' Papa said.

I stepped into the doorway beside him. Catherine was sitting on a couch, her head in her hands shrieking and wailing in a manner which, to my shame, made me want to cover my ears rather than to offer her comfort. Beside her was the large form of Thomas Monkton, leaning down to rest his hand on her back. Something had occurred at Whitehall.

Papa stepped further into the room. 'Thomas. What can have happened to–' he gestured towards his wife. 'To cause this?'

The lieutenant straightened, though Catherine seemed not to notice the absence of his hand. 'I have brought your wife bad news, as you can see. The worst I'm afraid. Her son James Villiers has been found dead.'

Catherine's shrieking became quite frenzied and worrying she was about to lose her wits entirely, I sat beside her myself placing my hand on her arm to belatedly offer what little comfort I could. She did quieten somewhat then, though whether because of my touch or to hear Thomas's words more clearly, I was uncertain.

All colour had drained from Papa's face 'What? How?'

'I regret to tell you he has been murdered.'

Catherine began to scream again, high and piercing.

Papa moved to kneel at her feet. 'My dear. I beg you. Calm yourself and allow the captain to inform us of the circumstances.'

She dropped her hands. '*Circumstances?* What does it matter? He is dead. My boy is dead. Don't you understand?' Her words were spat, leaving wet traces on my father's face.

Thomas straightened his back. 'James Villiers was found run-through by a blade within the confines of Whitehall Palace. Therefore, the King has ruled the murder high treason carried out against his person. The body was discovered this morning by *Signor* Raphael Rossi, a jeweller to the court, who is now held under guard whilst his movements are investigated. I shall make sure you're informed of any further developments.'

Catherine, silent suddenly, had watched him through red narrowed eyes.

He bowed. 'I'll take my leave of you, my lady. And once again you have my sincerest condolences.'

'Sukie, see Lieutenant Monkton out, would you.'

I stood, nodding to my father, and moved to Thomas's side, gesturing for him to proceed me.

Catherine leapt to her feet. 'Wait!'

Papa rose, too, looking ashen. He stood at her side without touching her.

'Find Samuel Carter.' With sudden composure, she told Thomas – in unexpectedly lucid detail – her own twisted version of both Sam's encounters with James. 'Raphael Rossi is undoubtedly involved also. And you should question that slut of a maid, she can tell you how she lured my boy–' Tears cascaded down her face, once more. 'To his death.'

My heart plummeted as she spoke, leaving me fearing I might vomit. 'Bess is visiting her family.' I hurriedly scribbled. 'Shall I bring her to you at Horse Guards when she returns?'

'Thank you. I'll need to speak with her.'

'Not Sam.' I wrote. 'Never. NEVER.'

He met my imploring gaze with kindly eyes. 'I must now speak with Master Carter. Would you be so good as to direct me to his home?'

Catherine's eyes were avid. 'The Carter house is further down across the street.'

I wondered how she could look both grief-stricken and gleeful at the same time. 'He too is away from home,' I wrote.

'Then, perhaps he could accompany you and your maidservant when they are both returned?'

I nodded.

'Where is he? You must send out men to locate him at once. The man's a murderer, you imbecile.'

Catherine had two spots of hectic colour high on her cheeks. I could not help but think she looked a madwoman. The death of a child would do that. Even one such as James.

After I had seen Thomas out to the stables to collect his horse, with more hasty scrawls insisting on Sam's innocence. Scrawls I truly wished could have been the spoken words he knew me capable of – shaking my head and pointing to my lips to convey that regret – tears came to my eyes seeing such compassion in his. He squeezed my shoulder, swearing to find the truth of it before I hurried across the street to Sam's house.

Though he had not yet returned from a rather mysterious trip to the country, I thought it prudent to leave a message with Connor to warn him of what was afoot. In the event, I was able to do so myself for as I sat at the table in the kitchen parlour writing my note, he walked in looking particularly happy and relaxed. I felt a lump in my throat that I was about to so cruelly shatter his mood.

'Join me in the drawing room, Sukie. Claret, I think, Connor.'

Once inside with the doors securely closed behind us, I flung my arms around him and burst into tears. 'Sam. Holy Christ, Sam. Catherine has accused you of murder.' And then I told him everything, only pausing briefly when Connor brought our wine.

He pulled me down beside him on the couch and held me. 'Well, if Thomas Monkton says he will uncover the truth, then we must take him at his word.'

I looked up at him. 'But you have people who can confirm your whereabouts, thank Jesu.

He frowned, looking oddly guarded. 'That's not possible, I'm afraid.'

'How can it not be possible? I don't understand.'

'All I can tell you is the person I was with is not in a position to assist me.'

Who could truly be unable to help in such a situation? Did Sam not understand the gravity of it? Surely not simply a married woman. How could her marriage be worth more than Sam's life? 'How can this be when you could face execution?'

He stood and walked to the window. 'I assure it is, so let us just leave it there.' He turned back to me, forcing a smile. 'I need to talk to Thomas myself.'

'But if you cannot say where you were, how can you prove you didn't do it?'

'By finding out who did.'

The next morning Bess and I travelled with Sam in his coach and four to Whitehall. No one spoke as wheels rattled and hooves clattered. Sam had little expectation of retuning to Henrietta Street with us. That Raphael Rossi had been held as a suspect simply for being unlucky enough to discover the body left him in little doubt he would be incarcerated also.

He had dressed simply in a plain grey worsted coat and breeches, chosen for warmth I imagined, together with stout jackboots. Bess was in her Sunday best, one of my gowns from two years before, she had altered to fit her tiny form. Its dun colour suited her dark curls far more than it had ever suited me. She also looked ashen with terror. I had written careful instructions for her the evening before. It was important she told the complete truth, so Sam could confirm it. I wondered if he understood just how determined Catherine was to have him guilty.

At Horse Guards, we waited outside the captain's office for some minutes while Thomas spoke with him, explaining our presence and the information we had. 'Courage,' I wrote, showing it to them both. When the door opened and Thomas asked for Bess to come inside, I rose beside her, shaking my head and gesturing at myself. She would not go in without me.

He appeared uncomfortable. 'Sir Henry wishes to speak with her alone, I'm afraid.'

I shook my head again and pushed past his bulk into the office. How infuriating I was unable to speak. I wanted to sweep his desk of all its contents. I wanted to fling his silver ink stand though the window down onto the parade ground. Again, I read Thomas's sympathy for my predicament.

Sir Henry stood, his expression thunderous. 'Madam, you cannot be the maidservant?'

Ignoring him, I sat before his desk and wrote, 'I am Sir Richard Gresham's daughter, Susannah. My maid will not be interviewed unless I accompany her.' I was also the King's Goddaughter and had dressed as such in lapis satin, rather than the soberly clad portrait miniaturist.

Sir Henry turned a particularly unhealthy shade of puce but appeared not about to challenge me. He turned to Thomas. 'Bring the chit in, if you please, Lieutenant.'

An additional stool was found for Bess, who was visibly trembling. I reached out to pat her hand and she looked up at me with the eyes of a trapped animal. Yet she answered all the captain's questions clearly though her voice was little above a whisper, giving a truthful account of what had happened between her and James. She denied Catherine's allegation of soliciting him and would not be pressed to change her answer even though Sir Henry tried his best to intimidate her in to doing so.

'You expect me to believe you did not see this young man as a potential source of supplementary income?' He blustered.

Bess stared down at her hands, as she had done throughout. 'If you means, Sir, t'was my intention to be his whore then I swear on my ma's life it were not. He forced his self on me.'

'Pah.' Sir Henry flicked his hand as though batting away the wrong answer. 'We only have your word for it, girl.' He steepled his fingers, watching her with a raptor-like glare. 'How, then, do you explain your lack of maidenhead before the incident.'

She looked up then, colour washing over her face. 'I don't know what ...'

I quickly wrote. 'How dare you? That is not a suitable question.' I pushed my notebook towards him and turned to Thomas in time to see the disgust on his face.

'I decide what questions to ask, Madam, not you.'

With that, Bess began to weep with complete abandon. I reached across to draw her into my arms, hiding my smile against her hair. Had I not known her to be entirely without guile, I would have suspected her sobs a tactic. And, of course, just the right one for the occasion.

Sir Henry stood, his face a picture of sneering contempt. 'In the name of God, get the snivelling wretch out of my sight.'

Back in the smoky hall again, we sat down as Sam was ushered inside by Thomas. I wished I could have stayed with him but understood we had no argument for it. He had my prayers, though I had little hope they would serve much purpose. Though Catherine insisted on his guilt, I had a strong feeling Papa would not support her. I knew the King had a soft spot for Sam and his father certainly had his ear. I also knew that murder made the King less likely to show leniency, especially with so much unrest amongst the people when courtiers often went unpunished no matter the seriousness of their offence.

Bess moved from my arms, drying her face on a tiny lace-edged handkerchief that looked barely up to the task. I noticed she had recovered almost immediately once we had escaped that room. I studied her face, her eyes red and swollen from crying, finding no artifice there, just relief.

I wrote, 'Forgive me, but we must remain here until I know Master Samuel's fate.'

She managed a wan smile. 'Of course we must, Mistress. Just as long as I does not have to speak wiv that man again.'

I shook my head, squeezing her hand for reassurance.

. . .

Now I must lift my pen to write the final line. Sam did not return home.

RAPHAEL

It all happened so fast, I had barely understood what was afoot when they hustled me out from the guardhouse and over to the Hall Stairs. Why was I taken at night? I could only think to make the experience more terrifying. Torches: flaming reflections on the black water of the Thames and in glittering streams from oars, dipping in relentless rhythm taking me those few short miles – and through the white-water race up against the looming mass of the great stone starlings beneath the widest arch of London bridge – downriver to the Queen's Stairs and the brutal bulk of the Tower under a black sky aglitter with frigid stars. I was as frozen in mind as in flesh; my heart pounds and my guts clench whenever I think of it.

And so, I was imprisoned in the Tower of London – not something I had ever foreseen for myself – and here I have been for well past ten days. At first, I found it difficult to understand why I should be treated as a traitor to the King until I remembered Catherine Gresham telling James about the possible consequences of using a sword within the palace precinct. So, James was killed with a blade. Unfortunately, I then remembered the punishment dispensed for such a crime. This took me to a cobwebbed corner where I puked, much to the disgust of my cell mates who shouted for me to use the slop bucket, though I had no intention of risking any splashes from that source upon my person.

They both looked rough men, dressed in ragged homespun coats with filthy hose much in need of darning. I wondered why they were in the Tower and not Newgate but what did I know of how such things were decided? And we were not housed in one of the Towers proper, but rather in a stone outbuilding up against the north wall, with Tower Hill beyond.

I had remained in the Horse Guards guardhouse for four days where both Tom and Giuseppe had been able to visit me, Tom with news of the case against me – or more accurately the lack of it, though Giuseppe's account would need corroborating by other servants, which alarmed me greatly – and Giuseppe bringing me food. Tom had told me of Sam Carter's arrest as soon as it occurred. I could only think his alibi must be as problematic as mine for he had not been released either. Maybe he had no witnesses to his whereabouts? Or maybe he was, indeed, guilty? Yet, somehow, I knew he was not. Well, I wished they would hurry up and reach a decision. The authorities could not think us both guilty, surely? I trusted it was only Catherine Gresham who thought that a reasonable position to take.

Home-cooked food had stopped, though, in the Tower where I was provided with a daily heel of bread and a bowl of greasy liquid in which unrecognisable objects floated on the surface like turds in the slop bucket. Not an appetising similarity. I believe it was intended as broth. After much persistence, I was eventually rewarded with a visit to Ned Henwood – the chamberlain to the Tower's lieutenant, Sir John Robinson's – in his office in the White Tower. Short, stout and disconcertingly good humoured, he handled my request for my own food to be brought in as though it could not be of higher importance to him. Even though this, as it turned out, was a common practice available to all for a fee. I was then able to send a message to Cheapside, so that the very next day Giuseppe was with me again, carrying a basket of bread, meats and cheeses including a fine bottle of Chianti.

He took some moments looking around at the damp stone walls, the high narrow window and the straw covered pallet where I slept. 'Well, at least you're above ground, though I doubt it could be any colder below.' His breath misted in the frigid air.

'Why Italian?' I answered in the same language, looking across at the two men lying on their cots showing every indication of being asleep, including loud rattling snores and the occasional wet fart. Since arriving in London we had spoken English as much as possible, firstly for practice and then because it felt discourteous not to.

He whistled through his teeth in a rather derogatory way. 'Because who knows if they are spies. Perhaps put here to catch you incriminating yourself?'

'Well, it seems unlikely they could as I have committed no crime.'

Whilst he watched me eat, he told me how things stood for me. Tom had visited the duchess and asked her, on my behalf, not to become involved and she had agreed for the time being. Her caveat being should my situation worsen, she would speak to the King. I prayed then it would not for I knew full well what worsen meant. 'What news of Sam Carter?'

'Signor Monkton, he is not talking of him. His oaf of a boss – that yard of cack – has instructed him not to.'

Before taking his leave, he held my face kissing me gently on both cheeks, causing the pair of churls – who had woken and watched me eat – to snigger. He responded with a grossly obscene gesture before rapping on the door, summoning a warder to release him.

Late the following afternoon – much to my startled surprise – when the door swung open with its usual reluctant screech as though the Tower itself had no wish to give up its prisoners, Sam Carter was thrust inside by ungentle hands, landing on his knees on the filthy rushes scattered over the flagstones. I quickly helped him up before the two guards returned with a fourth pallet to cram between mine and the wall. '*Santo Dio, cos'è questo?*'

Quite unexpectedly, he replied in excellent Italian. 'Nothing good, it would seem. Our acquaintance looks about to become a touch more intimate.'

When he smiled, I realised again just what an exquisite creature he was. For some reason I have not yet been able to understand, Englishmen seem reluctant to acknowledge beauty in their own sex. I wonder if they see it as the first step towards sodomy? Something they seem to fear a very great deal. 'It may prove useful we are able to converse in my language. My manservant is convinced our fellow guests are spies.' They were now looking at us and scowling, which did little to improve their countenances. Sam smiled at them, causing their identical frown lines to deepen before they looked at each other.

'What's you bout then, laughing boy?' said one.

'I've been held alone until now. Perhaps the authorities think we might discuss our crime should they put us together?'

'Eh? Why's you talking foreign at us? Do we look like we's foreign?' said the other.

'Well, we can hardly discuss a crime neither of us has committed, in any language.' Yet we continued to converse in my tongue. It provided a sense of privacy and I admit to enjoying the men's mumbled irritation that we did so. We lay down on our pallets side-by-side and I watched him as he told me of Catherine Villiers accusations against him, which consisted of our encounter with her son at the Twelfth Night Ball and another witnessed by Susannah Gresham, when Villiers had raped her maid. A vile act, which came as no surprise to me.

When he had finished his account, I scratched at my two-week beard, once again dearly wishing I could shave it off. He had received better treatment than I, for he was both clean and shaved. 'Well, I fail to see why anyone might imagine you would kill the man in defence of a maidservant's honour. She is nothing to you, no?'

'Susannah is fond of her.'

Once again, I felt a pang of jealousy at his closeness to her. 'Ah, and you are fond of *Signorina* Gresham. How long have you known each other?' I already knew the answer, for the duchess had told me.

He smiled. 'All our lives. We've always been close neighbours, first in Paris and Cologne, and then in London. Richard taught us portraiture together. We even shared a tutor for a time. And we share the King as Godfather, of course.'

Now that came as a surprise. 'Then why does he have you sent to this godforsaken stink-hole?' I gestured to the forbidding surroundings. I had stopped smelling the foul slop bucket and the unwashed pair who shared our cell – in truth, I had become one of the unwashed myself – though the miasma would be all too disgustingly apparent to him. 'Indeed, why has he allowed you to be imprisoned at all?'

'High treason. He cannot ignore the manner of Villiers' death. And Willets sees my guilt as an easy solution from his point of view. It is unfortunate my father is away in the Indies. He would challenge the King on my behalf.'

'Ah, well, I do see how that might be useful. They are good friends, yes? But can't you tell Willets you have witnesses who can vouch for you that night?'

'Can't you?'

'My manservant served me dinner at home, though he does not seem to quite satisfy them.' He raised his eyebrows and I read the question. 'No other servants were present.' I sat up, feeling there was nothing more I could say. It seemed we both had unsatisfactory alibies. I turned to him again. 'I have someone who can, should it prove absolutely necessary.'

He chewed his lip. 'I unfortunately do not.'

I woke from dreams of Frances and Susannah who had somehow become one person and so resembled neither, fearing I had called out. Sam's night-dark eyes were upon me, his expression unknowable in the moonlight.

We both sat up and I moved to sit beside him, our backs

resting against the icy stones, blankets around our shoulders. 'I hope I didn't wake you.' I whispered, my breath pluming, quickly wondering why I had bothered when the churls were clearly solidly asleep.

'No. Sleep is hard to come by. Our companions are not the most considerate. I don't believe I've heard such snores ever before. It almost appears they are competing to test who is louder.'

I smiled. 'I know it seems unlikely now, but you do become accustomed to it. The noise and the stink.'

'No matter. I hope to secure better accommodation once Connor can convey the fee to Robinson's chamberlain. I'm sure we can arrange for you to accompany me then.'

'Connor?'

'My valet. He was allowed to attend me daily in my last cell, which was somewhat more salubrious than this one.'

So being the King's Godson had some advantages. 'Why were you moved?'

'Christ knows. To unsettle me, perhaps? Or push me to pay for better.'

I felt certain additional remuneration would be required on my behalf if I were to be allowed to join him. I hoped I could meet it myself without the necessity of taking money from the business. I smiled at the very thought of it. My father would explode with rage that I had offended the King to the extent he must send me to the Tower of London.

So far, he would be unaware of any change in my circumstances as our trade continued quite normally without me. Giuseppe was a highly skilled jeweller in his own right – taught by my mother – something else my father was unaware of. And we have five more than capable apprentices, so there should be no need for him ever to know. I focussed my attention back onto Sam. 'You speak my language very well and with a Florentine accent, too. You must have spent considerable time there?'

'Never been. It was my mother's city. I learned from her. She always wanted to take me home to meet her family, but her health prevented it. I've not yet felt entirely ready to visit without her. I shall one day.'

'How long ago did you lose her?'

'Nine years now. I was fourteen and away at Winchester – at school – when she died. Papa came to tell me. Yet I knew as soon as I saw his face. Though I had never felt close to him myself, I was always sure they loved each other. He looked destroyed. And all I could think of was how I had not been there to say goodbye. I was very close to her.' He turned away.

'*Sì*. As I am with my *mamma*. It must have been difficult to lose that, especially if you did not have it with your papa.' As, indeed, I do not.

'It was. And he was so often at sea.' He smiled. 'But I had Susannah. And Jane was like a second mother to me in so many ways. Then, of course, we lost her too. Susannah, well.' He sighed. 'It's been difficult for her.'

'I'm sorry to hear it.'

He shook himself a little. 'So, I am yet to meet my Florentine family. I hope to one day, for they are the only people I have besides Papa.'

'Well, when you decide to go, I would be honoured to show you my beautiful city.' We were silent then, both no doubt questioning whether this would ever happen. Making such plans seemed fanciful locked-up in a cell and facing the possibility of death. Yet I knew his predicament to be alarmingly graver than my own, for should I be sent to trial, Frances would come forward. 'You cannot have been entirely alone for a day and a night. What about your valet? Mine has spoken for me. He must be better than no one.' But not much, without corroboration.

He looked down at his hands. 'I was away in the country. He did not accompany me there.'

'But why ever not?' I could not imagine staying away from home without Giuseppe. Chiefly because I felt certain he would not allow it.

He shrugged. 'It was a private visit.'

I knew from his tone I could press him no further on it. 'We should try for more sleep. I moved back to my own cot and pulled my blanket around me. He remained as he was, pensive in the spear of moonlight now shinning down upon him, silvering his chestnut hair. He looked like an elvish King was my last thought before sleep found me.

Three days later we were moved to a suite of rooms in the Beauchamp Tower.

SUSANNAH

Diary: March 28, 1676

In many ways, it has been an unnerving day. And, certainly, one I never saw coming. How did it happen? Jesu. How was it even possible?

I have at last been allowed to visit Sam again. He had refused to see me until better accommodation had been arranged once more. I could hardly bear imagining surroundings so bad he refused to let me to see them after that freezing bare cell in the Wakefield Tower. Connor had carried my notes begging to visit him each day and returned with the same answer, to wait.

Once again, I travelled there by hackney and went alone. If Catherine should discover I visited him, it would cause yet another frenetic scene of anguish. Many such had already occurred because of my support for him. And my father's refusal to condemn him.

The elderly, scarlet-uniformed warder summoned for his reading skills, guided me up an imposing staircase in the Beauchamp Tower, regaling me with a brief history of the place with particular emphasis on the more notable executions of those held there. Not especially what I wished to hear under the circumstances, but I smiled at him anyway. Finally, he unlocked a door at the top of a narrow flight of stairs and I soon found myself in Sam's arms. He showed me his set of rooms comprising a hallway, a parlour boasting a healthy fire and a large mullioned and transomed window facing towards the river, ruffled and glittering in the early spring sunshine, and a bedchamber with a smaller window overlooking Tower Green. A sight I found more than chilling, even on a cheery afternoon. The furnishings though worn were of good quality, the old-fashioned arrases softening the harsh stone behind them to some extent, so he would be comfortable in as much as he could be when held prisoner.

'So, I am not too badly off now am I, as you can see?'

I tried to smile despite the whiff of musty damp tainting the air. 'I'm sure it is a palace compared to where you were.'

'Indeed. And something of an improvement on the Wakefield Tower, don't you think?' He smiled, placing his hands on my shoulders. 'Try not to worry about me, Sukie. All shall be well, I promise.'

I looked around the chamber, noting the two cots with their meagre featherbeds and worn faded quilts and the garderobe that would contain the close stool, a significant improvement on the slop bucket Connor had told me of. Yet, however bearable the conditions of his imprisonment now were, he was still imprisoned. 'You must insist your companion from the country vouches for you. What can it matter if she is married? What is that compared to this? I simply cannot understand why you refuse.' I gestured around the small chamber. 'Look where you are. You should not be here when the means to leave are in your own hands.' Tears spilled but I did nothing to wipe them away. 'I beg you to save yourself.'

He pulled me into his arms again, holding me tight. 'It is not possible, Sukie. Believe me, it wouldn't help.'

'Why?' said a deep voice behind me.

I spun around to find Raphael Rossi staring at Sam, hands on hips. He must have been in the garderobe.

'Why would you not demand this woman admits you were with her? Have you lost your mind?'

I stared at Raphael with a mixture of horror that he had heard me speak and gratitude that he was pressing Sam to act, just as I was. Without thinking, I lifted my pad to write but Sam tore it from me.

'No, Susannah. Speak. Raphael has heard you. It is time to speak, damn you.'

I stepped back from him quite unable to comprehend his behaviour. His cruelty. I looked from his face to Raphael's and saw something pass between them. Had I fallen into a trap? I had never seen Sam's expression so cold. Yet he knew better than anyone I could not do it. I thought I might vomit then.

'Sam,' I mouthed, silently. 'Please.'

'I have nothing further to say to you until you speak.'

I began to pace. I paced for some considerable time before stopping to stare at them both standing with their arms folded. Implacable. I gazed at Sam, begging him with my eyes. Begging him with my tears, my heart racing and swooping. He knew I could not. He knew it. 'Christ. You despicable brute,' I croaked, finally. The words like shards of glass in my throat.

He pulled me hard into his arms, stroking my hair. 'You've done so well, my Sukie. So well. You must see how much you need to be able to talk to Raphael. He's soon to be released. He knows all about you and wants to help.'

I pulled away from him, and looking into his face, found only the usual kindness there now. No. Raphael did not know all about me because Sam did not, but he knew enough. 'Did it not occur to you to do me the courtesy of asking my permission first?' I rasped.

Sam smiled. 'It occurred to me briefly, yes, but as I knew it would not be forthcoming, I decided against it.'

'You have nothing to fear from me,' Raphael said, softly. 'I can offer you a friendly ear when needed. I think it must be difficult without one.'

Hearing the compassion in his voice, my thudding heart began to slow. I turned to him. 'Yes,' I whispered. 'It has been.' I was certain now they had planned this as soon as they learned of Raphael's release. And how was he suddenly able to secure it? I understood Sam's motives were kindly ones. He only wished for me to have someone I could talk to in his absence, especially under such dreadful circumstances. And he was right. I had found complete silence very hard, as I always did, even trying unsuccessfully to speak to Papa again. And why choose Raphael Rossi? He was simply there.

How though? How can I have spoken to someone else at last? Jesu, it makes no sense.

Diary: March 31, 1676

Today, Raphael called on me in Henrietta Street. He had sent a note saying he would collect me in his coach that afternoon, so I was able to intercept him at the door. As the steps were already down, I climbed straight inside.

Once we were underway, he turned to me. 'I thought perhaps a walk along The Mall. St James's Park appeals. Not unsurprisingly, I feel the need for open skies.'

I panicked, of course, fearing I would be unable to speak to him this time. Though I understood Sam had prepared him for it when he reached for my hand but did not look at me. I took a deep breath, my heart pounding. 'You must be much relieved to have your freedom.' Trite. But they were words and I had spoken them aloud. And in a reasonably normal tone.

He turned back to me, his face radiating pleasure, green eyes full of warmth. I studied him in a way I had never done before in daylight. His teeth were white against his tawny skin and his black hair, tied at his neck, gleamed sleekly in the watery sunshine. He had a captivating handsomeness made all the more so because he seemed genuinely unaware of it. More typically, men would use such looks as a weapon to win a woman's interest. Yet he seemed not to know he even had it in his arsenal. Or he had missed a vocation on the stage.

'Indeed, I am greatly relieved to be outside in the fresh air again.'

Then I watched something like regret pass fleetingly across his face.

He examined his fingers. 'I am a little sad that someone became involved when I had wished them not to.'

'I am sorry that is so but, for your sake, I am glad they did. I just hope another someone might do the same for Sam.' I chewed my lip. 'He didn't confide in you who that might be, I suppose?'

He shook his head. 'Perhaps it may be possible to find out? We might try at least.'

Of course that is what I should do. What we should do. Just knowing he has said 'we' made me feel more confident of success. Though he should not feel compelled to be part of such a search. 'Please do not feel you must become involved. I know Sam wouldn't wish to place you under any obligation.'

'I want to help. As you say, for me, the decision was taken out of my hands. We must try and do the same for Sam.' He squeezed my hand. His was warm, its strength somehow reassuring. 'He would do so for me if our positions were reversed. It is what friends do.'

'Connor. He is where we should start.'

'Well, should I ever manage to divest myself of Giuseppe in order to travel without him, I am certain by some alchemy known only to him, he would know where I was and with whom.'

This gave me further confidence we should be able to discover this mysterious woman if we could but persuade Connor to go against his master's instructions. Would he not do so now Sam's life depended on it? 'Surely it must be a wife whose reputation would be ruined should her affair with Sam come to light?' I turned to him in the carriage now moving slowly down The Strand towards The Mall. 'Perhaps you have had a similar experience?' He looked at me with such startled surprise, heat swept across my face. 'Forgive my impertinence.'

He touched my flushed cheek with a look of wonderment on his face. 'Not at all, *Signorina*. Please don't be embarrassed. Perhaps I should tell you my story? Especially if it might offer you some comfort. I must warn you, I don't come out of it well.' He rapped on the carriage wall. 'Pull up, Rory. We'll take a stroll in the park.'

'I don't wish to pry. I'm simply trying to reassure myself. If your lady came forward, then Sam's will too. Perhaps she's not yet aware of his circumstances.'

He helped me down onto the grass and took my arm in his. 'I am happy to tell you.'

So, we walked again beside the canal where we had seen Monmouth ride on the ice. This time watching the King's pelicans – with their long beaks and throat pouches – bobbing incongruously on ruffled water reflecting the sky like shards of blue glass amongst the sunshine glitter, while I heard a little of his liaison with the Duchess of Richmond. He spoke easily but not without considerable self-deprecation. I cannot deny I felt some admiration for her. I already knew of his affair with her, of course, having won my wager with Sam over it. Though I also knew he had many others.

'I understood what she risked with me, yet to my shame, I continued it.'

'She knew what she was risking, also. It was honourable attempting to protect her when you were arrested ... and to her credit that she would not allow it, I think.' I touched his arm, and he gave me a rueful smile.

'She went to the King in the end and told him everything. I think he will forgive her dalliance with me when her heart was not involved.' He took a sharp breath. 'Forgive me, *Signorina*, I should not say such things to you.'

How little he knew me. 'I have been at court since the restoration, Raphael. You would probably not believe some of the things I've heard or indeed seen there.' It had been but a pleasant diversion for them as all such affairs were. Yet they had both been reckless risking the King's anger. The duchess with her home and income, Raphael with his trade at court and, no doubt, his father's wrath. But if she could risk everything for Raphael, why could Sam's lady not do the same for him?

He gave me a speculative look before grinning broadly and I felt myself responding to him, and not just with an answering smile.

So, we are to meet again in three days to interview Connor together. I feel particularly unsettled and suspect sleep will prove difficult tonight. I am anxious to know whether he will be able to help and worried what to do next if he cannot. And, in truth, something about Raphael Rossi unsettles me, too.

Diary: April 1, 1676

I dreamt of him. Jewels and kisses, God help me.

With Bess's help, I dressed in my most fashionable gown. Pink floral satin. Skirts drawn back over dove-grey petticoats. A plum busk and full lace-edged sleeves gathered at the elbow. After commandeering Papa's coach, I went to petition the King.

I eventually found him in Portsmouth's grand chamber with Monmouth and York, together with his usual assortment of wits and ladies of the court, spread around the room at gaming tables. What a sumptuous and glittering place it was. Even in daylight, candles in golden candelabras were reflected in mirrors within framed silk panels embroidered in jewel-like colours, heavy with gold and silver thread.

The King sat with Louise at an ivory and ebony marquetry chess table where he appeared on course for an easy win. I looked at her with her creamy skin and gentian eyes, never to be mistaken for anything other than French. Was she really this unskilled at chess or did she seek to flatter him? It was impossible to know with her. They both appeared decidedly displeased to see me.

The King looked down his great nose, his eyes ice-cold. 'Yes?'

I wrote, 'I beg a private word with you, Your Majesty.'

'Come back later.' He gestured at the chess game. 'We are occupied, as you see.'

I made a deep curtsy before writing, 'I beg your indulgence, Your Majesty.'

He snorted and got to his feet. 'Pah. For your father's sake we shall then, but for a moment only if you please.'

He hurriedly moved a rook, yet that Louise failed to capitalise on this somewhat reckless error, left me none the wiser about her reason for such an omission. Holding me firmly by the elbow, he moved me outside into the Privy Gallery.

'Proceed, Madam.'

'Samuel Carter. You cannot intend he should remain incarcerated?' I scrawled.

Colour drained from his normally florid face. 'God's fish. You dare such impertinence?' he growled.

'Forgive me, Your Majesty. I meant no impertinence. I am just worried for my dear friend,' I wrote.

He slapped my pad away. 'It is time you stopped this childish petulance. Do you not apprehend how much it pains your papa?' He lifted his chin, his face appearing carved from granite, his lustrous wig flowing down over his shoulders. 'If Samuel Carter has committed treason against our person, he shall be subject to the law as would anyone else.'

I scribbled. 'But you know he would never do such a thing.'

He turned away without reading, stalking back to the duchess and his courtiers. When the door opened again, the scent of tobacco smoke and French perfume wafted out.

'Why?' I whispered in the empty gallery. 'Why turn against him now when he needs you? Why have you lost faith in him?'

RAPHAEL

I had used these past two days to confirm the smooth running of *Rossi & Son. Jewellers of Florence*, its workshop and salesrooms, before turning my attention to Samuel Carter and how to help him. Giuseppe, as I knew he would, had everything under control in the workshop and Mistress Kincaid supervised the ground floor showroom and our booths at the Middle Exchange, faultlessly.

My time imprisoned in the Tower with Sam had enabled a close friendship to grow between us, bringing the sort of intimacy that would have been difficult to achieve so quickly in other circumstances, for we had no one else to talk to for the larger part of each day. I knew of his family and upbringing in great detail. He knew all about my business and work as a jeweller. We had also spent a surprising amount of time talking about Susannah and he seemed happy to tell me of her life. I wonder now if his decision to ask me to help her was because he sensed I had feelings for her and, if he did, what then did he think of my confession about Frances?

Yet what exactly were these feelings? She had certainly filled my thoughts since the moment I first saw her. Was it possible that I loved her? It was hard to know for I had never been in love before. And I still bedded other women. Would a man truly in love behave in such a manner? Indeed, why might I love this woman and no other? Not simply because she was beautiful or because of her milk-white skin with its delightful blush? Or that I desired her more than any other I had ever known? Could it be because I understood she was in some way broken, without fully knowing why? I knew I wanted to help her. Did I love her because she needed me to? Christ, I wanted her to need me. Or might I hope for some sort of redemption through loving her because of Valentina? In truth, that struck me as self-serving enough to lie behind such fancies, considering how little time I had so far spent in her company.

So here I was finally on my way to see her and begin our quest on Sam's behalf. When Rory put me down outside her house the door opened, and I was shown up to the drawing room by a diminutive maid. Susannah rose to greet me but, of course, did not speak until the door closed behind the girl, who by then I knew to be Bess. The girl raped by James Villiers. Susannah looked pale and anxious, and it was all I could do not to pull her into my arms. Instead, I squeezed her hand, briefly. 'Don't worry, we shall find a way to get him released.'

She tried to smile. 'I want to believe it.' She returned to her couch, indicating I should sit beside her. 'I don't understand why the King refuses to help him. I saw him some days ago and he was unpleasantly hostile. Sam has always been a favourite of his, in his own right, and as Rupert's son. I've spent some time trying to understand it.' She chewed her lip as though trying to reach a decision. 'I'm going to tell you something you must never repeat to anyone. Will you give me your word on it?'

I stared into her storm-grey eyes, startled by their intensity. 'You have it.'

'Sam often travels to other royal courts across Europe, ostensibly to paint portrait miniatures but, more importantly, making informal diplomatic contacts on the King's behalf. The way he responded to my entreaty, I began to wonder whether unwittingly he had discovered something the King does not wish him to know. Or someone has suggested such to him.'

'And he is relieved to have Sam removed from circulation before he can reveal what he knows ... what he possibly knows. Has he said nothing to you?'

'Nothing, other than he had heard some interesting rumours from French patrons.'

Frances had already told me a little of this work Sam undertook for the King and for some reason, Susannah's suspicions heartened me. They gave us another avenue to explore at least. 'Well, let's see the valet first. Have you told him of our visit?'

She stood to ring for her servant. 'Bess took a note earlier.'

Once her cloak was fetched, we made our way across the bustling street with its clatter of hooves and iron-banded wheels and pungent whiff of horse shit. Soon, we mounted the steps to the Carter house where the valet, Connor, let us in. 'Is there somewhere we can talk privately?'

'Of course, Master,' he replied in what I assumed to be an Irish accent. He led us into the deserted kitchen parlour, gesturing for us to sit on chairs beside the fire as the day was somewhat chill. 'Can I offer you any refreshments Mistress Susannah?' He turned to me. 'Master?'

I held up my hand to decline.

Susannah shook her head before writing on her notepad, '*Signor* Rossi will tell you why we're here.'

He turned to me again, his back straight as a soldier standing to attention. 'Master.'

'I understand your employer has likely instructed you not to discuss what you know of his whereabouts at the time of the murder, but if there is anything that might assist us in freeing him – anything at all – I entreat you to tell us now before his situation becomes even more perilous.'

'Believe me Master, Mistress, if I knew I would've already told it. My master wished it not known, including not known by meself.'

I tried to square this with my relationship with Giuseppe but he, of course, was my friend since childhood. I would ask Susannah how close she thought them. 'You give us your oath you know nothing?'

'I do give it, Master. On my honour.'

His steady blue-eyed gaze convinced me he spoke the truth, however much I wished it otherwise. 'Well, I trust should anything occur to you, you'll inform Mistress Susannah?'

'Oh, I shall indeed, Master. You need have no worries on that score.' He looked down at the floor, relaxing his rigid stance at last. 'I visit him each morning and witness his spirits fading as each day goes by. If I could be helping him in any way at all, I would do so.'

Susannah rose and squeezed his arm. 'I know you would, Connor,' she wrote. 'We all would.'

I stood beside her. 'We won't give up.'

Outside again, I caught Susannah's arm to halt her as she headed off towards her home across the street. 'How do we get to the mews? I think a word with the coachman might prove useful.' She raised her eyebrows, following my train of thought, and turned to walk in the opposite direction. We passed Sam's house again and several others before turning into an alley leading to the row of stables and coach houses behind the grand terrace. She stopped outside the block belonging to the Carters.

'Call out for Joseph,' she whispered into my ear. The touch of her lips against it sent a shiver through me. I stared at her in surprise until she gave me a small shake, reminding me to get on with it. I pulled myself together, cupping my hands around my mouth. 'Ho there, Joseph. Are you within?'

A stable lad appeared, holding a brush and curry comb. 'He be at the Ordinary, Master. Ain't much need of him just now what with the admiral and Master Samuel both away like, as you might say.'

'Which Ordinary would that be?'

He pointed to the end of the mews. 'Bannister's. It be just around the corner, Master.'

When I handed him a groat, his face lit up with a wide smile which unfortunately revealed a snaggle of blackened teeth. He spat on the coin before putting it in his pocket. 'For luck, Master.' He touched his fist to his forehead and returned to the horse.

'*Grazie.*' I called after him. I was still a little uncertain of the value of such a coin. However, as Susannah had shown no reaction, I assumed it appropriate. She put her arm through mine, and I looked at her enquiringly. 'He might be of no help, but it is worth a try.'

'Yes,' she murmured. 'Anything is worth a try.'

Bannister's proved to be a low sort of place, not surprisingly, there to cater for servants and tradesmen rather than the occupants of the great houses. Well, ordinaries were never aimed at them. Hence the name, I imagined. 'Perhaps it would be better if you returned home–'

'No.'

Her fingers tightened on my arm, and I sighed rather theatrically. 'Very well, then. But stay close.'

She nodded.

I open the door, assailed by the aroma of roasting meat, ale, and tobacco smoke. Dirty sawdust covered the floor and Susannah lifted her skirts before following me inside. At the counter, the grizzled publican was engaged in a rather heated exchange with a customer about the quality of the ale. There was a noticeable lull in conversation when Susannah's presence was observed, causing the man to break off his diatribe to see what caused the sudden hush.

'No women served here.' He pointed. 'Over the food side. Off you go, Poppet.'

'She is with me.'

'Don't care who the trull's with, Sirrah. Get her out.'

Without thought, I crossed the floor and grabbed him by his grimy neckerchief, thrusting my fist in front of his face. '*Signore*, I strongly advise you not to refer to this lady as a trull.' My accent had become more pronounced as my temper frayed. While unsure of the exact nature of a trull, I felt certain it was not complimentary.

He pulled away, looking alarmed. 'No offence meant, milord, only I cannot serve her, like. 'Tis against landlord's dictate.'

Susannah joined me, glancing around the room. 'Not here,' she scrawled. 'Eating?' She gestured through to the other room.

In the event there was no need to look, for a man obviously returning from the privy, spoke up. 'Be that you Mistress Susannah?'

Susannah moved from behind me and hurried to him, touching his forearm.

'Might we have a word outside?'

'Of course, Sir.' He moved a little way along the street before turning to us. 'Is there news of Master Samuel, Sir?' His eyes flitted to Susannah while he spoke, understanding my role as her mouthpiece.

'Nothing, I'm sorry to say. But we are trying to help him.' I glanced at her. 'I understand you may be following your master's instructions, but it is vital you tell us anywhere he might have gone around the time of the murder. Perhaps somewhere you had not taken him before?'

'I took him nowhere all that week.' He shook his head, looking despondent. 'I only wish I could tell you somethin what would help him, Sir. It don't bear thinking of what they be doing to him.'

Susannah's shoulders slumped. I had known it was a long shot. 'Sorry to drag you from your drink, Joseph.' I handed him two groats. 'Get yourself another one.'

He made as though to walk away but stopped and turned back. 'One of the kitchen girls thought she saw Master Samuel gettin in a coach on the corner of the street early one mornin before, like–'

'Then, we must talk to her.'

'No need, Sir. Believe me I got every bit of what could be got from her. It were a dark coloured coach and four bays with not a thing to mark it different from any other. In other words, I got fuck all.' He reddened. 'Pardon my tongue, Mistress.'

Susannah waved it away, giving every indication of entirely agreeing with the sentiment. Yet I felt it might be worth talking to the maid again, perhaps using a gentler approach. 'Did she mention the coachman?'

'She never did, Sir.' He frowned. 'Though I did not ask her, thinking on such a cold morning he would have a scarf around his face, for I does myself on such days, like.'

I felt I was grasping at phantasms. 'Perhaps she noticed his build?' I looked down at my boots, feeling somewhat foolish. Just where would the shape of the man get us without facial features.

'Well, I know a great many coachman. If she saw anythin to notice about him, I'm sure to track him down.'

'Then we must speak with her.'

Susannah, still looking downhearted, scribbled. 'I shall return home. Call on me there when you have seen her.' She turned back, her eyes fierce suddenly, and wrote. 'Why must he be so damnably honourable? Has he no care for what he does to the rest of us who love him?'

I touched her arm. 'He is trapped by it, I think.' I watched her walk away towards the alley which would take her back to the street, her pale hair a candleflame in the murk, before following Joseph through the back entrance to the Carter house. Like all such places in grand houses, the parts only frequented by servants were far from that, but it was all generally clean and in good repair. Joseph took me through and up to the drawing room where no fire was lit. Why would there be when neither Sam nor his father were in residence?

'I shall fetch the girl to you, Sir.'

I wandered around the room, picking up objects – brass ships' lanterns. An astrolabe. A collection of what looked like carvings taken from ships' taffrails – and putting them down again. I tried to imagine Sam here but found I could not. It seemed so much his father's room, even down to a large portrait above the huge, corniced, marble fireplace. I saw nothing of him in the admiral's long stern face, either. Was there a portrait of his mother anywhere? I was startled from my musings by the sound of the doors opening and turned to see a young child guided inside by Joseph's hand firmly planted on her shoulder.

'Here be Annie, Sir.'

On closer inspection, I saw she was older than I had first thought. Perhaps thirteen or fourteen. Small and slight with bright ginger hair and a dark trail of freckles across her button nose and wide cheeks, she was not a pretty girl. I smiled at her. 'Has Joseph told you why I wish to speak with you?'

Her face flushed almost purple, and she bobbed a clumsy curtsey. 'No, Sir,' she murmured.

I told her my business as simply and succinctly as I could, pleased my English had improved to such an extent that I had choices about how to use it. 'Did you notice anything at all about how the man looked? Anything that caught your eye?'

She touched the hair escaping from her coif. He were a carrot top, too. He had a rat's tail down is back.' She looked up at me, meeting my gaze, less intimidated now she had been able to tell me something. 'I notice em like, coz of how I knows what it be like to be one, Master.'

'That's very helpful, Annie. Thank you. Is there anything else you can tell me about him?'

She looked at her boots again, shaking her head, 'I only saw it coz sun caught on it for a trice, like.'

Joseph patted her shoulder. 'Thank you, Annie. Off you goes now back to your work.'

'Well,' I said, when the door closed behind her, my hopes beginning to soar, 'do you know any red-haired coachman?'

'One or two. Leave it wiv me, Sir. I shall ask around a bit like, too. Try and get you a few names. Then I'll pass em on to Mistress Susannah.'

I shook his hand. 'Good man.' How could I not grin at how absurdly English I sounded? I hurried from the house, eager to tell Susannah that we might at last have a means of finding where Sam had been those fateful days. Whoever he might be protecting, she was not worth his freedom never mind his life.

NOAH

Noah read the letter again with rising dismay at what Sam asked of him. After learning of his imprisonment only days after he had been taken to the Tower, alerted one morning hearing his name spoken above the buzz of coffeehouse gossip was something of a shock. He had turned his head intent on knowing just what was being said. When he understood, he made his excuses and left his companions, almost overcome with the horror of it. With the letter's arrival some days later, he learned just when the murder of which Sam was accused had taken place.

Now, at his desk in his Rotherhithe office, the lad's written words again filled him with dread. He was under no circumstances to come forward with the information which would prove his innocence, for it would prove him innocent of one crime but convict them both of another. He urged him to leave the country for a while, perhaps to captain one of his ships himself again. Noah considered it carefully. It was certainly something he could arrange, but did he really wish to abandon Sam in such a craven manor? Yet he was right. The only sure way he could vouch for his presence with him then was to admit he spent it in his bed. There was no way to hide from that truth. And what they had done there was a crime punishable by death.

Sam knew how to affect him too, reminding him of what such a prosecution would do to his wife and sons. Their shame. He put his face in his hands in despair, unable to bear the thought of losing his sons' approbation. Well, Michael's anyway. He had expected Hal to tell his mother and brother of his confession, but he had not. Yet still he found himself trapped between his desperate need to help Sam and the knowledge it was impossible. He dropped his hands and sighed. For the moment he was only held on suspicion. If and when he came to trial, then Noah would have to think again. But for now, Sam was held under investigation. And the best way to put an end to that was to find the true murderer.

Noah stood. He would see Thomas Monkton, the Lieutenant of the Yeoman Guardsmen at Whitehall Palace. Sam's letter had mentioned his kindness. He took his coat down from its peg beside the door before sticking his head through the hatch to tell his clerk he was leaving. 'Send a lad to call my coach around.' The man was elderly now and getting slower by the day. By the time he had reached his feet Noah was already gone through the door, calling behind him, 'No matter, Jensen. I'll do so myself.' A lighter to the Hall Stairs would have been ideal, but they were all out. How bloody typical. And that the high tide now aiding his own boats upriver was too fast for the horse ferry. So, the bridge it would have to be.

The sight of Hal halted him in his tracks. He was standing on the wharf looking at the river so brown and solid on a grey morning, its race was barely discernible. His plain dark coat blending in made him almost invisible, except for his bright hair. Noah went to stand beside him. 'I am so glad to see you.' He did not touch him, though he wanted to very much.

Hal turned, his nostrils flaring. 'I need to ask your forgiveness, Papa.'

Noah gasped. 'No you don't. Not at all. I shocked you and you had every right to do as you did.'

'But I didn't. I behaved in just the way I accused you of. You told me the truth and I walked away. So, I ask you again. Can you forgive me for it?'

Noah smiled and shook his head. 'Forgiven, dearest lad. I love you. You're my son. But can you forgive me for … well, for what I am, I suppose? The shameful thing that I am.'

Hal grasped his shoulders. 'Papa. Don't you know how much I've always worshiped you. I prayed I might grow up to be just like you … well not that, obviously.'

They both laughed a little.

'No.' Noah said. 'Not that. Who would?' Sam's plight now

was a pretty illustration of just why not. 'You went back to Oxford, your mother said? I'm going to my coach. Walk with me.'

'Happily.' The walked across the dock towards the coach shed. 'I went to friends not to Corpus, obviously.' He stared hard at Noah. 'I'll not go back. I want to work for you, Papa. I'll do anything, but I am not going back there.'

They arrived at the substantial wooden building. 'Barnaby,' Noah called. 'Get the horses up. I need to go out.' He opened the carriage door. 'We can talk in here. He climbed inside with Hal following.

He stared at his father for a few moments. 'Did you know what you were when you married Mama?'

He should have expected there would be questions. 'Yes.' What more was there to say. He already knew the next one.

'Did you love her?'

'Many people marry without love, Hal. Most even.' He sighed. 'No. I didn't love her, but I tried to be kind to her. I tried to make her happy.'

'She's not happy though, is she? I can't remember her ever being truly happy.'

What could he say? 'I did the best I could.' How feeble it sounded. Yet it was the truth. And perhaps her unhappiness owed something to her nature, too. He studied his son's face. 'I used to wonder if I were even capable of love. My mother died in childbed. I went to sea on my father's ship when I was very young. Too young, in truth, and we were never able to become close to each other. I don't know why. So, I thought maybe I'd never learnt how, because he hadn't. But when you were born – and then Michael – I was overwhelmed with love ... and all the fear that comes with it.' He reached across to touch his son's hand. He could see more questions there still and steeled himself to answer them truthfully.

'Do you love this man?'

'Sam. Do I love Sam?' He closed his eyes for a moment. The truth. 'Yes. I do, very much.' Though he had never told him.

Why? Fear, of course. What if it was not returned? Yet that mattered nothing, he found, when he considered it.

'Have there been many of them?'

Christ. What the hell to say now? He felt his patience starting to wear a touch thin. 'Yes. But none I've loved.' Never mind those whose names he never knew, their faces unseen in shadowy corners. He held Hal's gaze. 'Have there been many lads for mutual pleasuring?'

Hal laughed. 'God, yes.'

They laughed together for a few moments.

'Thank you for not telling your mother. It would only hurt her–'

Hal's face fell. 'Why the fuck would I ever do such a thing?' He shook his head. 'You really don't know me at all, do you?'

'Christ, I want to, Hal.'

'Well, is not this your chance?' He raised his eyebrows. And then he grinned.

And Noah found himself bewitched by his own smile. He shook his head, gathering himself. Sam. 'I have to go to Whitehall Palace on urgent business. Wait in the office for me, please. We need to talk some more.'

'I'll come with you.'

'It's private business, Hal. Wait here, please.'

'Your Sam, perhaps?'

Noah rolled his eyes. What the bloody hell. 'Very well, I'll explain on the way.' That is, he would try. What a thing to discuss with a son. 'You curse too much, Hal.'

'Well, that's a little rich coming from you.'

Noah rolled his eyes again. Too clever by half.

His coach brought them to the stone gatehouse through to London Bridge, its spikes now flaunting only the bleached skulls of those long dead. How could he not think of Sam accused of a crime that could end here as carrion for the wheeling shrieking gulls? He clenched his jaw and looked towards the chaos of traffic, so sluggish they might swim across in less time than it took to get through the bottlenecks. So much slower than his early morning and late evening crossing though, Christ's wounds, they were bad enough, still usually preferable to waiting for the horse ferry too much in demand at such hours.

The coach inched forward through swarms of people and driven animals, in tunnels beneath fine houses – many five stories high – out onto open stretches some between semi-derelict buildings looking ready to fall backwards into the river at any moment. More fine houses and then across at last, passing Fishmongers' Hall in still seething traffic. Fleet Street. The Strand to King Street and the palace. London was becoming impossible to navigate. Too many damned people. Still, despite these tribulations, he managed to tell Hal his story as concisely as he could and, in the end, gave him Sam's letter to read. He watched his face closely while he did so.

Hal shook his head. 'So, this man's life is at risk because you cannot say he was with you?'

Noah rested his head back against the seat squabs. 'It seems so, yes.'

'Christ.'

'Agreed.'

'What can I do?'

'Why should you do anything? Sam's the King's Godson. There must be more going on here than it seems. So, it could be dangerous.'

'Why should I, Papa? Because I love you and for the very first time in my life, I can.'

Noah hugged him. What in God's name could he say to that?

Noah instructed Barnaby to halt as close as possible to the King Street gate into Horse Guards. At the sentry post, they waited while it was established whether the lieutenant might see them. He turned to Hal. 'I hope claiming to have information about Sam will not be too difficult to explain without incriminating us.'

'Then say I'm his friend. Less suspicious than an old man like you.' He grinned. 'He is twenty-three? Much closer in age to me.'

Noah raised his eyebrows. 'Old man, indeed.' He shook his head. 'Well, I now see the benefit of an Oxford education.'

'A very brief one, Papa.'

'Not necessarily, Henry.'

Hal rolled his eyes to the sky. 'A very short one indeed, I assure you.'

After waiting for what seemed an inordinate amount of time, the guardsman returned to say the lieutenant would see them and that they should follow him. The young man guided them inside the building, asking them to wait in a seating area, before knocking on an office door and putting his head inside.

'They's here, Sir.'

'Then show them in, if you please, Hunt.'

Monkton shook Noah's hand firmly and then Hal's, looking from one to the other. He was of a build and height equal to their own and Noah saw him appreciate this with an expression he felt certain was mirrored on his own face. Admiration tinged by a hint of disdain. 'Thank you for seeing us at such short notice, Lieutenant.'

'Not at all, Sir. If you have information about Samuel Carter, then I must hear it. I am in charge of the day-to-day investigation as you are no doubt aware.'

'Indeed.' Noah studied him for a moment. Dark hair. The strong features necessary for such a large man's face. Finding integrity in his steely eyes, he cleared his throat. 'Sam Carter is a friend of my son's and of mine because of it. He told us in a recent letter you had been kind to him ... that he sensed you wished to help him. Is that correct?' Noah watched, waiting for his response.

Monkton sighed, as though coming to a decision. 'It is my duty to remain impartial when conducting an investigation of this nature. However, the truth is, I do not believe Samuel Carter to be guilty, so someone must know where he was that night.' He sighed again, sounding exasperated. 'That he will tell me nothing makes his position extremely precarious.'

Noah shifted in his chair, knowing that was something he could never disclose. He glanced at Hal, who appeared very concerned. Just what was needed. How canny he was. 'Let me just say we know Sam to be innocent, in all truth we know it, but the only way open to us to assist him is to track down the true culprit.'

A brief flash of disgust crossed Monkton's face. He rose. 'Then I shall say good day to you, gentlemen.'

Noah stood his ground. 'I'm offering fresh eyes and fresh minds to apply to the problem ... from friends who could not hold Sam's interests dearer to them. Tell me what you know and what you think. What harm can come from our assistance?'

Monkton frowned. 'What harm? This is a palace matter and, as such, confidential to the King.' He studied his fingernails. 'What you choose to do outside the palace confines is entirely up to you, of course.' He wrote briefly on a sheet of paper and handed it to Noah. 'I have said the very same to other interested parties.'

Raphael Rossi. Susannah Gresham. No indication of where these persons might be found. Noah smiled. Well, he had claimed skills as an investigator. Tracking them down would be his first such task. And Hal's too, should he wish it. Susannah? He tapped the paper. The name seemed familiar for some reason. It would come to him.

RAPHAEL

Susannah sat in a state of agitation upon a mint-green damask sofa in my drawing room, eager I should read the list of names and addresses of red-haired coachmen put together by Joseph, making her reluctant to listen to me.

I held up my hand once more to still her. 'I visited Whitehall yesterday–'

'More gems for Richmond? And more of yourself in thanks for rescuing you, no doubt.'

Once again, I was grateful that the heat I felt flash across my face would be barely visible. For I had indeed ended up in Frances's bed despite my sincere intention not to do so, not least because of my feelings for Susannah. Now the King knew of our liaison, she felt no restraints upon her actions. And how was I to resist? Somehow, I contrived an affronted expression before replying to her questions rather primly. 'I often take jewellery to the palace. I have many patrons there.'

She raised her eyebrows. 'I'm sure they all enjoy your excellent service.'

I stared at her. 'Indeed.' Surely, she had made such a remark in innocence? But then, looking at her, I was not so certain. I frowned, lowering myself to sit beside her. 'If I may continue?'

She nodded though her eyes sparked fire.

'On my way out through the King Street Gate, I saw a black coach and four just ahead of me–'

'And the driver had red hair?'

'Well, of course he did,' I snapped. 'Why else would I mention it?' I held up my hand once again to forestall further interruption but seeing how little it was appreciated, lowered it somewhat sheepishly. 'Just as I approached, two giants-of-men overtook me and climbed up inside it without need of steps and off it drove. Father and son by the look of them.'

'So, you do not know who they are or where they live?' She waved her paper. 'Whereas I have names and addresses here.'

She was very angry now, yet those sparking eyes enticed me. The flush on her cheeks. God help me, I had a sudden and overwhelming desire to kiss her, which to my credit I manage to resist.

'I, too, have names and an address.' I sounded smug even to myself.

She snorted her derision. 'Very well, then. How?'

I understood her mood reflected her concern for Sam. But had we not at last something solid to work with? 'The guard on the gate told me the two men had visited Tom Monkton.' I snatched the list from her fingers. 'And he told me who they are and where they live. This Noah Bartholomew and his son have a fierce interest in finding the real murderer. So, they must be certain Sam is not guilty.'

'And Sam got into their coach – it must have been their coach – which means they know where he went and who he was with.' She jumped to her feet. 'Can one of them be Sam's lady's husband? Where are they? We must go to them at once.'

Unable to think of any reason why we should not, beyond the obvious one that I should be in my workshop, I stood too. 'Eastcheap. I'll have my coach summoned. Susannah had arrived in a hackney. Perhaps she did not wish her father to know she had visited me? It had never occurred to me just what valuable sources of information coachman could be. Indeed, all servants. By some strange means known only to him, Giuseppe seemed aware of everything I did, including that I had bedded the duchess again. He enlightened me of this in the crudest terms imaginable, accompanied by a vigorous gesture should his words not have had sufficient impact.

We were shown in by a liveried footman, who led us upstairs to a grand parlour overlooking the parterre garden in Bartholomew's elegant town house. After seeing us seated, the servant left to enquire whether his master was at home … that is, whether he wished to see us. As I had said we were here about Samuel Carter, there was little doubt that he would. I was soon proved correct when the door flew open and the large man I had seen the previous day strode into the room, his presence immediately diminishing its scale.

He bowed to us in turn. 'I already know your names, I believe. Susannah Gresham and Raphael Rossi. I had expected to come to you, but you have found me first. I think perhaps you will show yourselves the better investigators.'

I took a moment to scrutinise him. While he was another with Tom Monkton's mighty stature, his hair was the colour of buttermilk, fastened at his neck. His clothing, that of a wealthily merchant, was sombre but finely made. 'Regrettably not, *Signor*. We were given your name and where to locate you.' I looked at Susannah sitting beside me. She gestured to her lips, and I touched her arm to reassure her. 'Mistress Gresham does not speak, so I shall do so for both of us.'

Bartholomew looked at her intently, his pale blue eyes full of sympathy. 'I'm sorry to hear it, Mistress.'

'Thank you,' she wrote on her notepad.

I cleared my throat. 'I believe you know Samuel Carter is innocent?'

He nodded. 'I do, yes.'

'I should tell you now, he was seen getting into your coach early on the morning before the murder.' If this information surprised him, it did not show on his face. 'Where did he go that day and who was he with?'

He looked from one to the other of us, his expression closed and unreadable. 'Unfortunately, I'm not at liberty to say.'

Susannah wrote, 'Was your wife … or your son's wife with him that night?'

He appeared quite dumbfounded. 'No, Mistress. My wife is … unwell. And my son has no wife. He is but eighteen years old.'

Just then the door swung open and a frail woman leaning heavily on a cane, shuffled in. Dressed in black, her hair hidden beneath an old-fashioned white lace coif, I assumed her to be Bartholomew's mother. She had a pinched, high cheek-boned face, her large dark eyes hinting at some past handsomeness.

Bartholomew assisted her down into an armchair beside the fireplace. 'Have a fire lit, Husband. The room is chilled.'

I stood and bowed to her. Husband, was it? '*Signora*.' She turned to us as though she had been unaware of our presence, looking us both up and down with palpable distaste. I could understand Bartholomew's astonishment at Susannah's suggestion she may have been Sam's mystery woman. Poor lady.

'Who are these people and why have you allowed them into my parlour?'

'Mistress Gresham, Master Rossi, this is my wife, Margaret.' He turned to her, smiling with cold eyes. 'They are here on a business matter. If you'll excuse us, we shall continue our meeting in my office.'

'The fire.'

'I'll see to it, my dear.'

We followed him downstairs and across the black and white marble-tiled entrance hall to the other side of the house, where he showed us into a square room with a tall window overlooking the street, light reflecting off a large globe in a mahogany stand placed beneath it. The walls were lined with books, nautical objects scattered here and there on the shelves, reminding me of those in the Carters' drawing room. Then footsteps sounded behind us and Bartholomew's companion I had seen the previous day appeared in the open doorway. My God, they were alike, though he was dressed more stylishly in a shade of green that suited his colouring rather well.

Bartholomew raised his eyebrows. 'My son, Hal. This lady and gentleman are Sam's friends Lieutenant Monkton told us of.'

He nodded to us, warmly. 'He's a good friend of mine.'

Susannah, looking startled, wrote, 'Is he? He has never mentioned you to me. I know all his friends, I thought.'

I sensed all was not as it seemed. 'Susannah, we know that cannot be so or you would know who he was with on the night of the murder.'

She gave me a withering look. *Merda*.

'I know his friends. Not his lovers, damn you,' she wrote.

I shrugged a, *whatever you say, cara,* at her. When her eyes flashed daggers at me, I felt my lips begin to twitch a little which did nothing to sooth the situation. I looked away. Bartholomew stared at us both, appearing a little bemused for he had no idea what she had written, of course.

'Er, do forgive me. I haven't yet offered you refreshment.' He moved to a bellpull and was soon able to do so to the footman we had seen earlier, and also arrange for his wife's fire. 'Now, where were we?'

I smiled. 'I had just asked you about Sam's whereabouts at the time of the murder. Perhaps I might also put that question to. Master–'

'Hal, please.'

'Hal.'

He looked at his father, deferring to him, which seemed odd if he were Sam's friend. Some shared understanding flashed between them. Bartholomew delayed answering by moving to sit behind his large mahogany desk and indicating we should sit on leather upholstered chairs set before it.

Hal stood behind us so he could watch his father, I felt sure.

Bartholomew steepled his fingers. 'We do know where he was.' He looked up at his son. 'But I have given my word not to reveal it.'

I turned to him. 'Have you also given your word?'

'No. But I shall honour my father's.'

Susannah shook her head.

There was a loud rap on the door before the footman entered with a tray, holding a jug of wine and a platter of sweetmeats. We were all silent while he poured. As soon as the door closed behind him, I voiced my question to Bartholomew. 'You gave your word to Sam?'

He nodded. 'That's why my ... our only course of action is to find who is really responsible for this James Villiers' death.'

Susannah met my gaze and I reached across to squeeze her

hand, seeing the disappointment on her face. We had both imagined that once we found someone who could account for Sam's movements, all would be well. Now it seemed these people were as set on keeping this secret as he was. I looked at them, the father and son, and wondered how they were involved and why such a promise had been extracted. I sighed. Now what?

Chapter Six
SUSANNAH

Diary: May 5, 1676

Yet another day has passed with only bad news to tell. I try not to despair, but it is hard.

This morning I was astonished to receive a letter from the Duchess of Richmond. Bess brought it to me in the studio and I took it downstairs to my chamber, wondering why she would write to me of all people. With some trepidation, I broke the seal and unfolded the heavy sheet of paper.

> Richmond House
>   Whitehall Palace
>   May 5, 1676
>
> My dear Susannah,
>
> *I am writing to you, as I have already done to Raphael. I know you are both concerned to help poor Samuel Carter and today I*

have learned something most alarming to his situation and wish you both to know of it immediately.

A kitchen porter by the name of Hubert Winks claims to have found a sword hidden behind some casks in a storage area off Scotland Yard. How he came to be there has not yet been explained. My biggest concern is that it is monogramed SC and Willets sees that as Samuel Carter. A search party will be sent to his house to see if his sword can be located there. I pray it can, otherwise things begin to look very dangerous for him. I must say I find the King's lack of sympathy most puzzling.

I shall pray for your success.

Your friend,
Frances Stuart

I, of course, grabbed my cloak straightaway and dashed across the street to Sam's house, hoping to arrive before the searchers. Connor let me in, looking not a little unkempt. He had plainly not expected to receive visitors with neither master at home. Scribbling as quickly as I could, I told him what was afoot.

'I know his sword hangs in a press in his chamber, for I cleaned it only yesterday morning and replaced it there meself.'

'Fetch it, please.' I wrote, once again angrily frustrated by the delay caused by my lack of speech. 'We should have it here to show them at the door so they will have no need to cross the threshold.'

He grinned. 'Ah, now that will be a pleasure, Mistress Susannah, to prevent such unpleasantness, so it will.'

I sat down on an upholstered chair in the receiving hall, relief sweeping through me. The monogram was nothing but coincidence. And, again, Willets had made it fit his prejudice. Hearing a sound, I looked up to see Connor coming down the stairs empty handed. I stood, my heart beginning to pound. He was very pale.

'It's gone.' He shook his head. 'It makes no sense, for I put it there meself.'

We returned to Sam's chamber together and searched it thoroughly. His sword could not be found anywhere. I turned a full circle almost expecting to see Sam standing there, all his belongings so redolent with the scent of him. Clean linens and the musky perfume of his coats. An exotic new fragrance brought back from France.

Connor scratched his head. 'It makes not a jot of sense, Mistress. I knows as how I cleaned it and I know where I placed it, so how can it've disappeared?'

I clutched his arm before writing, 'I can think of but one way. Someone has taken it.'

'And hidden it at the palace? Why? Why would anyone do so wicked a thing?'

I wrote, 'To implicate him.'

At that moment, we heard loud knocking on the front door and Connor hurried away back to his duties. I decided to remain where I was. This room would now be searched again so I determined I would be present to make sure nothing else could be done to incriminate Sam. I did not trust Willets in any way. Whilst I waited, I looked around the well-appointed room, my eyes coming to rest on his large tester bed with its cobalt and gold hangings. I have my own long-ago memories of it. I touched the heavy silk fabric imagining Sam sleeping there, his chestnut hair loose on the white linen pillow. It was then I remembered the night he had a woman here. I retraced my steps to the landing, intending to ask Connor what he knew of her. Could this be whom he was so resolved to protect now? And what was her link to the Bartholomews?

When I arrived at the staircase, I saw not the search party I had expected, but Raphael and his manservant Giuseppe. When Raphael spotted me, he mounted the stairs two at a time and strode into the room, flinging open the door to the press and rifling through the clothing hanging there. I moved close to him. 'Do you really think you can find it when I could not?' I hissed. He had the good grace to look sheepish.

'Forgive me. I had to see for myself.' He gave me a quick hug.

I realised then the extent of my pleasure at seeing him, and it was far more than just the relief of being able to speak.

'*Dio mio.*' He shook his head. 'So, now we also need to find out who took the damn sword.'

'Ask Connor for a list of everyone who had access to this room yesterday or indeed the house. That is when it was stolen.'

He smiled. 'Giuseppe has already set him to the task.'

I glanced at the bed again before telling him of Sam's mystery lady, though there was very little to tell. 'Perhaps it has no bearing on this, but I think we must ask Connor about it.

'I agree.' He moved closer to me, studying my face. 'How are you, *cara mia*?' He ran a finger gently down my cheek, his eyes full of sincere concern. I hoped he did not notice my shiver at his touch. It was not difficult to understand how he made so many easy conquests. My eyes, of course, had to flit to the bed. Something else I hoped him unaware of. Yet I suspected very little escaped his notice. 'I am quite well, just anxious for Sam. We should go down.'

He nodded and followed me out.

Down in the receiving hall again, Raphael asked Connor what he knew of Sam's visitor the evening I had called upon him.

'I wish I could help you, Mistress, but I was instructed to remain below stairs on that particular night. The master told me he would have a guest and to lay out a cold supper in the dining room, where they would serve thereselves.'

Giuseppe's eyes narrowed. 'Reminds me of your evening of debauchery at Cheapside–'

'Though we tolerated your slapdash waiting service. Perhaps we should have served ourselves, too?'

Giuseppe shrugged. 'You? *Merda per il cervello.*

Raphael gave him a hard stare though his lips twitched, which I saw mirrored by Giuseppe. So, they were more than manservant and master, then? They were friends. And the duchess had been in his bed. I chewed my lip. I had assumed he had been with her at Richmond House. Still, why on earth did I mind? But for some reason, I found I did. Jesu. Then I felt myself blush. And, of course, his eyes were on me.

I tried to pull myself together and wrote, 'Why has Sam been so secretive about her?' I knew he trusted Connor completely and, whilst they were not as close as Raphael and Giuseppe, he was fond of him. I wrote, 'You fetched him down to see me that evening. Did you not see whom he was with then?'

'No, Mistress. I knocked and called through the door to tell him you were here.'

'And no one saw anything the following morning?' Raphael said.

'I didn't see my master again until I served him a late breakfast in his chamber. Who's were with him was long gone.'

We could talk no further, interrupted by the arrival of Willets' search party. Both Raphael and I followed the guardsmen upstairs to watch, Raphael instructing them to take care how they handled Sam's possessions with monotonous regularity, clearly enjoying their irritation.

Giuseppe had followed Connor down to the kitchens and I felt certain he would continue to probe him for more information, quite probably without Connor realising he was. Eventually, the search of the house was done for they had little incentive to look too hard as it suited Willets no sword should be found.

Raphael walked me across the street to my door. 'So now we must find out who has done this to Sam.'

I touched his arm with gratitude. 'Thank you for caring. What would I do without you?'

. . .

Now, as I finish my day's entry, I reflect on it all. Though it daunts me, I still believe however groundlessly, we shall succeed because of Raphael. I shall not question the why of this, I only know it is true and I take comfort from it. I try not to think of what might happen now for Sam. Was finding his sword enough to bring him to trial? Yet the sword is not proof in itself, for why in the name of God would he leave it there if he were indeed the murderer? So, everything rests on Willets and, most of all, on the King's pleasure.

RAPHAEL

Weeks have passed with nothing changed for Sam. Susannah and I visit him often, though not together to spread our company. The rest of my time has been taken up in the workshop and with trips to Whitehall after receiving a further shipment of gems. Patrons came to our showroom, and I couriered my pieces to the palace, visiting Frances and hoping to see Susannah. It did not escape my attention how shameful this conduct was, yet I seemed unable to change it. The duchess was irresistible when I was with her but at all other times, Susannah filled my thoughts. I felt my behaviour more than a little disrespectful towards both ladies.

I had not seen Susannah since the search of Sam's house and the hope of her company at the May Ball had been my chief reason for attending, together with my father's instruction to do so which came but a sorry second. I stood beside Tom in the great state hall of the Banqueting House, looking out across the packed stifling space redolent of hot flesh not quite subsumed in myriad perfumes. That evening Tom was not on duty so looked sombre in his dark green coat and breeches, with only cream silk embroidered lapels and cuffs to soften the effect.

At Giuseppe's insistence, I had dressed as a representative of *Rossi & Son. Jewellers of Florence,* though not quite so flamboyantly as some of the late James Villiers' foppish friends with their beauty patches and trailing lace cuffs. I brushed lint form my coat sleeve. Lapis-blue satin. The waistcoat edged in silver and stitched with Sapphires from our stock to form periwinkles, seemed appropriate to the role he had dressed me for.

I stepped through the line of columns towards the tall windows which for some reason remained closed. Perhaps a breath of air might be had from the staircase leading down to the ground floor where the great doors were wide to the outside, and spring twilight still lingered? The hall was ablaze with candles making all the bejewelled clothing sparkle, rivalling the glitter from the crystal chandeliers. Many of the pieces were mine, I saw with no little satisfaction. And some were even paid for.

Tom turned to face me, grinning. 'Perhaps I should act as your bodyguard with all those gems upon your person.'

I laughed. 'There are many more valuable than me here tonight.' I ran my fingers lightly across them. 'Most of these are not of the finest either but good enough for this.' He moved to stand at my side, and it was then I saw the duchess approaching. Just the sight of her made me smile, hers quickly mirroring mine. 'Frances.' I lifted her hand to my lips, admiring the magnificence of her gown. White, dripping with diamonds, golden petticoats and a violet mantua matching her eyes. 'You look enchanting.'

She caressed her jewel encrusted stomacher. 'We both display your wares to their best advantage.'

'You far more so. Mine are but chips in comparison.'

She took my arm and together we surveyed the room. Thomas had moved discreetly away but she beckoned for him to join us.

'I spoke to the King again yesterday. He joined me for dinner at my house after one of his tiresome squabbles with Portsmouth over money. As you know, I am something of refuge from the mistresses and their endless demands. So, I was cautious about raising the subject of Samuel but felt I must.'

I moved closer to her. 'Do not risk his anger. We have friends who are determined to find the true culprit. Once we have him, Sam must be freed.'

She smiled. 'I think I know the King well enough by now to avoid displeasing him. I was able to lead him around to talking of Samuel's plight by asking if he had seen his father who is recently returned from Port Royal in Jamaica. He appeared decidedly uncomfortable admitting he had not. Then, without any further prompting, he seemed to feel compelled to justify it.' She paused, opening her fan, and looking around warily.

I followed her gaze. 'I think no one will hear us above the clamour. Go on.'

Even so, she lowered her voice. 'There was some complicated evasion about the crown not appearing open to influence from vested interests–'

I snorted. 'I've not heard fatherly affection termed a vested interest before.'

'Just so. Rupert has always been his dear friend, so I found it hard to understand what was really going on. Unravelling it all in my mind later, it seems to me Louise de Kérouaille is somehow part of it. She is pressing him not to let personal affection for Samuel and his father come before treason against his person. Now he has resolved that's what it is.'

I frowned. 'But why? Why should she be involved at all?'

'France. I cannot help thinking this is somehow linked to France.'

I nodded. 'It is where Sam spent several months last year. Susannah wondered if he had somehow discovered something he should not have.'

Frances eyes roved over the room, once more. 'Perhaps she is correct and interests there wish Sam silenced.' She fanned herself briskly for a moment. 'Is it possible the King knows what this secret is and also wishes Sam silenced … permanently?'

'*Dio mio*. If so, what can it be that he would sacrifice a life because of it?'

The duchess closed her fan with a snap and tapped me on my arm before pointing to a group gathered at the end of the same wall where we stood. 'Susannah.'

She was pressed into the corner surrounded by James's foppish friends I had noticed earlier. Though her face was pale, her posture was defiant. I set off towards her without a backwards glance and soon felt Tom's presence close behind me. I pushed my way through the men. '*Andare indietro, figli di maiali.*' Tom made sure none rounded on me. 'Susannah?' I put my arm around her waist, gathering her in. 'Are you all right, *cara mia*?' I turned back to the men. 'What's happening here?'

One particularly rouged and powdered gentleman pulled himself free of Tom's restraining hand upon his shoulder. 'You ... you shopkeeper. You are as complicit in James Villiers's murder as this cunt. Samuel Carter will die a traitor's death. You have my oath on it. We have influence close to–'

One of his friends grabbed his arm. 'Hold your tongue, Mark.'

'Carter has yet to be charged with anything, gentlemen. I'll thank you to remember it,' Tom said.

Mark looked at him with disdain. 'For now, Lieutenant, but moves are afoot to change it very soon.' With that they turned, as one, and strode away.

The shortest fop winked at me over his shoulder. 'Got no bubs that one but her cunny's slick enough.'

When a tide of red flowed across Susannah's face it took Tom's retraining hand to stop me going after him. '*Vaffanculo*,' I shouted, drawing many disapproving glares. I pulled her into my arms. 'Would you like to leave, *cara mia*?' I felt her nod.

After collecting Susannah's cloak, I placed it about her shoulders over her simple gown of soft blue silk draped with a cream lace mantua. We walked down the staircase and out into The Court, remaining silent as we threaded our way through the crowd spilled outside for some relief from the heat. As the tangle of revellers began to thin, I took her arm in mine. 'My carriage waits on The Mall. I'll take you home.' I pulled her closer. 'The duchess had some interesting thoughts which I must pass on to you.'

She nodded. 'I don't wish to impose upon you, but might we not go directly to Henrietta Street? I cannot risk an encounter with Catherine. It was she who insisted I attend tonight, and I realise now it was so James's friends could accost me.'

We walked out through the Park Gate employing a linkboy to light the path, his torch trailing a frantic wake of moths as we made our way towards the line of coaches. The park, of course, became a very different place after dark with sounds of debauchery – shrill cries of female laughter and male jeers – coming from the shrubbery and groves of trees. We were brought to a sudden halt when a large woman in a state of undress ran across the path pursued by two men, one without his breeches and in an overt state of excitement. The link boy jeered. 'I wonder the King permits this outdoor brothel in a royal park.' Somewhat hypocritical of me, considering my own activities within, no? She obviously shared such thoughts.

'What, when much the same goes on inside Whitehall?' She shook her head. 'Though I believe efforts are made to clean it up from time to time, but it never stays so for long.'

I waved to Rory, gathered with other coachman sitting on a grassy bank with a brazier to light their gaming. He was quick to take his leave, clearly glad to have had a shorter wait then many would that night, and we were soon settled inside and on our way. 'Would you care to come back to Cheapside for a while, I can offer you refreshments and Rory can take you home whenever you wish?'

She gave me a cool grey stare. 'Very well. I cannot expect you to drive around London until I am certain Catherine will have retired for the night.' She seemed to remember herself then and smiled. 'Thank you. It is most kind of you.'

Strangely, we did not talk for the remainder of the journey.

Perhaps because I knew we had time to do so in the comfort of my drawing room away from the clatter of the coach and team, and the bells and clappers warning of approaching rakers' carts, taking their stinking cesspit dung-pots to laystalls outside the city. So, instead, I was able to think of what I wanted to say to her. Reporting my conversation with Frances would be straightforward enough but finding out what had occurred with the fops would not. Still, it felt important to know exactly what they had said. I turned to her and in the dim light from the single candle-lantern, could see her eyes were closed, though there was a tension about her which told me she did not sleep.

I stood beside the carved Carrara marble fireplace, ornate as anything to be found in our Florence home. 'Do you really believe Catherine sent you there so those men could harry you?'

She lifted her glass and took a sip of Chianti. 'I do. She persuaded Papa I should go, and I couldn't understand why when she insists the whole household be in mourning. Then, quite suddenly, I'm to dress in finery and go to the May Ball.'

'Can you tell me what happened with them? What did they say to you?'

She held my gaze and nodded. 'But first you must tell me what you learnt from the duchess.'

I took a long drink and told her all I knew. 'Are you sure Sam has said nothing of any rumours he might have stumbled across at the French court?'

She rubbed her forehead, looking tired. 'He hinted at something as I told you, but I never pressed thinking him not at liberty to say more. I shall visit tomorrow and see what he will say when he knows it might be relevant to his trouble.'

'I have not seen him for some days, I'm afraid. I've been needed here. Giuseppe has already been too much burdened by my absences. But I shall try to visit him soon.'

'His father spends time with him each day now, though I

haven't seen him there. Sam tells me he is devastated by the King's treatment of him, poor man. Loyalty travels but one way it would seem.'

I sat beside her, and she turned to me, her expression remote. I wanted to hold her face and smooth away the frown between her fair brows with my thumb. Why was I so hesitant? She plainly found my gaze uncomfortable, so I looked away. Yet I found her intoxicating even though my attention seemed unwelcome. What would she do if I kissed her? Had she ever been kissed?

I had sensed something between her and Sam at first but now it seemed they were little more than brother and sister. I downed my glass and stood to refill it. It occurred to me as I did so that all my women had been married and flirted with me to let me know they were available. And willing. Christ. It was a most unpleasant thought, leaving me uncertain what to do. Was I really wondering whether I might find out if she were interested before ending my liaison with Frances? And, yes, I was all too aware such speculation was inappropriate while her thoughts were so consumed with Sam. Yet knowing this was not enough to stifle it, God help me.

I refilled her glass and sat beside her again. 'My concern is Sam knows nothing, but others think he does. There is no way to prove he doesn't, which is dangerous for him and leaves us little to bargain with.'

'We need to find the wretched murderer,' she said, softly.

'Is there truly no one to be found in Connor's list of those with access to Sam's house that day?'

'I fear not. None with any motive to harm him.'

'Coin, perhaps? Or loyalties elsewhere?' I put down my glass.

'Straws.'

'*Che cosa?* Forgive me, I don't understand.'

'We're clutching at them, like those men about to drown.' She smiled, seeing my puzzlement, still. Then she touched my face, feather light. 'Your English is so good, despite your accent, I forget.'

That touch was enough. I leaned in then to kiss her,

knowing straightaway she had been kissed before. I found the simple clip that held up her hair and let it down to cloak her like wheaten silk. Sweet Christ, I desired her and that until now would be enough. But I found myself uncertain what to do, afraid of alarming her. I ran my fingers through her hair inhaling the scent of rosewater, whilst hers moved tentatively to my neck beneath my ribbon-clubbed hair. I shivered at her touch, wanting to undress her and kiss her breasts, to part her thighs. Gently I found her breast and felt her stiffen, though she pressed closer to me with a small gasp of what sounded like pleasure.

By now, I had her lying back on the couch and had moved over her, kissing the swell of her breasts before lowering the fabric of her gown to uncover them. When I raised my head to look at her, white as an alabaster statue, she met my gaze before turning her head away and closing her eyes, tight. What did she think she had found in mine? 'You are so beautiful.' I wanted to tell her I loved her then, but how could it sound anything other than self-serving? Just an oily lie to have her.

'No. This ... this. I cannot.' She sat up, covering herself. 'This can't happen.' She struggled away from me and stood. 'It's time I returned home.'

I closed my eyes and gave myself a moment before rising to stand beside her, turning my body to hide that part of my anatomy which remained stubbornly hopeful. 'Please forgive me.' I watched her face, not knowing what more I could say.

She picked up her jewelled clip and made to wind her hair. I took it from her and quickly fastened it back in place. 'Susannah–'

She placed a finger on my lips to silence me. 'We must forget this and save our friendship.'

But how could I forget? 'I shall always be your friend, *cara mia*. Always.'

She took a deep breath. 'Those men. They said there were powerful people wanting Sam dead, people who could put particular pressure on the King. Now, have someone fetch me a hackney.'

SUSANNAH

Diary: May 22, 1676

Raphael sent me home in his coach and I arrived to a silent house, thank Jesu. No sign of Catherine for I would not have held my temper with her. Had she told them to take such liberties with my person? How glad I am to have newer memories to overwrite those impertinent hands. Though I know I should not be.

With a night candle left for me in the hall, I was able to see my way to my chamber where I lit another on my desk to write a few words here whilst my feelings are still so fresh in mind. And my mind is full of Raphael. Does he have the slightest idea how close I came to capitulation? I was so overwhelmed with desire for him. Jesu, why does my body betray me so? For I would have been but one more conquest, though for those few short moments I had truly wished to be. And I would, had I not seen how differently he looked at me – his need to possess me ... but something else, too, I cannot yet place – though I understood our friendship would not survive it.

I refuse to be one of those women who see achievement in winning such attention from a man. He said I was beautiful. And he wanted me. But he would not be mine for he has not given up the duchess and I doubt he ever will. However harshly I view myself, I know I deserve more. I wonder how many of his faded ladies he continues to bed. Has he truly given any up for Frances Stuart? He still sells gems at court and needs such women to become his patrons. Does he have them all? And why would he not if such were offered? Even knowing all this, my mind is full of him.

Diary: May 23, 1676

After sending Bess out for a hackney, I appraised myself in the hall mirror. The dark circles beneath my eyes were hardly surprising considering my lack of sleep. Even though I had eased myself, imagining a touch that was not my own, it was not enough to bring me peace.

I pulled my light cloak more closely around me over my simple gown of russet silk. Bess had fastened my hair at my nape with curls arranged from my crown to my forehead. Did it look overdone for a visit to the Tower? I doubted Sam would notice when he has far more pressing concerns.

The hackney smelt of tobacco smoke and sour wine, which did little to settle my belly, made queasy by lack of sleep and worry for Sam ... and a horrible unease about Raphael. I found myself dreading his company, fearing what I might reveal about myself. Bess sat pale and still beside me, looking as anxious as I felt. I wondered why this should be but could not summon the orderly mind needed to question her then. It would keep.

She would accompany me to the Tower and then take the carriage on to Southwark to visit her mother. Later, I would have to find another one myself and return home alone. Sometimes there was a friendly yeoman warder on the Postern Gate who would summon one for me. I had, at first, speculated I might be able to speak to a coachman on Vine Street who did not know me and whom I would likely never see again but, alas, found I could not – I had never even tried on King Street, for walking home from there was not arduous. But it had, of course, proved testing when so many could not read, forcing me to resort to asking aid from passers-by until one was able to tell the driver I wished to go to Henrietta Street. And the whole process had left me red-faced and trembling. I hoped fervently a kindly warder would be there today. My heart sank, finding none were.

The guard who followed me up to Sam's quarters was young, grossly stout, and taciturn. I was glad. It would save me the unpleasantness of trying to communicate. I sensed, too, his desire to shove me inside and be rid of me. Then all thoughts of him left me when I saw Rupert Carter sitting beside his son on the narrow cot, both looking grey and haggard. In that moment I saw a likeness between them I had never noticed before until they smiled such different smiles, and it was gone. They stood as one and hugged me, first Sam and then his father. Of course, his presence meant I could not speak. No matter. 'Any news?' I wrote.

Sam touched his father's arm. 'Papa had tried several times to get an audience with the King but has so far been unsuccessful.'

'I shall not give up. This cannot be Charles's doing. Someone else is behind it.'

Sam nodded. 'But who? And more to the point, why?'

Screaming inside at the absurdity of my silence, I wrote of what I had learned yesterday.

'Someone with influence over the King. Just as I surmised.' Rupert straightened his back. 'Very well. I shall wait on him until he consents to see me.'

'Remember France,' I wrote.

Sam shook his head. 'I learnt nothing of note in France. There were rumours of a secret pact with the King but about what I never could discover.'

I scrawled in my frustration. 'But you tried? You tried to find out?'

Rupert's nostrils flared. 'So, someone thinks you did.' He pulled Sam to him and kissed him tenderly on both cheeks. 'I'll do my best to convince the King you know none of his secrets. And, believe me, I shall get the chance to tell him.' He hugged me quickly and was gone.

I sat down on his bed and Sam came to sit beside me, taking my hand in his. 'You look tired.'

I touched his face. 'You look worse. The trouble is we are no further forward. If the King is under pressure to rid himself of even the smallest risk you might know something secret, your father will never persuade him to release you.'

'I fear you're right.'

'So, we must do all we can to find the murderer. I think it is time to visit Noah Bartholomew and ask for his help once more.' Yet, in truth, he would have no more idea where to start than we did.

His sigh sounded closer to a groan. 'Tell him again I'm most grateful for his concern.'

I grasped his arm. 'For the love of God, Sam, please tell me who you were with that night. And why are the Bartholomews sworn to secrecy about this woman?'

He shook his head.

So, I would challenge him more harshly over it. Surely, I must use any weapons available to me? 'Why put your father through this when you have the means to stop it? How can you be so cruel?' I watched pain sear his face, colour flooding his cheeks. Jesu.

'I swear on my life; I can do no other.'

'Then you might pay with it. And your father will pay, too.' My gut clenched to speak with such brutality.

He blinked, chewing his lip hard, before looking away. 'How is Raphael?'

'We're not talking of–' My mouth snapped shut as the door to the hallway behind me was flung open.

'Speak of the devil.'

I spun around, my face aflame, and was in his arms before I could utter a word. 'Raphael,' I said, as the outer door slammed shut. He kissed me softly on both cheeks before turning his attention to Sam and repeating the hugging and kissing. I noticed Sam shut his eyes as Raphael's arms closed around him, just as I had done.

'I have news.' He held Sam away from him, smiling broadly, both hands grasping his shoulders. 'I ran into Tom Monkton at Whitehall earlier. He told me Hubert Winks, the kitchen porter who found your sword, has disappeared. He has not turned up for work since the day Willets questioned him. It was only by chance Tom discovered it when he read through all the statements again and saw Winks had never been asked to explain why he was in Scotland yard at all. Then, when he tried to find him to inquire, he discovered him gone.'

I took a deep breath, hoping my blush had faded. 'Does he know where the man lives? It must be suspicious for him to disappear like this.'

'Well, I still wish to know how anyone came to get their hands on my sword in the first place? And surely the fact he has vanished suggests he put it there himself.'

'The man comes from Southwark. That's all Tom knows.' He turned to Sam. 'Agreed. How can it not be suspicious that he's gone?'

I looked at them standing side by side. Two beautiful men, although only one seemed to know it. 'The hovel courts of Southwark and Bankside are good places to disappear. Searching for him there would be like hunting for an angel in a cesspit.'

Raphael raised his eyebrows with a slight smile, puzzled again by an English saying.

'The gold coin not the celestial being.'

'Ah, I see.' His smile widened. 'Tom has questioned everyone who worked in the kitchens with him, but no one seems to know much. He has a brother.' He shrugged. 'Of no relevance, I'm sure. So, we must discover how the sword was taken from your chamber. How it then found its way inside the palace precinct. And the whereabouts of our mysterious kitchen porter.'

How daunting it all sounded.

Sam returned to his place on the bed, chewing his lip. He looked up at me then, as though reaching a decision. 'Hal Bartholomew's father does business in Southwark occasionally. He might be able to help. You said you were planning to visit him again soon?'

Raphael nodded. 'I have my coach. We could go right away if Susannah is agreeable?'

I nodded. 'Indeed.' And remembering I had brought Connor's list of those with access to Sam's house on 4th May again, I sat beside him to pull it from my pocket. 'One more look. Is there anyone here who should not be?'

He quickly scanned it before shaking his head. 'No, I'm afraid. I have given it plenty of thought, believe me. They are just the trades people and servants I would expect to see. Your Bess, of course, but she often calls in for Sarah and they run errands together.'

'So, it would seem Noah Bartholomew is the way forward. We need to find this Hubert Winks.' I kissed Sam's cheek. 'We will tell you as soon as we have any news. You have my word.'

He nodded, looking melancholy. 'Let's hope Papa gets to the King.'

'He shall, I'm sure of it.' What I was not so sure of was just what good it would do.

So, I spent time alone with Raphael in his coach, and we seemed at ease with each other again, as though nothing had happened between us. How strange to find myself in such a situation once more, as I had been with another long ago. Part of me was grateful for it and part was not. Just as before.

RAPHAEL

How strange to sit alone with Susannah in my coach yesterday, knowing what had so recently happened between us. I had feared she would be cold towards me, but she seemed her usual self and because of it I acted as I always did in her company. I questioned whether I should apologise again for my forwardness of the night before but, on balance, it seemed best not to raise it.

Yet it was not only friendship I needed from her, and nothing could change that. I decided to ask the duchess for advice, admitting I knew little of virgins. I could not decide whether this was a good thing or not, though she would be sure to put me straight on it, but I must renounce her bed for good before raising it. And, of course, I knew still less of love. Indeed, it was not something I had given much thought to until now. Unrequited, it seemed a treacherous thing. I quickly moved my thoughts back to the previous day.

When we halted outside Bartholomew's Eastcheap house, I had taken Susannah's hand to help her down and our eyes met for an instant. I hoped she could not read the longing in mine ... or did I, in truth, hope she might? She did squeeze my fingers briefly, though I thought it more about our joint hopes for Sam than any acknowledgement of my own. We were shown directly into his study on this occasion, and I was glad that meant we were unlikely to encounter his wife.

'You're lucky to find me home at this hour. I'm usually at my Rotherhithe office, but I'd foolishly left some manifests I needed here, and it seemed easier to return and collect them myself rather than send a clerk.' He grinned then, rather disarmingly. 'Especially as I was not altogether certain of their whereabouts.'

As soon as we were seated, I brought him up to date with how things stood for Sam.

He rubbed at his face, absently. 'So, he wishes me to locate this Hubert Winks in the slums and stews of Southwark?' He looked from me to Susannah. 'Are either of you familiar with the tenement courts of Abbot of Battle's maze behind Tooley Street? Some of the poor folk living there would sell their children for a gold coin or someone else's for a pint of genever.'

I did not wish to confess I had never been south of the river. Well, to Kew Palace only, which would contrast rather starkly with the place Bartholomew described. 'I can't say I am familiar with it, no.'

Susannah wrote, 'I have been there a time or two with my maid to visit her mother. Their court is in a better way than most.' She turned to me. 'If you want to see how much of London looked before the fire, you will find it there.' I read aloud for Bartholomew.

'Perhaps the worst of how it was? But I do have business contacts there. I'll ask around.' He stood. 'Now, if you'll excuse me, I must return to Rotherhithe.'

Just as my mind arrived at our silent journey back to Henrietta Street, Giuseppe flung open the door, startling me. 'Not in the mood for knocking today, eh?'

He narrowed his eyes. 'Fuck you, Sirrah.'

I raised my eyebrows, applauding his fine attempt at a London accent. '*Molto buona.*'

He made a courtly bow. 'A Lieutenant Monkton to see you, *Signore.*'

I rose and met him at the drawing room door; he had not waited to be shown up and his grave face had my belly clenching. 'Tom?' I turned to Giuseppe. 'Wine, I think.' Giuseppe relieved him of his hat and went to the consul table to pour for us. He was still in uniform so had come directly from the palace. 'I already know it's bad.'

He sighed and shook his head slightly, before looking down at the floor. 'He is to go to trial.'

'*Merda.* So, the King has decided. Do you know when? Where?'

'Westminster Hall. No date as yet.'

Giuseppe handed a glass to Tom and then one to me, which I downed and held out for him to refill. 'How long, do you think?'

Tom drank deeply before looking at his glass, regretfully, and setting it down on the table beside him. 'I must return to duty. As for when, that's at the King's pleasure, of course. I would like to say weeks rather than days.' He shrugged. 'But all depends on His Majesty. I wanted to tell you in person, my friend.'

I squeezed his arm. 'I am truly grateful. Now I must do the same for Susannah.'

He nodded. 'I think it will be easier for her to learn of it from you.'

And preferable that Catherine did not know of his consideration towards us. I walked with him to the stables behind my house, watching him fetch out his horse and ride away. Then instead of returning to the workshop for the afternoon, I wrote a note to Noah Bartholomew and sent Giuseppe to deliver it to him in Rotherhithe.

∽

NOAH

After the visit from Raphael and Susannah, Noah had dreamt of Sam. He had thought himself awake in the dark of his chamber and found Sam beside him, pale and supine, arms folded on his chest like a knight carved in stone upon his tomb. When he felt the chill coming off him, fearing him dead, he fought hard to move his leaden limbs, desperate to take the lad into his arms. To warm him. To breathe life into him. And then he woke alone in his bed, his face wet with tears, sure he could smell Sam's scent on the pillow where he had seen his resting head.

He came back to himself sitting in his warehouse office, looking out towards the wharf where two of his ships were tied up. The tide was low so the gangways leading to them were at their shortest and cargo was netted onto one and off the other with greater ease than when hulls rose higher above the dock. The Gillyflower and the Cloverleaf. They were both fine three masted brigs built for him not far away down river in the Deptford shipyards. He ran his fingers through his loose hair, glad to be free of his wig for a while.

Sam. Dear God, what could he do? A part of him said if Sam must die then he should have the courage to do so with him. At least then they would both die for the crime they had committed. But once again the reasons why he could not were all too apparent. All this in front of him. All this for his sons. But not if he died a sodomite when it would be subject to attainder and forfeit to the crown. Hal was here somewhere in the warehouses doing everything he could to learn. And how could he not thank God for it? He thought, too, of Michael with his glorious auburn hair just as his own mother had. He was the kindest soul. Noah could weep just thinking of him.

He sighed, tying back his hair before picking up his damn wig and putting it on. And sighing again, though louder this time, he grabbed his coat from the hook by the door. It was time for his visit to Tooley Street to draw upon the skills of his friend, Jacob Gold, banker and trusted fixer of myriad eclectic problems. If Jacob could not locate this Hubert Winks, then no one could. Christ, it felt good to have a reason to act. Until this, there had simply been nothing he could do. No means of helping Sam at all. He would catch a lift to the St Mary Overie Stairs on one of his lighters going up west with cargo.

The morning was sunny and warm, and he shaded his eyes against light reflecting off the water. The rhythm of the sweeps dipping into the sparkling river lulled him into a brief doze before he hauled himself out of it and stood to talk with the bow-legged skipper, trying not to gape at his purple potato of a nose. Noah pointed to the barrels of small beer stacked in the boat's well. 'Where's this lot for, then?' The ale had been picked up at Deal on the Cloverleaf's return from Scandinavia with a cargo of pine.

'St James's Palace, Master.' He scratched amongst his greasy wisps of grey hair.

Noah resisted the urge to scratch beneath his wig in sympathy. 'How many loads are we taking up?'

'Another ten.' He grinned showing a few sparse tobacco-stained teeth. 'There be many guardsmen, Zur.'

'Undeniably so.' Noah jumped ashore easily at the dock so the lighter could continue on its way upriver. He moved quickly through the shouting, milling crowds of hawkers and cockle-sellers, weaving around cargo sheds, some built out on stilts over the river with overhanging upper stories added one atop the other to increase floor space.

Soon the pungent odour of fish gave way to the eye-watering stench of tanneries and musk from the Bankside bear pits, thriving again since the restoration. Cromwell had the animals shot but only to save men from enjoyment, not the bears from their suffering. He looked for a sedan chair as the most easily acquired means of transport and spotted one on the corner, quickly agreeing a price to Jacob's Tooley Street house. He sat back against the grubby squabs, the distance to Jacob's premises soon covered by the striding men eager to carry as many customers as possible after him.

Inside gloomy oak-panelled rooms redolent of diligence with the dust of mouldering leather acrid at the back of his throat, quills scratched in ledgers and silent clerks barely looked up as he passed. For he was well known here and left to make his own way upstairs. He tapped on Jacob's door not waiting for a response before letting himself in. He had sent a note and his friend expected him, moving slowly around his cluttered oak desk to take Noah in his arms.

Jacob kissed him warmly on both cheeks. 'Good to see you. Sit. Sit, my dear.' He pointed to an elderly sofa guarding the smoky fire. Though it was warm outdoors, this room was always chill and damp. A small window facing north, looked out over the shadowy squalor of Abbot of Battle's maze.

Noah lowered himself beside Jacob. 'How are you?' He studied his friend's swollen and twisted fingers wondering, as he always did, why he did not find premises more conducive to his health. Yet his black eyes still twinkled beneath a mane of white hair, falling loose to his narrow shoulders.

Jacob shrugged. 'I am, as always. Now tell me why you're here.' He tapped Noah's knee with a gnarled finger. 'Not to ask after my health, I'm certain.'

Noah smiled. 'You know how much I value your friendship–'

'But ...'

'But I need your help.'

Jacob raised his eyebrows, his eyes full of compassion.

How had he read so much in those few words? So, he found himself telling him of Sam and all that was at stake for him. Jacob knew all about Noah and had always accepted him as he was. As a Jew, he understood what it meant to be despised for something beyond his control. He had changed his name in an attempt to hide it, just as Noah had tried to hide himself in marriage. 'Now finding Winks is all I can do for him.'

'I hear something different in your voice when you speak of him.'

Noah met his gaze. 'His life rests in my hands. That is a huge thing, Jacob.'

'It is. Oh, indeed, it is. Yet what I heard, my dear, was love. And it gladdens my heart to hear it.'

Noah stiffened, frowning, ready to deny any such thing and then he slumped. For it was the truth. Of course, it was. Had he not already admitted so to Hal? It was little short of madness but there was nothing to be done. 'Not sensible of me, I know. And I've always tried to be sensible.'

Jacob touched his arm, gently. 'We all need to know love, Noah. However unlooked for. I once loved a gentile. It didn't end well.'

'No, I imagine it wouldn't.'

Jacob took a long breath. 'Hubert Winks. Tell me all you know of him.'

'That's simple. I know little beyond his name, his work in the palace kitchens and that he lodges somewhere in Southwark.'

Jacob tilted his head. 'Well, that must be enough then, my friend.'

He walked Noah to the staircase, but he insisted the old man should not accompany him down. Back out in the sunshine, he prayed it would indeed be enough. For if they could not locate the man, what then?

Chapter Seven
RAPHAEL

The very next day after telling Susannah of Sam's trial, I found myself knocking on her door for a second time hoping she had not received a letter too. In my workshop earlier that morning, a servant had brought me a simple folded paper without a seal, my name scrawled on it in an unformed hand. I opened it with little interest, imagining a note from a shopkeeper or a tradesman chasing a bill, only to draw a sharp breath for it was not that at all. Giuseppe stared at me, frowning. '*Leave Samuel Carter to die or die in his stead,*' I read aloud.

Giuseppe snatched it from my fingers. 'What this fucking thing about, eh? Who write something like this shit?'

'That's a very good question.' I took it back to examine it again holding it up to the light, but there was nothing more to see. Still, my instinct was to take it at face value. We already suspected powerful forces were at work behind Sam's imprisonment, so this could easily be a real threat. But who knew of my interest in freeing him? And who knew I was seeking the real murderer? I wondered then whether the others had received such letters.

'You should go to her.'

So go I did, and with all haste in so far as that was possible through the thronged streets. Bess opened the door. 'Is your mistress at home?'

'She be working in the studio, Master.'

It was then I spotted the folded paper on a silver tray atop the hallstand, almost hidden amongst other letters waiting for the family to claim them. 'Will you ask her to spare me a moment. It's important.' I waited where I was while Bess went to fetch her. Should I remove the note and leave her unaware, and so unworried by it? Yet I knew I could not for she must be warned that someone might mean her harm. Maybe someone powerful enough to inflict such. I took it from the tray and slipped into my pocket before glancing up at the sound of footsteps on the stairs. She looked entirely beautiful and not a little alarmed.

'Raphael? What's happened?' she wrote.

'Might we go to the drawing room?'

She nodded and led me back upstairs. Once the door closed behind us, she spoke. 'You look worried. Tell me. Tell me what in the name of God has happened now?' She shook her head. 'Not his trial date?'

I took her hands in mine for a moment. 'No. Not that. This.' I took the paper from my pocket and held it out to her.

She took it, her fingers shaking slightly. 'I find myself reluctant to open it. Must I?'

'Forgive me, I think you must.'

She read it, frowning. 'Why, it's nonsense, surely?'

'I fear not. It seems entirely possible that those behind Sam's imprisonment don't wish us to find the murderer, so are warning us off.'

She stared out of the window. 'Catherine. This is just the sort of thing she would do. She knows you and I believe him innocent.'

'Well, the test will be Noah. She can't know of him. And, come to think of it, how can anyone?'

'They can't.'

Just then a soft tap sounded on the door and Susannah moved

to open it. 'A letter just come, Mistress.' The maid held it out. 'Boy say you must see it quick, like.'

When the door closed behind her, Susannah broke the seal. 'Noah. Jesu, he's had one.'

I took his letter from her. 'So, someone must have followed us to him. That's the only explanation.'

She clutched my arm and I pulled her to me. 'Jesu, Raphael. What can we do?'

'Tom Monkton. I should tell him.'

She drew away. 'Then I'll write to Noah. He needs to know we have all been threatened.'

We parted then, and my desire to kiss her was so strong I fear I fled rather abruptly, seeing myself out and hurrying to my coach.

Luck was with me, and I found Tom at his desk in his Horse Guards office. He rose as I entered without knocking. 'Raphael. What's happened?'

I handed him the two notes. 'Noah Bartholomew has one.' I said nothing more, wishing to hear his thoughts first.

He closed his eyes a moment. 'I feared something like this might occur. Willets has harried me about dilettantes interfering in a case already solved. His temper on it suggested he's being pressed himself from above–'

'Sam Carter is innocent.'

He sighed. 'I know it. Believe me, I do. But it's now clear someone thinks him guilty of something and it's for this he's imprisoned.'

'The King.'

His expression darkened. 'Raphael. This is dangerous talk. I warn you, if you mean to go on with it then you must take the utmost care.'

'We are already being followed. That I do know.'

'Well, then, you must take precautions. Hackneys are more difficult to trail.'

'I worry most for Noah. He's the one trying to find Hubert Winks in Southwark.'

Beyond warning us to be careful there was little more Tom could do, and I pondered this as I made my way back to King Street.

'Raphael.'

I turned to find the duchess beaming at me. 'Frances. I'm glad to see you.' And I was. I would tell her everything. Maybe she could help?

I lay on my back staring at the ornate gilded ceiling covered with colourful frolicking cherubs and putti, while Frances dozed pressed close against me. So, if I now loved Susannah, what in the name of holy God was I doing in her bed? And had I not decided, once and for all, to end it? When I accompanied her to Richmond House intending to discuss Sam Carter how instead had I fallen into her bed? Again. How could I love one woman yet swive another? It was beyond dishonourable and should never have happened. Said before, of course. Many times. So, this time I must tell her it at once.

Frances sighed, her fingers beginning to caress my chest. 'What is it, Raphael? Your thoughts are so fierce, I can hear them growling.'

I turned to look at her, and her eyes widened enticingly. 'Frances, I–' God help me, I kissed her again and had her, hard. So much for honour.

Finally, when she lay beside me once more, our bodies hot and slick from well-sated lust, I was able to tell her about the letters. 'Susannah wondered if her step-mother might be behind them, but I can't think she has the influence to do any real harm.' And, yes, I felt mortified talking of Susannah with my arm around another women, my fingers resting on her naked breast. Shame hot on my face because of it, but I did not remove my hand.

'I wouldn't be so sure. Castlemaine has decided to acknowledge their kinship, though it was her late husband who was the distant cousin. Very distant indeed, I believe. She's moved into Barbara's rooms, and they work together to ensure poor Samuel is found guilty.'

I frowned, looking down at her. 'But why? What is Castlemaine's motive? I thought it more likely Portsmouth if France is involved.'

'Well, I imagine Louise knows the French secret – whatever it may be – and so is warning the King of the danger to him. Barbara? Who knows with her? She's out of favour with him more often than not. Perhaps she tries to draw his attention?' She laughed. 'For a different reason than the usual one.'

I knew Castlemaine was ostentatiously flaunting her many lovers in competition with the King who did the same. There were rumours he was tired of her greed, too, and planned to send her from court. I worried for Frances. Another reason why I should stay away from her bed.

'If we find the murderer would the King release Sam?'

She was silent for a time, chewing on her thumb nail. 'I think he'd have to, providing the case is well known – which is something you and Susannah must see to. A pamphlet perhaps? But he'd soon be taken up again so should leave the country quickly.'

That would not prove difficult with Noah's help, providing we could get him released. 'I'm sure it could be arranged.'

She turned on her side to face me. 'How goes it with Susannah?'

'You think it appropriate for me to lie with you and talk of my situation with her?' I sounded pompous even to myself.

She tapped me on the nose with her index finger. 'I know you don't love me, Raphael. You wouldn't be here if you did, believe me. And when you leave me for her, I shall be very happy for you both.'

I closed my eyes. 'I don't know how to act with her.' And then I told her of our kiss. 'Virgins are something of a mystery to me,' I added, sheepishly.

She laughed though her eyes slid away.

'I know I'm dishonourable.'

She blinked and focussed on my face again. 'No. I don't believe so. Virgins can be damaged too easily. They should be left safely to husbands.'

'So, I must marry Susannah before I touch her?' I could not help remembering the feeling of her body responding to mine in that instant before she pulled away.

'I'm not saying that at all.' She moved away then, leaving the bed to fetch her robe. 'Now, my dearest, you must go as I've guests coming for luncheon and with that, she left the chamber.

I tried to make sense of what she had said while I dressed hastily, but it seemed oddly contradictory. Susannah was the King's Goddaughter so marriage to me could never be possible, anyway, could it? Just what was Frances trying to say?

She was nowhere to be seen when I descended the stairs. I let myself out, still buttoning my coat as I walked towards the bowling green … and almost cannoned straight into Susannah. I watched her take in my tousled appearance before her gaze moved to Richmond House behind me. 'Susannah. What are you doing here?'

Her face was quite blank. 'Portraiting,' she wrote.

Heat burned on mine. 'Are you arriving or leaving? You didn't tell me you were coming here today. You could have shared my coach.'

She scribbled crossly on her pad, though whispered the words through her teeth. 'I thought you would have left long before I needed to be here.'

'So, you're leaving then?' When she shook her head, vigorously, I knew it was not the truth. 'The duchess has told me much of interest–'

'I'm sure she has,' she hissed, not bothering to write this time before turning on her heel to hurry away.

'*Merda*.' Now what could I do?

SUSANNAH

Diary: May 26, 1676

There is another fire. I cannot believe I write such a thing. God has truly turned his back upon us. I heard the King and York oversee the battle against it themselves. All I know is it is over the river in Southwark. My hands shake. Where is Hubert Winks?

It was Bess who told me after her brother had arrived at dawn. A servant to a wealthy family in Bermondsey, he was woken by a red glow in the sky in the early hours. Bess sat beside me on my bed, my arm around her, feeling her tremble.

'He weren't sure if our ma's place be caught or not.' She dabbed at her tears with a ragged handkerchief. 'He be gone to find out what's what. He'll come tell me when he can.'

I doubted he would learn anything for quite some time, remembering the chaos after the fire ten years before. Nothing would be known until it was put out and the devastation cooled enough to be surveyed before the clearing could start. I prayed this fire would not prove so destructive. I wrote, 'Your sister and her husband got her to safety, I'm sure.' I knew they lived with Bess's mother since her brother had gone into service but had never met them.

She found a wan smile from somewhere, nodding. 'Yes. Yes, they would've.'

I pulled her close, touched by her trust in my words. Please God, the fire had not started in Abbot of Battle's maze where the old, crowded, timber-framed buildings were much the same as those destroyed so easily before. 'Try not to worry,' I scribbled, my thoughts turning to the man Noah was searching for in Southwark. I went cold at the prospect he might be lost to the flames.

Jesu. What would we do then? With little thought, I wrote, 'Do you know a Hubert Winks?'

She shook her head, her face suddenly white beneath the red blotches from weeping. 'I must be gone, Mistress.' She scrambled away and fled.

I frowned. Was that a reaction to the name or shock because her mother was in danger? I hoped she was safe and for a very different reason that Winks was also. I wondered if Noah had found out where he lived. If he had not, we would likely never know if he were alive or dead.

Did Raphael know of the fire? And then, of course, my mind returned to our last meeting outside Richmond House thanking God, once again, I had resisted him. And, yes, I have lost a great deal of sleep over it. I had even begun to wonder if I had seen tenderness in his eyes when he looked at me that night, leaving me to question if he might even love me. Or did he feign it to have his way with me? Could he really be so deceitful and cruel? Yet how could he love me and still go to her? Or was I simply naïve? It was what men did, after all. Why should he be any different?

I made a mental effort again not to imagine him with her, with little success, until I watched the scene as though present in the room with them. Their nakedness, his black hair loose against her skin as he kissed her breasts. Those kisses moving down her body, her small hands upon his tawny back. How was it possible to be revolted by this vision and aroused by it, too? How was it possible not to imagine myself in her place? Then, the bubble burst with a flash of rage. God damn him. I no longer even wished to be his friend.

Though it was very early still, and with even the thought of breakfast making me queasy, I ran up to the studio. I needed to lose myself in work, which was easier when I had the place to myself. I mixed my red paste before sitting at my table to begin transferring the watercolour image I had done of James Scott the day before – resplendent in the scarlet and gold uniform of Master of the Horse – to a gold oval. He wished is as a gift for his father.

It was there that Raphael found me. A kitchen maid had let him in and left him to come up alone. How did servants know where I was? Yet, somehow, they always did. He pulled a stool across from another worktable to sit beside me, watching me in silence until I had finished and moved away to place the miniature into the kiln for the first firing.

'I'm glad I've seen you work, at last.' He lifted my watercolour to study it. 'Monmouth is ... but I can see the King in him. His mother must have been very beautiful. I–'

'She was, I believe.' I walked slowly back to my table, seeing him properly for the first time. And he looked utterly wonderful, damn him, dressed in that shade of green which seemed to match his eyes to such perfection, his black hair gleaming in the early morning sunshine. His expression, though, was pensive. 'Raphael. What do you want?' I felt colour upon my face, remembering my earlier imaginings.

He looked up at me with a fierce intensity. 'I need to speak with you about yesterday–'

'Indeed, you do not.'

He returned the painting to my table. 'I must tell you what she said ... the duchess.' He looked at me again, his expression both contrite and defiant. 'Castlemaine is helping Catherine to have Sam found guilty. She is staying in her lodgings. You didn't tell me she no longer lives here?'

I sat, rather abruptly. 'I knew she spent a great deal of time at court. I didn't know she was with Castlemaine. Why? Why on earth would she take an interest in Catherine?'

He moved his stool closer to mine. 'She has acknowledged some kinship.'

Seeing me about to speak, he held up his hand. I narrowed my eyes.

'Don't ask me why. Frances has no real idea. Perhaps she competes with Portsmouth to dispose of Sam for the King.'

Frances. The sudden intimacy of her name enraged me. 'Did you need to swive her to get this information?' I saw the absolute shock my words caused when deep colour spread across his face. I had never seen that intensity before on his dark skin. It was not enough though. 'Did you sell her more jewels, too? Do you still serve all your faded ladies with your body or is she lucrative enough alone?'

He stood, the stool crashing to the floor behind him. '*Dio mio. Voi mi pensi una puttana?*' He stared hard at me, his eyes narrowed, before taking a sharp breath and bowing low. '*Signorina.*' He turned on his heel and made for the door.

Jesu. I had wished to hurt him yet when I did, I wanted nothing but to have it all unsaid. I chased after him, catching his hand. 'Raphael. Forgive me, I beg you.'

He pulled me into his arms and kissed me fiercely, his tongue deep inside my mouth. I kissed him just as passionately and found myself pinned against the closed door, his body crushing mine, his arousal hard against me. Thank God, he had no such proof of the extent of mine. Though he was quite aware of it, of course. Then he moved me aside without a word to open the door, closing it quietly behind him, leaving me listening to his footsteps as he ran down the stairs. I covered my face with my hands and wept. It was only when I was able to think coherently once more, I remembered I had not spoken of the fire.

How shall I sleep tonight with my thoughts full of that coming together? The fierceness of it. The desire. Why have I tried to turn him against me, when it is the very last thing I wish for? God help me. Have I completely lost my wits this time?

RAPHAEL

In my drawing room, I poured myself a large glass of brandy though it was not long past nine. I had recovered my composure on the carriage ride home and even been distracted by a group of cattle hurtling down Long Lane, having escaped their drover on the way to the shambles. Good thinking on their part, though I doubted their freedom would be long-lived and nor indeed would they. Poor beasts.

Now in the privacy of my home, I could not help but relive my encounter with Susannah. Both her words and her body pressed against mine. Just the thought of it made me hard again. Christ, I wanted her ... and without doubt I loved her, too.

The door opened behind me, and Giuseppe strode in dressed for the workshop. 'You a man of leisure today, eh?' He grinned taking in my state of excitement, which was enough to have it subside almost immediately. 'Brandy and a bone? You had some adventure, no?'

'No. Now bugger off and leave me in peace. I shall be out to the workshop shortly.'

'After, eh?' He pointed to his crotch and made an obscene gesture depicting onanism.

What was there to do but laugh? 'In my drawing room? *Really?*' And then I told him all about it. 'I can understand why she thinks so badly of me. Perhaps others do, also? That I'm some sort of prostitute. Which is amusing when you think of it, when so many are still to pay me. Whores are not noted for working on credit as far as I'm aware.'

He shook his head. 'She jealous, is all. And no one think what you do is whoring. Is business. If women want you then *fortunato*. Men, they wish only to be you with an easy way to a woman's bed.'

'She's not jealous. She despises me.'

'And then kiss you like that? Pah. She wishes to be the duchess you *idiota*. You blind you cannot see it.'

I gulped the last of my brandy. 'Then I am blind.'

He picked up my empty glass. 'You want more?'

I shook my head, feeling a little nauseous. 'Wish I hadn't had it, in truth.'

He nodded, sagely. 'French piss, no?' He made for the door carrying my glass but looked back, speaking over his shoulder. 'You heard about the fire?'

'Fire?'

'Southwark. Is a bad one,' he said, closing the door behind him.

I dropped onto a chair, closing my eyes. *Merda.* Southwark. Hubert Winks. How would we find him now?

I would go to the workshop and finish the last pieces for Frances. The next time I took them to her that would be all I would do. I must prove to myself it was possible. It struck me like a physical blow when I walked in, how similar my workplace smelt to Susannah's. Hot mettle. Men toiling with heat. Old sweat. Christ, it flung me back there and I smelled her hair, felt her body constrained by mine. Giuseppe, rising from his bench startled me out of it, and I watched him fetch the last of the duchess's pieces from the strong room. He handed them to me with raised eyebrows over sceptical eyes. I knew what he thought and was determined to prove him wrong. Frances would understand. She had said she would be pleased when I left her for Susannah. But would Susannah?

Later, after mounting the final emeralds extracted from a heavy gold cuff into their new setting of a filigree necklace, I studied it carefully with my lens before accepting it was finished. Then, returning it together with the other completed pieces to the strong room, my mind still on Susannah, I picked up the ring I had been working on ready for some mythical time when I might give it to her. This seemed further away than ever now. Holy God, how could I ever win her? Perhaps all I could do was attempt to help Sam in some way? That would mean more to her than anything. Quite how this might be achieved was uncertain, I only knew I must try. I dropped my leather apron onto the workbench. 'I'm going out.'

Giuseppe bowed. '*Grazie* for all the work you done today, *Padrone. Grazie mille.*'

I ignored him, heading for the stairs back up to the house where I donned my coat again before leaving to find a hackney. Noah. I would start with him. If I hoped to get across the river today the bridge would be out of the question, though I soon learnt from the helpful coachman that I could take a wherry from Wapping to Noah's wharf. Had he discovered anything about Winks? There seemed little hope of finding him now with a fire raging in Southwark, but maybe there was something about him that might help us. Was Winks himself the murderer? And the question still remained, who had taken Sam's sword from his chamber?

At Wapping, I had to wait a tediously long time amongst shrieking fishwives and hawkers, cutpurses circling whilst I ate a rather good oyster pie – guilty for my enjoyment of it on such a day – before I could finally secure a boat to row me downriver. The Thames seethed with wherries, lighters, and barges, crossing to and fro. With the bridge out of action, it was the only way to get to the south bank. What a scene it made, even here the sky was dark with billowing smoke carried on the wind with water the colour of blood reflected from the fiery sky. I imagined many were seeking loved ones and pitied them for it. I crossed myself, commending the dead to God.

For reasons I was unable to ascertain, the wherryman insisted on putting me down at the Salt Stairs in Rotherhithe. I could only imagine he regarded additional lucrative passengers more important than fulfilling his contract with me to go further downriver. Not unreasonable under the circumstances. I should have expected to be gulled on such a day.

After trying to secure a sedan chair with little success though, again, not entirely unexpectedly, I found myself walking to Bartholomew's wharf in the late afternoon. There was a passable track, mostly through orchards and market gardens, away from the road winding its way through the warehouses crowding close beside the river, which I was informed would shorten the distance considerably.

Walking beneath sweet apple blossom was a small relief from the taint of fire. And, yes, I did ask myself what I hoped to achieve by coming here when Southwark was ablaze. With no real answer, I turned back to look at the burning skyline, noisome smoke again filling my nostrils, borne on a strong west wind. A single question now filled my thoughts. Had the murderer already been consumed?

∽

NOAH

Noah had complete faith the fire could not reach them. So much had been learned from what happened ten years before and buildings had already been demolished upwind to create a wide swathe of open ground where the fire could not cross, with numerous beaters in place ready to stop any windborne sparks catching hold.

His clerk, Jenson, told him he had seen the King and the Duke of York supervising the demolitions, cheered on by a throng of onlookers who would have done better to look to their own well-being. How brave the King was. Fear for his own safety seemed never to occur to him. Perhaps he believed himself under God's particular protection? Perhaps, indeed, he was. Even when silencing inconvenient Godsons.

The tide was high, though on the cusp of turning, and first mates were hastily finishing loading readying their ships to catch it in order to speed their passage downriver and out into the North Sea. His view of them was somewhat obscured by the haze of smoke today. He looked away when a loud rap sounded upon the door which was slightly ajar, quickly followed by Jenson's head poking around it.

'A person for you, Zur.'

'A person? What person?' For some reason, his clerk never thought to ask. Noah sighed. 'No matter, send the person in.' He stood ready to greet whoever it might be, though this particular person turned out a mighty surprise. Christ's wounds, had he come to press him again for Sam's whereabouts on that fateful night? If so, he was wasting his time, of course. He forced a smile. 'Signor Rossi? You've chosen a sad day to cross the river.' Noah studied him. It was the first time he had seen him alone and he was struck afresh by his dark, sultry handsomeness. There was something truly captivating about him. Well, that smile returning his, for one thing.

'Indeed. I must admit it is the fire that has brought me to see you. I ... we ... Susannah and I fear this man Winks may have fallen victim to it.' He appeared uncertain for a moment. 'I wonder if you have had time to learn anything of him?'

'I had a note from my associate yesterday evening with an address in Abbot of Battle's maze. It's too soon to know if Winks escaped the flames. He lived there with his wife and her mother, apparently.' Noah sat at his desk once more and after gesturing for Raphael to sit on a chair beside the window, he opened a drawer to pull out a scrap of paper and a sealed letter. 'I made a note of the address for you, though I fear the tenement is unlikely to have survived. The houses there are, well ... very like those lost in the fire ten years ago. Wood framed wattle and daub structures crowded together, many upper stories added to overhang out across narrow streets and sheds turned into ramshackle dwellings. So, another tragedy, alas.'

Rossi watched him intently. 'I trust your friend has not been affected?'

'Another note arrived this morning. His house on Tooley Street backs onto the maze but it's stone-built, and enough fire breaks were made in time to protect it. He's in poor health, I'm afraid, so has moved out for a time as the street is badly troubled by smoke.'

Rossi studied his fingers. 'Forgive me for pressing but is there anymore known of Hubert Winks beyond his lodgings? Things could go badly for Sam at any time when the King decides on a trial date.' He looked up sharply, as though struck by a sudden thought. 'Do you know anything of pamphlet printing?'

Noah listened, nodding, while Rossi told him of the Duchess of Richmond's suggestion to get Sam's case known to the public. He lifted a bottle of Bordeaux down from a shelf and poured two glasses. 'I can see how it would make the King think twice before keeping him imprisoned if he is found innocent.' He rubbed his face. 'Still, we mustn't back him or those advising him into a corner and force them to dispose of him in some other way.'

'Wouldn't public interest make that a bigger risk for them, too?'

'Public interest?' Noah nodded again. 'Aye. His father, the admiral, is something of a hero I believe, after his feats against the Dutch. That would definitely work in our favour.' Noah picked up the sealed letter. 'Perhaps you might pass this to Sam on your next visit.' He looked at it, keeping his expression neutral. 'He asked me only to write to him when my letters could be handed over in secret. All are read now he's to go to trial.'

'I didn't know that.'

'They're careful to reseal them, but Sam is something of an expert on that sort of thing, I'm given to understand. He got a note out to me with Connor, telling me ... and Hal to be cautious.'

Rossi raised his eyebrows and took the letter. 'I. We plan to visit him tomorrow.' He stood. 'I don't suppose you know the mother's name? Though it will be of little use if she has perished, of course.'

Noah shook his head. 'Regretfully I don't, but I shall see if I can find out regardless.' He moved out from behind his desk. 'I'll walk you to the dock. One of my lighters can take you back across.

Save you a deal of time today, *Signor* Rossi.' Noah wondered why he had come, for it had not been what he thought, of course. It seemed a lot of trouble on such a day and for so little reward.

'Raphael, please. And I'm most grateful to you.'

They walked outside together into murky air that now seemed a mixture of acrid smoke and fog, their footsteps echoing. Great hulls and tall masts soon appeared, ghostlike out of the gloom. As they passed, Noah eyed his men still busily loading goods winched-up in nets to be stowed below.

When he turned to make sure Rossi was still with him, he let out a startled cry before drawing his sword. He watched him hold up his hands in alarm at this, with no attempt made to draw his own weapon. 'Stand aside,' he barked. The Italian obeyed. Though, just as he lunged his blade at the masked man who had moved in behind him, another appeared and clubbed Rossi over the head. Both men then disappeared into the swirling mist as Noah dropped to his knees beside him. 'Raphael. Holy Christ, man.' He thought for a moment he was dead until he felt him breathe. 'Raphael. You're all right. Wake up now, there's a good lad.' Again, Raphael obeyed, his eyes fluttering open. '*Quello che e successo?*'

'A club to your head is what happened.' Noah bent and scooped him up in his arms as easily as lifting a child.

RAPHAEL

I woke to light stealing in around the canopy and bed drapes. Coarse ones I did not recognise, which was disconcerting enough without the raging headache I had no explanation for. As I tried to make sense of my situation, the curtain closest to me drew back and sunlight blinded me.

'Raphael, how are you feeling?'

I closed my eyes, heart pounding, needing some moments to

even realise Noah had spoken in Italian. 'Confused. Where exactly am I and why does my head hurt like damnation?'

He handed me a cup of small beer and sat down on the quilt beside me. 'You're at my warehouse. It has a pair of rather basic bedchambers for when dawn sailings mean we must stay overnight. So, I was able to keep an eye on you.'

'Then you have my gratitude.' Thinking of Noah's wife, I could imagine why such an arrangement might prove useful for other reasons. 'What happened to my head?' I touched it feeling a lump the size of a hen's egg. Perhaps something of an exaggeration, though it was certainly painful enough to be such. I closed my eyes. '*Merda*. I remember.' I gulped down the beer. Well, I remembered something cracking my head from behind, which explained the searing pain.

'I don't think they meant to kill you. They would have had blades for that.'

'Good to know,' I said, dryly, fingering the damage again with some trepidation. 'When you drew your sword, I thought for a moment you were going to run me through.'

He grinned. 'I saw you think it.'

'Well, I must thank you. Had you not been there it could have gone much worse for me.' I watched his face as I spoke. 'Do you think this is about Sam? Or were they just footpads out to rob me?'

'I don't think we can dismiss those letters. If someone threatens to kill you and then you are attacked it seems likely the two are connected, doesn't it? Though this was perhaps more of a warning.'

'Well, then, I'm entirely warned.'

Noah frowned. 'Of course, we have no way of knowing which of us was their intended target.'

'I imagine if it were you, your sword proved something of a deterrent.' I handed him the cup and tried to sit higher against the pillows, but dizziness swept over me, and his large hands gripped my upper arms to steady me.

'*Merda*. I think I might puke.' He quickly found the piss pot beneath the bed and handed it to me just in time. I remember my head throbbing against the pillow and then I knew no more.

The second time I awakened, the change in light told me quite some time had passed. I sat up to swing my legs out over the side of the bed waiting for dizziness again but feeling steady, I crossed myself as a courtesy for it. Cautiously I got to my feet and though the room spun for a moment or two, it quickly passed. When a few tentative steps proved uneventful, I padded over the rough wooden boards to the window which gave me a view out over cargo sheds and an oblique sight of the river now bare of ships, the winches idle beasts awaiting new arrivals.

Someone had undressed me down to my shirt, hanging my clothes on a peg beside the door, but when I lifted my coat it slipped from my fingers onto the floor. I stooped to pick it up and then feeling a touch light-headed, sat down on the bed again, where Noah's letter slid out from my pocket onto the quilt. The seal must have shattered when I fell the day before and the drop to the floor had flipped open the top fold. I read the words without intention. They were just there in front of my eyes. '*I love you, Sam. I can no longer deny it, for why would I? Especially now.*' I folded the flap down again and replaced it, wishing with some intensity I had not seen them. Though I could not wipe them from my memory, I could ensure they never left my lips.

And, of course, Sam's refusal to reveal his whereabouts made complete sense if he had been with Noah. I could not believe my stupidity. That Sam had been in his coach made this possibility blindingly obvious from the start. Yet it had simply not occurred to me. However, I saw no reason to tell Susannah of it, for what purpose would it serve when our objective was still solely to find the murderer?

Dressing then proved more difficult than I had anticipated

when dizziness hit me yet again after managing only my breeches, so I lay back down accepting I must take longer over it.

After a brisk rap sounded on the door, it opened to reveal Hal Bartholomew this time. 'Papa sent me to see how you fare.'

'I fare rather damn poorly just now. But thank him for his concern.'

He sat down on the bed. 'I am sorry to hear it. Can I do anything for you?'

'No. I think I must just lie still for a while.' I looked up at him. Perhaps conversation might prove a distraction. 'So, you work for your father?'

'Now, yes.' He appeared a little embarrassed. 'I was up at Oxford until recently ... I was rusticated for the remainder of Trinity.'

Had my mind been affected by the blow? For I found myself quite unable to understand his last words.

He read it on my face. 'Forgive me. I mean I was sent home for the rest of the term.' He met my gaze. 'Unacceptable conduct.'

I raised my eyebrows, quickly wishing I had not when pain stabbed me in the back of my head. *Merda*. I looked at him again. 'That can't have gone down too well, I imagine?'

'No.' His eyes slid away. 'Whore in my rooms.'

Well, that was not true. 'You can go back next term though, I'm sure.'

'Yes, but I shan't. I want to work for Papa ... I'm sick of being treated like a child. I thought it would change after school.' He shrugged.

'Well, perhaps a slight improvement? I most certainly couldn't have smuggled a whore into school.'

He laughed. 'No. But I did expect university to be different. We're not bloody monks for Christ's sake.'

I stopped my eyebrows just in time. 'I know quite a lot about monks. My school was run by them. It was a seething hotbed of lust.'

Hal laughed. 'Aren't all schools?'

'I suppose they must be. Boys are boys, no? But monks take vows of celibacy, which does not mean only forswearing carnal knowledge of women.' I sighed. Not quite fair, not all. But enough.

'At mine, of course, masters had no objection to women either. Christ, if my papa had the slightest idea of what really went on, he would demand my fees repaid.' His eyes went soft. 'My brother is there now. But he's very religious, so his friends are rather different to mine.'

'So.' I tried to sit up higher against the pillows, and he helped me in a practiced way. His mother, I imagined. 'Now you'll work for your Papa – as I do for mine – and be free to have whores whenever you wish.'

'Master Rossi–'

'Raphael.'

'I live at home with my mother.' He sighed. 'And I can't see how I might work for him when everything here runs so smoothly because he's so often away at sea. How can there be any place for me?'

'Then might you not go to sea with him?'

He shrugged. 'It's a possibility, but will he take me?'

I closed my eyes for a moment. The time had come to resume my efforts to dress.

'Raphael, may I ask you something?'

I opened my eyes again. 'Of course.'

'What is Samuel Carter like? I know Papa is very fond of him?' His eyes widened and colour swamped his face 'Fuck.'

I touched his arm. 'I already know he's your father's friend, not yours.' Noah's letter had opened my eyes to that, finally. Did he know the truth about them? I rather thought he might. 'I like him very much indeed. You know he's in the Tower?'

He nodded, looking very serious.

'Well, I was there with him for a time and got to know him. Susannah Gresham has known him all her life and loves him dearly. He is a good man.'

He nodded again. It seemed enough. 'I can help you finish dressing if your wish?'

I held on to his arm and stood shakily whilst he towered over me. 'You have my word I shall do all in my power not to puke over you.'

'Obliged to you, Sir.'

Fully dressed at last, I made my way down the narrow flight of stairs to find Noah, as expected, in his office. And there sitting where I had sat the previous day, was Giuseppe. They both stood.

'What are you doing here?'

'I sent for him,' Noah said. 'You can't possibly travel alone after what's happened to you.'

Giuseppe crossed to me and pulled me into his arms. 'What you doing get hit on the head? Your papá, he flay me alive if you have a bashed-in head, eh? You stupid bugger.'

'Thank you, Giuseppe. My health is much improved. I appreciate all your heartfelt concern though.'

'Your man crossed in a tilt-boat.' He gestured towards the river. 'It's waiting. I've sent out notes trying to discover more about Winks and his family, and I'll get word to you as soon as there's anything to tell–'

'If there is anything to tell,' I interjected, gloomily. Suddenly it all seemed so futile, and I was mighty tired of it.

Noah grasped my arm. 'We mustn't lose our resolve. We can't for Sam's sake. I'll get someone looking into pamphlets as that's something we can do directly.'

I took a long breath. 'You're right.' I touched the lump on my head. 'Addled still.'

He bowed. 'Good day, Raphael. We'll talk again soon. Watch yourself.'

I touched my hat. 'Good day, to you.' I pointed to his sword hanging on a peg. 'Don't go out without it.'

'I won't. You must do the same.'

'Indeed.' Quite what good it would do me remained doubtful. I turned to Hal, and we nodded to each other.

Giuseppe held my elbow to lead me away, though I shook him off as we crossed the wooden quay towards the river. 'I'm not an invalid.' Yet I had to reach for his hand to duck beneath the boat's awning to sit. I was especially relieved when, after our journey up the smoke-shrouded river, I found my coach waiting for us. I had never been so grateful to lean back against that cushioned leather.

Giuseppe persuaded me to take to my bed on returning to Cheapside. In truth, I needed very little encouragement for my head pounded and I felt on the verge of puking again. I allowed him to help me undress, which he did without any of his usual insulting banter. Unexpectedly, this rather alarmed me. Did he think me at death's door? After ten Hail Mary's I had finally begun to doze when a sharp tap on the door startled me, making my heart race and jump. I wondered then if I were indeed about to expire. That Giuseppe's face appeared around it grinning was reassuring.

'You have a visitor.' And with that short announcement, he flung the door wide allowing Susannah to walk in.

I struggled to sit up fearing I was truly about to puke, and all too aware of my déshabillé with my nightshirt open to my navel. I drew the quilt up over my chest, grateful for the gloom provided by the closed window drapes. She hurried across the room and quickly located the piss pot beneath my bed – empty, thank Christ – and thrust it at me just in time to catch my spew. How did she know? I closed my eyes and waited for Giuseppe to relieve me of the horrid thing, before easing back against my pillows. 'Forgive me,' I croaked.

When the door closed behind him, she spoke. 'Giuseppe told me what happened.' She sat beside me on the bed, placing her hand gently on my forehead. 'Raphael, I am so sorry. I should never have allowed you to get involved in Sam's trouble.'

'I chose it for myself.' My voice sounded more my own and

my thoughts had begun to coalesce again. 'Why are you here? Not because of this?'

She chewed her lip. 'No. But finding you hurt makes me question whether to tell you.'

I now realised just how distressed she was. 'You must. Let me help if I can.'

She sighed, pulling a crumpled paper from her pocket. 'Read it.'

I unfolded the note and gasped. *How would your sister be without you? How would you be without her?* 'Holy God. When did you get this?'

'I came to you as soon as it arrived. And finding you like this makes such a threat all too real.'

I reached for her hand. 'What can I do?'

She closed her eyes for a moment before taking a long breath. 'I must get her out of London.' She chewed her lip. 'I shall take her to my grandmother's estate in Hampshire. She'll be safe there.'

'What does your father say?'

'He doesn't know.' She shook her head. 'He's distressed enough over Catherine's behaviour at court. He can't bear how she works against Sam.'

I sat up higher against the pillows, closing my nightshirt across my chest, desiring her touch on my skin. How could her presence arouse me even with a cracked skull and the taste of puke in my mouth? And when she was so distraught. I was clearly recovering. Christ, I wish I could be a better man. 'When will you go? You shouldn't travel alone.'

'Bess can accompany us.'

'I shall accompany you. We'll leave tomorrow if we can.'

She smiled a little, studying my face. 'You're hurt Raphael … and after my unforgivable words to you yesterday I would not expect it of you.'

'There is nothing to forgive … and I'm coming with you. I shall be fully recovered by tomorrow.'

'But should you not be here in case there is news from Southwark?'

'I'll write to Noah and ask him to pass anything of interest on to Tom Monkton in our absence.'

She blinked. 'But he works for the King.'

'He works to find the truth as much as we do, believe me. He's an honourable man.' And with that it seemed we had agreed to travel to Hampshire together with Susannah's sister. Where the devil was Hampshire? How far was it? How would we get there? With my head still pounding, I decided to leave it all in Susannah's hands. She stood and bent to kiss my forehead. Christ, I wanted to pull her into my arms.

At the door she turned back. 'We'll go by public stagecoach. We are less likely to be noticed then. I shall have my maid arrange it.'

SUSANNAH

Diary: June 1, 1676

Raphael. I must write his name before I begin. Raphael.

Well, we are at last arrived at Chewton Court – of which more later – after a four-day journey, three aboard a stagecoach accommodating eight souls, tightly packed, which bumped and rattled abominably over the terrible roads we were forced to travel upon. We are so spoiled now in London. The only thing to be thankful for was the lack of rain though, of course, this meant considerable dust forcing us to keep the blinds down across unglazed windows and, thus, to travel in crepuscular gloom, only relieved by regular stops to change the horses. I must note here how poor Raphael suffered with the jolting. His head pained him dreadfully.

 Having crossed the river by wherry, we had taken the coach from the Queen's Head Yard in Fox Hall instead of embarking from the George Inn in Southwark, because of the fire. Our first overnight halt was at the well-appointed White Hart Inn in the village of Frimley Heath. After Raphael used his charm upon the innkeeper's wife, we were able to secure a chamber to ourselves though the other passengers were consigned to communal ones where a bed could be shared between any number of strangers.

I was quite entertained watching him and began to further understand just how he attracts so many women. And I cannot pretend I am not among them. In truth, I fear I am now entirely infatuated with him however much I feel it a mistake. I shake my head as I write, for I have not forgotten that kiss or indeed the cruelty that proceeded it. How has he forgiven me? Yet I am entirely sure he has.

In our commodious chamber we found an enormous elaborately carved four-poster with a featherbed, a walnut table and chairs, a brocade upholstered settle and even our own close stool inside a garderobe. There were sufficient beeswax candles and a small fire burnt on the hearth, though it was a mild evening. Raphael threw open the casement, allowing rose-scented air to cool the room.

He chatted easily to Penny about his childhood in Florence while we ate the excellent game pie fetched up from the kitchens. I watched her fall under his spell until her eyelids began to droop and I carried her to the bed, where she fell almost instantly asleep as soon as I got her into her nightgown. I closed the bed drapes around her, and we were able to talk quietly, finishing the wine. 'It must seem a great unkindness that I don't speak to her.'

He placed his hand over mine. 'Don't talk of it if it's distressing.'

I removed my hand. Jesu, but I deserved such distress. 'Grandmamma hates my silence with her. It has caused something of a rift between us. Perhaps she'll be a little less disappointed in me, now I can tell her of the difficulty I still have.' Had my mind truly done this to somehow save me from guilt … or censure? 'I'm quite terrified I might be unable to speak to her, just as I cannot to Papa.' How self-serving and mad it all sounded.

'Sam told me something of how it began.'

'Did he? Though I'm sure he was far too kind to me.' I sighed. 'At first, after Mama died, I couldn't speak at all. It was a frightening time until I found I could with Sam. I didn't see my papa though, before I left for Grandmother's. In fact, I hadn't seen him at all since she died. He never came to me even when I was ill myself ...' How to say my next words when I never had before ... to anyone. And why now to him? 'I thought perhaps he wished it had been me and not her–'

He reached across to grasp my hand, holding it in both of his. 'No, *cara*. It was grief. It does strange things. It is hard to think clearly. It meant nothing like that, I'm certain of it.'

Who had he lost to understand so clearly? 'Grandmama said he was afraid to see me. Afraid I would die too.' I raised my eyes to his then. 'I didn't tell her what I'd imagined lay behind it. I knew she was right, though.' I looked away again, chewing my lip. 'When I arrived home, finding the Villiers there truly did rob me of my voice again. I was quite literally speechless with shock. The servants assumed I had still not regained it after my illness and, God forgive me, I went along with it. So, I could speak to no one. And Penny just seemed to accept it. I'd spoken at grandmother's but could no longer. Poor little girl. The Villiers were hard for her, too.' Jesu, how mindlessly I had trapped myself.

He squeezed my hand still held inside his. 'I am very glad you found your voice with me.'

I smiled. 'Sam forced me, didn't he, in the end? When I believed he would abandon me, I was completely terrified. Even now I still can't quite understand how I did it.' I chewed my lip again, remembering my turmoil then and needing to change the subject because of it. I pulled my hand free from his. Reluctantly, in truth, for I enjoyed their warmth and, God help me, that some intimacy still remained between us. 'I think we should retire. We have an early start tomorrow.'

He moved the food tray outside the chamber door. 'I shall sleep on the settle. Perhaps I might have a pillow and quilt from the bed?'

I nodded. 'Take what you need.' I watched him close the shutters and go into the garderobe. Never a wholesome place to linger no matter the number of pitchers doused through it. Though I knew he would remain in there long enough for me to prepare myself for bed. Then without a word we swapped positions and I held my nose as, no doubt, he had done. When I came out, he was lying on the settle covered with a quilt, looking most uncomfortable. His poor head. How would he ever sleep? 'Goodnight, Raphael.' I snuffed all the candles bar one, which I carried to place on the table beside the bed.

'*Buonanotte, cara mia.*'

I climbed onto the soft mattress, feeling guilty at leaving him in such discomfort. Sighing, I pushed my head around the drape. 'You may sleep there,' I whispered, gesturing to the far side of the bed.

He sat up. 'I don't want to invade your privacy.'

But when we lay far apart on either side of Penny, sleep found us both with ease. I heard his breathing change before I felt myself follow.

After a breakfast eaten in the inn's parlour, we all climbed back onboard the coach sharing matching expressions of reluctance. The day grew hotter as we crossed the desolate expanse of Bagshot Heath, and the fear of encountering highwaymen became the sole topic of conversation amongst our fellow passengers. I was able to see them clearly this time as the blinds were open, with dust seeming a lesser threat than being held-up unawares.

There were two prosperous-looking elderly married couples who talked of returning to their families in Winchester and Southampton. The man travelling alone was quite monstrously stout and clearly took up the additional space freed-up by Penny's smaller needs. It most certainly did not help Raphael's recovery that he was forced to sit beside him. He was visibly dripping sweat in the heat and Raphael moved tight against me to escape him. When I turned to him our eyes met, and we smiled at each other. It occurred to me the others must think us a married couple traveling with our daughter. Who could imagine we were taking Penny to her grandmother's because of a threat to her life? I thought then of Sam and prayed the King had not yet set a date for his trial.

Once again, we stopped for the night with our six horses rested there until morning, on this occasion at the Crown Inn overlooking the River Lodden in the village of Old Basing. Here, though, no innkeeper's wife appeared, and we were forced to share a room with the couple on their way to Winchester. They were both small and stick thin with the same long faces and fine white hair, they could almost be brother and sister. Our room was cramped and sparsely furnished, the bed small and the wool mattress lumpy. I suppose I should be grateful there were two chamber pots though little privacy to use them beyond a rudimentary curtain, all of us relying on each other's courtesy not to notice. Both our bedfellows snored and farted, too, not infrequently. I lay with Penny in my arms and Raphael close beside me. Oddly, though, we slept soundly.

After another monotonous day of travelling in perpetual shade we arrived at the Mitre Inn on St Catherine's Hill overlooking Winchester. Our bedfellows were met there by a fine carriage and swept away back to their home. I hoped we would do the same the following afternoon near Southampton, where my grandmother's carriage would be waiting to meet us should my couriered letter have reached her as speedily as I hoped. Inside, Raphael quickly discovered another innkeeper's wife and deftly secured us a separate chamber again. It was, however, small and none too clean.

He saw me look with horror at the stained bed linen. 'Shall I try to do better?'

I wrote, 'No. We'll manage. Just imagine a larger version of this shared with others?'

Somehow that night sleep eluded me. Penny lay curled-up like a dormouse beside me and Raphael slept as close to the far edge of the bed as was possible, facing away, as he did when we were alone. A faint sweet musty odour tainted the air unpleasantly. I slipped around the drape and out of bed as quietly as I could, going to the window to throw it open. I leaned out to look down upon the city with the great bulk of its cathedral dominating a skyline dazzled in moonlight, breathing in the cool air. I heard his light tread on the bare boards behind me and moved aside enough for him to lean out, too.

'It's a lovely night,' I whispered.

'*Bellissima.*'

I turned to look at him, finding his eyes upon me instead and felt heat on my face. 'You must miss Florence ... it looks a beautiful city from what I have seen of it in paintings.'

'It is. I should like to show it to you one day.'

'I'd like that.' I do not know whether I moved to him or he to me, but I found myself in his arms, pressed against his heat, kissing him and so weak with desire I believed my knees would buckle beneath me had it not been for his grasp. I knew my thin linen shift did little to conceal my body just as his shirt did nothing to conceal the obvious presence of his arousal. One hand moved hot down my back pushing me harder against him whilst the other found my breast beneath my shift.

When Penny let out a piercing shriek my heart swooped, and we jumped apart. I ran to the bed, ripping back the drapes and pulling her into my arms. She was weeping then, and I rocked her until she began to quieten. Once again, I railed against myself for being unable to offer her any words of comfort.

Raphael arrived beside me and reached down to stroke her face. 'Just a dream*, il mio piccola amore.*'

She looked up at him, her face soaked with tears. 'Wolves came in through the window. The big one was going to eat me.' Her lips trembled. 'I screamed.'

'Well, that's a very bad thing to dream of so it's lucky I know how to banish such wolves for good.'

'How?'

'I say the banishing words, *tutti i lupi devono andare.* And there it is, all done. They're gone.'

She gazed at him, wide-eyed. 'They really are? You promise, Raphael?'

He kissed her forehead. 'I promise, *piccola.*'

I stood to climb in beside her again and pulled her back into my arms until she fell asleep there. Raphael lay on his side facing us. 'Thank you,' I mouthed.

'*Non è niente.*'

Moonlight shone through the open bed curtain lighting his face and I watched his eyes slowly close, his lashes casting shadows on his cheeks as he slipped into sleep. He really was the most beautiful man. And a gentle one, too, I now knew. Was I glad Penny's nightmare parted us? In truth, I do not know. And I am under no illusion where that kiss would have led. And thinking of it kept me awake for quite some time that night. As it does, still.

The next morning, we ate breakfast in the inn's parlour and again I sat in my hellish silence whilst Raphael and Penny chatted together. He was good with her, talking easily without talking down to her. Putting her at ease. He was used to children. Nephews and nieces, I imagined.

Inside the coach, we found the stout man had left us too, and we had acquired three additional gentlemen for the journey on to Southampton. They were content for the blinds to remain open, so we were at least able to see the countryside we travelled through. Penny and Raphael resumed their conversation, and I might have felt invisible had he not turned to me often, smiling and making me feel part of it.

Penny began to tell him of Chewton Court, her excitement at the upcoming visit clear in her voice. 'It is on a cliff looking over the sea with steps down to the beach. There's a pony called Lilly I can ride. Grandmama rides with me sometimes, or Susannah.'

'Not this time, I'm afraid. Raphael and I must return to London.' I wrote.

She frowned. 'Because of Sam?'

I nodded.

'But why must I stay with Grandmama?'

'She wishes it. You don't mind, do you?' I wrote.

She shook her head vigorously, her flaxen hair flying. 'I love Grandmama. But when shall I come home?'

Aware my lack of speech made us the focus of attention for our fellow passengers, I quickly scrawled, 'Soon. After she has enjoyed your company for a while. We'll write to each other.'

She turned to Raphael. 'Will you write to me, too?'

'Of course, *piccola amore*.'

'Shall you and Sukie both come to fetch me home?'

We looked at each other and I nodded. His smile made my heart lurch and I had to turn away.

'We will,' he said, softly.

We found Grandmama's carriage waiting for us outside the Swan Inn at Eastleigh and her coachman, Fenton, was able to move our boxes directly across from one conveyance to the other, securing them on the roof. Once inside, we could spread out and take our ease in much more luxurious surroundings. Yet, strangely, I found myself feeling guilty over it. That we had rattled along in the noxious overcrowded public coach seemed right and proper while Sam was imprisoned. This carriage and my grandmother's house to come felt like inappropriate indulgence. Even my feelings for Raphael felt frivolous, somehow. I looked at him then, and finding his eyes on me, this time I did not look away.

'Does your grandmother expect me?' He said, quietly, with Penny sleeping pressed against him.

'Not you specifically. She knows I travel with a friend.' I gestured at Penny. 'You're good with her. She has already grown fond of you.'

That smile again. 'She's delightful. I have many nephews and nieces. I miss them.'

'You have a large family?'

The pain crossing his face was impossible to miss. 'Three older sisters ... two only, now, sadly.'

I reached across to touch his knee. 'I'm so sorry, Raphael. When did she die?'

He took a long breath. 'Gianna ... smallpox. Last November.'

'You were close. I can see that.'

'We were the nearest in age. Artemisia and Claudia are many years older.'

I wondered how it would feel to grow up in such a family. I had always been alone. Well, until Penny anyway. I watched her stir beside him, and he put his arm around her looking down, his eyes soft with kindness. And it was at that moment I knew with certainty, I loved him. Christ help me, what was I to do now? Love and desire. Jesu.

My grandmother, Lady Sylvia Marshall, waited for us on the pillared and porticoed porch in front of her grand cliff-top house. When the coach halted at the stone steps, Penny jumped out and rushed up to launch herself into her arms. Raphael helped me down and I took his arm to follow her. After brief introductions, which my grandmother took entirely in her stride, I led him through the entrance hall with its double staircase soaring up on either side leading to a gallery above. Guiding him on into the drawing room at the back and watching him look around, I saw it all with fresh eyes. It truly is a sumptuous house. He stood before the great window that stretched near enough from floor to ceiling, looking down at the view of the sea, the sky turquoise and gold as twilight began its advance upon it.

'What is the land we see?'

'The Isle of Wight. Those white rocks jutting from the water are the Needles.' When I gazed at the groups of sofas and chairs all upholstered in shades of blue and gold, with a huge Chinese pot of blue and yellow flowers filling the empty fireplace, the room fragrant with their scent, I realised just how special this house is to me, glad I had brought him here.

Raphael turned to me, shaking his head. 'What a sight. It really is quite ... sublime.'

My grandmother joined us then though Penny was not with her.

'Where is she?'

She looked from me to Raphael, eyebrows raised. 'I left her in the kitchens with Cora. Cake was mentioned. Not terribly sensible so close to dinner but I wished to speak with you alone.' Her eyes turned to Raphael. 'But I see you speak in front of *Signor* Rossi. I hope this means you are now quite recovered?'

I chewed my lip. 'No. I'm afraid it doesn't. I tried so hard with Papa. It breaks my heart that I cannot.' I sat and covered my face with my hands briefly, trying to compose myself. When I looked up again Raphael moved to sit beside me. 'I need to tell you everything.'

Grandmama took a chair opposite our sofa, anxiety etched on her face. 'You must. Your letter alarmed me, Susannah. Why would anyone threaten Penny with harm?'

I took a deep breath and told her all I knew. 'We believe the King is acting against Sam, which makes his position extremely dangerous.'

She narrowed her eyes. 'But why has he lost trust in him after placing so much secret foreign business in his hands?'

'Portsmouth–'

'Louise de Kérouaille. The French whore. Yes, Yes, I can see that. I've heard the King is very susceptible to her. Who thought of her in this?'

I turned to Raphael to indicate he should answer.

'The Duchess of Richmond.' He cleared his throat and looked at me. 'Catherine Villiers is involved too, working with Castlemaine.'

My grandmother's face softened. 'Oh, Susannah that must be so difficult for your papa. I never did like that woman.' She smiled. 'And you, I know, always loathed her.'

'It seems we are both fair judges of character, Grandmama.'

'Well, I understand your need to get back to London. Tell Sam I shall pray for him next time you visit and keep me informed as much as possible. And keep pressing him to say where he was that night. I understand why he refuses, that he's protecting a woman … which is, of course, laudable. But whatever the King's agenda, her word would surely get him released and give him a chance to escape the country.' She rose and moved across to me, bending to hug me. 'Don't worry about Penny, she'll be happy here until it is safe for her to return to you.'

'I know,' I said, hugging her tight. We parted and Raphael stood, taking my hand to assist me.

'Your boxes will be in your rooms by now. I'll ring for someone to show you up.'

I patted her arm. 'I know my way. Where have you put Raphael?'

'Across from you.' She gave me a hard look before moving away towards the doors. 'Penny is in with you. It will be easier for her there after you've gone.' The door closed behind her.

'She's very like you.'

'And my mother. When I was young, they looked like sisters both so tiny and fair. Come, I'll show you upstairs.'

I worry about tonight. About what I might do with his chamber so close. The door opens as I am about to write my final words for the day.

Grandmama closes it behind her, checking Penny sleeps before speaking. 'Leave him alone, Susannah. Have not you brought enough trouble already?'

I put down my pen and watch her leave without another word. So, I am not allowed to fall in love? Anger surges hot as fire.

Well, we shall see about that. But it is short lived. Because, of course, she was not talking of love, was she? A woman's lust is not frowned upon now. St Augustine might have seen desire as a rebellion against God, but our King does not. Indeed, he expects it displayed most wantonly for him. Provided maidenheads are saved for the marriage bed.

∼

NOAH

Noah had come to Lieutenant Monkton's Office with Hal at his side again. It was time to share what he had and, as Raphael Rossi and Susanna Gresham were still not returned, it must be with Monkton.

He carried with him a copy of his pamphlet detailing the false accusation of murder made against Sam, with the only evidence being a sword stolen from his house after he had been imprisoned. It also made much of Admiral Lord Carter and his heroic feats against the Dutch in the Battle of Solebay. Noah was more than satisfied with it.

The lieutenant came out from his office. 'Good day, gentlemen.' He gestured towards the room.

Noah sat whilst Hal remained standing in front of the door. The office was too warm despite the open window. 'It's good of you to see us. Signor Rossi asked me to come to you.'

He nodded. 'He wrote to me. So, there've been developments?'

Noah handed him the pamphlet. 'This for a start.'

Monkton studied it with some care. '*In all Innocence: A declaration of false accusation and malicious imprisonment.*' He looked up. 'A clever title. How many have you printed? How are they distributed?'

'Enough. Coffeehouses, taverns, theatres. Everywhere. They've already gone out.'

Monkton leant back and dropped the booklet onto his desk. 'Very well. I'll show it to the King. He needs to know Carter's case is now public knowledge.'

'Good. Let's hope it will make him more circumspect. Am I right in thinking there is some ill will towards him when so many courtiers appear above the law?'

The Lieutenant shrugged slightly. 'I can't deny it, Sir.'

Noah placed his hands flat on Monkton's desk. 'Yet I don't believe those same people will think an innocent man such as Sam should be one made an exception.'

'Agreed.' He placed the pamphlet into a drawer and locked it. 'Have you anything else for me?'

'Not as much as I would wish, unfortunately.' He leaned forward. 'I've learnt Hubert Winks has a brother called Joseph who is married to Elizabeth. I've not yet been able to discover her mother's name and we don't know if any of them survived. But we have names, and my associate has men out searching for them. The fire was a damned tragedy for those caught-up in it and ill-luck for us trying to find the truth.'

'It was certainly that.' Monkton stood. 'I'm sure I need not remind you to be vigilant.'

'No, indeed. I was with Rossi when he was attacked, as you know.' Noah rose to take his leave. 'Still no news of a trial date?'

'No. I don't know which is worse for Carter, knowing or not knowing when it is to be.'

'Knowing must be worse. Until then he can still hope for release without one, if we're successful on his behalf.' It occurred to Noah then that his pamphlet might force the King's hand and hasten it. But it was too late, they were already in circulation. And it was right they were. 'Good day, Lieutenant.'

'God go with you, gentlemen.'

They made their way back to the coach, both wearing swords and both extremely proficient in their use, ready and able to rebuff any threat of violence.

Once inside, Hal cleared his throat. 'I'm sorry, Papa. This must be very difficult for you.'

Noah looked at him in surprise. How extraordinary to be able to speak of it. 'Aye. With that damn fire making it feel like the very gods themselves are against us.' Yet the gods had smiled on him with Hal.

'May I ask you another question?'

Christ. He nodded. What else could he do?

'Do you know why you should love Sam when you never have before?'

It was a good question. 'I'll need to think a bit.' That recognition had come only when Hal had made him consider it. As for why? He rested his head back against the squabs. And again, found he did know when he thought about it. Sam's integrity. His absolute decency. Noah had never heard him rude or impatient with anyone without reason and not often with it. His smile. His touch. His complete abandon in bed. His beauty. Christ, his body. 'I should not talk of this with you.'

'Why? Is it different falling in love with a man?'

Noah laughed. 'How the devil am I supposed to know that? Perhaps when you fall in love with a woman, we can test it?'

RAPHAEL

When the door closed behind Susannah and she left me alone, I sat down on the mattress. Horsehair. Hardly surprising in such a very splendid room with its blue velvet draped gilded bedstead and furniture upholstered in cream silk embroidered with blue flowers. The view from the window was the same, though naturally more spectacular a floor higher even though the window was not quite so expansive. The sky was already fading fast to dusk, but there were sufficient candles burning to adequately compensate for it. I rose to wash with the hot water waiting for me and began dressing for dinner.

Did Lady Sylvia think me Susannah's lover? Was that why Penny would share her room? Though we had come close to it despite her presence. But it must not happen. I had been shamefully careless with her. And it mortified me to think I had expected her to hold back because she had done so before. Yet I had quickly known this time she would not. I knew enough of a woman's desire to sense when she passes the point of no return. What would I have done? Taken her maidenhead up against the wall? Or on the fetid floor? That was not love. It was not even decency. I crossed myself. Thank God it had not happened. And never would.

The court had tempted me, taking me back to a life I had once vowed never to live again. But I could not withdraw from the place. Perhaps now I faced what I had become, I could find some integrity again. Just as I had done before in Florence. But I could not think of that now, not when Susannah filled my thoughts. Still, when I held her … so, Christ help me, I must not.

I quickly dressed in my coat and breeches with the sapphire studded waistcoat. *Dio mio*. Would Susannah think I wished to sell her grandmother gems? Well, it was all Giuseppe had packed for me. I tied my hair with a matching blue ribbon and was apprising myself unfavourably in the cheval mirror when a soft knock sounded on my door. I moved to open it and Susannah slipped inside.

'I'll take you down.'

'You look very lovely, *cara*. Dark colours suit you.' She did indeed look wonderful in indigo satin and silver mantua. And my waistcoat went unremarked, thank God. I reached out to touch her moonbeam hair held up with a single silver pin and closed my eyes for a moment, feeling the same need to pull her into my arms. Her blush told me she felt it too. 'We should go down,' I said, my voice husky.

In the lavish dining room with its own great window looking out over the sea, Lady Sylvia sat at the head of a long walnut table set for just four, with Susannah and Penny to her left. The meal was a light one of clear soup followed by fricassee of chicken and a fruit jelly under an elaborate spun sugar dome. Penny was unusually quiet, and it was clear how tired she was when her eyelids drooped as she struggled to stay awake. Sitting beside her sister wearing a matching blue gown, her pale hair hanging to her waist, it was impossible not to be struck afresh by their remarkable resemblance, though Susannah's eyes were grey and Penny's blue. It was not long before Susannah rose to take her to bed, leaving me to continue my conversation with their grandmother about the foibles of my patrons and the vagaries of the jewellery trade at court. To her credit, she had managed to appear moderately entertained by it.

When the door closed behind her granddaughters, however, she turned to me, her blue eyes suddenly hard as ice chips. 'You're from Italy?'

It was as though she asked if I hailed from darkest Africa or the moon. That she could imagine nowhere more dubious. 'Yes. From Florence.'

'Are you Susannah's lover?'

Well, she was nothing if not direct. 'No.'

'Do you intend to be?'

I blinked, more than a little disconcerted. 'I would never do anything to harm Susannah.'

'I am glad you recognise it would harm her. It would harm her a very great deal. More than you know. So, I'm thankful life at court has not yet jaded you completely.'

'Court ways are not mine.' Though, Holy Christ, they have been. 'It's my place of business.'

'Perhaps you need to remember that's all it is. Your place of trade.'

. . .

I lay awake for some time thinking of Lady Sylvia's words, reminding me the court was a very different place for Susannah as the King's Goddaughter than it was for me. They also brought to mind Frances's advice that virgins should be left to husbands. And, of course, all my women at court had those as did all the others having their own brief liaisons. Just as most men had wives. How sordid it all seemed to me now. How desperate and sad. I truly wished never to have been part of it.

Yet how could my thoughts not turn to Susannah, sleeping so close. Would she come to me tonight and, if she did, what would I do? I hoped I would not be tested for it was not possible to imagine sending her away, however much I knew it to be right. I scrubbed hard at my face. Fuck right, though. Fuck it and damn it to hell. But I would not go to her. I would not. I gasped a breath and crossed myself in determined contrition. I had lived a celibate life before, as penance, and could do so again. I tried to pray but, in truth, it did not seem a suitable matter to raise with God.

Sleep found me, finally, but I woke early ... and alone. Though I had dreamt of her too vividly and was aroused by it still, a condition easily taken care of. I took a long breath then, allowing regret at her absence and the relief of it to sweep over me in equal measure. Moving to the window to part the drapes, flooding the room with early morning sunshine, I saw a figure sitting on a boulder close to the breaking waves. Even from such a distance I knew it was Susannah. I dressed quickly to go down to her.

The air was fresh and pungent with the smell of the sea as I walked across the close-cropped grass to the cliff edge, seeking the flight of steps Penny had told me of, gulls wheeling and shrieking overhead. In my haste, I had left my hair untied and the gusty breeze tossed it around my face until I held it away to watch my footing. At the bottom, although my feet crunched loudly over pebbles, the sound was subsumed in the boom of the sea pounding over stones and the rattling suck of it drawing back. She sat looking out over the water. The heavy childlike braid hanging to her waist filled me with a sudden aching tenderness. It was only at the last moment she heard my approach and turned, her face wet with tears.

I sat beside her, pulling her into my arms. '*Cara?* Susannah. What's wrong?'

She struggled away, scrubbing her face hard on the sleeve of her gown. 'Many things. Too many things, Raphael.' She shook her head. 'Sam. We must get back to help him.'

The thought of more days in the discomfort of a stagecoach horrified me. Not to mention the nights we would need to spend in coaching inns. Alone or with others? Both seemed equally undesirable. 'Then, we must leave straightaway.'

She turned to me, her face tear-streaked and pinched with misery. 'Grandmama has arranged our passage aboard ship from Southampton to St Katherine Dock. It will get us home far sooner.'

I could not help but wonder if this were so, why the coach journey had been necessary at all. She answered before I asked.

'Penny is seasick so unfortunately it was not possible on our journey down.'

After a hurried breakfast and quick tearful goodbyes between Susannah, her sister and grandmother, we were again in the carriage and on our way back to Southampton, this time going as far as the docks on what Susannah told me was Southampton Water. Like all docks, it was noisy, malodourous, and chaotic, with a forest of soaring masts and furled sails silhouetted against the milky morning sky. However, that ships were steadily loaded and unloaded with crates, bales and casks moved by handcarts and horse carts, proved there must be some semblance of order to it.

When the coachman, Fenton, left us to find the captain of the Godolphin and secure us cabins, Susannah frowned at his retreating back moving up the ship's gangway. 'It is unlike her to leave such a detail undone.'

I shrugged. 'Is this a river port?'

'It's a deep-sea inlet from the Solent, which is the channel between the coast and the island.'

We waited, watching the line of merchant ships out on the water, their sails filled and pennants flying, until Fenton returned trailed by two obviously reluctant sailors press-ganged to carry our boxes.

He bowed. 'Master, Mistress. The captain can offer the first mate's cabin or a hammock between decks with the crew for Master Rossi.'

Ah, so all was explained. Lady Sylvia had arranged one cabin for Susannah and her expected female travelling companion. 'A hammock is perfectly acceptable.' I would not force such on the first mate.

She touched my arm when we were alone. 'I'm sorry, Raphael. I should have told her you would accompany me.'

I smiled. 'I feel certain it will present no more hardship than some of the rooms we have endured so far.'

And it did not.

At last, with Southampton Water behind us, we rounded east into the Solent and then beyond the island out into the English Channel in late afternoon. We would then hug the coast before turning north up towards the Thames estuary. The ship was carrying a cargo of bricks from Liverpool, and paper loaded in Southampton – which had caused the delay in sailing – both always in demand in London. The captain had invited us to take our ease at the table in his cabin, where he joined us eventually for a hearty supper of beef stew, coarse bread, and strong ale.

Though Susannah and I had spent so much time in each other's company of late, we did not find conversation difficult in those hours alone together in the cabin or strolling on deck. She did not speak of Sam, so I did not. Perhaps this gave her a little respite. A time to gather strength. We watched the passing coast and were entertained by a pod of dolphins racing us for a while, leaping out of the water precariously before the fast-moving bowsprit.

Then, after supper, I walked on deck beside her once again before I would see her safe to her own cabin in the aftcastle though it would be some hours before full dark. A brisk wind kept the sails taut and straining, so we made good time through undulating waves, which began to make us clutch for the taffrail to keep our footing when the deck plunged beneath our feet. 'The sea is getting rougher, I think.'

She grabbed my arm to steady herself. 'Maybe a hammock might prove the better berth, after all.'

'I shall not mind it, I'm sure.' The swell really was increasing, with water splashing onto the deck when we pitched into a larger wave. I took her arm. 'Come. You should get below.' Her cabin on the lower deck was accessed via stairs little better than a ladder, which proved hazardous for her with skirts to contend with. I led the way to help her, catching her into my arms when she missed her footing at the bottom. I wanted very much to kiss her but instead released her to open the door into the musty, airless space. There were two bunks, one atop the other and a small window, opaque with salt spray.

'Neither of us fare too well with our sleeping arrangements.' She chewed her lip. 'In truth, I see no reason why you shouldn't take the upper bunk–'

'No, Susannah, it's best I don't.' I closed my eyes and kissed her cheek before leaving her there. *Cristo. Cristo.* '*Buonanotte, cara mia.*'

∽

SUSANNAH

Diary: June 5, 1676

So, returned to my own chamber in Henrietta Street, I sit at my desk to write another entry. Once again, I ask myself what am I doing? Once again, I ask if I have finally lost all reason?

On disembarking at St Katherine Dock, we agreed to go immediately to Thomas Monkton at Horse Guards, trusting he already knew of any recent developments, so saving us the time it would take to visit Rotherhithe. I prayed for good news. Then we would go to Sam.

I watched Raphael across from me in the hackney a porter had efficiently secured for us. He looked tired, with dark stubble on his face. Perhaps we should have returned to our homes to refresh ourselves before calling on the lieutenant? Yet I could not shake off my sense of urgency. We had been away too long.

He scratched at his beard and looked up to see my eyes on him. 'Shaving on a pitching ship seemed an unnecessary risk.'

'You look like a pirate.'

He laughed. 'I feel like a vagabond.'

'Well, I imagine neither of us looks at our best.'

He tilted his head, considering me. Caressing me with that damnable smile ... and watching me blush. I do believe he enjoys it. And he knows what it does to me. Of course he does.

'You look wonderful, *cara*.'

'And you, Raphael, are in need of eyeglasses.' I turned away to look out of the window at a drab street, crowded with carts and carriages, horses' hooves clattering along the drizzle-soaked cobbles. I knew my gown was creased and somewhat travel stained, and my hair poorly pinned-up. I patted at it hoping it was not too disreputable, for a pitching ship had been of no help to me, either.

He moved across to sit beside me and began unpinning it. 'Allow me to help.'

'What on earth are–' Then I felt how expertly he took each section and pinned it in place. I patted it again. He had caught it up simply once before. How was this possible? 'I don't know what to say.'

'*Grazie mille*, perhaps?'

'Thank you, I'm grateful. Truly I am.' I gave him a searching look before I understood. 'Ah, I see. You have sisters.'

'And I was their dear little slave boy.'

How could I not love such a man? But could he love me? And could I ever trust him if he did?

At Horse Guards, Raphael helped me down from the carriage and I shook out my skirts. I was horribly afraid though, somehow, he seemed to sense my reluctance to talk of it. He took my arm firmly in his and we walked on together in silence.

I understood immediately we sat before Thomas at his desk, something serious had occurred. And that could mean but one thing. I wrote, 'When?'

'It's most unfortunate. I had hoped ... well, we all did.' He straightened his back. 'The trial will be on the 10th of July in Westminster Hall.'

I lifted my notepad. 'But that leaves us so little time.' How mortifying I still wrote despite him having heard me speak, however sympathetic he was towards me. I glanced at Raphael. They must both think me quite mad. And rightly so. Raphael's light touch on my arm felt like reassurance. That he understood my shame over it made me want to weep with gratitude.

'Especially with the fire, Tom. Has Noah found anything? Does he know of this?'

'I've written to him.' He opened a drawer and removed a pamphlet placing it on his desk. 'Winks's brother has a wife, and I had a note from Bartholomew this morning saying they now know her mother still lives but have not yet found her. So many people are displaced.' He lifted the pamphlet. 'And he had this printed.' He handed it to me and Raphael leaned-in to read it. 'When I showed it to the King, he was angered by it, of course.'

He sighed. 'But he had to know there would be public scrutiny of his actions.'

I wrote, 'And in his anger, he set Sam's trial date?'

'I feared he would keep him locked up indefinitely as he has done with others. Though, admittedly, I had not expected him to act with quite such haste.'

Raphael squeezed my shoulder. 'Let's hope Noah can come up with more information. Finding this mother quickly might help us.'

I nodded. What else could we do but hope?

Thomas rose to his feet to show us out. 'I'm sorry to have given you such distressing news. At least he's not often alone. His father or his manservant keep him company.'

When the door closed behind us, I whispered to Raphael. 'We should go to him straightaway.'

'Yes, we must. But first we need a change of clothing and, in my case, a shave.'

That I did not wish to be parted from him must have shown on my face.

'Perhaps we might go to Henrietta Street first, then to Cheapside and on to the Tower?'

'Yes. Yes, that seems sensible.'

I led Raphael into the hall and rang the bell to summon Bess. Once inside the drawing room with the door closed, I was able to speak quietly before she appeared 'You will still be here when I come down?' I would have taken him up to my chamber, but Bess would be scandalised. Yet after we had shared beds, such segregation now seemed nonsensical.

'I shall be here, *cara*.'

Bess knocked and came in, bobbing a curtsey to both of us.

I looked to Raphael to be my mouthpiece and he nodded slightly. 'Fetch hot water for your mistress and help her dress in a fresh gown.'

'Master.'

'I shan't be long,' I whispered, after she had gone.

With another knock, Bess's head appeared around the door. 'Alice is takin it up now, Mistress.'

I touched Raphael's arm and left the room to follow my maid up the stairs. It felt a long time since I had last done so. In my chamber, I selected a dark green silk gown and a cream lace gorget and Bess helped me remove my soiled clothing.

'Does you wish a clean shift, Mistress?'

I nodded. Well, this I could not have done in front of him. I would have liked to bathe but grudged the time it would take, making do with a quick wash instead. After dressing again, I looked at myself in my long mirror, seeing how well my hair looked and how horribly pale I was.

I took a deep breath, smoothing my skirts, and returned downstairs to Raphael.

The hackney was forced to pull up a little way beyond his Cheapside house as the road was choked with traffic. I had only ever entered from directly outside his front door, so looked with interest at the discreet shop front with its gold lettered sign, *Rossi & Son. Jewellers of Florence* on its wrought-iron bracket. He guided me back past it and up the familiar stone steps into his home.

'Come with me.'

I followed him along a corridor to a short flight of stairs leading down to his workshop. How interesting it should smell so familiar. This was somewhere I had never been before. I looked around at several men and boys busy at the long benches, all glancing up at me surreptitiously. Already I found the heat coming from a small furnace in the corner more oppressive than that from our kiln which, though of a similar size, was built to keep it inside as much as possible, of course. I watched, fascinated, as liquid silver was poured into moulds by one man while another drew malleable gold out into long thin strands.

'Giuseppe,' Raphael called.

He emerged, looking irked, from what appeared to be a small cupboard. 'You look like shit.' He gazed at me then, his eyes alert with speculation. 'She here again.' He grinned.

'Susannah Gresham meet once more my most charming manservant and workshop assistant, Giuseppe Giardini, for however many times it is. I apologise again for his many shortcomings.' He turned to him. 'And it is because I look like shit, I need your attentions.'

Giuseppe removed his leather apron and bowed. 'Whatever you wish my *padrone*. It will be my pleasure.' He walked across to steps that must lead to the kitchens and bellowed, 'Hot water for the master's chamber.' There were some grins and chuckles as he did this. He watched me again. 'She come up?'

I nodded. Why did I feel I could not be parted from him? It was reckless, I knew, but I would do it anyway.

Raphael searched my face, unsmiling. 'She is,' he said, softly.

Our eyes held and I wondered if he saw I loved him. Jesu. Did I wish him to?

Giuseppe tilted his head, giving Raphael a knowing look. 'Thought so. You gonna bathe?'

I pointed to the clock.

'No time.'

He shrugged. 'So, stay *puzzolente*, yes?'

Raphael stared hard at him. 'Shall we just get on with it.' He grasped my hand to take me with him up the two flights of wide stairs to his large chamber at the front of the house. The furniture was of pale gilded wood, the hangings and upholstery embroidered silk in rich, deep colours. I had not seen it properly the last time when the window drapes had been closed.

He saw me eyeing it all. 'My father had it shipped here. He wanted the house to look just as it would in Florence.'

'Strip. You in hurry, *si*?' He glanced at me. 'Just big cock she already know, eh?'

I blinked. *What?*

Raphael's eyes flew to me, wide with embarrassment. '*Cristo*. No, *idiota*. Just clean clothes and a shave. Now get on with it. *Subito*.' A burst of Italian invective followed from them both.

I walked to the window looking down on the busy wet street, the cobbles dark and dull as coal. It looked like chaos in some version of Hell. Jesu. I gripped the sill before turning back to the room and watching Giuseppe rifle through presses and cabinets before making his selection in assorted blues and greys. 'These?'

Raphael waved his hand impatiently. 'Fine.'

'So, you gonna put em on over them ones?'

'*Cristo mi preservi*.' Raphael took off his coat and waistcoat, letting them fall to the floor before sitting on his bed to remove his stockings.

Still at the window, I saw the rain had now become a deluge and I closed my eyes, praying I was not about to weep. Sam. Dear God, we had to do something for him.

'*Cara*?'

I glanced over my shoulder and shook my head, seeing he now wore only his shirt and Giuseppe was about to begin his shave.

'You want this, or no?'

I heard Raphael sigh and then the scraping of a razor.

'She no much to say for erself?'

Another loud rancorous dispute in rapid Italian commenced, which I thought posed as much threat as a pitching ship when one party held a razor.

'Giuseppe, *ti ordino di tacere*.'

'Order me shut up you little shit, see what good it do.'

But he said no more.

'You may leave us now. I shall dress myself. Take the dirty clothing and water away.'

'Course I take em. What you think I fucking do, eh? Kick em

in a corner?' He scooped them up and left, muttering darkly in Italian.

I turned back to the room, finding him pulling on a clean shirt.

He shrugged. 'We can be a little fiery.'

'I think you are good friends.'

He laughed. 'Though he does occasionally pretend to be my manservant. He's also an excellent jeweller.'

'I don't suppose I should be in here with you. It was probably a mistake. Servants will gossip.' They would make assumptions about us just as Giuseppe had.

He held my gaze, putting on his waistcoat. Serious now. 'Perhaps they will. Forgive me for not minding it when I should have done.' He frowned appearing a little puzzled. 'Giuseppe is usually more perceptive.' He moved to the mirror to tie his cravat. 'We must be away.' He pulled on his coat and after a final cheek in the mirror, we went down.

Sam was philosophical about the trial date, but his air of melancholic acceptance made my heart ache for him. Jesu. I am too tired and dispirited to continue. I rub my blurring eyes. How sad it feels to be alone in a bed chamber after so many nights when I was not. And how much I would welcome Raphael's arms around me now but that cannot be for I know all too well where it would lead. I think of Sam in his prison and Raphael in his gilded room. I know who should fill my thoughts but, to my shame, I know who truly does.

Chapter Nine
RAPHAEL

We had visited Sam each day in the weeks since our return to London and I found it hard to witness Susannah's distress afterwards, though she kept it hidden from him. Worse, his trial was upon us and still we had nothing.

Now, after spending our usual time with him, we made our way to see Noah in Rotherhithe, having received a cryptic note summoning us to discuss certain plans.

Susannah sat beside me in the hackney, looking desolate. 'Plans for how we shall bear to see him die?'

'Let's hope he has some good news.'

'Then he'd have said so in his note.'

What could I say to comfort her? 'Try to stay hopeful, *cara*.' Impressive, no?

However, she did turn to me with a wan smile. 'Yes, I shall try. You're right. I cannot be any help to him if I despair.' She chewed her lip. 'Jesu. Will he die rather than give up this damnable woman?'

'It would seem so.' That there was no woman to reveal meant, of course, any such disclosure would only provide another route to a convenient death.

The carriage stopped at Shadwell Stairs where one of Noah's

lighters waited for us. I helped Susannah down and took her arm, leading her through an alley between ramshackle sheds – crowded with watermen, raucous fishwives, and assorted ruffians – and beyond onto the wooden wharf. As it was low tide, the slippery jetty taking us to the boat crossed a stretch of reeking mud scattered with silver pools reflecting the bright overcast sky and strewn with detritus carried by the river. Bloated dead fish. Other drowned things considerably fouler. Wading birds abandoned their feasting when mudlarks moved in to delve, while gulls swooped overhead, their one-note cries filling the air.

A stiff breeze out on the river, brought welcome relief from the stench. With light sparkling on the wind-ruffled water, Susannah sat pressed close. 'Whatever he wants with us, it'll be important and in Sam's very best interests.' Noah's feelings for Sam made that a certainty.

She patted my hand. 'Yes, I know it will. He's a good friend to Sam.'

We were soon across the Thames and making our way to Noah's office, where we were expected and quickly taken in to see him.

He stood, briefly, gesturing for us to sit. 'Forgive me for bringing you here rather than coming to you but I've a ship just in and a fragile cargo to see unloaded. Hal's there in my place for the moment.' He cleared his throat. 'I've given much thought to what can be done for Sam when he's released. How we can get him to safety.'

I glanced at Susannah, seeing her frown. 'Noah, unless we find Winks or one of his family who knows where he is, Sam's in the gravest danger. His trial is tomorrow.'

His eyes narrowed. 'I know when his fucking trial is, Raphael, and I still intend to find the killer. I learnt this morning we have the wife's mother, and someone is questioning her as we speak.' He took a deep breath. 'So, the King must release him, if only briefly, until another false charge is brought.

That's why we should act immediately. And we can't do it without a plan already in place. So, this is what I've done. I hope you'll see why I couldn't write to you of it.' He looked from me to Susannah. 'Complete secrecy is vital. Letters can be intercepted.'

Well, Noah had not given in to despair and I saw how his words affected her, with real hope there on her face now. I felt it too. This woman, pray God she would somehow give us proof of Sam's innocence. 'Perhaps you might tell us what you propose.'

'Sam will exchange clothing with Connor in his coach before meeting you, Raphael, in Whitechapel. You'll be waiting in a hackney which will take you to St Katherine Dock while Connor returns to Henrietta Street as Sam.' He raised his eyebrows. 'I thought it rather fitting as the King escaped disguised as a manservant after Worcester. I shall be at the dock with my lighter ready to take us to the Mirabel.' He gestured towards the river. 'Already berthed here with some boxes of Sam's possessions to be loaded onboard shortly. It's not without risk, of course. It seems likely the Carters' coach will be followed so speed is of the essence. Should the transfer be witnessed?' He shrugged. 'Well, then, we might encounter a few problems. But if we're quick enough, all should be well.'

Susannah's eyes shone, brimming with tears. She wrote, 'I pray it will be so.'

I cleared my throat. 'I think Sam is extremely lucky to have you as a friend.'

'Debatable,' he murmured. 'Don't tell him of it yet. I shall have a letter with Connor, so he understands exactly what is to happen. I think knowing it all now would unsettle him. He knows only that I have a ship waiting for him.'

Susannah wrote, 'Where will he go?'

'Port Royal in Jamaica. He should be able to disappear with ease in that lawless place.'

We stood to leave. I shook his hand and he kissed Susannah's. 'I'll pray for your success.'

'I'm still waiting to hear what has been learnt from the woman, but I'm more than hopeful. I'll keep you informed.'

Back inside a hackney, Susannah turned to me. 'If ... when it happens, I shall go with you to Whitechapel–'

'No. You heard what Noah said. It could be dangerous if things don't go to plan.'

'For you also.' She gestured at my sword. 'You're prepared to use that, are you? Do you even know how?'

I frowned. Why would she presume me unskilled with a sword? The fact she was correct was of less importance than her reason for making such an assumption. 'Why on earth would you think such a thing?'

She blinked. 'You don't touch it. You're not aware of it. Men who know a sword as a weapon rather than attire, do. Noah does.'

Merda. Of course, everything she said was entirely accurate. I was no swordsman, though the term had an additional connotation at court which she might think more appropriate in my case. Though, I hoped, without the touching tell. 'Susannah, this has nothing to do with my swordsmanship or lack of it. It's simply not safe for you to be there.'

She lifted her chin. 'I shall say farewell to Sam. How can you even think of denying me such a thing? You have no right to. Neither does Noah.' She blinked back tears. 'I don't believe you'll be so cruel.'

I grasped her hand. Christ. What could I say? Should they not have the chance to say goodbye? In happy circumstances ... or not. I sighed and smiled. 'Well, I suppose we must take our chances together, then.'

She flung her arms around me. 'Don't worry, Raphael, I shall have a phial of poison with me so I can defend us both.'

I laughed, enfolding her in mine. Holy God, how good it felt to hold her again. 'Then, I'm sure we'll be entirely safe.' In truth, it would likely be more useful in that regard than my sword.

. . .

The evening found me back at the Tower. Sam had asked me to stay with him overnight and it seemed the least I could do if he felt my company might help him. How could I even begin to imagine his suffering on such a night? They had changed his lodging to a finer one. Why? It would do naught but disorientate him. Was that the intent because his trial was tomorrow? Or so he would not see the scaffold already there on Tower Hill? Pragmatism or the outcome a certainty? Then it occurred to me it might not be for him if Tyburn was his destination.

He had dressed in fine clothing – a damson brocade coat and waistcoat edged in gold – and had shaved his beard, revealing deep hollows in cheeks. *Cristo.* How thin he had become. His eyes, sunken and bloodshot, were those of a man who looked to close at death.

'Papa wished to stay again but felt compelled to try for one last audience with the King. He'll beg William Chiffinch for it though he detests the man, for unfortunately he guards the King's time as diligently as he procures him women.' He sighed. 'His conscience demanded it of him, yet I'm certain it will serve no purpose. Even Monmouth has been unable to sway his father on it and if he cannot, no one can. Connor offered to stay in Papa's place but ... I don't mean to belittle him. I need talk to distract me tonight.'

He looked up at me, briefly, from his chair beside the window with a view out across the Thames, glossy and benign in the early evening light, and then back down at his hands. 'For I am afraid, Raphael. I couldn't say that to him. To either of them, in truth.' He held his forehead. 'I fear I'm quite unmanned by it.'

I squeezed his shoulder. 'As anyone would be.' I wondered if speaking in his mother's native tongue brought him comfort? I rather thought it must. The language that had soothed him as a child.

'I don't fear death ... a quick death. But the one the King

wishes for me? Christ, I thought he loved me. He always said he did.'

I pulled up a chair and sat facing him. 'I've spoken with Frances again and she's doing everything she can to remind him of it. You're his Godson, Sam.'

'Does Susannah know you visited her?'

'What?'

He tilted his head. 'You must know she loves you? She near swoons every time she looks at you.' He shook his head. 'Jesu, man. And your eyes barely leave her. Tell her. Time is precious, I know that now. Neither of you should waste another moment of it.'

Dio mio. I was desperate to tell her, but it must wait until Sam was safe – please God it would be so. He was foremost in her mind now, and so he must be in mine. And he was for his own sake. I could not allow myself to imagine how she would be if he were executed. Such a thing seemed unimaginable. I already felt the weight ... the privilege of her dependence on me. We had grown even closer over the last weeks, and it terrified me I would not be able to help her then. That what I had to offer her would not be enough.

I looked away. 'She accompanied me to see the duchess.'

He snorted. 'Well, of course she did. Though I doubt Frances Stuart can influence him now, any more than the others. He's made up his mind and won't change it. He's stubborn ... even for a King.'

'This mother will know something, I'm certain of it. Then he'll have to release you. Noah's pamphlet will help, too. Is it not so you've been talked of in Parliament?'

'So my father tells me. Yet it seems unlikely you'll find the man whatever this lady knows.' He slumped further in his chair. 'Perished in the fire, most like.'

I reached across and grasped his upper arm, giving him a slight shake. 'Noah is still working for you. Don't give up, Sam. Put your trust in God.' I crossed myself.

'His Will? Perhaps it's for me to die. Have you thought of that?' He scrubbed at his face. 'But enough of my melancholy. I reek of self-pity. 'Have you a family, Raphael?'

'I have. Parents. Sisters.'

He relaxed back in his upholstered chair. 'Well, you have heard something of mine, so tell me of yours.'

So that is what I did. *Mamma*, daughter of the Moretti dynasty of Florentine jewellers. *Papà's* drive in business and indifference to his family. His mistresses. Gianna's death. Artemisia. Claudia. My many nephews and nieces. My Moretti cousins.

'Sounds like your family gatherings might be a touch chaotic. But nicely so, I would think.'

'Oh, yes, definitely chaos but a special kind of Florentine chaos which is at a different level altogether. Often involving competitive shouting to drown each other out.'

He laughed. 'Our family gatherings always involved too much silence. I should love to witness your kind.'

'I think you might change your mind about that with some rapidity.'

His face became wistful. 'What will Susannah make of them, I wonder?'

'Susannah?' I closed my eyes.

'I want her to be happy, Raphael, and you can make her so. I know you can.' He leaned forward to place his hand on mine. 'I've tried to care for her … to help her. She was quite unwell after her mother died and especially so when the Villiers invaded her life, as I'm sure she's told you.' He held my gaze. 'But we both know I'll no longer be able to do so, for I shall either be dead, which is the outcome I would wager upon, or I'll flee. Noah has a ship already waiting to spirit me away to the West Indies in disguise, I don't doubt, for there are those who will not easily see me go.'

'What can I say? You're right about my feelings for her … and seem confidant of hers for me–'

'I know her very well indeed, so I'm entirely confidant, Raphael. You should marry her.'

I smiled. I shrugged. 'Perhaps.' He would never see it. Though her grandmother had. Clear and plain. 'Why would her father see me as a suitable match for her? I attend court as an artisan ... a tradesman, and she is the King's Goddaughter.'

'I think you might be surprised.' He tipped his head back, his eyes fixed on my face. 'Our parents followed the King around Europe before the restoration, where he lived on the generosity of others. It was entirely possible he may have remained in exile for the rest of his life. Susannah and I were both born in Paris. It was not a conventional life or a conventional choice to remain with an exiled King. So perhaps Richard is not a conventional man.'

At that point, a supper of cold pigeon pie, bread and cheeses arrived for us, together with a very large jug of strong ale. I poured for us both and we drained our pewter tankards, sitting opposite each other at the gleaming mahogany table. I poured again. 'Eat,' I said, pointing to the pie. He cut a slice and bit off a small mouthful, chewing in a desultory sort of way before putting it down to drain his tankard again. 'You must eat.' But neither of us showed much appetite.

When – after some considerable time filled more with increasingly meandering conversation than eating – the ale jug was empty, he stood a little unsteadily, his chair scraping sharply on the oak boards when he pushed it back. I had allowed him the larger share as his need seemed somewhat greater than mine, though I doubted he would thank me in the morning. Yet a pounding head would likely be the least of his concerns then.

'Have you the hour, my friend?' Back to English in his cups.

For a moment, the river caught my eye where night seemed to rise-up from its depths like black satin streamers amidst the sun-glittered ruffles. I blinked. So to consult my timepiece – that is – to squint at it until I could discern the roman numeral for ten. 'Ten, Signore.' At that moment, the bells of St Peter ad Vincular, facing Tower Green, struck ten. I felt absurdly pleased I had it correct.

'Ha. It is so.' He shook his head as though shaking loose a lost train of thought. 'Then, good sir, we should retire.' I followed him through to the bedchamber with its impressively large four-poster, which it seemed we must share. Somehow, he managed to struggle out of his clothes without falling over, dropping them onto the none to clean floor. I retrieved them to lay over a chair. If he were to wear them tomorrow the floor seemed hardly the best place to overnight them. I did the same with my own, for they were definitely required. Giuseppe would never believe it of me.

Then, in our stale shirts, we lay far apart in the wide feather-bed, the drapes open to allow in a little air from the casement left open a crack. I settled back into the deep goose down. I had not expected such ease. The room spun a little. It would be worse for him. I hoped he would not puke. But, instead, he wept. I moved close to him.

'Forgive me.' He wiped his face on the lace cuff of his sleeve. 'I am very horrible drunk and full of stinking pity for myself.'

I raised up on my elbow to look down at him. 'There is nothing to forgive. I should not have poured you full of ale.' And who would not pity themselves now?

He chuckled, wetly. 'Pissing all night.'

'We both shall.'

He turned to look at me. 'Favour of you, Sir? Not offended if you refuse.'

Knowing what I knew of him ... of his secret predilection, I began to feel a little uneasy. 'I hope I can. What is it?'

'Arms around me?'

Merda. Dio. 'Sam. I'm sorry, I don't ... I can't do–'

'Christ, not that. Not asking that. Why in name ... in God's name would I? It's comfort. Touch. Feeble, I know. Papa holds me in the night till sleep. Christ. So very fucking drunk. Please God, not remember in the morning. And don't you.'

But when I pulled him into my arms, he did not resist. With his bones so sharp beneath his shirt, I felt only an aching tenderness for him. And such pity for his unimaginable plight. 'Try to sleep, *amico mio*.'

'Raphael, let me tell you, something, yes? Three types of men at court, yes? Men like you. Men like me, and fucking men like James Villiers who'll fucking fuck anything with a heartbeat ... or without one, yes? You and I, we know who we are. What we are.'

When he finally fell into sleep, I moved away from him a little. Jesu, it was so much easier to be my kind than his. I prayed for him and then, God help me, I thought of Susannah.

The next morning, I travelled with Sam inside the carriage taking him to Westminster Hall and his trial. We were taciturn when we woke, both hungover. He more so than I, of course. In truth, I could not think what to say to him. Indeed, what was there to say? The lieutenant generously arranged a manservant to shave us and help us dress and a good breakfast was served but, again, we ate little.

The carriage had barred windows and a burly guard sat opposite, sneering. 'Top to see a gent be getting is, like.'

I turned to Sam, speaking in Italian. 'Seems we have a prick for company.'

The guard scowled puffing out his chest, relishing his tiny taste of power. 'Oi. Speak bleedin King's English.'

Sam folded his arms. 'Really? When he seems incapable of it himself.'

Somehow, it felt easier to talk to him in my own language and maybe it offered him further comfort. And I was certainly perverse enough to do so because it aggravated the churl who now rummaged in his nose with his forefinger, examining the result with interest before disposing of it in his mouth. 'How will the trial work? Who sits in judgement?'

'The Lord Steward. James Butler, Duke of Ormonde. A good friend of my father's and of the King's. There will be two lesser judges sitting with him.'

That should help you, surely. That he is your father's friend?'

'And the King's. I think one friend is somewhat more influential, no?'

The guard thrust his face towards us. 'Speak bleedin English, you buggers.' Spit was sprayed.

Ignoring him, I punched Sam's arm, lightly. 'You look a little better, I think.'

He shrugged. 'Rather a low starting point, so probably doesn't signify.'

We talked then of Florence and all the places I would show him when we travelled there together, provoking regular commands to speak in English which we continued to disregard. He spoke of his mother's family estate in the hills near *Maiano*, seeming to walk in olive groves he had never seen, both of us hearing the calling song of cicadas and feeling the heat of fruity-spice scented air. I wanted him to hold on to it, keeping his mind there as long as he could.

On arrival at our destination when we had to part company, I kissed him on both cheeks. 'Go with God, dear Sam.' When the churl led him away rather roughly, I was pleased to see it made him smile. I crossed myself, discreetly, asking for the Holy Mother's intercession. *O mother of the Word Incarnate. Despise not my petitions, but in your mercy, hear and answer me.* Well, it helped me compose myself if nothing else.

Inside the long hall, the tiered benches were filling up beneath high windows where light flooded in under the soaring oak ceiling arches. Lord Carter sat beside Susannah's father. I was contemplating joining them when I felt a light touch on my back and turned to find her there, dressed in grey, sombre as tears. She glanced at the door, still open for people to enter, and gestured towards it. We moved outside to a quiet corner of the lobby.

She turned her back to the crowd and rested her hand on my arm. 'They wouldn't let me see him. How is he? How was he last night?'

'I got him drunk.'

She frowned.

I shrugged. 'At least he slept. I held him in my arms until he did. Christ. How unimaginable it is. I try to put myself where he is, but fear pulls me back.' For I am, without doubt, a coward. She looked pale and tired. And much too slender, just as he did. '*Cara*. Let's hope Noah finds something, even now. There is still this Elizabeth's mother. Maybe the answer lies with her.'

'Why does he still refuse to name the woman? Why, in the name of God, is he ready to sacrifice himself for her?'

'I have no answer.' None that would save him. I took her arm, leading her back inside the hall to sit beside her papa. She hugged him and Sam's father, too, then I heard her gasp. The Countess of Castlemaine had arrived beside Catherine Villiers Gresham both in full finery, enough so to stand out against the more soberly attired spectators. They were clearly dressed to celebrate. Cunts.

Susannah wrote, 'No words are adequate to convey the depth of my loathing.'

I turned back to the door in time to see Frances enter, dressed in plain indigo. After scanning the crowd, she smiled heading towards us. When Susannah stiffened, I stood.

Sir Richard and Rupert Carter rose to greet her formally. 'You Grace.'

'Duchess,' I said.

She kissed me on the cheek. 'Raphael. This is a sad day I hoped never to witness.'

Then she bent to kiss Susannah who had remained seated. 'I wish I could have prevented it, my dear.' She turned to the two fathers. 'Truly, I do.'

When we were all seated once more with Frances beside me, she spotted Castlemaine and Catherine and tilted her head in towards me. 'Never have I seen two ladies display such surfeit of bosom and deficit of intellect.'

The doors to the hall were closed by an attendant and a buzz of excitement travelled around the room, followed by a collective gasp when the door behind the dais opened. The Lord Steward and the two judges – red robed with grey rice-powdered peri-wigs – took their seats, the Duke of Ormonde tall and commanding on the high-backed chair in the centre, the great chain of state resting on his black velvet-clad chest. Above him the King's full-length portrait stared sternly out at us.

Another door at the top of the hall opened then and Sam was led in by a guardsman with Sir Henry Willets following. Susannah began to tremble, and I took her hand bringing it down against my thigh, hidden in the folds of her skirts. 'He looks composed,' I whispered. I saw her eyes were fixed on him. In truth, everyone's were.

Sam took his seat in the dock. And so, it began. Willets stood at the table between the two banks of tiered seating and began to sort his papers.

Frances leaned in again. 'He will put the case for the crown. Read out statements. Call witnesses.'

'Who?'

She frowned. 'I don't know. Considering the agenda behind this, perhaps anyone ready to traduce Samuel.' She looked across the floor at Catherine Villers on the front row. 'She's certainly dressed for the occasion. So her, I'm certain.'

And, indeed, she was the first to be called. But before that Willets outlined the case, describing how I had found the body and how later, Sam's sword had been discovered.

Eventually Catherine Villiers, standing at the table below the bench, spoke her name, swore an oath on the bible, and proceeded to tell a pack of lies. Richard Gresham watched her with a look of utter contempt upon his face. I saw it replicated on Susannah's.

Willets eyed her. 'Can you describe a confrontation between the deceased, your son James Villiers, and the accused Samuel Carter at this year's Royal Twelfth Night Ball?'

She lifted her chin and stared hard at Sam. 'I saw an argument between them.' She pointed. 'He spoke to my son in a low manner, telling egregious lies about him. Then he drew his sword.' There was a gasp from the onlookers. She looked up at them on both sides in turn, nodding. 'And I told him to put it up, for to use it was a treason against the King. When he did so, I took my son away to ensure his safety.'

The place erupted in uproar. I squeezed Susannah's hand 'None of that is true. I was there. It was Villiers who began to draw; she made him stop. Sam told Tom this. Why is it only her twisted version we are hearing?

Frances tilted her head. 'Why do you think, Raphael?'

The clerk called for order again and again until there was silence once more.

Willets lifted another paper from the table. 'Will you now tell the court about a second occasion when the accused was violent towards your deceased son, James Villiers?'

Her eyes narrowed. 'My son was enticed to commit an act of fornication by the whore employed by Susannah Gresham as her lady's maid.' When her gaze found Susannah, heads turned, following it.

Susannah gasped a breath though she met Catherine's regard unflinchingly.

Satisfied, Catherine turned back to the judges. 'I heard sounds of a struggle and shouts from the kitchens and found my son collapsed upon the floor having been punched on the nose by him.' Again, she pointed.

Susannah wrote, 'No. He raped Bess.'

Next, Willets began to read out the written statements about the case – including my own – with each accepted into evidence by the duke. Connor was called to tell the court of the whereabouts of Sam's sword at the time he was arrested. I watched the spectators continue their chatter, taking little notice. He was but a servant after all and he did not present himself with any confidence, mumbling and difficult to follow. So, when someone spoke the truth, it seemed no one listened.

Willets read out more statements. The coroner's detailing the cause of death. Courtiers confirming last sightings of Villiers that night. Palace guards on locating the sword. Hubert Winks was named but no mention was made of his disappearance. That was when I ceased to listen, though Willet's voice droned on and on. '*Merda.*'

'Precisely,' Frances said.

Susannah began to tremble again, though with rage this time. I could tell by her clenched jaw, though there were tears still. I felt it, too, because I could do absolutely nothing.

The two fathers talked quietly together; Lord Carter voiced bewilderment that his son would not defend himself, while Sir Richard stared across at his wife with pure malevolence etched on his face. How he must regret bringing her into his family and introducing her and her abhorrent son at court. An act that would likely cost his dear friend his only child. I pitied them both. But most of all I pitied Sam. It was hard to imagine how it could have gone worse for him unless someone had claimed to witness the act. I turned to Frances. 'What will happen now?'

'James Butler will confer with his two lackies over wine and cakes before finding Samuel guilty.'

I looked at the others. They already knew this to be true. When a tear ran slowly down Rupert Carter's cheek, he did nothing to halt its progress.

The proceedings were at last wound up. The duke and the judges left the hall by the door at the back of the dais and Sam was led away while they deliberated. Most people stood to stretch their legs with others leaving the hall. I looked at Susannah who told me with her eyes and a slight nod she wished to leave also. When we did Frances moved to the men, ready to offer what little comfort she could.

We wove our way through the throng to find our quiet corner again. I wanted to take her in my arms. 'Are you all right?' It was an idiotic question. I shook my head. 'Of course you're not. Is there anything I can do for you, *cara*?'

She stared at me, her face white apart from two spots of hectic colour high on her cheeks. 'I really don't think there is, Raphael.'

I moved closer to her, and she pressed hard against me briefly before stepping away with a sigh. She needed comfort from me, but I had none to offer her. We stood close, isolated in our private silence for a while, for there seemed nothing else to be done. How could I love her this way yet be quite unable to help her? When people began streaming back inside the hall my gut clenched in shock. 'Christ. They can't have made a decision already? *Santa Dio.*'

She grasped my hands. 'I cannot– Raphael, how shall I bear it?'

'With me beside you. He'll need to see you there, *cara.*' Especially as Noah was not.

She nodded, standing straighter and lifting her chin. I knew Noah's absence meant he had not yet given up the fight. For, how could he? Please God, we had not run out of time. I took her arm to lead her back to our places. Frances now sat between the two fathers. Both had composed themselves and seeing this Susannah, by sheer force of will, did the same.

The Lord Steward led the return. Soon Sam sat in the dock, once more. Willets took a paper from the duke and read it without reaction. 'The accused will rise.'

He did, looking distant. I prayed he had his mind in *Maiano* again, standing in the olive groves his mother had told him of so vividly. '*Santo Cristo.*' I crossed myself, doubting any eyes were upon me.

'The verdict of this court is that you are found guilty of high treason against the King.'

Uproar once more. Susannah slumped against me. I bowed my head and prayed, quietly. '*Ave Maria, gratia plena. Benedicta tu mulieribus, et benedictus fructus ventris tui, Iesus. Sancta Maria, Mater Dei, ora pro nobis peccatoribus, nunc, et in hora mortis nostrae. Amen.* I crossed myself, again.

When James Butler, Duke of Ormonde, Lord Steward of

England stood to pass sentence, the hall became silent in an instant. He looked down at Sam, his expression cold and hard as granite. 'Samuel Giacomo Rupert Carter, you shall be taken to a place of execution where you shall be hanged by the neck, then cut down alive, your privy-member cut off, and bowels taken out to be burned before your face, your head severed from your body and your body divided into four parts, to be disposed of as the King should think fit.'

Sam showed no reaction. Catherine Villiers and Castlemaine smiled. Fucking cunts. Susannah rocked forward and I thought she would swoon. *Cristo.* I held on to her, meeting Frances's gaze. 'When?'

'Soon. Days, only.' She rose. 'Now I shall return to Whitehall and beg the King for the mercy of the axe.'

∼

NOAH

Noah climbed the stairs to Jacob Gold's Tooley Street office, this time with Hal beside him. Two swords again, especially when he knew there were those determined to prevent help being found for Sam in Southwark.

'We must get something from this woman. I won't accept it's not possible.' He cleared his throat, hoping it had covered the catch in his voice, though Hal's expression told him it had not. 'I cannot accept it.' Jacob's note maintained the old woman had lost her wits and would be of no use. 'His trial is today for Christ's sake. So, she is my final hope.' Which was why at the last moment, rather than going to Westminster Hall, he had set out for Southwark instead. To fight for Sam until the end. And he refused to believe this was it. They now knew her daughter Elizabeth still lived, too. The landlady where she lodged had told Jacob's man so. And this Elizabeth was married to Hubert Winks's brother Joseph. The woman needed to be found so her mother must tell him where she was. It was as simple as that.

They found Jacob standing at his window looking down on the devastation from the fire behind his house. Noah moved to stand beside him. 'They've cleared a lot in so short a time.' On his last visit the site had still smouldered with no bare ground visible amongst the great mound of blackened timbers.

Noah gestured for Hal to come forward. 'Jacob. My son, Hal.'

'Master Gold. I'm pleased to meet you, Sir. Papa has told me much about you.'

Jacob smiled, looking from one to the other. 'But how wonderful you are so alike. Two giants, eh?'

'Everyone is a giant to you, Jacob.' He tried to keep his face impassive though he seethed with urgency.

Hal looked down at the scorched ground. 'Will they rebuild it, Sir?'

'They will. In bricks and stone so lives shall not be so easily lost again.'

'But where will the poor go? Hal asked.

Jacob shrugged. 'They'll move on to another warren until it, too, burns. Perhaps when there are no more such places, they might be more safely housed at last.'

Noah turned to look down at him. His face was scourged by the pain he endured day and night from those swollen and twisted joints. How could they still function? 'The man who spoke to the Smallwood women? Is he sound?'

'He is very young but knows what he's doing.'

Noah wondered how much he knew of bereaved mothers. 'Where might we find her? She must be worth another try.'

Jacob touched his arm with gnarled fingers. 'Things are getting desperate. I pity you, my friend.'

Noah's sigh sounded closer to a groan. 'Sam will be found guilty even though the valet knows his sword was still in his house after the murder was committed.' He shook his head. 'But the King wants him silenced. God's wounds, why would he leave his sword there anyway? No one has explained that assumed piece of idiocy.' No. That hiding was a careful thing. Horror at the act would have left it dropped at the scene. Mindful concealment would have had it safe away.

Jacob hobbled to his desk to open a drawer. 'Grace Smallwood's address. Her lodgings are not far.'

Noah looked at the paper. 'I know it.'

'Go with God, my dears.'

He patted his friend's shoulder gently. 'You too, Jacob, and thank you for all you've done. Come, Hal.'

Out on Tooley Street, they kept up a fast pace to get to Kettle Court. Ahead was a barrow selling oranges. Noah stopped, arrested by their brightness on such a grey morning. They glowed. If hope had a colour, then this was it. He bought two and put one in each pocket of his coat. They would eat them on the Mirabel, sailing to Jamaica.

Hal said nothing.

Grace Smallwood slept, her cheeks hollow, her toothless mouth so caved-in she appeared entirely lipless. When the landlady opened the door to the tiny dark chamber Noah had thought her dead, turning to the woman in some alarm.

'She be all good, Sir. If you lets her wake when she be ready, she will talk to you. Loses her wits if woken. The lad before were irked by her. She screamed her bleedin' head orf, she did.'

So, Noah waited at her bedside. It was the opposite of what he wished to do. Fizzing with anxiety, he needed to act. He stared at the cot and the filthy threadbare blanket covering the woman. There was barely room for the battered table beside it with its rushlight and the stool upon which he sat. The walls were water-stained and streaked with black mould in all the corners. It smelt of damp and piss, and something else pungent he could not identify. Mercifully, he imagined.

Hal stood beside the narrow unglazed window, facing into the room. There was nowhere else for him. 'I thought her dead,' he whispered.

'So did I. Thought the game was up for us for a moment there.'

Hal scrubbed at his face. 'Christ. I hope she knows where her daughter is?'

'I'm with you on that, lad.' Time passed slowly. Noah closed his eyes and tried to slow his breathing. The landlady knocked and carried in a tray with a jug of small beer and three wooden cups. Well, she clearly expected the old woman to wake. God's blood. Sam's trial would be over before she did at this rate.

'Who be yous?' said a querulous voice. 'Why yous in here?'

Noah looked up. 'My name is Noah Bartholomew, Mistress Smallwood.' He gestured towards Hal. This is my son.' There was no time to gentle her. 'I urgently need to speak with your daughter Elizabeth Winks. Can you tell me where I might find her?

'Betsy? Why you wants her?' Then she remembered her family's tragedy. 'My poor girl. Her man, he seems gone in the fire. His brother too. And my poor little scrap.' Tears spilled, pooling in the hollows of her cheeks. 'My other babe ... I thinks–' She closed her eyes while tears streamed.

Noah bit his lip hard, knowing he must remain patient. 'I am sorry for all your terrible misfortune, Mistress. But it is very important I find your daughter, Betsy.'

She frowned, dabbing at her dripping nose with claw-like fingers. 'Why?'

'A man's life depends on it.'

He saw some sympathy in her waterlogged eyes then. 'She be a maid for the Gresham's of Henrietta Street–'

'Fuck. Sweet holy fuck.' They ran. Down the staircase barely wide enough for their shoulders, their feet turned sideways on narrow treads which groaned like living things bearing their weight. Then outside into the street and back towards the St Mary Overie Stairs where their boat waited. 'Whitehall. Tom Monkton.'

Noah gasped. He looked up at the sky where the sun had at last broken through. Midday. The oranges bounced against his thighs as he ran.

When others saw them approaching, they moved out of their path. Two men of their size were weapons moving at such a speed. Soon they raced across the dock before jumping down into the lighter. 'Hall Stairs. Quick as you can, lads.' Noah collapsed at the back of the boat, dropping his head into his hands, trying to catch his breath. 'God help me. God help me.' He gasped over and over.

Hal knelt beside him. 'What do you need from me, Papa?'

He looked at his son, his eyes brimming, and for the first time in his life he knew he needed him more than he was needed. 'Stay with me, Hal. Please just stay with me.'

Hal hugged him. 'I'm here for however long you need me.'

As soon as the boat touched the quay they were over the side, up the stone steps and running for Horse Guards and Monkton's Office. The guardsman at his desk outside tried to bar their way. Noah shoved him aside. Hard. 'Can't allow it, lad,' he said with the last of his breath.

Thomas appeared momentarily stunned by Noah and Hal's abrupt entrance. 'What the–'

The guardsman stood in the doorway. 'Tried to stop em, Sir.'

Thomas waved him away. 'Close the damn door.' He waited for it to be done. 'Bartholomew? What in the name of Christ has happened?'

He was still trying to find his breath.

'Susannah Gresham's maid is Elizabeth Winks. Married to Joseph Winks brother to Hubert,' Hal said.

Noah stared at him. Well, he was twenty years younger. Nice and succinct, too. Oxford or Harrow, perhaps? Money well spent. His bloody mind was rambling. He tried to pull himself together.

Tom sat down. 'And she stole Carter's sword?'

Noah took a deep breath. 'I'm sure of it. She was on the manservant's list several times that day. She is always in and out of there.'

'I shall send men to fetch her in. I need to hear what she has to say for herself.'

Noah collapsed down onto a chair at last. 'I should like to hear that, too.'

Tom left the office to set the wheels in motion.

Hal sat close beside him, their silence allowing Noah's mind to turn to Westminster Hall where Sam would have long noticed his absence. Should he send Hal with word? But nothing was yet certain, so he was afraid to offer false hope. He scrubbed at his face. 'Fuck this.' He stood and began to pace the small office like a caged bear hungry for the dogs. He believed he had rather the smell of such, too. Though there was nothing to be done about it.

Hal watched him, his eyes soft with compassion.

Time passed, and Noah felt every moment of it. But he could not leave until he knew there would be enough to free Sam. He stood at the window for a while looking over the parade ground towards Westminster. How was the lad holding up? His plight seemed unthinkable. The threat to him.

When Tom returned to his desk, he cleared his throat and turned to Noah. 'I think you should know James Villiers raped this girl–'

Noah whipped around. 'Holy God.'

Hal sat up straighter in his chair. 'So, her husband had a motive to kill Villiers.'

Noah feared he might weep, taking several deep breaths through his nose. Christ. From just hoping to find the sword thief there was suddenly the prospect of the murderer himself. 'Why the hell did we not know this before?'

'Susannah Gresham knew. She witnessed it. So did Carter. But there was nothing to connect it to the murder until I knew about the maid's husband. Willet's uses it in The Crown's case because it provoked Carter to use violence against Villiers.'

Noah raised his eyebrows. 'He did, did he?'

'Punched him.'

'Good.' Noah knew everything had changed, excitement fizzing inside him. God's blood. They were going to do it. They were going to get him out. 'You need to be careful how you handle her–'

'Indeed.' Thomas cocked his head. 'Well, I shall begin by writing a plan of what I need from the interview before listing the questions to get me there. It usually helps.'

Noah grinned. Just his own approach to a voyage. Start with a plan of the profit needed then work out steps to achieve it. 'Then don't let me interrupt you any further.'

Thomas picked up his pen and the ensuing silence was soon broken by the sound of a quill scratching on paper. After a time, he wiped it on a rag and carved a sharper nib with a penknife before dipping it in the silver ink well and resuming.

Eventually, Noah returned to his chair in front of the desk. 'How much longer, do you think?'

Thomas looked up. 'Difficult to say. Depends if she were at the Gresham house.' He had just begun to write again when there was a sharp rap on the door. 'Yes.'

Noah turned to see a tiny girl with a comely face stumble in, looking completely terrified. Her eyes were red from weeping. The guardsman escorting her fetched her a stool.

'Sit,' Thomas said. 'Tell me your name.'

'Bess Smallwood, Master.'

'That's not quite right, is it?'

She bit her lip hard enough to draw blood. 'No, Master.'

Noah had never heard a voice shake quite so much.

'I already know of your marriage. Tell me your husband's name.'

She gasped a breath. 'Joseph Winks, Sir.'

'Can you tell me the whereabouts of your husband and his brother Hubert, Bess? Thomas's voice remained soft.

Tears rolled down her face. 'I believe them gone in the fire, Sir, for no one as seen em since. Nor my sweet sister.'

Hal leaned across to hand her his large pocket handkerchief. He smiled at her. 'Take it.'

She did. 'Thank you, Sir.'

Noah wanted to growl with impatience.

'Yet their names are not on any of the lists.' Thomas waved his hand. 'But many could not be identified.'

Bess began to weep again. 'My poor Joe. Im all burnt up like that.'

Noah tapped his foot on the floor.

Thomas stared at him until he stopped. 'Very well, Bess. I know you stole Samuel Carter's sword from his bedchamber. Please explain how and why you did this?'

The girl appeared resigned and then even relieved, Noah thought. Well, thank Christ for that.

She sighed. 'I told Ma what Master James did to me, Sir. How he forced his self on me.' She sniffed and blew her nose on Hal's now rather soggy handkerchief.

'Go on.' Thomas said, gently.

'I said how he kept telling the mistress I were sped ... well, I were coz I'm married a course. I were worrit like, for if they believed im, I would lose my post. Married girls is not allowed as maidservants, Sir.' She seemed not to know what to say next.

'And then did you not tell the same thing to your husband?'

'Oh, no Sir. I would never have done that. He has ... had.' She wiped her tears and blew her nose again. 'He had a terrible temper, Sir. When he ad drink in im, he'd use his fists on me something shocking. But never my face, however drunk he were. I ad to work, Sir.'

This was not going as planned. Noah looked at Hal and read the same concern.

'So, who told him, Bess?'

'Ma. I don't know why she did it.' She shook her head. 'For ad she not, none of it would've appened.'

'What did happen?'

'My Joe used his fists on me for it for a start, and then he swore he'd kill the bugger. A course, when he told Bert they sets about working out how it might be done, like. Then they did it.' She swallowed. 'They killed the bugger. They only told me of it when they ad to, for they needed me to get the bleedin sword.'

Noah let out the breath he had not realised he held, and Hal touched his arm, grinning.

Thomas cleared his throat. 'Why did they kill him in Whitehall Palace?'

'You know Bert were a kitchen porter? That bugger, he be very much ated by the servants there. He once chopped off a potboy's ear with a carving knife for knocking wine over im. Bert were appy to elp. He told Joe how the place is dim lit at night and how it is a lair of passages and courts. He took im there to point the bugger out and show im where he'd hide the sword he were going to pinch from where they's kept. The Arm ...'

'Armoury,' Thomas said. 'Why did they choose a sword to kill him?

'They thought as ow it would seem a scrap between gents, Sir. They knew Joe must kill him, like, not just urt him. Joe could only be safe if he was dead.' She shook her head. 'Though he did think to balk it when he followed is lantern to an alley an watched im piss against the wall but when he turned and saw im, he ad to. For when he sees the sword he shouts–' Bess mimicked a cultured voice. '"You there, churl. How dare you hold a sword like a gent'-man. Give it to me at once." So, Joe does give it im, just not how he thought. Joe tossed it in the river off Hall Stairs. He kept the bugger's lantern.'

'Bess. Will you explain why your husband and his brother sent you to steal Samuel Carter's sword? I'd also like to know how you managed to get it out of the house. A sword is not easy to conceal I would imagine.'

'I wrapped in a blanket and chucked it from a window down into the backyard. Then I puts it in a chest in the coach house where Joe got it.'

'And why did they want it?'

She sighed. 'They got worrit coz the bugger's having his way with me was known of. And how I wasn't ...'

'Virgin.'

'You was there when that other one asked of it, Sir, wasn't you? So, Joe might be found as my husband and then.' She shrugged. 'So, when Master Samuel be took, they thought as how if they id is sword rubbed wiv pig's blood and Bert found it, well, they'd not look no more. And they was right, wasn't they?'

Thomas sighed. 'They were indeed, unfortunately.' He had been taking notes as she spoke and put down his pen. 'So even though Samuel Carter came to your rescue when James Villiers assaulted you, you helped your husband and his brother try to have him found guilty of a murder he didn't commit? You were willing to see him executed for it?'

She shook her head. Tears again. 'I had to, Sir. It don't matter no more, do it? They're gone to God. Can Master Samuel be let go now?'

Noah spoke for the first time. 'He fucking well better be.' He looked hard at Thomas.

The Lieutenant stood. 'I shall speak to the King.' He opened the door. 'Get this girl locked-up in the guardhouse. She'll stand trial for theft and perverting the King's justice.'

Noah and Hal pushed past him and ran.

RAPHAEL

Still reeling from the horror of such a death sentence, we arrived outside swept along by the surging crowd. I held Susannah tightly around her waist, fearing her legs would buckle beneath her. Lord Carter would follow his son to the Beauchamp Tower to be with him there, but I had lost sight of Sir Richard. Then I spotted two fair heads standing out above the crowd as the Bartholomews ran towards us, people scattering to let them through like the parting of the Red Sea. I do believe they would have been trampled had they not. The men stopped before us, winded. One look at Susannah was enough for them to know the outcome. Noah fought to find sufficient breath for speech.

'Bess Smallwood,' Hal said.

Susannah raised her head.

Noah gasped another breath. 'Is Elizabeth Winks. She has confessed to stealing Sam's sword.' He gasped again. 'Her husband killed Villiers because he raped her.'

I closed my eyes in a silent prayer of thanks, sufficiently overwhelmed with the relief of it that my mind went suddenly quite blank. 'What must we do?'

'Go to the King,' Susannah scribbled so wildly I could barely read her words.

I shook my head as though to spark thought again. The King, of course we must. All at once our surroundings became starkly heightened in the light of such hope. In New Palace Yard, rainbows danced in mist around the cascading spouts of Henry's VI's fountain inside its domed pergola. Under the Gate House through to King Street, with its tall crenelated towers and niched statues, a blind man squatted ringing a bell that echoed painfully beneath ancient stone arches. A small, ragged girl tried to waylay travellers for alms, gesturing towards his empty sockets.

Out on King Street, Hal set a brisk pace, Noah keeping up though winded still from their run. 'Sam's conviction should be overturned now, surely? The King must agree it.'

'God's wounds, he must,' Noah said.

I touched his arm. 'We should find the Duchess of Richmond. She has easier access to him.' Susannah nodded vigorously. I never thought to see her so eager for Frances's company. In the Stone Gallery, we found Tom waiting outside William Chiffinch's office, talking with the very lady we sought. They turned hearing our approach, both their faces grave.

'I'm sorry. But it was the outcome I feared.' Tom sighed. 'It occurs to me the name Winks might never have come to light had they not stolen Carter's sword. So, we must, I think, be especially thankful that they did.' He nodded towards Frances. 'Her Grace and I both seek the King now, but he is proving somewhat elusive and Chiffinch is not in to share knowledge of his whereabouts.' He handed Frances the papers he carried. 'You shall have his ear more readily than I.'

She quickly scanned them. 'When I find him, I shall see he knows all of this. I trust him to do what is right whatever pressures are upon him.' Tom bowed and she turned to us when he walked away back towards Horse Guards. 'First, though, I must see to your comfort at Richmond House. Susannah looks ready to swoon.' She eyed Noah shrewdly, her head tilted to one side. 'So, you are Samuel Carter's friend who has done this for him. I think he owes you a very great deal.'

He bowed. 'Your Grace. This is my son, Hal.'

'Yes, I had rather assumed him to be.'

I sensed she knew the nature of the friendship existing between Sam and Noah.

How strange it felt to enter Richmond House with my arm around Susannah's waist, climbing those wide stairs to the drawing room and seeing her in the setting where I had begun my affair with Frances. When I found her eyes upon me, I knew she thought of it too.

After wine had been brought and poured. Frances turned to me and spoke in Italian. 'Take Susannah to my chamber where she might rest, and you can talk.'

I smiled. 'You know? Why would this surprise me? Yet it has.'

'It really should not, my dear. I've been acquainted with her for quite some time.'

Susannah stared at us coldly and wrote, 'If you are going to talk about me so I cannot understand perhaps you might care to do it elsewhere.'

The duchess patted her hand. 'Forgive me, Susannah. So thoughtless. Now I must leave you and resume my search.'

I moved to the window to watch her go. 'Pray God she finds him quickly.'

Noah closed his eyes. 'Christ, make it so.' He turned to me raising his eyebrows because, of course, he had understood everything we said. '*Vai a parlarle.*'

I nodded and held out my hand to her. 'Come, *cara*. Frances suggested you use her bedchamber to rest.' I led her up the marble staircase to the floor above. Again, it felt odd and strangely transgressive to take her there.

'She only spoke in Italian so I wouldn't know you were familiar with her chamber. Jesu, why would she think I didn't?'

I shrugged. What could I say? For that was not the reason at all. When I pulled her into my arms, though, she did not resist. 'Lie down for a while. You're exhausted, *cara mia*.' She did not demur and was soon settled against the pillows, her face pinched with anxiety. I looked down at her there just as I once had at Frances. 'I'll fetch more wine.'

'I don't want to be alone, Raphael. Please.' She held her hand out to me.

'I took it and brought it to my lips. 'I know. I shall be but moments.' She closed her eyes and I hoped she might sleep a little, for she would not have done so last night.

In the drawing room Noah waited at the window and did not turn when I entered. Hal was stretched out on a sofa watching him. I refilled our glasses and took one to Noah, touching his back to bring him out of his reverie. 'She'll find him. I know she will. She is nearly as stubborn as the King though a little more subtle about it, perhaps.'

'You know her well, I think.' He took the glass. 'How is Mistress Gresham?'

'Exhausted. Sick with worry.'

'Then I understand just how she feels.' He turned to Hal. 'We both do.'

Hal nodded obediently – and unnecessarily as far as I was concerned – draining his glass before pouring himself another. 'Why can she not speak?'

Noah looked at him, frowning. 'Please forgive my son. As soon as a question enters his head, he seems compelled to ask it.'

'It's what a good education will do for a man, Papa.'

'Then perhaps I should have saved my bloody money.'

I spoke to Hal in Italian. 'Do you understand what I say to you?' He looked blank.

Noah, refilling his glass, replied in my language. 'Not such a good education after all, then.'

'Perhaps best if he doesn't know she can.' I shrugged. 'It's complicated.'

'And up to her if it is known by others.'

I nodded picking up our glasses. Hal stared at us wide-eyed. 'And now I must return with her wine.'

'I didn't know you spoke Italian?'

'There's a lot about me you don't know, lad.'

'And quite a lot I do, dear Papa.'

I heard them as I left the room. So, he did know of his father and Sam. In truth, how could he not?

Returned to the bedchamber I found her sleeping, a slight frown between her fair brows. My heart ached for her, but I was as powerless as ever. I placed a glass down onto the table beside her and went to stand at the window as Noah would be doing on the floor below. I thought of my last time in this room. Though I loved Susannah, there I had been in Frances's bed. How had I strayed so far from the man I wished to be? The man I had once been.

I sipped my wine, watching shadows grow beside brick buildings glowing ruby-red in the late afternoon sunshine. It was at that moment Frances came into view, walking quickly beside the bowling green. Deciding not to rouse Susannah until I knew whether she had found the King, I hurried down two flights of stairs to meet her at the door. Noah watched me from above. 'Well?'

She shook her head. 'Though I now know where he is and have been assured he'll return today.'

'Where?'

'Greenwich. John Flamsteed – his Astronomer Royal – starts his work today. It has been the King's obsession for the year it has taken to begin it. So, he and Monmouth sculled down there with the tide early this morning. I expect they wished to offer their assistance with the setting up. The royal barge followed behind to fetch them back when they are done.'

She sat down on a flimsy-looking ornate chair close to the door. 'I shall leave you to tell the others. I must get back. When the King arrives, I intend to get to him before Louise does. She is jubilant, of course. Not often she and Barbara agree on anything.' She pursed her lips. 'Sometimes this place wearies me, Raphael. I should give it all up and go to my house in Kent. I could be content there, I know.'

I rested my hand on her shoulder and she placed hers over mine. 'Then why don't you? Though I'd miss you, Frances.'

'Why don't I? You probably won't understand, but I stay for the King.'

'You love him? I never knew that.'

'No, my dear. I don't love him, but I know he needs me. And that's why I stay.'

She stood and I kissed her forehead. 'I'll pass on what you've told me.' And then she was gone.

Noah accepted the news stoically. Holding on to Frances's words that she trusted the King to do what was right. Susannah slept still, and I did not wake her. Let her sleep until we knew Sam's release had been granted. Finally, I lay beside her and after a time slept too, waking in darkness to find her pressed close to me. When she whimpered in her sleep, I closed my arms around her. I did not wake again until dawn.

· · ·

Susannah watched me. Christ, how I loved her. And how I loved waking to her eyes upon me. I smiled until our circumstances came crashing back.

'Why has the duchess not returned?'

I tried to gather myself, addled still by sleep. 'The King had gone to Greenwich but was expected back yesterday.' I left the bed, crossing to the window to draw back the drapes. Someone had been in while we slept to close them. The sky was full of pink-tinged puffball clouds against palest blue and there was a slight mist hazing the ground. Susannah came to stand beside me. Most of her hair had come unpinned and hung in a tangle down her back. She looked ... everything I could ever desire. 'I can only assume she has not yet spoken to him.'

'Then, where is she? She cannot have waited-up all night for him, surely?' On catching sight of herself in the cheval mirror, she let out a small cry. 'Jesu. Why did I sleep in my skirts?' She tried to smooth out the creases from the grey silk with her hands. 'You, at least, had the sense to take off your coat.'

'You hadn't planned to sleep, and I hadn't the heart to wake you. You needed it, *cara*.' I went to the bed to recover her hair pins from the pillow, and she sat at the toilet table. When I opened a small drawer to take out a hairbrush, our eyes met in the mirror.

'Did you do this for her?'

What could I say? The truth, of course. 'Yes.'

She closed her eyes for a moment, then looked at me again in the glass. 'You untied yours.'

She watched me brush hers out. I wanted to lift it to my face and feel it against my skin. But, instead, I quickly pinned it up before re-tying my own with the ribbon I had put in my pocket. I scrubbed at my face. I needed a shave but there was nothing to be done. I put on my waistcoat and coat. 'I wonder how Noah and Hal have fared?'

'We should go down.' She chewed her lip, looking out at the

ever-brightening sky. 'Nothing will happen ... Sam. They won't. I mean–'

I pulled her into my arms. 'No, *cara*. Frances will get to the King in time, I am certain of it.' I could see trust in her eyes. She believed me because she wished it so, of course. I took her hand, and we went down together. Noah slept sitting on a chair he had pulled up to the window. Hal was stretched out on the floor, his head on a satin cushion. I was about to back out again and leave them to sleep when I heard the front door open and spun around. 'Frances.' She looked tired but perfectly groomed as she always did. Susannah tried to smooth her crumpled gown once again as the duchess came upstairs to drawing the room. Noah was already on his feet while Hal rubbed sleep from his eyes like a child.

'I've just spoken with him. He's read the lieutenant's notes and wishes to see you. He has questions. I'm sorry you've waited all night. Monmouth told me he'd returned but was already gone to Louise, so I waited in his bedchamber for the night. At least there I could sleep. I knew he would leave her for his own lodgings by dawn at the latest. James said they'd had a successful day, so I counted on his good temper in the morning unless Louise had managed to sour him.' She took a quick breath. 'Which, fortunately, doesn't seem to be the case.'

Noah looked eager for action. 'Well, then, let's go to him and answer his damn questions, and get Sam away to my ship.'

Frances turned to Susannah with her eyebrows raised. 'He has questions for you in particular.'

I thought for a moment she might swoon, what little colour she had draining from her face. I took a step towards her. '*Cara*?'

Her eyes remained on Frances, and she nodded stiffly.

Frances knew she was able to speak which surely meant the King did too. *Merda*.

The duchess led us back along the Stone Gallery to the King's apartments off the Privy Gallery, close beside the river. We followed her inside and up two expansive flights of marble stairs to his chamber. Ornate golden candelabra. More sculpted and gilded marble. And on a dais in a wide alcove, an elaborately carved tester bed swagged in gold embroidered carmine silk. No surprise I had not seen its like, for I had never before entered a King's bedchamber.

Frances rapped on ceiling-height double doors of equal splendour, and a gruff voice bid us enter. Hal remained outside when we stepped into the King's study, where I was startled to find shelf upon shelf of clocks. Jewell-studded gold. Translucent jade and onyx. Gleaming Venetian crystal. How would it sound when they all chimed the next quarter? I sincerely hoped we would not find out.

He sat behind his great oak desk – inlaid with intricate gilded tracery – dressed in a scarlet banyan and as yet unshaven. Without a wig his hair was closed cropped, grey and thinning. He appeared tired and decidedly vexed by our intrusion into his morning routine. Tom Monkton's papers were spread out in front of him and, viewing them, his expression was as stern as in his Westminster Hall portrait. We bowed. Curtseyed. He gestured at a chair before his desk for Susannah. Frances left us, closing the great doors behind her. Noah and I remained standing.

His eyes were now fixed, ominously, on Susannah. 'This maid of yours has confessed to theft and names her deceased husband as James Villiers' murderer?'

She nodded, chewing her lip.

He narrowed his eyes. 'Why would we not conclude this is something concocted by you and this girl to help Samuel Carter? We are very well aware of your close connections with him.' He put noticeable emphasis on 'connections.' Why, I wondered?

She looked startled before lifting her notepad to write, 'Your Majesty, I swear before God, I have not induced her to make such a confession.'

He slapped her notepad away. 'God's fish, why do you

continue this charade, Susannah? We know you speak. Do you think it acceptable to insult us with such behaviour?'

Susannah turned to me, panic in her eyes.

I knew I must speak in her stead, and my mouth turned dry as ash. 'Your Majesty.' I bowed.

Dark, heavy-lidded eyes turned to me. 'We know who you are,' he said, before lifting his hand and gesturing, irritably, for me to continue.

Of course he knew who I was, for had I not been his mistress's lover? 'Susannah's ability to speak is limited to but a few persons. She wishes nothing more than to change this yet, so far, has been unable to. It's not in her control.'

He shook his head, the disgust clear on his face. 'Well, we suggest she gets it in her control before our patience is no longer in ours.'

Susannah wrote, 'I try, Sire. I swear it.'

His eyes softened a little, then narrowed again when he turned to Noah. 'You spoke to this Smallwood woman, the maid's mother? She told you her daughter was employed at the Gresham house?'

'She did, Your Majesty.'

'And you are responsible for a pamphlet accusing us of,' he looked down, 'sanctioning false accusations and malicious imprisonment?'

Noah straightened his back and met the King's hard stare. 'Your Majesty, Samuel Carter is innocent of the murder of James Villiers.'

'Hmm.' He tapped his fingers on the desk. 'We have already sent an equerry with an order to commute the sentence to beheading.'

We all gasped, and then Susannah began to weep. Noah was clearly fighting to keep his temper. I touched his arm. He must do nothing to anger the King further.

Charles growled a long sigh before dipping a pen to sign a document prepared ready before him. 'This is an order for his release, but he must leave the country immediately. In this we are unequivocal.'

Noah grinned, bowing. 'He shall, Your Majesty. Arrangements are already in hand. He shall be away today.'

'Very well.' He gestured impatiently for us to leave him.

And we did, with immense relief.

Frances waited with Hal outside the door. One look at our faces told them all they needed to know before Susannah flung her arms around her. The surprise on her face, I felt sure, mirrored that on mine.

Noah and Hal hugged each other, too. 'Get to Rotherhithe and see the Mirabel is ready to sail and have a lighter sent to wait at St Katherine dock.'

Hal nodded. 'I'll see to it.' He punched Noah lightly on the arm and strode away, grinning.

'Is there anything I can do?' Frances said.

'I'll need to get a note to Sam's manservant to bring his coach to the Tower, Your Grace.'

'Come. We'll return to my house where you may write it. I'll send an equerry with it.'

Noah reached out to grasp her but stopped himself in time. 'How can I ... can we ever thank you for all you have done–'

She smiled. 'I'm fond of Samuel and much relieved you can get him to safety.'

Noah rubbed at his face. 'How long before they might release him, Your Grace?'

'It is difficult to say.' She shrugged. 'Two hours? Perhaps a touch less.' Her eyes found mine. 'I feel sure the King will see it expedited.'

We were all aware there were those who would not welcome his decision.

Noah looked at me. 'Then we shall leave it an hour before we go to our places. I'll be with the lighter waiting for you to bring him to me.' He sighed. 'But first I must see my wife.'

Christ. I did not envy him that. I took Susannah's hand and

smiled. She looked heartbreakingly beautiful; her eyelashes still jewelled with tears. 'That leaves us time to get to Cheapside. Will you wait for me? You'll be safer there.' Our eyes met, for we knew she would not stay.

Frances watched us. I thought she appeared a little smug. Yet how could I object?

Susannah remained with me, this time sitting beside me on my bed for my shave and change of clothing. Our eyes barely leaving each other while Giuseppe thought to entertain us with a convoluted tale of some childhood idiocy of mine when he was called upon to save me from certain death. Needless to say, I have no recollection of it. That neither of us laughed seemed not to concern him. In truth, we paid him very little heed. We both thought of Sam, I knew. And I thought of her ... Christ, I loved her. But did she truly feel the same?

Before we left, I pulled her into my arms then held her away to look at her face, and seeing both hope and dread there, kissed her forehead. 'We'll get him safe away, I know it.' She waited on the steps while I hailed a hackney to take us to the rendezvous place in Adler Street, until I helped her up inside and sat close beside her. Was I right to take her with me? To risk her like this? I crossed myself asking for God's mercy before I grasped her hand, feeling her tremble. 'Courage.' I could think of nothing more to say.

Though the journey to Whitechapel was a short one, I paid the coachman handsomely to wait, for I had no real notion of how long the delay might be. He halted in the shadow of St Mary's church to give himself and his horses some shade. Though early still, it was already hot. The carriage held an unpleasant odour of sweat and spilled ale, underpinned by a hint of piss. I climbed out and helping Susannah down, we walked a little way to sit on the stone wall surrounding the churchyard breathing in the scent of freshly turned earth from a nearby recent grave. We held hands, still. I closed my eyes turning my face up to the sun, having made sure she remained in shade, and bringing her hand to my lips. 'The sun is not so kind on your skin, *cara*, I think.' I watched her smile a little, her eyes focused in the direction of the Tower.

I tried not to think of what might happen between us now. I knew what I wanted but did she feel the same? Yet Sam had been so certain. In truth, it was better not to think of it. We would soon return to Cheapside where I must say words I had never spoken before. And find the courage to risk myself by saying them. Knowing this made me suddenly anxious for an entirely different reason, and oddly disconcerted with myself because it did. The sound of hooves brought us to our feet. Sam's coach. So, sooner than Frances had thought. Joseph pulled up behind the hackney and I ran across to open the door, leaving Susannah to hang back in the shadows. Sam jumped down, dressed as his servant, and I hugged him. He was very pale but grinning, with light back in his eyes at last. 'You look rather better than when last I saw you.'

'I feel transformed, dear Raphael.'

Susannah rushed to him then, flinging her arms around him.

'Sukie? I didn't expect you here.' He clung to her.

Lord Carter climbed out, embracing Susannah and then his son. They would part company now, but Sam being safe would be all that mattered to him. 'Go with God, my dearest, dearest boy.' They held each other briefly, both faces wet with tears.

Holy God, I hated to chivvy them, but Noah had stressed the importance of speed in case of pursuit. It was time for Sam's father to return to Henrietta Street with Connor disguised as his son. 'We must be on our way and get you to the ship.'

Sam helped his papa back inside. 'Go, Joseph.'

We ran to the hackney and set off for St Katherine Dock, Susannah sitting between us.

She held his hand in both of hers. 'Jesu, Sam. I cannot believe you are truly free.'

He shook his head, smiling broadly. 'I feel much the same.'

'I think Noah might be a touch surprised to see Susannah. She wished to say goodbye.' I shrugged. 'What could I do?'

He laughed. 'Very little I would imagine.' He turned to her, pulling her into his arms. 'I shall write when I can. Don't ever forget how much I love you.' He gave me a very direct look. 'Tell her,' he said in Italian. 'Give me your word.'

'You have it.'

She moved away from him to look at me. 'What?'

Sam touched her arm. 'Sukie, please stay away from Henrietta Street for a while. If anyone comes for me again, they will come there. And our friendship is well known.'

What he said, though entirely true, was not his only reason for pointing this out. I smiled. 'Susanna can return home with me, should she wish it.' I watched her blush.

'I'm happy to. You have my gratitude.'

When we pulled up at the dock, the boat was already there with Noah standing on the pier smiling his relief. I watched Sam's face light up at the sight of him. Susannah and I followed him out and down onto the wooden boards.

Noah's grin faded on seeing her. 'What the fu– hell are you doing here, Mistress Gresham?'

Sam took a step towards him. 'Saying farewell to me, Noah. Because of Raphael's kindness we have that chance.' Their eyes held for a moment, the love unmistakable.

Cold eyes again though when he gave me a hard stare. 'Raphael's kindness, is it?' He shook his head. 'I should describe it as Raphael's recklessness myself but see I would be in a minority of one.' He gestured to the boat. 'Come. We mustn't tarry.'

He made no comment when I helped Susannah down into the lighter. What could he say? Sam was happy she was here. We would go with them to Rotherhithe. Sam's father needed to know we had seen his ship sail safe. He sat close beside Noah in the boat's well. Neither spoke, both tense, still. So much could yet go wrong. I took Susannah's hand, uncomfortably aware of what I risked, bringing her into danger. But the men rowed hard, and it seemed little time until we arrived at Noah's wharf. As we did so, the Mirabel's sails began to unfurl on all three masts, men darting across the rigging like squirrels in the treetops. Noah intended no time should be lost.

He turned to us on the wharf. 'The lads will take you back up to St Katherine.'

Susannah and Sam clung to each other, murmuring softly. I moved away to stand beside Noah.

His eyes were fixed on Sam. 'I must thank you for bringing her, I think. He needs this time with her.' He looked down at me, grinning. 'Still reckless, mind.'

'We'll write.'

'Bartholomew, Port Royal will find him.'

Susannah and Sam came to us then, both smiling, both tear streaked.

Sam hugged me one last time, whispering in Italian. 'Remember your promise.'

'I shall, Sam. Go with God, my dear friend.'

Later, we stood side-by-side watching the lines untied from the mooring bollards and, with her sails already filling, the Mirabel moved out into the river to ride the current of the ebbing tide. Now I must take Susannah back to Cheapside, which brought a different kind of trepidation. Time for a little more recklessness, perhaps? I placed my hand in my sword's basket-hilt with some flamboyance. She shook her head and laughed.

Chapter Ten
NOAH

It was some time before Noah joined Sam on deck where he stood leaning on the taffrail, watching the passing marshes as the Thames widened towards the sea. Ahead the water gleamed like quicksilver with cloud shadows scudding across it like great beasts beneath the surface. On either side the mudflats were pocked with pools of tumultuous sky under spears of white light seeming to escape through chinks in the walls of heaven.

He wanted to give him time alone to adjust to such a huge change in circumstances, to steady himself, but he had work onboard, too. As his own super-cargo on this voyage, he needed to satisfy himself that all the bills of lading were in order for the tin, bales of fine woollen cloth and casks of whisky filling the holds. He rested a hand on Sam's shoulder, shocked by how thin he had become; they had been apart a long time. And he became suddenly conscious of how little time they had spent together before that. What they had been to each other then seemed distant. Almost another life. 'How do you feel?'

Sam looked up, his face pinched and pale, loose chestnut hair windblown. He had changed his clothes, looking more himself now in sapphire blue that matched his eyes. 'I don't know. It's hard to take it in. Yesterday I faced death. Today I have escaped it ... because of you.' He looked away.

'Not me alone, you know that.'

He turned back. 'Susannah and Raphael. But you most of all. You fought for me right to the end, Noah.'

He heard it. The way he spoke Raphael's name; the slight catch in his voice as he did. Well, here was a thing. Had Raphael stolen a part of his heart? He understood how it might be possible for he was a young man with a great deal of charm and no little beauty. Noah looked up at the sheets. The light sparkled on benign waters for the moment, though they were sailing towards much darker skies out into the North Sea.

Sam moved away. 'Noah, you needn't stay with me in Port Royal. I'll be fine there alone.'

He shook his head. 'We'll make a life together–'

'No. I can't let you do that. You have a wife, sons, a merchant business. I won't allow you leave your life for me.'

'It's already done, lad. I l-love you.' The words tripped his tongue for he had despaired of ever saying them out loud and now it almost felt they were spoken to a stranger. 'We'll stay together.' He frowned, disconcerted by a new notion. 'Unless you don't want me?'

Sam clutched his arm. 'Christ, no. How could you think it?'

There were sailors within earshot now. 'Come. Let's go to the cabin.' He led Sam to the aftcastle and into his private space. It was a generous one for a ship, full of sunlight from the broad expanse of tall windows. It seemed strange to be in here with him again. Who could have imagined how things would turn out for them on that short sail back from Le Havre? Or how excruciatingly difficult their path would prove. But they had survived it. Just. Now, he had to do something to get beyond this awkwardness between them. 'May I kiss you?'

Sam smiled. 'I've never known you ask before.'

Noah held his face. When Sam's lips parted beneath his he knew him again, and the relief of it sweeping through him made him gasp. Sam's arms came up around him. It was a long kiss. 'I've got you now, laddie. Your safe. I'll take care of you.'

Sam stepped back, smiling, and swiping tears from his face. 'See how easily you've unmanned me. I do believe I have become overly accustomed to weeping.'

'Weep if you need to. It's only me here.' He gestured for Sam to sit at the big table and lowered himself down opposite him. The chair creaked a little accommodating his bulk. He reached overhead and brought down a bottle of brandy from a shelf, followed by two pewter tankards, pouring and pushing Sam's towards him. 'There is but one life for us and it's time I have the one I want for myself.' He met Sam's gaze. 'A life with you.' He closed his eyes for a moment. 'Michael is almost grown, and Hal is already working in Rotherhithe. There are three of my own ships left for them and good contracts in place, with sound people able to keep it going until Hal's ready to take control. I shall miss them both. Christ. But there you are. Never can have everything.'

'So, you don't believe there is a God? An afterlife?'

'Oh, I believe in God well enough, I just don't expect to meet him.'

Sam smiled and sipped his brandy. 'The idea of heaven has been rather helpful to me of late. And I refused to even contemplate any notion of Hell for it seemed to me I already lived it.' He closed his eyes for a moment. 'Do the crew know who I am? I presume I have a new name on the ship's manifest?'

Noah grinned.

'Ah, I've missed that wolfish grin.'

'You are Samuel Bartholomew, my long-lost and now much beloved half-brother.' It had seemed a good solution. They could spend time together aboard ship without attracting attention. Sodomy was not unknown, of course, but rarely love between men he felt certain. He reached across to take Sam's hand. 'Well, Master Bartholomew, what do you think?'

'I like it.' He laughed, raising his eyebrows. 'I think our

mothers must have been somewhat divergent in appearance, though. And will it not be incestuous to swive as brothers?'

Noah barked a laugh. 'I hadn't thought of that, lad.' He watched Sam's eyes slide away, his expression wary all at once. He was troubled. Well, there was plenty of time – seven or so weeks onboard ship for a start – to find out exactly why, and a stay in the Tower under threat of death would do that to a man.

Sam yawned. 'I barely slept last night. Well, not for many nights, in truth. Nothing like contemplating a grisly death to make sleep elusive ... or undesirable.'

Noah stood and moved to him, pulling him to his feet and into his arms. 'Christ's wounds. I can scarce get my head around it.' He rested his cheek against Sam's hair.

'I, unfortunately, had little choice in the matter.'

Noah felt him slump. 'Get up on the bunk. You can sleep there safe. I shall keep you so, you have my word. He helped him out of his coat and waistcoat before pulling off his boots, then watched him collapse onto the bed and it seemed but moments before he fell into slumber. 'Christ, laddie. I can't imagine the horror of such a night,' he murmured. His father had sat vigil with him sharing it all, tormented by what awaited his beautiful and most beloved son. He thought of his own boys then and could not bear it.

Noah looked in on him several times as the afternoon tidied away slowly into evening. Later he brought bread and cheese ready for him when he woke. He sat at the table again just watching him. Loving him. And thanking God for his deliverance. Later still, he took a rolled mattress from a cupboard beneath that high bunk to lie beside it on the floor. He could no longer see him but left a lamp alight. Sam must not wake in darkness.

How had he arrived here loving this man, and the life they would now have together? A lad on a ship. A lad in port. Tall and fair, turning heads. Women's heads. Yet it was a man who first showed him visceral desire. And this one who brought him to love. He thought of Margaret and her contempt at his choice to go. A coward's choice. What would her response have been had she known the truth of it? It was not hard to picture the depth of her repugnance.

Settled on the thin mattress, he had little expectation of sleep for himself but was mistaken, waking with a start to the sound of stifled weeping. He was on his feet with Sam in his arms in moments. 'Hush, laddie. Hush now. You're safe.' He rubbed his back as he had done for Hal and Michael when they woke from night terrors. Sam had lived one.

'Forgive me.' He bit his lip, hard. 'It will not leave me. What if it never does?'

Noah fetched a cloth to dry his face. 'It's too raw. Only hours have passed. But it will. In time, it will. I promise you. We shall make a life together and this will fade, lost beneath all our good new memories.' His heart ached for him. Christ, he vowed to make it so.

Sam sat up and moved to make room for Noah. Though quite generously sized, the captain's bed proved a tight squeeze when one of the occupants was Noah Bartholomew. Sam took some long breaths before finally composing himself. 'How lucky for us, those divergent mamas of ours. In truth, mine was quite tiny.'

He sounded so fragile. Holy God. Would he break? Noah smiled though, touching Sam's face. 'Do you want to talk of it? It was a nightmare just now? Well, you have plenty of material for such. Look at me, laddie.'

Sam did as asked. 'I don't know if I can yet.' He closed his eyes. 'I told Papa of you last night.'

'And?'

'He minded less than I thought he might. I think it helped that he could at last understand why I'd been unable to save myself.'

'He loves you. He'll only want your happiness now, I'm sure.

Now it's over. Sam, it is what I intend for you. I'll see you happy, I swear it.'

'I'll miss him. All the time we've spent together over these last weeks brought us close in a way I never thought possible for us. I think we got to know each other for the first time. I was close like that with my mother. It was good to feel it again.'

'I'm glad. I never managed it with mine.' He stroked Sam's face, still. 'Though it is a pity then, that you've had to part so soon.'

'Well, at least we found each other in the end.' He managed a smile. 'And writing to him will be easier. I used to find it quite difficult to know what to say.'

Noah blinked rapidly, hoping Sam had not seen his eyes brimming with tears. 'I've never felt so helpless, lad, when I could do nothing for you.'

'Just knowing you were there helped me. Knowing you loved me.' Noah cupped his face. The moon was full and high now, casting a swathe of silver light over the undulant sea, shinning in through the aftcastle windows above the bunk and haloing Sam's hair. 'Can you sleep again, do you think?'

'I hope so. I want to.'

Noah made to return to his mattress.

Sam grasped his shoulder. 'Stay please. There's room enough if we lie close.'

Noah reached over him to open a small casement letting cool air into the stuffy cabin. He pulled Sam into his arms, feeling his ribs sharp through the thin linen of his shirt. 'Sleep, lad. You're safe now.' How was it possible to feel such love? Why this sudden overwhelming certainty of it? Then, of course, he understood. Sam needed him and what could be more potent than that?

Noah woke alone, bolting upright. Sam? Had he harmed himself? With a pounding heart, he leapt from the bunk, pulling on his shirt as he dashed from the cabin. He found him on deck amidships in much the same place he had been the day before, watching the dawn, the sky a lambent cerulean with a rind of moon and a scattering of stars still. He turned at the sound of Noah's bare feet slapping on the deck boards. The sea was calm with sails hanging limp, only flapping a little from time to time when a small breeze stirred them. The ship's timbers groaned in the slight swell.

Sam moved closer so their arms were just touching when Noah arrived beside him. 'We make little progress. I have such a strong desire to get away from England as quickly as possible, but the wind refuses to cooperate, it seems.'

'You scared me, lad. When I found you gone.' He took a deep breath and turned to look around them at the dawn sky. 'It'll pick up later when the sun's up. But it is the same wind for any ship if you fear pursuit.'

'Reason tells me it is unlikely. Sam Bartholomew isn't known to anyone. Yet I'm uneasy.'

They stood a little longer watching the pinks and golds build across the sky until the orange ball of the sun appeared above the horizon in a great flash of light. Noah slapped him on the back heartily enough not to draw attention. 'Come brother. Tanner,' he called, walking back towards the aftcastle. 'Have someone bring breakfast.'

'Aye, Sir. Done.' He brought his fist to his forehead.

When the food arrived – coddled eggs and fresh baked bread with a generous dish of butter – they ate in silence. Noah poured them each a horn beaker of small ale, glad to see him eat with some enthusiasm. He really was far too thin. He pushed his empty plate away. 'Have you any idea what it is the King thinks you know?'

Sam looked up, studying him with some care before he spoke. 'He was correct about it. I know exactly what it is and why it is undesirable that I should.'

Noah's eyes widened. 'Christ, lad. Then you've had an extremely lucky escape. I wonder why he allowed it?'

'Because he was being pressed to dispose of me by the Duchess of Portsmouth, who in turn was pressed by agents of Louis of France. Yet, in the end, when you gave him the opportunity to act, the King knew he could trust me.' He shook his head. 'I had never given him cause to doubt my loyalty to him. In truth, he would see how this ... matter would be distasteful to me. Very distasteful indeed. But I am his Godson, and my father is one of his oldest most loyal and most beloved friends.'

'Then, I suppose you can't tell me what it is?'

That stare again. Calculating. 'I believe I can, Noah. I trust you and I also think someone should be aware I know of it.'

'You really believe you might still be in danger?'

'I do. From England and from France. Louise de Kérouaille was sent by Louis to become the King's mistress.' He smiled a hard, cynical smile.

Noah had never seen it before. This was a Sam unknown to him.

'When Louise spread her legs for Charles, France fucked England. Before long she had his agreement to negotiate and, believe me, he is most accustomed to indulging his mistress's requests. There was a treaty made between England and France that in exchange for a very substantial sum of money, England would support France's interests against the Dutch. And the King is ever in need of funds when so much is diverted to all his grasping duchesses and even his silly little actresses, never mind those all but pimped off the streets for him by Chiffinch.' He shook his head. 'He's allowed Portsmouth to raid the public and privy purses on a scale more massive than even Castlemaine managed.'

Noah drew his fingers down over his stubbled cheeks. 'Well, fighting the protestant Dutch for papist France was never much popular until their navy began to trounce ours again, of course. And the humiliation of Medway lives long in people's memories ... when they took the Royal Charles as a trophy.' He shrugged.

'But I can see how it's unpalatable that our Royal English were made mercenaries had they but known–'

'No. What's truly repugnant is the second and most secret condition for receiving the money. England must return to Rome. For this the King will receive an additional £160,000 when he converts.'

'Fuck. No. He can't do it, though, surely? The people would never accept it. And he knows only too well what can happen to an unbeloved King.'

'He can't now. There's far too much anti-Catholic feeling. All his attempts towards religious freedoms have been overturned by parliament. But we don't know if a time might come when he can. He signed his name to it.' Sam chewed his lip for a moment. 'You probably know the Duke of York is already a convert. Their mother – like mine – was Catholic, of course, and he is Charles's heir if the Queen doesn't produce one.'

Noah shook his head. 'Which can't be very likely now, poor woman. And you were put through such fucking ...' He struggled for words. 'Suffering because at the bottom of it all, the King needed coin? God's blood. I think we are well rid of England, lad.' He had a strong sense there was something more left unsaid. Though he found it difficult to imagine what could be more alarming or secret than what he had just heard and in view of that, had no desire whatsoever to know what it was.

When the breakfast dishes were collected, Noah stood to stretch. The ship began to pitch a little as the wind took her again. He grinned. 'Told you so.'

Sam rose and came to him, placing his hands on his chest. 'Well, you are somewhat more experienced with such matters than I.'

'Can't say I'd like your sort of knowledge. Not when it can cost your life.'

'But the sea takes lives, too, does it not?'

'It does, indeed, but quite without malice.' Noah bent to kiss him before pulling his shirt up over his head. 'Christ, look at the state of you.' He hoped he had concealed the full extent of his shock.

'I don't think you mean that in a good way, do you?'

'No, Sam, I do not.' He ran fingers down his visible ribs to his concave belly. 'It's just more proof of what has been done to you. He pulled off his own shirt before kissing him again, needing to feel his naked skin against his. Wanting to gift him something of his own vigour, if such a thing were possible.

Sam pulled away and placed his palm on Noah's face. 'Forgive me. I don't think I can ... I–' He dropped his hand, closing his eyes.

'Come.' Noah helped him up onto the bunk again and held him in his arms. 'There's nothing to forgive. I love you. You know that.' He touched Sam's face gently, to hold his gaze. 'I love you,' he said, again. 'I need nothing more until you want it, too.'

Sam took his hand and kissed it. 'What if I never do?' Noah chuckled and Sam soon joined in. 'It certainly doesn't sound like me, does it?'

'No, it most surely does not. What do we have now but time? And time is just what's needed. Can you tell me ...? Do you know why you feel this way?'

'Something closed inside me. I was afraid for so long.' He looked up at Noah. 'The truth. The truth is ... I was facing the traitor's death and it began to fill my thoughts the closer it came. The closer my trial came. Though I was never alone, I couldn't talk of it. How could I to Papa or Connor? Raphael stayed with me on the night before the trial. I might have done so with him but got unpleasantly drunk instead and wept. He was very kind to me.'

'He's a thoughtful fellow.' And Sam was clearly fond of him, yet he found it mattered nothing. Indeed, it pleased him to know he had his company on the night he needed it.

'You took care of him when he was attacked, didn't you? And you were kind to him.' Sam sighed. 'He is besotted with Susannah. No, they're besotted with each other as you probably noticed. I hope everything goes well for them now and they can stop worrying about me.'

But Noah's thoughts had gone elsewhere. 'Castration?'

Sam blinked. 'What?'

'The traitor's death. That's part of it, no?'

Sam blinked again. 'Indeed, as I was so recently reminded, it is the first joy to be experienced prior to the gutting.'

Christ. What a thing to anticipate. 'Well, I can quite see how a cock might go absent without leave after contemplating such as that for any length of time.'

Sam raised his eyebrows. 'And do you think such a soldier might be brought back to barracks?'

Noah grinned. 'I know he can, dear lad.'

'Good. Then I shall leave the matter entirely in your hands, Sir.'

They laughed a little and held each other for a while. Then Noah sat up, opening a cubby to bring out two rather wizened and battered oranges.

Another dawn when Noah found himself alone, he knew where to go. Yet he stopped in his tracks when he saw whom Sam stood next to leaning on the taffrail. Hal? 'What the fucking Christ are you doing here?'

Hal turned, smiling. 'Meeting my old friend and now newfound uncle, Papa. Sam, I must apologise for my father.' He shook his head, loose flaxen hair swinging on his broad shoulders. 'Such coarse sailor's language. What he meant was, 'How pleased I am to see you my dearest son.'

Sam grinned, his eyes shining.

Noah slumped a little before grasping Hal into his arms. 'God almighty. You know my intensions with this. You know what Sam and I are doing.'

'Papa, of course I do. But, well, I won't—' He shrugged. 'I won't be in your way. You have my word.'

He watched Sam laugh. Holy Christ. They were already friends.

'I want to go to Jamaica ... I don't know after that. I shall wait and see what happens.' He shrugged again. 'I'm not Michael.'

'Michael? What the f–' With Sam's eyes on him, he bit back his cursing as he always tried to do. 'What has Michael to do with it?'

'God. You really don't know either of us, do you?'

Giving his son a dirty look, Noah began to feel more than a little irritated. 'Perhaps you might care to enlighten me then.' Eyebrows up, Sam watched him with indulgent interest and Noah gave him a hard stare, only to get a wide-eyed look of innocence in response. The little shit. He swallowed. How he loved him. How he wanted him. He had to take a sharp breath, his nostrils flaring.

Hal sighed. 'Michael has his life already mapped out. He is very clever. You must know that, yes?'

Noah nodded, unconvincingly.

Hal sighed again, rolling his eyes, clearly enjoying his father's discomfort. 'Well, he is. He'll go up to Oxford to read Theology and then become a minister.'

Noah was vexed by Hal's insinuation he knew nothing of either of them. A minister? Fuck. 'Perhaps you'd care to explain why you've abandoned duties you had accepted on a whim it seems? You agreed to represent me in Rotherhithe and to take care of your mother.'

Hal's eyes narrowed. '*What?* What the devil are you talking about? Rotherhithe is already running like a well-oiled wheel. There was never any need for me there because I was supposed to be up at Oxford.' His nostrils flared just as Noah's had. 'And as for Mama, she has Michael who'll be there just as often as I would have been. He's her favourite, anyway.' Eyebrows up. 'I'm sure you can guess why?'

Noah's patience deserted him completely. He stepped close to Hal. Face to face. 'How the holy fuck should I know, unless it's that you are an unreliable fucking–'

Sam moved forward, grasping his arm. 'Noah, please.'

He clenched his jaw. 'Very Well. Tell me. I can see you're itching to, lad. Let's have it, then.'

'Because dearest Papa, I remind her too much of you.'

Noah tilted his head back to look up at the sky shaking his head a little, feeling it like a physical blow. Christ's blood. That Hal should be thought less of ... loved less because of him. It pierced his heart.

Hal touched his shoulder, visibly mortified. 'God, I've hurt you. Forgive me. I didn't mean–'

'No!' Noah closed his eyes for a moment before grasping Hal hard into his arms and holding him tight, his cheek pressed against his son's. 'No. No you haven't. Not you.' He gasped a breath. 'I should be asking your forgiveness, Hal. 'I'm glad you're here, of course I am. How could I not be? You're my son and I love you more than you can ever begin to understand ... until you are a father yourself.' He had asked him to stay with him. Said he needed him. Holy God. Then he remembered Hal telling him how he had always wished to be like him. 'We'll find your place. Maybe it'll be a ship. Maybe it won't. But we'll find it together.' When they moved apart, Noah looked at Sam who smiled, his eyes definitely a touch moist.

'You were a ship's captain at my age, though. Perhaps it is already too late for me?'

'Hal, I should not have been. It was my father's ship, and he was dead. I had no choice. But it was far, far too soon and it terrified me.'

Hal smiled a little shakily. 'Well, now I no longer have to hide from you, I shall find more food. I'm monstrous starved.'

Noah and Sam stood side by side watching him stride away towards the galley.

Sam touched his back. 'It will be good to have him with you.'

When Noah thought of it properly without surprise or rancour, what more could he ever want? He felt blessed to have them both. For however long it might be.

'He is wonderful, isn't he? And so like you. Wild. Reckless.'

'*What?* I'm not those things at all. Just the opposite, in fact. What the f– devil are you talking about?'

'No?' Sam gestured at the ship, at them together. 'Really?' Raised eyebrows. 'Cabin, perhaps?'

Noah shrugged. 'Can't hurt.'

Inside, Sam moved to kiss him. It was a long kiss. He shook his head. 'Let's just go to bed and, well ... *vedere cosa succede*. See what–'

'*Perchè no?*' Noah shrugged again and grinned. Sam's eyes widened in surprise. 'There's a lot about me you don't know, laddie.'

'Well, I'm sure to enjoy finding out.'

SUSANNAH

Diary: July 12, 1676

Sam is safe away. I witnessed it myself. Thank Jesu I can write these words, at last. He came perilously close to disaster; I can hardly bear to think of it, haunted still by that sentence to take his life by torture and mutilation. And I have so much more to write, it almost overwhelms me. God help me. So much has changed.

We returned to Cheapside yesterday, having spoken little in the carriage. Raphael's eyes were closed, and I could not tear mine away from his face which seemed already imprinted on my soul. I knew we shared the same relief at Sam's deliverance, but did we share the same feelings for each other? My heart swooped with fear, for I loved him so helplessly it made me afraid.

I walked into his drawing room, its familiar white marble and gilded carvings gleaming in the afternoon sunlight, desperate to feel his arms around me. I took a deep breath to compose myself before I spoke. 'I'm so grateful you took me with you. I needed it.'

'I saw you did. Sam too.' He handed me a glass of wine and sat beside me on the sofa. 'Noah said to write to him in Port Royal. The Bartholomew name will be enough to find him.'

'I shall.' I placed my glass down onto a side table and covered my face with my hands for a moment, trying to gather myself still, before I turned to look at him. 'I can scarcely believe it's over.' Joy and fear were uncomfortable companions in my heart. Penny could now come home, thank Jesu, but would we fetch her together as we had promised?

He touched my face with his fingertips. 'He's safe. Noah will take care of him.'

I closed my eyes as his fingers moved down my throat to find my collarbone, tracing its line before he moved in to kiss me. We kissed then for quite some time, and it was easy to lose myself, I had wanted it for so long. Yet, this time when I wished his hands to find my body, they did not. Why? I pulled away, searching his face. Our eyes held. But how could I ask him such a thing? I stood and moved away to the window, looking out over the busy street. The commotion out there seemed part of a dreamscape. I heard his footsteps as he arrived behind me, closing his arms around me, pressing his cheek against mine.

'I need you to know I love you, Susannah ... it's time I found the courage to say it.'

I pressed back against him, taking a moment to breathe as the relief of it flooded through me. 'I prayed you did.' I turned to place my palm on his face. 'Because I love you very much.' Still, it felt a dangerous thing to love him like this, never mind that I had no choice and had not for quite some time, for would he want me when he knew my secret?

'I've loved you for so long. Perhaps, since I first saw you at court? The night before last with Sam, he said you loved me too – he swore he could see it – I, well, I was.' He seemed to search for words. '*Molto felice* ...very happy.'

He smiled his smile, which had its usual effect upon me.

'He said, too, we should waste no more time because it is so precious.'

My Sam. Another gift to treasure. 'Let us not, then. Let's not waste any more of it.' With that, I surrendered myself to him. Whatever it meant, I was his ... if he wanted me.

He moved away. 'Will you excuse me for a moment? There's something I must ...' Then he was gone.

I returned to the sofa, finishing my wine, and refilling both our glasses before taking some deep breaths to compose myself. He loved me. 'Raphael loves me,' I whispered, smiling like a simpleton. My life was about to change, and I was on the cusp of it wishing only to launch myself. I tried again for calm and then, of course, knowing what I must tell him, fear found me again. I am sure I appeared quite my usual detached self by the time he returned.

He sat beside me and drained his glass. 'You look a little uncertain. You have concerns about me, I know–'

'No, it's not that.' Not just then, anyway. I looked away, unable to find words to soften what I must say and while I struggled, he moved down onto his knees before me.

'Susannah. I know I must prove myself faithful to you. You have my word I shall be. I swear it, before God. Will you ... can you say you'll be my wife? Will you? I know your family might find me ... well, perhaps a touch too artisan, but I love you. This is all I can offer you.' He held out his hand to me and on his palm was an exquisite diamond and sapphire ring, a delicate open lattice of gold set with glittering stones. 'I made it for you. Though without any real expectation of ever being able to give it to you.' He smiled. 'It was a way to use my love. To dedicate it to you, I suppose.'

I took it from him. Felled again by his smile, though silent still. Jesu, I had to tell him. I could hear my heartbeat and feel its thud and swoop.

He moved back onto the sofa beside me. 'Susannah, please

look at me. I know you think me a libertine ...' He shook his head. 'But I shall never be so again. I love you.' He took my hand and closed my fingers over his ring. 'But if you need time, you shall have it.'

'Forgive me.' My voice sounded strange to me. I opened my hand to look at it again. 'It truly is the most beautiful ring I've ever seen. And you made it for me?' I looked up at him, meeting his gaze and trying to hold on to it. 'But before I can accept it, there's something I must tell you ... about me.' Again, I searched for better words.

'I love you. You need tell me nothing.'

What could I do but say it? Straight and plain. Words I had never spoken before. 'Penny is my daughter not my sister.'

I watched his face as he understood. 'Tell me,' he said, softly.

'I've never spoken of it before, but I shall now.' I waited for the question that must surely come.

'Who is her father?'

'I cannot tell you that.' I have never told.

His eyes widened. 'Are you saying you don't know?'

I gasped. I truly had not expected such a question from him. 'No, Raphael, I said no such thing. I was never a whore. I mean I won't tell you. I've never told anyone.' Tears. How humiliating. How damnable. He thinks me a whore and I cry.

'No, *cara*.' He pulled me hard against him. 'Christ. No. I didn't mean that. I thought, maybe an attack by men. I would never think such a thing of you. How could you believe it for a moment?'

Indeed, he never would, though I had called him such and it shamed me still. I moved away to look at him again, brushing away tears with my fingers. 'Forgive me. It is difficult. No. It's ... Jesu ... when I never have before.'

'Then don't say it all now. We have so much time.' He crossed himself. 'Your pardon. A habit I've found difficult to shed.'

'You're Catholic. You should be free to do so.'

'Perhaps not in England.'

I took a long breath. I needed to finish my confession while I still had the courage. Catholicism in England was for another time. 'Raphael. I'm going to tell you all of it. I love you and I want you to know.' I took a deep breath. 'I need you to.' And I did, for if he was to be my husband, he had that right.

He lifted my hand to his lips. 'Then tell me, *cara*. Say everything you need to.'

I had to watch his face while I did. He held my hand, stroking it lightly with his thumb, which helped as well. 'I was very young ... well you know that, obviously. I was sixteen when I gave birth to her, fifteen when ... we were both fifteen. Little more than children. It happened once.' I looked away for a moment, biting my lip. 'It wasn't enjoyable and, well, there was never a suggestion of repeating it. Later he behaved as though it had never happened, so I did too. But it had, of course. And for me there came a time when denial was no longer possible.'

His eyes were full of compassion. 'Susannah. *Cara*. And you have never spoken of it to anyone?'

'Only my mother. Well, she spoke of it to me first.' I laughed, mirthlessly. 'I honestly didn't know I was with child. I'd become friendly with a group of unmarried ladies at court. You know the sort.'

He nodded.

'I was distracted. I understand now why I was drawn to them. They were older and knew so many things I did not. How to make men notice them. Desire them.' I looked away for a moment. I could not tell him how important such things had become to me then. 'Even how to pleasure a man and how he might do so for a woman without–' His blink of surprise made me smile. How I had admired it all then and how much I despise the abject complicity of it now. Women so eager to offer themselves.

Our eyes held again, and I chewed my lip. 'When my mother came to my chamber one night and asked if I were with child. I was ...' I shook my head, remembering. 'I was stunned. Shocked beyond imagining. Then, of course, came the questioning. What had I done with him? An explicit description of what was needed to get a child. Had I done that? Jesu. I shall never forget what I felt when I understood. I was sick with terror.' I bit my lip hard this time. Do not weep. Do not dare weep again, damn you.

'*Cara.*' He pulled me close. 'I don't know what to say to help you. It seems unthinkable you went through such a thing alone. Where was Penny's father? I know you were both so young, but could you not have married? Christ knows I'm glad you didn't, but wouldn't it have been best for you? Please don't tell me he refused?'

'He never knew. And he would not have done if he had. He loved me. We loved each other.'

'Then I don't understand.' He moved away to pour more wine.

We drank in silence for a while. What a strange self-inflicted woe it must seem to him. 'Raphael. There is an explanation, and I will tell it. When I can.'

He searched my face. 'Of course, *cara mia.*' He took my glass from me, returning it to the side table before kissing me. His mouth tasted of the fruity wine. 'So, how did she become your sister?'

I met his gaze again. He was a man. How could he ever truly understand the vitriol and contempt directed at a woman found to be with child outside marriage? Though, of course, it was not a state achieved alone, she alone was condemned. 'Well, I could not be a mother without a husband first, so I was hastened down to Chewton Court and hidden away by my grandmother while Mama went through her pretence. When I still refused to name Penny's father, she knew the King would learn of my condition and marry me off to some aged widower in the fenlands or some such.' I touched his face. 'For she had married for love and wished it so for me.' Jesu, how little sense this must make to him.

He kissed my fingertips. 'I'm glad.'

'She wrote to Papa telling him she found herself with child

and too unwell to travel home. She begged him not to visit her because she did not wish him to see her in such a poor state. She said being with child at her age was an abomination and had left her bedridden. She hated deceiving him.' I shook my head. 'I still feel guilt she had to because of me.'

'You should not. She needed to feel she protected you as much as she could, I think.'

'Yes, but she loved him very much. It cannot have been easy for her.' I closed my eyes, doubting I could go on.

'Tell me, Susannah.'

I took a long breath. 'After Penny was born. After the three days it took ... when I feared I would die ... and then prayed for it–'

'*Cara* ...'

'After that – when I had fallen in love with her – and was sufficiently recovered, a wet-nurse was found, and we returned to London with my sister.'

'Well, then.' He took my hand and kissed it before sliding his exquisite ring onto my finger. 'And this, *amore mio*, makes you my wife. We shall have a ceremony as soon as it can be arranged. This ring is made from my love. I made it for you, Susannah, *il mio amore più cara*. You are already my wife in my heart.'

'Why would I need anything more?' I touched his ring 'This means we are handfast. We are bound until death just as we will be before God.' I felt the wine in my blood now. There had been quite a lot of it. I closed my eyes for a moment. 'Forgive me, I know you didn't expect a woman already sped. I–'

He barked a laugh. 'I'm not sure I'd know entirely what to do with a virgin, so you've nothing to regret. In truth, it is something of a relief.'

Now I laughed, for I had not seen that coming. 'You'll take me to bed, then?'

He took the glass from my hand again, smiling. 'Well, might we not wait for our blessed wedding, *cara*? It'll not be long away, I'm sure.'

'So you can swive all those fat faded ladies but not me who is already your handfast wife?'

He tilted his head, still smiling that damnable smile. 'Faded ladies? *Really?* Again?' Another long kiss. 'I can make love to you, *cara mia*, but should I? Should I when you're so much the worse for drink?'

'Yes. Damn you. And I am not the worse for drink.' Though, I cannot deny I was almost euphoric – having told him my secret – with simple relief at finally having spoken of it. I had claimed my daughter. And thank Jesu, he had claimed me.

He stood. 'Very well then, *mia moglie*.' He took my hand and pulled me to my feet and straight into another long, long kiss, pressed hard against him. Then he grasped my hand and led me up the white-marble stairs and into his chamber. Again. Though, full of sunlight now. 'You truly want this, *cara*?'

I blinked against the sudden glare. 'I desire you, Raphael. Are women not supposed to feel lust?' What I could not say was I needed something more from him. Something he would never understand.

He searched my face and closed his eyes for a moment, oddly serious. 'Lust is a part of love, Susannah, so why should I not wish you to feel it for me?' He took off his coat and waistcoat and tossed them onto a chair, pulling the tie from his hair to let it fall, black, below his shoulders, and came to me untying his cravat.

I had seen him do these things many times but never like this. Never feeling like this. And then I was in his arms again. And afraid ... again. He unpinned my hair, lifting it to his face to brush it against his skin. When he undressed me, he showed all the skills I expected of him. Buttons. Laces. Until I stood before him in my shift as I had done once before.

'Now you.' I dropped to my knees to peel off his stockings. He sat on the bed so I could pull them from his feet. Kissing his shins. His calves. All the while he watched me, his expression unreadable. He stood again, taking me up with him and I began to fumble with the buttons on his breeches. My efforts were so clumsy, he quickly unfastened them, pushing them to the floor himself.

We stood before each other in shift and shirt, once again, and I understood this was that precipice edge from where I must launch. I trembled with, well ... overwhelming desire, barely able to breathe and utterly disconcerted by it. He loosened the ribbon at the neck of my shift and eased it down until it pooled at my feet. I closed my eyes and felt him pull his shirt up over his head. My heart thumped and swooped. He must see it in my chest, surely? My mouth was dry as sand.

'*Dio mio, quanto sei bella*. Your skin is pale ... as moonlight. Your breasts. You take my breath away. Open your eyes, Susannah.'

I opened them and fell against him finding his mouth before burying my face in his neck, smelling his fragrance and the musk of his desire. A scent I would soon come to know rather well. He took my hand and moved it down to hold him, grasping it under his own around himself. 'Well, then, the big cock.' I don't know why I said it for I had no way of knowing if it were even true, but the words arrived before thought and I clamped my other hand over my mouth.

'*Che cosa?*' With his eyes round with astonishment he appeared stuck dumb, before roaring with laughter.

So, I laughed too, and we fell back onto his bed still laughing, until he rolled over me.

He hesitated when I flinched, though I would not allow him to stop. With our eyes closed then, both lost in our own desperate need for release it was fast and hard, and we made a lot of noise at the end which made us laugh again because we had.

My God, it was like nothing I had ever imagined. Jesu, I had wanted him so much it felt visceral. How was such a thing even possible? The nearest I had come to such intensity of desire before was on the night of Penny's nightmare. We lay on our backs now, breathing hard until he moved onto his side to face me.

'*Dio mio, cara*. How can you possibly be mine?'

'I am, Raphael, and you are now *entirely* mine.' I raised my eyebrows.

'Everything I am is yours. Always. I love you, Susannah.' He stroked my hair back from my forehead and kissed me. 'Forgive me for hurting you.'

I caressed his face. 'You didn't ... well, for a moment only, perhaps. It didn't matter. I desired you very much.'

He smiled. 'I think I may have caught an inkling of it.'

'What about earlier when we kissed?'

'What do you think?'

I smiled. 'Why, though, when you knew how much I wanted you?'

He shook his head. 'I had to kiss you for love. I didn't want you to misunderstand what I needed from you. To think I talked of love to have you.'

'Is that what you do?' All men did, surely? It was how conquest worked.

'Christ, Susannah. No. I've never told a woman I loved her until you because I never have before.'

I rolled, moving close and pressing myself against him. I understood at last. They simply desired him. Look at him. Yet he had no idea. 'Well, I'm most impressed and grateful, but please don't do it again.'

'I think you need not be concerned, cara.'

The afternoon was fading when I woke and moved to look at him. I had slept deeply, needing it after so many nights when it had escaped me entirely or haunted me with anxious dreams. His eyes were closed but fluttered open while I watched. With a shaft of soft golden light on his face, I marvelled again at their colour. Deepest green flecked through with amber. 'Thank you.'

He looked startled, again. 'What? You cannot be thanking me for making love?' His voice was husky, his accent more pronounced.

I nodded.

He chuckled. 'Well, I have never been thanked for it before.' He reached to push my hair away from my face, his thumb stroking my cheek. 'It was hardly a burdensome task, *amore mio*. But I promise we can do better now things are not quite so ... fraught.'

And he was right. This time was all about love. When I took him inside me again, feeling the heft of him there, we stilled to hold each other's gaze. I touched his face in sudden understanding of who he was to me now ... and of who he would be. 'Oh, it's you, my love.' No one but him would ever know me like this or lie with me like this. He was the father of my children. He was the only man I would ever love. 'My Raphael.'

He kissed me, gently. 'I love you, Susannah. My heart overflows with it.'

I tightened my legs around him then and we took our time, sharing sensation and finding each other. Getting to know each other. Noise at the end but no laughter this time, only love and an unexpected special closeness I knew would never leave us. 'I can tell you why I didn't want to wait now if you wish?'

He raised himself up on his elbow to look down at me. 'You needed to know you might enjoy it more than your first time, perhaps?'

'Yes, that, of course. But I also needed to know it wasn't like that with him because of me.'

He bent to kiss me. 'Susannah.' He kissed me again. 'So, you had some notion I might not enjoy you?' He shook his head and began to laugh.

I think he tried not to but ... 'Well, I don't think it now, obviously.' I felt more than a little vexed he found it so amusing.

He moved onto his back; a hand arched on his forehead. 'Shall I tell you something? I probably shouldn't because it doesn't show me in a particularly favourable light.'

I raised my eyebrows. 'I feel sure it won't surprise me, then.' Of course it would not. I knew very clearly what he had been.

He sighed. 'Very well, I probably deserve that. Well, here it is. After I first saw you at court, I spent time with someone – and please don't say a faded lady – and imagined she was you.'

It was my turn to laugh. 'Poor, sweet, faded lady. There she was believing your ardour was all for her.' I did put particular emphasis on the faded lady part.

He rolled over me again, grinning. 'Actually, I think she did rather well from it.'

'What, with your big–'

He put his hand over my mouth. 'I'm your husband and forbid you to say it.'

He removed his hand, his eyes dancing with mirth. 'Cock.' I held up my hand up to admire my beautiful ring. Then my eyes widened. 'Jesu, I saw you in Wood Yard. You were dressing as you walked.'

'Susannah, I most certainly was not dressing. I was buttoning my coat.'

I shrugged. 'It appeared so to me. Definitely dressing.'

There was considerable kissing and then, well …

We slept entwined for a while, and I woke to find him watching me this time. The day had tidied itself away, with light faded to a soft blue twilight. I reached across to touch his face. 'It's wonderful to wake and find you with me like this again, so overwhelmed with love. We've woken together before but never like this.' We had done so at dawn that very morning. How could I ever have imagined this, then? It seemed to have happened in a different lifetime.

He watched me, still. 'May I ask you something?'

I nodded, my heart already fluttering with vague anxiety.

'Is Sam Penny's father?'

This secret treasured thing that was mine alone and he had spoken it aloud. 'What?' He saw my distress instantly and pulled me into his arms. Yet why was I surprised he had guessed? Thinking rationally, it was not difficult when he knew us both as he did. I chewed my lip. 'Yes,' I whispered. 'But please don't ask me why I didn't want to marry him.'

He kissed me, tenderly. 'I think I understand.'

I gasped a breath. 'You can't possibly.' How could he when I barely understood it myself?

'He's ... No. You already said you know nothing of his lovers?'

'Indeed, and why should I? Well, apart from that damnable secret woman of his.'

He sighed. 'Not a woman, *cara*. Noah.'

I had truly not expected that and took several moments to absorb it, though it made perfect sense, of course. And I felt not a little foolish for being so blind. 'How could I not have known.'

'I didn't see it either. Not until I accidently looked at a letter he had written to Sam and then the rest fell into place.'

'So, he prefers men?' I shook my head. 'All this time thinking it was my fault. That there was something wrong with me. Why hasn't he told me?' There were many at court quite open about such preferences, even though it was against the law and ostensibly punishable by death. The King's grandfather had been such a one.

'Perhaps he didn't know then? I cannot think it an easy thing to face. And he never knew it was anything more than a botched attempt at finding out with you.'

'No, he didn't.' Sam. Oh Jesu, Sam. Tears spilled, finally. Shed for us both, held in Raphael's arms.

After a while he spoke. 'You did right not to marry him. Many like him do but they tend not to have very happy wives ... or find much happiness themselves. If there are children, the stakes become so much higher.'

I sniffed noisily and nodded, thinking of Noah's wife. But he has sons. And Sam has a daughter. 'When I understood what happened between us wasn't how it should be, how could I not wonder why?'

He left the bed to fetch a handkerchief, holding it out to me. 'We should eat.' He pulled the bell rope for a servant.

How beautiful he was naked. Mane of black hair. Tawny skin. Fine-boned and hard-muscled. I blew my nose. Something impossible to do discreetly. I honked again. Jesu.

His lips twitched as he moved back beside me. 'Better now?'

I nodded, again. I must look atrocious. Then I bit my lip, remembering. 'You know, I couldn't decide what I would do if ... if the worst happened. If a time had been set for ... it. Would I tell him Penny was his? Which would have been easier for him? Knowing or not knowing.'

'I think it is a very good thing it was a dilemma you never had to face, *cara*.'

After a knock, Giuseppe's head appeared around the door followed by a burst of rapid Italian from them both, with something said by a grinning Giuseppe that clearly referred to me and just as clearly vexed Raphael. He was different speaking his own language, using more gestures, his face noticeably animated. In English he was the perfect court gentleman, as he needed to be, though with a rather alluring accent. I thought. God. How I loved him.

'*Grazie*, Giuseppe.'

'*Prego.*'

'What did he say about me?' Giuseppe had closed the window drapes and lit the many candles liberally placed around the room in floor-standing, now glowing candelabras, and wall sconces, so I was able to discern the slight darkening across his skin. 'My God, you're blushing. Tell me what he said.'

'No need. Just more of his idiot nonsense.'

'Then I shall ask him.'

'Can you?' He must have seen my doubt and also my resolve to try. 'Don't make me say it, Susannah. He heard us and made a coarse joke about your enjoyment. He is a stupid, irritating man.'

'Not your big–' He gave me such a despairing look, I took pity on him, kissing him instead.

Then, after a short while – well, it seemed so filled with kisses – Giuseppe returned bearing a laden tray and again their exchange was in Italian with eyes flashing. Platters of bread, cheeses, cakes, and fruits were slammed down hard onto the table while Raphael glared. A jug of wine and glasses followed. Grazie. Prego.

He held out his hand to me. 'Come.'

I followed him to the table, where we sat facing each other. He poured the wine and handed me a glass. '*Saluti.*'

'*Saluti.*' I took a long drink. 'That sounded interesting.'

He grinned. 'I told him to put the food on the table. He asked if I thought he would put it on the fucking floor. He told me to leave the tray outside the door. I asked if he thought I'd throw it out of the fucking window. That, I think, is about the gist of it.'

I rolled my eyes. 'Jesu. Then you thanked him, and he said you're welcome.'

He shrugged.

I finished my wine, watching him eat, candleflames reflected in his eyes. He refilled my glass before spreading soft cheese onto crusty bread. He had a pretty mouth. I laughed. He would likely not appreciate such a description.

'What?'

'I was thinking you have a pretty mouth.' I reached across the table to touch his lips.

He looked pointedly at my wine glass and tilted his head back. 'So, you think a pretty mouth a good thing for a man to have?'

'Oh, I do. It begs to be kissed.' And it had been. Often and by many. He shook his head, smiling, and handed me the bread. I put it down onto my plate and lifted my glass. 'We should drink to Sam.' We touched glasses with a rather loud clink. His eyes widened yet again. I had been a little too enthusiastic and felt myself blush. 'I pray he's happy now with Noah.' I closed mine for a moment, thinking of him.

He put down his knife and looked at me. 'Will you tell him?'

His words sobered me. 'I think I must. Yet to know and never to see her again.'

'We cannot be certain of that, *cara*. Perhaps he can come home one day. Until then, she can write to him.'

I refilled our glasses. 'She will. And one day she'll understand who he is.'

He pointed to my plate. 'Eat, Susannah.'

I lifted the bread and took a small bite, quickly followed by another when I realised just how hungry I was.

'Tomorrow we must see your *papá* so I can ask for your hand, and then we shall fetch Penny home.'

'Bit late for that.' I took another bite, chewed, and swallowed. 'My hand. Not Penny.' He watched me cramming food into my mouth, with a slight frown between thick black brows. I tried to remember when I had last eaten. Sometime the day before? Perhaps not even then?

'Are you waiting for me to tell you when to stop?'

I chewed and swallowed before gulping down more wine. 'No.'

He laughed, shaking his head, but became serious when he spoke. 'You think your *papá* will approve of us?'

I nodded, still chewing. 'I know he will.' Food flew from my mouth onto the table in front of him. I froze, watching it land. And, of course, he looked startled again. Might I have had a little too much wine?

'What about your grandmother?'

I put down the honey cake I was about to cram ... put into my mouth. 'I hope she will. She had plans to marry me into the aristocracy a long time ago ... but all that changed, of course. When I became spoiled goods.'

'So perhaps a humble Florentine jeweller will be enough? She warned me off you. Now I understand why she said I could harm you.'

'She told me to leave you alone ... that I had brought enough trouble–'

He reached across the table and squeezed my hand. '*Cara.*'

'She meant another child. That I would do it again.' I stood, feeling a little sick.

He came me to me quickly, taking me into his arms. 'She asked if I was your lover. She should have asked if I loved you.'

I climbed back into his bed thinking of my grandmother while he disposed of the tray. Outside the door I was glad to see. He kept the wine jug and brought us each another glass. I took a sip and placed it on the table beside me. 'Maybe I have already done it again ... we have? I want our child, Raphael.'

He closed his eyes for a moment before moving to me, kissing my forehead, and placing his hand on my belly. 'It is possible as you know too well. But it is not always so. Or even often so, perhaps?'

I took his hand and kissed it. You know all about it, do you?'

He hesitated for a moment, his face frozen. What was this? Some fleeting anguish. There and then gone. Jesu.

He smiled his distracting smile then. '*Cara*, you have no idea how much I know. Most of it I wish I did not.'

'Why? How on earth–' Then, of course, I understood. 'Sisters.' Had I finally lost my mind completely? That was what I saw. Yet, disquiet still, because I saw pain. I knew it. But I pushed it away. Hard.

'*Sì*. Sisters. My mother.' He held my gaze, drawing me back into his story. 'Any time away from the workshop. Reticence ... privacy are unknown concepts to them. Winters in the kitchen where it is warmest. Summers on the terazza under grape vines.'

He clasped his hands behind his head. I wanted to kiss his black tufted underarms, but it was not difficult to imagine his wide-eyed look of surprise if I did.

He touched my face, reclaiming my attention. 'They talked and I was always there until, finally, I escaped to school.' He stared up at the ceiling, remembering. 'Claudia did not get with child for over a year. Christ. The questioning, though she showed no signs of objecting to it. Perhaps she enjoyed the attention?' He shrugged. 'Monthly courses. How often they made love. Did he finish. Did she.' He shook his head, laughing.

'Finish? ... ah, I see. Well, we did that.'

He turned to kiss me. 'We certainly did, *cara mia*.'
'Where was your father when all this was going on?'
He shrugged. 'Never there. Mistresses.'
'Did they never talk of that?'
'I'm sure they did. But they had one sure way of getting rid of me.'
'Well, if you could sit through all of that what could possible drive you away?'
'Their costive bowels. *Cristo*, I was away as fast as my legs could carry me.' He laughed, rolling his eyes. 'It was clearly a ruse to get rid of me. *Papà's* affairs were a closely kept secret. It was many years before I found out about him.'
'Your family sounds, well ... interesting,' I said, a touch uncertainly. 'I can't wait to meet them all.'
'That's one way of describing them.
'You love them very much.'
He smiled. 'I do. My dear *mamma*, especially.' He shrugged. 'With *Papà* it is a little more difficult. I talked of them to Sam. He wondered what you would make of them.'
'He was so certain we'd find each other.' I lay pressed close to him my head on his chest, listening to the steady beat of his heart, thinking of his childhood, and contrasting it with my own. I was glad he knew all he did of a woman's body, so there would be no awkwardness between us about such things. Every new thing I learned of him made me love him more.
Yet how much did I really know of men? Well, I would learn from him and, thinking of it, I already had. I was beginning to understand his complexity. I thought of his kindness. I already knew what sort of father he would be. We would become Penny's parents together now. I thought of his charm. His power over women. I moved away so I could look at him. 'Tell me about yourself. I want to know everything.'
He turned to face me. 'Christ. You must narrow it a little, no? I can tell you I hate the cold and like dogs, but I think it's not such as this you wish to know?'

He used his accent to distract me. I gave him a hard stare, which made him smile. Dear God. I closed my eyes. 'Tell me of your first woman?'

'Ha. Now I understand the territory. But will you like what I have to say?'

'I fear I shall not, but please don't let that stop you.'

He chuckled and kissed the tip of my nose. 'Well, *cara*. I was fourteen and she really was a woman. She would have been about your age. Very old to me then.'

'I'm listening,' I said rather coolly.

'She instigated it, of course. She was one of Claudia's friends. Married. Even now I can't imagine what she hoped to get from me.' He saw me take a breath ready to speak and put his finger to my lips. 'Don't say it. Fourteen-year-old boys are not a good choice as lovers. She took me to her chamber, shed her clothes and told me to do the same. Just seeing her naked would have been enough. My school friends made prolific use of my descriptions of her.'

I snorted. 'They talked of such things?'

He raised his eyebrows.

'Not ... in front of ...?

'You really don't want to know.' He rolled his eyes. 'Boys are filthy creatures, Susannah. But pragmatic.'

'Jesu. I– Go on.'

'Well, she told me what to do for I was not entirely confident about it, believe it or not, and while I did as instructed – very briefly mind – she told me not to spit my stuff inside her. Her words.' He shrugged. 'Mattered not a jot to me to do as she asked. I was in paradise. This went on for several weeks until she tired of me. I wonder, still, why it lasted so long. She got nothing from it. I never once gave her a thought other than to use her.'

Our eyes held. I bit my lip. 'Well, that was an interesting start, was it not? What next?'

He blinked. Then he ran his finger over my chewed lips. 'Very well. I make it brief, yes?' He raised his eyebrows.

'We shall see.' I sensed I was amusing him, which was not my intention. When I tried to look stern, his mouth twitched, damn him. 'Go on, if you please.'

Those thick black brows up again. I wanted to kiss them. 'After that, only the kind of activities your friends at court told you of. In truth, quite a lot of it but nothing more. The young ladies of Florence are fiercely protective of their virtue–'

I gasped.

'Christ.' He clutched me to him, stroking my hair back from my forehead and kissing me. 'Forgive me. It wasn't the same for you. You and Sam. You loved each other. I knew nothing of love.'

Yet this was not all of it. There was much left unsaid. Though I understood not to press him, feeling his tension while he waited to see if I would, I kissed him until I felt it leave him.

He sighed. 'So that was all until I came to London.'

Well, it was all he would tell me even though I had told him everything. I closed my eyes. 'And to all those desperate married ladies just waiting for you.' Were there none in all of Florence? Jesu. Had he not found one at fourteen?

He pursed his lips, clearly not happy with my choice of words. 'Quite so. I think you know the rest.'

I looked away. 'I really don't want to know how many there were.' He touched my chin, gently turning me back to him. I knew what I had done to him with my accusation. I had seen the hurt stark upon his face before he had kissed me that day.

'How many I sold gems to in exchange for my body?'

I closed my eyes for a moment wishing once again that I could take back those words. 'Raphael, I knew it wasn't true. I wanted to hurt you and I don't even know why.' But I did, of course.

He moved closer to kiss me. 'Because of Frances, *cara*.'

Who else? 'I suppose it was. I know you gave up all the others for her.' But not her for me. Had he even now?

He seemed to read the question on my face. 'It is over between us. I swear it.'

'Since you knew you loved me?'

He blinked. 'Not entirely. I couldn't believe it possible for you to love me until Sam insisted you did ... but I was never in her bed again after you saw me that day. You have my word. Nor in any other,' he added, seeing me think it.

I lifted a strand of his silky black hair, smoothing it between my fingers. 'You did this for me?'

'It's a little difficult to explain. I suppose I'd grown tired of feeling dishonourable. Tired of being disappointed in myself if that makes any sense. I love you, Susannah. I needed to feel worthy of you, even believing you could never be mine.'

'What? Worthy of me who had a child out of wedlock at barely sixteen–'

'Yes! *Still*. Worthy of you and of your daughter.' He crossed himself. 'And I thank God for you both.'

How could I not weep a little? He held me close, stroking my back. 'But I do understand how you drew them all, my Raphael.' He looked a touch wary. 'I have seen how you charm women, how you smile at them. I've watched you do it.' A slight frown appeared between his brows, again. 'I saw, too, it wasn't artifice. You talk to women as equals. You are truly interested in what they have to say. You don't talk down to them, just as you don't to Penny. And that, my dearest, is how you win them.'

He ran his hand down over my hip and left it resting, hot, on my thigh. 'So, Englishmen talk down to their women? Why should this be?'

'Because they own us and choose not to educate us so they can deride us for our stupidity and ignorance.'

His eyes widened. 'But this is not all men. You are as educated as I.'

'Raphael, have you not seen how most men at court treat their wives? How they speak to them?' I sighed. 'So, they seek something kinder from a lover. Who only gives it to them for another conquest to add to their tally. They squeal how could it possibly be true that such a man might love and desire them? How can they ever deserve such a thing?' I shook my head. 'What man ever thinks himself undeserving?'

He gestured to himself. 'This man does of you.' He grinned. 'Though I might convey such in a manly growl rather than a squeal.'

I laughed. 'Why do women choose it, though? Or, at the very least, accept it as their lot. Surely there must be a better alternative to exchanging an abusive husband for a calculating lover?' Jesu. Did he think I spoke of him? 'It's strange because the King never really behaves in such a fashion to any of his women ... well, not gratuitously. Castlemaine would try a saint. God knows, he buys their bodies with sometimes unbelievable generosity, so it's even possible to ask just who is exploiting whom.'

He barked a laugh.

'And he is always kind to his wife, though he spends little time with her. In most things, the court follows his example but, alas, not with this.' I pushed his hair back from his forehead, kissing him there. 'Though he might wish, more than a little unkindly, to rid himself of a troublesome Godson.'

He rolled onto his side to look at me. 'Tell me about you and Sam, *cara*.'

'Sam. Jesu. There is so much. We've known each other all our lives. We even shared the same tutor until he went to Winchester–'

'His school. He told me.'

'And I moved on to a governess. No more Latin and Greek for me, sadly.' I smiled remembering. 'We were always together.'

'Then you fell in love?'

'There was always love, it just changed. I remember so clearly the first time we kissed. He'd had a letter from a schoolfriend. I took it from him, and he tried to take it back. We laughed. There was nothing in it he did not wish me to read. Just a boy's letter about boy things. I'd read them before. Hunting. Eating. Shit– Anyway, I held it over my head and, well, we kissed. We spent a long time kissing that afternoon. I loved the feeling of promise it gave me. Of it being the start of something and a delicious longing to find out what it might be. How it might end.'

He moved in, overwhelming me with kisses ... again. I closed my eyes and took a long breath. 'Yes, just like that. That feeling.' We smiled at each other. 'Well, lots of kissing and touching over the next few weeks. Always at Sam's house. His father was away. Then late one afternoon, I felt him change.' I needed to gather myself before I could carry on.

He stroked my face. 'You needn't say any more, *amore mio*. I know the rest, I think.'

'No. I must. I want you to know what happened afterwards.' I took a deep breath. 'I felt it too. It wasn't enough for us. We went to his chamber.' I started to chew my lip. He put a finger there to stop me. I sighed. 'Nothing was right after that. We didn't undress. We were on his bed, and he just lifted my skirts. We didn't speak or kiss. There was ... well, considerable pain.' I took a breath. 'Though I never wanted him to stop. Then it was over almost before we had begun, and he collapsed onto me. I held him. I thought ... hoped if we tried again, it might be better.' I frowned. 'I didn't understand then quite when that could be, but I held him and told him I loved him. He rolled away from me, and I could see he was crying. I tried to comfort him.' Even now it still pained me to remember. 'He said not to touch him. Then he got off the bed and told me to go home.'

'Christ, Susannah.' He held me tighter.

I laughed, mirthlessly. 'So, home I went, and straight up to my own chamber where I wept, too, for a while before spending many hours trying to understand what had happened. But it was impossible. I decided I must talk to him, so the next day I crossed the street to his house as I did almost every day. And he'd gone. I never knew where. And I never saw him again before he returned to school. So, of course, I didn't see him until after Penny was born.'

'*Santo Dio*,' he said, softly.

'How could I have made him marry me when he bolted like

that? That I repelled him seemed obvious.' I sighed, looking up at the ceiling. 'Yet he fell in love with Penny the moment he saw her. I used to watch him holding her and wanted so much to tell him. Mama noticed it one day and whispered, "don't." She knew Penny was his by then but didn't want him to know. I suppose she must have understood about him?'

'It would seem she must have done. So, you've never spoken about what happened between you?'

'No. We just went back to where we were before the kissing. And we loved each other just as we had then.' I sighed. 'In some ways I was glad and in others not.'

'Well, *amore mio*, it saddens me to think you blamed yourself for what went amiss between you.'

'Hmm. I didn't want to think it, but it seemed the only explanation. When I understood more about what ought to happen, I knew he should have wanted me again ... and soon. But he didn't. I tried to tell myself he had been humiliated because it was over so quickly–'

'No. He would have expected it. Boys talk of little else in the dormitory after dark, believe me. They have older brothers. Sisters.' He shrugged. 'All information is welcome. Then as they get older, they have their own experiences to share. By fifteen they are usually experts.' He laughed. 'In theory if not in practice.'

'Like you were with your lady?'

'Well, I knew enough to ready myself beforehand.'

'What? How is that– Oh, I see.'

He grinned and kissed me. 'But if that was not possible, then, well.' He shrugged. 'Everyone knew it. Including Sam. So it wasn't that and it wasn't you.'

'No. He just prefers men.'

'I'm sure he had no more idea what went wrong then than you did.'

'Poor Sam. I would like to talk with him about it now. Just when I can't.'

'Perhaps you shall one day, who knows?'

He held me close for a while, stroking my back. Jesu. How I had unburdened myself to him, leaving me feeling both drained and peaceful ... and so grateful for it. All those things I had found so difficult to understand felt, somehow, resolved through the lens of his scrutiny. Perhaps that is what love does and he would let me do it for him one day, for I knew he held secrets still. Yet he must choose when, just as I had done. I moved his hair away to kiss his neck, touching his skin with the tip of my tongue, tasting the salt of his sweat.

'Did you just lick me, *cara*?'

I smiled, kissing and licking down over his chest through his thatch of black hair following its line down his belly, watching his desire grow and hearing him groan. 'Tell me how to please you.'

Then, sometime later, we finally slept in each other's arms.

Chapter Eleven
RAPHAEL

I left the bed, careful not to wake her, and used the piss pot before opening the window drapes. Though early still, the street was already busy with merchants' carts in the soft milky sunshine. A small grey mongrel hurtled down the middle of the road barking. What did he chase? I moved back to stand for a few moments looking down at Susannah, pushing my hair from my face before slipping in beside her again, content just to watch her sleep. I found it hard to believe we were together. Sam was sailing to Jamaica and Susannah was mine.

Could it be everything in my life so far had brought me to her now as prepared as I could ever be to make her happy ... in every way possible? I smiled, wryly. Impressed I could find such a justification for my life of sin. It was remarkably self-serving even for me. Yet was there not some truth in it? Villiers' body. A prison cell with Sam where she was forced to speak to me, making me a part of her life. Something I had longed for though she had not known it then when I meant nothing to her.

I understood my life would never again be as it had been – and thanked God for it – and for all that she was to me now, and all she would be. This was the only woman I would ever love or whose body I would ever touch. And how could I ever have imagined the difference love would make to the physical act? How could I when I had never known it before? Every caress, every touch born of love and at the end the sense of oneness remained ... even grew after the physical joining was over, after my abandon with her. I shook my head smiling at the wonder of it. That she would be the mother of my children felt a holy thing. A benediction of forgiveness. Yet how could it not fill me with gut-wrenching fear?

I closed my eyes forcing my mind away, thinking instead of all the things she had told me about her life and how much it helped me to understand her. I could see the devastating blow her mother's death must have been, not just the loss of her dearly loved *mamma* but of a confidant. Someone who knew about Penny and how could that not have contributed to her shutting-away her voice? I took a long breath. What a thing to have gone through so young. It was hard to even imagine her turmoil, and it was not a little disconcerting to realise that all her distress was now mine also. Past and future.

I truly hoped she could talk of it with Sam one day. It was probably something they would both need, for learning of her would surely take him back to her difficult beginning. But I had told her next to nothing of my past. Why? Like her, I had never spoken of it – my own beloved child – to anyone since. A coward's excuse, of course. Christ. My heart clenched thinking how much this would hurt her when she knew what I had done. What I had withheld. Tears pricked my eyes and I quickly swiped them away, seeing hers flutter open.

She smiled, stretching like a cat, and reaching up to touch my face. 'You look very serious, my Raphael.'

I smiled, too, stroking her bright hair back from her forehead. 'No, Cara. Just thinking how much I love you.' I moved in to kiss her, inhaling the scent of her sweat and my seed, until I felt her with me before moving my hand lightly over her breast and down between her thighs. She moaned. And I broke away from the kiss to look at her, at the colour on her face.

That delicious blush against the milky whiteness of her skin. I nuzzled her ear to whisper. 'Tell me what you want, *cara mia*. Tell me.'

She closed her eyes. 'I want you.'

'*Dillo a me.* Tell me.'

Her eyes flew open. 'You know full well what you're doing to me. I want you ...please. In the name of–'

I rolled over her. 'This? You want this, *cara*?'

'Yes, this now. If you please.'

She was breathing hard, clutching me. Running her hands down my back and over my arse. I began to move and watched her smile. Christ, I wanted it too. But I knew what I could do for her. Later, we lay on our backs both panting a little. I grinned 'That went well, I think.'

'How did you do it? Bring me there–'

'Twice? It was good, no?' I knew it had been. I'd heard her.

She turned on her side to look at me. 'Yes, it was. Thank you, kind sir.

I smiled, enjoying the effect it had upon her. I knuckled my forehead. 'Your servant always, *Signora*.'

I rolled so we were face to face. 'You're so beautiful. I could look at you forever. Look at you and have you. Look at you and have you. On and on.'

She laughed. 'Sounds wonderful to me. Let's give it a try.'

A knock on the door saw us fly apart, pulling the quilts up over us. '*Sì*.'

Giuseppe strode in with a large tray of breakfast things. '*Buongiorno Signore e Signora.*'

'*Buongiorno*, Giuseppe.'

He bowed, smiling and began unloading the contents of the tray onto the table. 'Will there be anything further, *Padrone*?'

'You're remarkably polite this morning? What's the matter with you?'

Susannah nudged me.

I shrugged. 'What?'

Giuseppe bowed and left the room with the tray balanced on his palm over his shoulder.

'What,' I said again.

She laughed. You know perfectly well. You were trying to provoke him.'

I put my hand on my chest. 'Me? Never. I was genuinely concerned for him.'

'Ha.' She tilted her head, looking at me. 'Wide eyed innocence suits you. You look more handsome than ever.'

I ran my hand through my hair. 'Now you're teasing me, Cara.' Perhaps love truly was blind?

'Why on earth would you think such a thing? I meant every word.' She moved in to kiss me. 'Might we see what we have for breakfast?' Her stomach chose that moment to gurgle insistently, and she clutched it, looking mortified.

I threw my head back, laughing. 'I think we must, *cara mia.*'

She rolled her eyes. 'It was lucky he chose the right time to bring it in. Any earlier might have been a touch embarrassing.'

'I don't suppose luck came into it; I imagine he listened outside the door.' I left the bed and stood beside it. 'Come.' I held out my hand, pulling her into my arms when she took it. We kissed again and there was nowhere to hide what it did to me. I saw her eyeing me, speculatively. 'No, *amore mio.* Breakfast.' I grinned. 'And please try not to spit food at me.'

She followed me to the table. 'Raphael, I most certainly did not spit food at–'

I held up a letter. 'Frances.'

She frowned hearing her name. 'Open it then. Let us see what she wants from you.'

Gesu Cristo. There was heavy emphasis on 'wants.' Would she ever trust me? I snapped the seal.

Richmond House
    July 12th, 1676

My dearest Raphael

It might interest you to know the King chose not to informLouise of Sam's release, so, she learnt of it from one of her French spies some hours after the event. As you can imagine, this caused a vituperative outburst of monumental proportions followed by floods of tears, which meant the King came to me again for peace, as he always does. You see, once again, why he needs me and why I must stay.

Yours, with much affection
Frances

Post scriptum. Some news of another lady. Barbara has left Whitehall and taken herself off to France, I am told. Her children, though, all remain at court. The King seems delightfully cheerful about it. As, of course, does Louise ... and a number of others.

I handed it to Susannah to read.

She placed it back onto the table when she had, smiling. 'Well, Catherine will be out on her ear or perhaps she has followed Castlemaine to France? Either way, good riddance to her.' She sighed. 'Why does he tolerate such women, never mind indulge them the way he does?'

I shrugged. 'Because he shares their beds? And perhaps loves them?'

'How could he when they are all so odious? Which makes me glad he has Frances to escape to.'

Now, that was something I never expected to hear her say.

SUSANNAH

Diary: July 12, 1676.

When he helped me dress in my freshly pressed gown, I found him just as adept with buttons and laces in reverse. After he had finished my hair, I brushed his and tied it for him bending to kiss the top of his head. 'It is black as night.' His hand came up over mine on his shoulder. I kissed it. Jesu, I felt giddy with love.

Giuseppe arrived then, with shaving water. 'Leave it. I'll do it myself.'

'But I do it so much better, no?' He winked at me before speaking again in Italian.

'English so Susannah understands, if you please.'

'So, you wish her to learn how to insult you, eh?' He smacked his forehead. 'Fucking excellent idea.'

'She has no wish to insult me.' He raised his eyebrows. 'Have you, *cara*?'

'Well, it cannot hurt to know a few of Giuseppe's better ones, just in case the need arises—'

'Susannah?'

He looked at me with wide-eyed astonishment. Rather an overreaction? I shrugged.

Giuseppe put down the shaving brush to devote his full attention to an extravagant bout of laughter, which necessitated bending down to clutch his thighs.

'Imbecile.'

The laughter stopped, abruptly. 'You no call your *sposa* an imbecile, you little shit.'

'You, *idiota*.'

Eventually, Raphael was shaved and dressed and managed not to tell his manservant to remove the water bowl and wet towel. I do believe he left looking a little crestfallen because of it. He had seemed back to his old self after his politeness with the breakfast tray. Perhaps it was the duchess's letter? Then I realised he would have brought breakfast to Raphael when she had been in his bed. As I watched him tie his cravat at the cheval mirror, two things occurred to me. He truly did not see his own beauty and no one other than I would ever share his bed again. I knew it because I knew with utter certainty, he loved me.

The coach waited for us in the mews behind the house and we set off for Henrietta Street, moving out of shadow into sunshine on Cheapside. I thought of our journey here the day before and how much had happened since. We sat side by side holding hands and I looked at him, finding his eyes already on me. 'Absurdly, I keep wanting to thank you.'

'Why? Yet if you must thank me then must I not thank you in return?'

When I smiled, his still had its way with me. Would it ever stop? 'Thank you for loving me and making me so happy.'

'Thank you for this too, *amore mio*.' He squeezed my hand. 'You think your *papá* will be at home?'

'I would expect it. He doesn't usually go to court until later.' Was he apprehensive about the meeting?

He held my gaze. 'Susannah, you spoke to Giuseppe this morning without noticing you had, I think.'

'No, I didn't ... I couldn't have ...' I had no idea what to say. What to think. And that, of course, was why he had looked so astonished.

'You did, *cara*.'

'How was I able to? I don't understand.'

'Maybe you gave it no thought? I was there. Giuseppe just thinks you reserved. You simply forgot it.'

'But why? When I've tried for so long.' I shook my head. 'Why now without me even realising I had?'

He tilted his head. 'I wonder? Could it be because you've told me about Penny and Sam and everything that's been secret for so long? You shut it all away. You shut your voice away to keep it so.'

I wrapped my arms around him, burying my face against his chest. Maybe that had been part of it underneath all that anger? 'Jesu. I belonged in a madhouse.'

He rested his hand lightly on my neck. 'No, Susannah. You lost your mother so suddenly and when you came home from your grandmother you found the Villiers. I don't believe you chose silence, the circumstances you found yourself in, did.' He moved me back to kiss me. 'But it's over.'

I placed my hand on his face. 'Because of you, Raphael.'

'No. Because of us. Now, will you try to speak to your *papá*? It is time, yes?'

I took a long breath. 'I pray that I can ... and he must know about Penny. It will be distressing for him but it's not right for things to go on as they are.' How completely everything had changed. Nothing was as it had been. It was hard to comprehend. 'But what if I still cannot? How shall I bear it?'

He took both my hands in his. 'Can you trust me now?'

'Yes.' With my life and with my heart because I loved him.

'You will speak to him; I give you my word. Because everything preventing you is over. It's done. It left you when you talked of it.'

'Yes. It must be so. It has to be.'

I sat close to him, his arm around me, looking out of the coach window at the busy streets thronged with people strolling in the sunshine. Carts and carriages clattered past, coachmen greeting each other. On through Ludgate circus passing the new St Paul's with its scaffolding and men moving like ants across the burgeoning structure. I had seen the scale model at the site. It would be truly glorious.

I turned back to Raphael. Though we had not discussed it, I knew we would live at his house and Penny would be with us there. I was leaving Papa alone and it saddened me, yet it was the way of things. And how could I not dread telling him he must lose Penny, too? For he loved her dearly and she loved him, though it would be as grandfather and granddaughter now.

When the carriage turned from The Strand into Bedford Street and on through Covent Garden piazza before rounding into Henrietta Street, I gazed out at Sam's house as we went by. Rupert would be there alone just as my father would soon be, although we were not far away and could see each other often. Poor Rupert. But he knew Sam was safe and that was all that would truly matter to him.

The coach pulled to a halt and Raphael stepped down before offering his hand to help me alight. We kissed briefly – well, a little more than briefly – before going inside. It was strange to arrive home and find Bess no longer there. I wondered what would happen to her now. Nothing good, I imagined. I led Raphael upstairs to the drawing room, pulling the bell rope to summon a servant. 'Perhaps you will ask for him to be fetched down? If I am to speak then I must try in private.'

'Of course.'

But when the door burst open it was Papa himself and I ran to him, hugging him tight.

'I saw you arrive, Sukie. It is such good news Sam is safe away.' He turned to Raphael. 'And my gratitude to you for having a letter couriered to Rupert. It was good to know of it so speedily.'

'*Prego.*' He bowed.

I had no idea he had done that.

'I shall have coffee sent up. Sit. Sit.' Papa gestured towards a sofa and, not bothering with the bell, poked his head around the door and called, 'Coffee. Drawing room.'

I sat beside Raphael, and he took my hand in his before clearing his throat. '*Signor* Gresham ... Sir Richard, I–'

'If you love my daughter then you have my blessing.'

'I love her with all my heart, *Signore.*'

'Well, I saw you kiss her outside and it certainly looked that way to me.'

I stood and went to him, kissing his cheek. 'I love Raphael, Papa. I didn't know it was possible to feel such love.' My voice was quiet but steady. I held out my ring. 'He made this for me.'

He lifted my hand to see more closely. 'It is very fine indeed, Sukie.' He glanced at Raphael before pulling me into his arms. 'I'm so glad, my sweet girl. And so glad you have found your voice again.' He turned to Raphael. 'Which I imagine has much to do with you, *Signor* Rossi?'

'Yes.' I said, before Raphael could speak. I took a breath. I should tell him now while he held me. 'There is something I must say to you, Papa. I know it will shock you ... and hurt you and I'm sorry for it but ... Penny is–'

'My granddaughter.'

I staggered back. 'You know? How long have you known?'

'Always.'

I turned to Raphael, who appeared as stunned as I. He was quickly up to grasp me to him. So how many others had lived a lie around me because it had been more comfortable for them? And Papa had carried on even after Mama died. Why could he not have told me he knew then? Could he not imagine how alone I felt? Instead, he had shunned me. 'Mama told you? Why did she never say she had?'

'Because she didn't, Sukie. I was with her when you were born in Paris. She wanted me there, so I was. Her French was poor, and it made her more fearful. Midwife kicked-up a fuss, mind, but there I stayed. I saw you born and held you before your mother did. So, a letter telling me she was with child and did not wish to see me? I knew it for the nonsense it was, and the rest wasn't difficult to guess. It has been done before, sweetheart. Many times, I'm sure.'

'But you never spoke of it to me. Why? When I was so lost without her. Why?' Tears fell. How could they not?

The pain scourged upon his face tore at my heart yet more. 'You'd gone before I came to myself after losing Jane.' When he closed his eyes, his own tears spilled. 'And after you returned ... it was not something I wanted them to know of.' He gently took me from Raphael's arms and back into his own. 'Can you ever forgive me for them?'

'I should not have left you. Can you forgive me for that?'

'There's nothing to forgive. I understood how much you needed Sylvia when I couldn't help you. It felt like betraying Jane to speak of it to you when she had not wished me to know ... and I was so afraid of losing you. I think I'd lost my mind a little then.' He tried to smile. 'But not so much as I did later.'

I took a shuddering breath, knowing I need not ask. 'Sam?'

He smiled, his face still wet with tears, both his and mine, and cupped my face. 'Well, who else would it be, my Sukie. Though I think he does not know, does he?'

I shook my head.

'Probably for the best, now, perhaps?'

I took another deep breath. 'He should and so must Penny.'

'Well, it is your decision to make. Not mine. You must do what you think best.' He held my face in both his hands again. 'But to hear your voice once more, my little one, is simply wonderful.'

I left Papa and Raphael with their coffee to come up to my chamber for the final time, for I will never be parted from him again. I look around, saying goodbye to it all. Alice is packing clothing for me for Cheapside and our travels as I write my last entry. The diary has served its purpose mapping my journey to this day when I no longer need it. Soon I will set out to fetch my daughter home with my husband at my side. The bells of St Paul's in Bedford Street chime midday – those bells, so much part of the fabric of my days – sound a fitting note to mark the end of one life and the beginning of another.

Author's Note

Some of my fictional characters were prompted by real people who lived and worked in London's Henrietta Street in the 17th century. Susannah and Raphael are based on married couple Susan and Michael Rosse, a portrait miniaturist and jeweller to the court. Susan Rosse's father, Richard Gibson, was – like Susannah's – a miniaturist himself. Samuel Cooper, my inspiration for Sam Carter, was another portrait miniaturist resident of Henrietta Street and Susan's close friend all her life. Interestingly, Cooper painted Barbara Villiers in 1661 and James Scott, Duke of Monmouth in 1659 aged ten.

The Palace of Whitehall was the principal royal residence in London during the Stuart period, and, as such, the effective seat of government, sprawling over 26 acres from Westminster to the City. At one time the largest palace in Europe, with more than 1,500 rooms, overtaking the Vatican before itself being surpassed by the expanding Palace of Versailles, which would eventually reach 2,400 rooms. In 1698 it was almost completely destroyed by fire with the Banqueting House being one of the few buildings saved.

On June 1st, 1670, a secret treaty was signed between Charles II and Louis XIV of France. In its terms, Charles agreed to

AUTHOR'S NOTE

support Louis's expansionism in Europe, to renounce the Anglican faith, to become a Catholic and bring England back to Catholicism. In return, Louis would subsidise Charles, so enabling him to rule without recalling Parliament to raise taxes for the Exchequer. Charles received an initial payment in excess of £100,000.

The Southwark fire began on 26th of May 1676 and burned for 17 hours. The King and his brother did indeed fight the flames themselves, ordering fire breaks to be created by blowing up buildings in the path of the fire. It is believed that more people died in this fire than in the Great Fire ten years earlier.

Monmouth's ride on the frozen canal in St James's Park took place in the winter of 1676, after a thick fall of snow turned Whitehall white, he rode the length of the frozen canal, though no one believed the ice could hold.

The Astronomer Royal, John Flamsteed, began his work at the new Royal Observatory in Greenwich, taking up residence there on 10th July 1676. The King's visit on the day of Sam's trial is, of course, fictional.

Some time sequences have been adjusted for narrative purposes, and some linguistic choices are intentionally modern. Any historical errors or inconstancies are entirely mine as are errors in Italian translation.

About the Author

Dodie Bishop grew up in St Annes on Lancashire's Fylde Coast – where her family have a long history – and in the New Forest in Hampshire, spending much of her life there before moving to Devon. Now living in the Blackdown Hills with her husband and an overindulged cat, she has grown-up sons in London and Sydney. With a First-Class Honours degree in English Literature, she completed a Master's in Creative Writing and discovered her metier in historical fiction, so much so she now calls herself a time-traveller to the 17th century. She is a full-time writer, following an earlier career as a company director and an independent bookseller, so books are very close to her heart.

To learn more about Dodie Bishop and discover more Next Chapter authors, visit our website at www.nextchapter.pub.

Printed in Great Britain
by Amazon